SOLDIER Boys

G. F. McCauley

Published by

 GENERAL STORE
GSPH PUBLISHING HOUSE

Box 28, 1694B Burnstown, Ontario, Canada K0J 1G0
Telephone (613) 432-7697 or 1-800-465-6072

ISBN 1-894263-78-2
Printed and bound in Canada

Cover by Tara Graphics
Layout and Design by Derek McEwen
Printing by Custom Printers of Renfrew Ltd.
General Store Publishing House
Burnstown, Ontario, Canada

National Library of Canada Cataloguing in Publication

McCauley, G.F., 1940-
        Soldier boys / G.F. McCauley.

ISBN 1-894263-78-2

        1. World War, 1939-1945--Fiction. I. Title.

PS8575.C4417S64 2003   C813'.6   C2003-901463-0
PR9199.4.M25S64 2003

The greater part of the human story of wars becomes lost because it is kept in the memories of the many thousands who go their separate post-war ways. Some is kept in the diaries of those few who had the secretarial mind. Those accounts which were gathered by reporters in the field are generally overwritten although based on fact. Most of the best of this adventure, the human part with its excitement and boredom, skill and blundering, courage and failure, and all the rest, passes out of our consciousness. Most that is recorded on the printed page is read and then forgotten. The mediaeval world did better, as the troubadours took up these themes and gave them form, singing them from court to court until the hardy exploits of brave men passed into the literature and culture of an age.

What Time the Tempest: An Army Chaplain's Story

Waldo E.L. Smith

Acknowledgements

This book could not have been written without the help of many, including other writers (published and unpublished), benefactors and friends too numerous to mention. But I would be remiss if I did not thank by name those veterans of the Algonquin Regiment who took me into their confidence and shared their memories with me. As listed in the Regimental history *Warpath*, they are

Allard, E. L. Pte. B55432
Batty, L. R. Cpl. B54670
Beauchesne, C. Cpl. B55371 *
Belair, L. Pte. C121657
Caya, G. L. A/Sgt. B55632 *
Conroy, G. J. Cpl. B55268
Geisler, A. Pte. B55654 *
King, D. L/Cpl. B54551 *
Laut, A. Sgt. B55002
Leathem, K. Pte. B55194
McCauley, L. S. Sgt. B55379 *
McNeil, N. J. A. Sgt. B54799
Paget, N. W. Lieut.
Regimbald, M. T. Capt. *
Smith, A. G. Sgt. B55394
Vallier, W. D. Cpl. B55192
Williamson, W. V. Sgt. H17351

* Now deceased.

Prologue

The boy stood with his grandfather on the hill watching Hitler, Mussolini and Tojo burn.

Watching with them in the dark was a cheering crowd of townspeople standing in front of a grove of birch trees, sentinels in white, guarding the stone memorial with its brass plaque inscriptions marking the dead of the First World War. In front of the crowd, on the crest of the hill, just before it dipped toward the cold green waters of the lake, were the leaders of Canada's enemies in the Second World War, their flaming, straw-stuffed effigies strung up on a gibbet. It was Tuesday, May 8, 1945. It was Victory in Europe Day in Lowvert.

Lowvert was a small town in the north of the province of Ontario. First settled by the French trading for furs with the Cree Indians of James Bay, it was called L'Eau Vert or Green Water because the water in the lake was the green colour of weathered copper. But when the English came L'Eau Vert became Lowvert.

When the English came they brought the railroad and the railroad brought the boy's grandfather, who came just as the First World War was ending. He was the baggageman. The baggageman ran the baggage room in the train station. The baggage room was where travellers brought their bags and traders their supplies to the boy's grandfather, who gave them a claim check and then loaded bags and boxes on an iron-wheeled wagon, which he hauled to the baggage car of the waiting train.

That evening at Lowvert's *auto-da-fé* the boy was in uniform. He was a five-year-old sergeant in the Algonquin Regiment, his father's regiment, his father's rank. The boy's mother had sewn the uniform for him, telling him it was for the day when his father came home from the War. But he had asked his mother if he could wear it to the victory party and his mother had said he could.

He'd been told his father was somewhere in England recovering in a hospital after being airlifted out of Germany by the Royal Air Force following his liberation from a prisoner-of-war camp. He still had bullets in his neck— Schmeisser machine pistol bullets—wounds received when his reconnaissance patrol was ambushed in the village of Damme just north of Bruges, a city in Belgium described by the tourist guides of the 1930s as being "a city of the Middle Ages, with brick houses bearing the wear marks of centuries, noble looking buildings, churches with clear, melodious chimes."

In the month of September 1944 the boy's father didn't get a chance to stop and admire the wear marks of centuries or listen to the melodious chimes of the bells. On the day he was ambushed and wounded, four of the men with him were killed. Two were Belgian resistance fighters, a father and his son. The other two were Canadians, privates in the Algonquin Regiment, one, three months short of his eighteenth birthday, the other, a life-long friend. Only three of the ten-man patrol escaped.

The boy's father was a prisoner of war for eight months and when he was liberated by GIs from General George Patton's Third Army, he was starving and lice-infested and so weakened by dysentery that he weighed only ninety pounds.

This is his story.

PART ONE

Chapter One

SEPTEMBER 18, 1940. *My name is Barney Berman and this is the first entry in my diary, the beginning of my account of the war against Hitler waged by the little league of nations which includes me, Al McDougal, Tony Foligno, Billy Assad, Reggie Carriere and Frank Archibald, whose nickname is Crow because of his ability to mimic the language of the noisy birds so well that even they can't tell the difference.*

The little league is the name Al's father, Sandy, gave us in the winter of 1930/31 when we were all in Grade 8 and playing hockey for the Lowvert Maple Leafs. As Sandy saw it, our team had representatives from six different nationalities. Al was the Irish ambassador, Tony the Italian, Billy the Lebanese, Reggie the French and Frank the James Bay Cree. I represented the Jews even though our family came to Canada from Russia.

When Canada declared war on Germany on September 27, 1939, all of us were up on the Lowbush hunting snow geese. We came home and sat in the Empire Theatre to watch Movietone News, *the Blitzkrieg cutting through Poland, tanks roaring down dusty roads through thatch-roofed villages past frightened refugees fleeing for their lives. It was damn quiet in the Empire when the ruins of Warsaw came up on the silver screen, bombed-out buildings looking like upright pieces of a jigsaw puzzle standing guard over the rubble of streets littered with dead bodies.*

Nothing much happened after Poland and so we all got on with our lives. Billy returned to work with his father at Assad's Northern Meats, a wholesale operation supplying construction camps and stores throughout Northeastern Ontario and up the T&NO line to the Bay. Tony took off to play hockey for the Cleveland Barons of the American Hockey League and Frank started to get ready for the winter trapping season. Al went back to waiting for a call from the railway. His dad, who is the baggageman at the station, said the CNR was getting ready to hire locomotive firemen. Yours truly returned to Berman's Men's Wear where Dad was still cutting prices because of the Depression, a three-piece suit that used to sell for $10.98 was down to $9.98. Reggie didn't have what you'd call a regular job but managed to pick up a few dollars here and there with his guitar in

9

the town's beer parlours, where the patrons were partial to the songs of those two Nova Scotia cowboys, Wilf Carter and Hank Snow.

The winter of 1939/40 was a time of waiting to see what Hitler would do next, but it was Stalin who was first off the mark. Russia invaded Finland in December. We sat in the Empire and cheered the plucky Finns but it wasn't enough.

At Christmas we did our usual rounds on Boxing Day, stuffing ourselves on kibbeh *washed down with dandelion wine at Billy's house, where his dad told stories of the old days, coming to Canada with gold coins worth more than $500 and getting into the meat business, cattle shipped in by boxcar and herded off to the small lake just outside town, where they were butchered. And that was how the lake got its name. Slaughterhouse.*

Then it was off to our place. By Christmas of 1939 we had moved from the lane behind the store (Jerusalem Alley to the locals) to our present house above the lake, on Seventh Street across from Veterans' Park. Reggie was hoping to hear more about the 1919 fire that wiped out Berman's Lumber Yard and caught Reggie's father trying to save the family's Rooming House on Railway Street. His body was never found. But trying to get Ben Berman to talk about the past was a lost cause. Mameh always said talk of the past, any past, brought back bad memories for him.

After schnapps and potato latkes at the Bermans it was on to Italian at the Folignos. Spaghetti. Lasagna. Chicken Cacciatore. You name it. And grappa *to aid the digestion. We finished off at Reggie's with* tourtière *at midnight.*

In April Al's wife Beth presented him with a son, who was baptized Sanford after his paternal grandfather and Berkett after his maternal grandmother, whose husband was the first farmer in Northern Ontario to own a cow. Because the baby weighed in at eleven pounds plus, Billy called him Two-Ton Tony.

In May, Hitler invaded Holland, Belgium and Luxembourg and that's when we started to talk about doing something. I didn't need any persuading given Kristallnacht *and the activities of the Nazis in Canada, the German Canadian Bund marching in Toronto in their brown shirts and swastika armbands giving the stupid stiff-arm Hitler salute. But Al was a reluctant convert. Or at least he pretended to me he was, going on and on about what bastards the Brits were and why should he go and fight their war after what they'd done to his ancestors in Ireland. He liked to quote a Quebec Member of Parliament who wanted to know why Canada was obliged to fight every time England went to war and I liked to quote right back to him another Quebec MP who said that Canada, by doing nothing, by being neutral, would be taking the side of Adolf Hitler.*

But after Dunkirk and the fall of France and pictures of Der Führer gleefully goose-stepping in Paris, we talked it over among ourselves and with our fathers over a few beers and decided Hitler had to be stopped because he was a bully and the little league should do our bit to take care of him just like we took care of Tubby Martin at Victoria Public School the day after he beat the shit out of skinny little Reggie, just for the hell of it. The six of us kicked Tubby's fat arse till his gums bled and Al said we'd do the same to the Nazis.

Excerpt from Barney's Diary

"I joined the army to serve my country, not ta eat it." Billy Assad was insisting there was Camp Borden sand in his mashed potatoes.

"Yeah, you're right, Billy. Somethin's gritty."

"Shit, I think I just cracked a tooth."

"Goddamn army food."

Ever since stepping off the train at Camp Borden, the Canadian Army's basic training facility north of Toronto, food had been the little league's constant source of complaint. After one mouthful of their first supper, a gelatinous blob they were told was lamb stew, Billy's strangled voice was heard to say that the only time the glop had been lamb was when Christ was a kid. The stew had been made that morning right after breakfast, when the cooks dumped 600 pounds of mutton, and thirty pounds each of carrots and onions together with five gallons of Caper sauce into big aluminum pots and boiled it for three hours.

Arnie Christensen, taken under the little league wing as the ambassador from Sweden, was used to eating in the logging camps of Algonquin Park where good meals were so important that every camp had a pastry cook. He took Billy's gritty complaint as his cue and started banging his cup on the table and chanting, "Army food is shit. Army food is shit."

A grinning Reggie Carriere followed suit, then adjoining tables, then the whole mess, hundreds of cups banging on scores of tables, "Army food is shit."

As the rhythmic shouting got louder and louder, a lone soldier stood on his bench and, with great care and ceremony, dumped his evening meal on the floor. Before you could say, "Jack Sprat could eat no fat," everyone followed suit. It came to be known as the night of the Great Food Fling and the participants were fondly remembered as Those Who Flung Dung.

Tony Foligno wasn't with them at Borden. He'd been the first of the gang to sign up, joining the Sand, Dust and Gravel Brigade, an Eastern Ontario regiment otherwise known as the Stormont, Dundas and Glengarry Highlanders. The rest of them had thought it better to stick with their own so had taken the oath of service with the Algonquins, a Northern Ontario regiment recruited from the farms and towns along the railway line south from Lowvert and including Timmins, Kirkland Lake, New Liskeard, Haileybury, Cobalt, North Bay and

Huntsville. The regimental badge was a moose with the motto, *Ne-Kah-Ne-Tah*, an Algonquin Indian phrase meaning, "We lead, others follow."

Along with the representative from Sweden the little league had grown to include a representative from Poland, Stanislas Popovich, who'd come to Canada in 1935 from a village outside of Warsaw to work in the Porcupine gold mines outside of Timmins. Stan had been one of the first to join the Algonquins, lusting for vengeance against the "bastard Nazis" who'd savaged his country. When he spoke of the bastards his face grew dark and his hands, each the size of a catcher's mitt, flexed as if he were in the act of strangling one of them.

Popovich was a cowboy and Indians movie buff and couldn't understand why Frank's family name was Archibald. He thought it should be Crazy Horse or Tonto or some such and Al had to explain that somewhere in the roots of Crow's family tree was a Hudson Bay fur trader whose marriage to a Cree woman had scattered a Scots name among the native settlements around James Bay.

The third Camp Borden addition to the league was Davey Ross from just outside Kirkland Lake, a place called Swastika. When the war started, pressure from the hoity toities of Southern Ontario to change the town's name had been something fierce but the townsfolk said to-hell-with-Hitler-we've-had-the-name-since-1906 and tore down the sign the Southies had put up saying henceforth and forever and ever amen the place would be known as "Churchill."

Ross was too young to be a delegate from anywhere, Billy kidding him about shaving without a blade in his razor, but just how young was the question. When Billy asked him directly the kid stuck out his jaw and said he was nineteen.

"Sure ya are, Davey old boy, and Barney's the pope's brother." Billy put his arm around Ross's neck and squeezed hard. "Listen, son, we figure you're about sixteen but we're not gonna say nuthin' ta nobody. You're not gonna get sent home, got it?"

Ross, who was only fourteen, nodded his head, his face creasing in an ear-to-ear grin.

The little league, newly configured, was just getting used to Camp Borden when the bush telegraph conveyed the news that by the end of the week the regiment would be moving on to another base, this one on the outskirts of Port Arthur, a town on the northwestern shore of Lake Superior. They would take to their new camp two lessons from the old—the basics of soldiering and pride in what they were all about.

Sergeant Gill had taught them the basics. Gill hailed from Kirkland Lake where he'd taught high school history and been in charge of the cadet corps. His Christian name was "Matt" for Matthew but he told them to call him "Gillie" whenever the brass weren't around. The little league liked Gillie.

Their days at Borden were days of repetitive exercises and drills, beginning with a bugle wake-up call at 0600 hours followed by their sergeant stomping through their H-hut and yelling at them, "Drop your cocks, grab your socks and get vertical, you horizontal bastards."

Gillie showed them how to salute, right hand flat, thumb tight, fingers extended and joined, palm out. He gave them World War I Ross rifles and told them what to do with them when commanded to "Order Arms!" or "Slope Arms!" or "Port Arms!" He took them through the Ps and Qs of close order drill with particular attention to those a little slow on the uptake when it came to the command, "By the left quick march!" Gill took care of that little irritant with white adhesive tape, marking the toe of left boots with a big "L."

From close order drill they moved on to route marches starting with punishing twenty-mile treks with forty-pound packs and eventually graduating to thirty and forty miles. On every march, at the noon break, off came the boots to swap socks from one foot to another, an old army trick to prevent blisters and foot rot in general.

On Sunday mornings it was church parade, the Christ Eaters off to the RC chapel and the Song Singers to the Protestant. Barney hung out with the Song Singers and belted out "Onward Christian Soldiers" with the best of them.

The pride that came from pleasing Gillie was reinforced by the culture of Borden where all the street names in the camp were reminders of epic Canadian battles—Lundy Lane, commemorating the famous showdown with American invaders in the War of 1812; Batoche, where the Riel rebellion was broken in 1885; Cambrai, where native sons fought so bravely in the First World War, 18,000 killed, wounded or missing. The message was clear. Whoever marched through these streets and drilled in this place were part of a brotherhood with a long and glorious tradition.

On the weekend before the move to Port Arthur, forty-eight-hour passes were issued from Saturday at 0600 hours to Monday at 0600 hours. With Gillie's connivance the boys from Lowvert sneaked away Friday night, catching the evening train that got them home at nine on Saturday morning.

The crew that arrived home in October was a lot different from the gang that had left home in September. After a month at Borden they were tougher, more disciplined, more close-knit. Al found it easy to explain why they were tougher and more disciplined but had a hard time understanding how they could be more close-knit. He knew it was true because he could feel it but it made no sense to him, especially for the original little leaguers who'd grown up together, gone to school together, played sports together, hunted and fished together, eaten and drunk together, chased girls together. They were, as the saying went, "thicker than thieves." So how could they possibly be any closer?

On the train home it took him a while to puzzle it all out. He figured it had a bit to do with being together twenty-four hours a day, seven days a week, eating at the same table and sleeping in the same hut, drilling and marching together, and something Barney had said about the uniform binding them together.

So that was part of it. But the more he pondered, the more he thought there was more to it. He remembered the sermon from their last church parade, the padre quoting from the twelfth chapter of First Corinthians, Saint Paul writing about the human body: "There are many parts, yet one body. The eye cannot say to the hand, 'I have no need of you,' nor again the head to the feet, 'I have no need of you.'" A time was coming, the padre said, looking at them directly, when their lives would depend on the men beside them. They had need of each other.

As the train pulled into Lowvert and he reached up to the luggage rack above his head for his kit bag he saw that his comrades were standing in the aisle forming a mock escort for him and Barney.

Just before they'd left Borden, Gillie had been promoted to lieutenant and the two of them to lance corporal, which accounted for the fact that when Barney and Al got off the train in Lowvert they outranked their comrades, a single stripe on their arms so signifying.

On the platform, in the midst of all the laughing, hugging and kissing, Al turned to his son, who was nestled in his mother's arms with his head shyly buried in her neck. Beth turned so Al could see Sandy's face and he reached out a finger to tickle the boy's cheek; but when he stepped back and held out his arms, his son turned his head away.

"Wait a bit. Give him a chance to get to know you again."

"Hey, I've only been gone a month, Beth."

"Yes, dear, but a month is a long time for a baby."

He supposed his wife was right but it rankled until he got home and Tippy, the family mutt, tail wagging, was barking and jumping all over him.

Home for the duration was his father's place on the east side of Ames Lake, a body of water divided by the ridge of Veterans Memorial Park sloping north to a narrow channel bridged by a structure that looked like a little pagoda. Billy and Barney lived in the older part of town on the west shore of the lake facing the park. Sandy McDougal had built his house overlooking the lake on the east side, a two-storey green clapboard with two bedrooms on the second floor, Al's and Beth's window with a view of the back yard and the victory garden planted by the women in response to the government's urging to grow "Vegetables for Victory."

In the living room the new lance corporal was down on all fours wrestling with the dog when he heard his mother tell him he had company. He turned to see his son crawling to join the fun and Al spent the rest of the morning with Sandy Jr. in his lap playing with his rattles but not before extracting a promise from his mother that she would cook all weekend for him. She smiled and told him they were going to have an early Thanksgiving—turkey and all the trimmings today, and tomorrow a roast of beef, which, because of the rationing, she'd had to finagle from a farmer friend of Gramps.

"Gramps?"

"That's your father's new name, Allan. We can't have two Sandys around. It's too confusing."

After playing with his son he announced he was going to do something he'd wanted to do for a month. Take a long, hot bath. He said he was damn tired of two-minute showers in lukewarm water.

Beth let him soak for fifteen minutes or so and then knocked with an offer to wash his back. When she reached over him to get the soap from the wire basket hanging on the tub, he grabbed her arm and half-heartedly tried to pull her in. She pushed him away laughing and then turned serious.

"Allan, do you mind if I go back to nursing school?"

Al straightened up, curious. "They'll take you back?"

"Oh, yes. There's a shortage of nurses, you see. And it's going to get worse. More and more girls are leaving to volunteer as army nurses, and hospitals all over the country are screaming for help. So the nursing schools have changed their tune about married women."

"What about the baby?"

"Oh, I think the one person in this family who really wants me to do this is your mother so she'll have little Sandy all to herself."

Al started to laugh. "Yeah, with you at nursing school she'll be able to dress him up and take him to all the IODE teas. He'll be an honorary Daughter of the Empire in no time."

"Oh, she loves to show him off, doesn't she?"

After the evening meal Al dug out the snapshots from Borden and told them about young Ross, Popovich and Christensen, especially Arnie's logging stories, felling trees—white and red pine—for Gillies Brothers at forty dollars a month plus room and board. It was winter work at forty below zero, so cold that at the end of the day the laces on his John Palmers had to be thawed beside the bunkhouse stove before he could untie his boots.

Al told them about the horses in the camps, how Arnie said they used big 1,700-pound Clydesdales, Percherons and Belgians for hauling or "skidding" out the logs to the Nipissing River. Reggie had pronounced it "Ni Pissing" which had quickly become their private little joke on the route marches. Whenever they stopped for a leak one of them was sure to go round and stop guys in mid-stream with the mock command, "Soldier, there is ni pissing around here."

At the Nipissing the logs were stacked on the river's edge waiting for the spring thaw in May, sometimes June, when the lumberjacks took their bars and peaveys to the frozen stacks and levered them into the water.

Al laughed when he mentioned how Arnie couldn't stop talking about how good the food was in the shanty camps, roasts and steaks and chops and homemade bread and cakes and cookies fresh from the oven. Every day.

Sunday morning both he and Gramps tried to get out of going to church but Myra, whom he'd taken to calling "Gram," wouldn't hear of it, so off they went.

The Reverend Mr. Payne, the Church of England minister, preached about Christian fortitude in the face of the Blitz, citing the brave people of London night after night enduring the terror of German bombs. Al heard his father muttering something about the fortitude of the Irish forced from their lands by English landlords. Payne quoted the American broadcaster, Edward R. Murrow, talking about looking out over London from a rooftop. "I saw many flags flying from staffs. No one told these people to put out the flag. They simply feel like flying the Union Jack. And among all those flags, not one was white."

After church, father and son walked the long way home wandering leisurely through the park, the town's memorial to the dead of a war that was supposed to end all wars. It was a sunny Indian summer day and Al kicked at yellow mats of damp birch leaves scattered here and there on the path. His wife and his mother with the baby in his carriage had gone directly home to cook the Sunday roast, a last meal for the condemned man soon again to be damned to the army's table d'hôte. *They say that in the army/ The food is very fine/ A bun rolled off the table/ And killed a friend of mine.*

They talked about the war and the bombing of Buckingham Palace, pictures of George VI and Queen Elizabeth inspecting the damage. Sandy, a little cynical as he was every Sunday he was forced to endure Reverend Payne, thought it was all propaganda, trying to make people think the royals had it just as bad as the poor buggers in London's East End where most of the bombs seemed to fall and most of the people definitely died.

They talked about the RAF, the gung-ho Spitfire and Hurricane pilots and how they seemed to be winning the war in the air if you could believe the newspapers and the radio consistently reporting Luftwaffe losses two and three times higher than the Royal Air Force. Sandy said the German papers probably had it the other way around.

Once they had scouted out clean spaces among the dirty white smears of bird droppings on the wooden bench near the memorial cairn, they sat and talked about Londoners using the tube, the city's subway system, as nighttime bomb shelters. Sandy figured you only saw the happy pictures of life underground, the spirited communal singing, the buskers entertaining laughing people and the visits of famous movie stars like Laurence Olivier and Vivian Leigh. He said you didn't see pictures of people packed in like sardines as they must have been, you didn't see harried mothers trying to nurse their babies, worried fathers trying to keep children away from the tracks.

Where did they all piss? Where did they shit? He couldn't imagine the smell. But you didn't hear anything about any of that. No siree! Mr. Edward R. Murrow wouldn't say anything about any of that! Wouldn't be good for morale, would it?

When Al turned to look at him and caught his eye Gramps shook himself and laughed. "Shouldn't go to church, son. Brings out the worst in me."

He sighed and, hands on knees, pushed himself up. "Come on, let's get on home. They'll be wondering what's happened to us."

After Sunday dinner, which Al ate slowly, savouring every mouth-watering bite, it was time to go and he said goodbye to his parents and son on the front steps of the house. It was his father's idea. He thought Al and Beth, just the two of them, should go to the station alone and take their time walking around the lake and up the hill to the waiting train.

Gram was holding Sandy Jr. and Al leaned forward to kiss him on the forehead, then his mother's cheek, then turned and shook his father's hand. Hoisting his kit bag to his shoulder, he swung round and went down the steps. At the bottom he hesitated, then dropped the bag to the ground, turned, went back up the steps and held his arms out to his son. As soon as he did, the boy reached out and Al took him, hugging him for a moment, and then handed him back to his grandmother.

Once across the road to the boardwalk circling the lake, the two of them turned and waved before walking briskly until they were out of sight of the front steps. At that point they slowed and began to stroll, hand in hand, toward the south end of the lake while Al told Beth about the walk home with his father after church that morning.

"Gramps was a bit testy, Beth. More so than usual. He okay?"

"He's fine, dear. He's just very worried about you."

Al shrugged. "How come? I'm just doing what we decided I should do."

"Yes, and he still thinks that way because deep down inside he believes that what you boys are doing is the right thing. But it doesn't mean he isn't worried. For your father, every time you leave Lowvert it's a step closer to when you leave Canada, a step closer to going overseas and that's a big step closer to his son being shot at."

Al was silent for a moment, the kit bag at his feet. They had stopped and were leaning on the wooden railing separating the boardwalk from the drop to the water ten feet below. He turned and bent to the gravel road behind him and picked up a flat stone, which he tried to skip over the water. But he was up too high for it to work. The stone went straight in and he stood there watching the ripples. "You think that's the real reason he isn't coming to the station?"

"No, I don't think so. Maybe partly, but I think he knows it's not easy for us to have the two of them around all the time."

Al turned to his wife and grinned. "Did all right last night, though, didn't we?"

Beth giggled as she ducked under his arm and snuggled close. They were looking out over the lake, remembering, and neither spoke for quite some time until Al began reciting.

"A friend is a gift that you give to yourself, that's one of my old-time songs. So I put you down with the best of them . . ."

Beth cut in and continued, ". . . for you're where the best belongs. Among the gifts I have given to me, most comforting, tried and true, the one that I most often think about, is the gift to myself of you."

It was what Al had written in her autograph book before he left for basic training; and when Beth finished the last line of the verse, he took her in his arms. They held each other for a long time until Beth squeezed him and said he was going to miss his train.

The gang on the train kidded Al all the way down to Toronto because every once in a while he'd drift away from them with eyes closed and mouth creased in the biggest smile they'd ever seen.

"There he goes again," said Billy. "Every half hour he's doin' it. Hey, Al, it's us—yer old buddies. Tell us what yer thinkin' about. As if we don't know."

Al just smiled some more and, eyes still closed, slowly shook his head. The pictures he was looking at in his mind were not just images of him and Beth in bed but also of holding his son, playing with Tippy, and gorging himself at tables of turkey and mashed potatoes, roast beef and Yorkshire pudding, pumpkin and apple pie. It was as if the war had never happened.

When their train arrived at Toronto's Union Station, they saw that the military police were posted at all the exits leaving no opportunity for them to reconnoitre the fleshpots of Hogtown. So they spent their time, the rest of the afternoon, exploring the nooks and crannies off the cavernous high-ceilinged hall of the biggest train station most of them had ever seen, except for Popovich, who said London's Liverpool Street Station was just as spacious.

If Union Station was something new, so was the train they boarded at suppertime. It was the first time any of them had travelled on the Canadian Pacific Railway, the other transcontinental route, the southern line linking the Maritime Provinces to Ontario and Ontario to the Prairies and British Columbia. The CPR brought about the discovery of nickel in Sudbury, carried British Columbia timber to the treeless Prairies, and central Canadian goods to supply the gold rush in the Yukon. It was also the railroad that made possible the port of Port Arthur where Western wheat was off-loaded from rail cars and on-loaded to Great Lakes ships.

But the CPR moved more than freight; it also moved people, immigrants to settle the West, more than two million of them over the years, settlers from the United States, Great Britain and continental Europe crowded together on the railway's "colonist cars," the same passenger coaches that were waiting for the Algonquins, coaches with toilets at one end and a coal-burning stove at the other. The lads were used to toilets in the cars but not to stoves. When they asked they were told that the stove was to heat the car but could also be used to make tea in the big tin pots hanging by the coal bucket.

Instead of CNR seats covered in a kind of ruby-red melton, CPR colonist seats were cane-backed and brown leather-bottomed. Folded down, the seat made a narrow bed that could sleep two if they were skinny. There was a top bunk above that could be pulled out and down from the wall near the ceiling and secured by a hook to the floor seat.

The lights were coming on in the city as they pulled out of the station through the Toronto marshalling yards, parallel tracks on either side, freight trains being assembled and freight trains being disassembled—cigar-shaped oil tankers, open-top coal cars and flatcars loaded with military vehicles, Jeeps, trucks, lorries and tanks, American-built Renaults from the First World War on their way to Borden to be used to train the newly formed Canadian Armoured Corps.

But mostly they passed boxcars, hundreds of them, empty ones with open sliding doors, and loaded ones, doors locked and sealed. Most of the boxcars were from Canadian railroads with the logo of the CPR, the CNR and the line from Toronto to Lowvert, the Timiskaming and Northern Ontario, the T&NO, stencilled on their sides. But there were also many from American railroads: Union Pacific, Illinois Central, New York Central, Western Pacific. Things were booming. The Depression was over. Happy days were here again. Thanks to the War.

Al's reverie was interrupted by the first call for dinner. They were eating in shifts and when it was their turn they found themselves in a dining car with linen-covered tables set with CPR cutlery and CPR china. But the meals were courtesy of their own Algonquin Regiment cooks. Tonight it was fish—"Ni Pissing Pickerel," according to Billy. But it was pretty good, "a helluva lot better than Borden," and they left their tables satisfied. Even Arnie Christensen.

The rest of the evening was spent passing the time playing cards or checkers, reading or just shooting the bull about their weekend adventures. Barney was sitting with Al, the two lance corporals going over their instructions from Gillie, who was travelling with the officers in another car. His orders were to keep the peace in their colonist car. No shenanigans he said.

There were no shenanigans. It was all quiet on the Algonquin front. Barney worked on his diary while Al leafed through a copy of *The Saturday Evening Post,* reading a review of the new Charlie Chaplin movie, *The Great Dictator*, which apparently was a grand spoof of Hitler. There was also an article about American public opinion. In 1939 it had been firmly against any involvement in another European war. Now, a year later, it was finally coming around in support of the British war effort. Al thought of the Reverend Manson Payne quoting Mr. Edward. R. Murrow.

A couple of seats forward Reggie had unpacked his guitar and he and Arnie were fooling around with some shanty songs. Once Reggie got the chording right, Arnie would sing, in a deep baritone, story songs of life in the camps, sad songs, rollicking songs, catchy tunes. Al soon lost interest in his magazine. For a while he stayed where he was and listened but soon got up and moved closer to hear better.

In the early days, lumbering was dangerous work, particularly in the spring when logs were levered into swollen rivers then poked and prodded through swift and treacherous currents to sawmills miles away. The logs often jammed on these river drives and men had to walk out on the jam and break it up with their peaveys. If the jam broke suddenly with a groaning roar they had only seconds to scramble back, leaping from log to log to the safety of the shore. Lots of times they didn't make it and when they didn't they were buried on the banks of the rivers where they died, their boots subsequently nailed to a nearby tree. In 1846, in and around Algonquin Park, 130 pairs of boots were nailed to trees on the banks of rivers flowing into the mighty Ottawa.

Other boots were nailed to other trees in other provinces and northern American states, the Miramichi in New Brunswick and the Penobscot in Maine. One of Arnie's songs was about the Penobscot where

. . . six of our Canadian boys did volunteer to go,

And break the jam on Gerry's Rocks with their foreman, young Munro.

They had not rolled off many logs when they heard his clear voice say,

"I'll have you men be on your guard for the jam will soon give way."

These words were hardly spoken, when the mass did break and go,

And carried off those six brave youths and their foreman, Jack Munro.

This was the song Arnie was singing when Al put down his magazine and moved forward in the swaying car. He wasn't the only one to gather round. There were more than a dozen soldiers leaning on adjoining seats or standing in the aisle keeping their balance by hanging onto upper bunks. Some of these bunks were occupied and men in their underwear leaned out to listen.

The sad ballad of "The Jam on Gerry's Rocks" was followed by a foot-stomping "How We Got Up to the Woods Last Year." Then there was a spirited version of "The Gatineau Girls," followed by a hand-clapping rendition of "The Winter Camp," with Reggie singing harmony. When the entertainers finally stopped to catch their breath there was hearty applause and piercing appreciative whistles of the two-fingers-in-the-mouth variety.

They sang for another hour or so until Barney came along in the middle of "You are my sunshine, my only sunshine," and told them it was time to pack it in. Later when Al was settling down in his upper berth he found himself humming the haunting tune of "Peter Emberley," the story of a young man from Prince Edward Island who left his home and family to work in the lumber woods by the Miramichi. He was killed there. Crushed to death by a falling log.

"Peter Emberley" was the one of the last songs Arnie had sung and when he finished the boys asked him to sing it again. And again. Until they knew it well enough to sing along with the chorus.

There's danger on the ocean where the waves roll mountains high,

There's danger in the battlefield where the angry bullets fly,

There's danger in the lumber woods for death lies silent there

And I have fell a victim unto danger's deadly snare.

When he fell asleep Al dreamed of fighting German soldiers at night in a forest where trees, huge white pines, were uprooted by violent explosions and the dark sky was flashing red with tracer fire. There were shouts and screams and cattle drowning in a water-filled ditch. When he lifted his head he saw Billy and Reggie and young Ross lying dead on either side of him, their eyes open, staring at him, condemning him. He heard a voice behind him shouting his name and when he turned there was Tony, a soldier's tin hat on his head and skates on his feet. He was wearing a Toronto Maple Leaf uniform, waving his hockey stick at Al and laughing. But the laughter was cut short by the sound of a referee's whistle. Two long blasts. Then a short. Then another long that got louder and louder until Al woke up and heard the train thundering through a level crossing.

He sat up dripping with sweat. Giving himself a shake, he looked at his watch, a rectangular Bulova his parents had given him on his twenty-first birthday. It was almost 0400 hours and he knew there would be no more sleep that night so he rolled into his pants and clambered down in search of a cup of tea.

Frank had already fired up the stove and was standing beside it waiting on the kettle. When he saw Al coming toward him he held up his hand, palm out, the signal to stop. "I know what you're gonna say, Al."

So they said it in unison as they grinned at each other. "A watched pot never boils."

"Whataya doin' up so early, Crow?"

"Billy snores. Sounds like a bull moose in mating season. What about you?"

"Bad dreams." Al looked at Frank then quickly turned away to peer out the train window at the passing night. "Ya know where we are, Crow?"

"Just west of Sudbury. Next stop Chapleau. Should be there around noon."

After Chapleau, where they disembarked with the bugle band to march to the ball field and do a few drills to show the locals what a spit and polish Northern outfit really looked like—the idea being to encourage enlistment—their next stop was White River, the station long and narrow with red brick siding and a slate roof. They knew from winter weather reports on the radio that White River was always the coldest spot in Ontario—Billy said Canada, but Barney said it couldn't be because Yellowknife in the Northwest Territories had to be colder. As if to confirm its chilly status there was a giant thermometer mounted on the station wall just under the black lettering on the white board sign identifying the town. Al figured the thermometer was there to let people know how cold was cold.

Standing at ease on the station platform waiting for the order to quick march to the town's hockey arena, where they were to repeat their earlier Chapleau performance, they were surprised to see the locomotive engineer, his fireman, conductors and brakemen walking along their ranks shaking hands. White River was a CPR divisional point where locomotives took on water and coal and trains changed crews, so the departing crew wanted to wish them well and tell them to give Hitler hell.

"Wonder when that'll be." Barney had left his section and sidled up to Al.

"When what will be?"

"When we give Hitler hell."

"Hey, Barn, I'm just a lance corporal. How the hell would I know? Ask the CO."

"I hear other units are goin' over."

"Yeah, but they've been trainin' for a year, Barn. Jesus, we haven't even fired a rifle yet."

Once back from the arena, no time was wasted lining up for the dining car. When the last meal had been served to the last hungry soldier the train was still in the station—some problems with the coal tender—so it was almost ten o'clock before they heard the two quick signal toots and felt the first lurch as the train got up steam powered by the *Royal Hudson*; the same locomotive, they were told, that had hauled the king and queen from Quebec City to Vancouver during the royal visit of 1939.

This was the last news of a long day. Especially for Al. By eleven he made sure everyone was tucked in before he climbed up to his own bunk and went out like a light.

The next morning at breakfast in the dining car, drinking tea and looking out the window, he had the same feeling he had when first coming into Borden: he was entering a foreign country. At Borden the muskeg and stunted firs of the North, balsam and spruce, had given way to a flatter landscape dotted with elms and oaks and Jack pines, straight and tall, nearer the camp. But on the way into Port Arthur, the foreign country on one side of the tracks was a land of rocks and cliffs, tree leaves in the colours of autumn, bright reds and yellows, while the other side, when he got up to look through patches of early morning fog, was the vast inland sea of Lake Superior, the water the same weathered copper colour as Ames Lake.

Once past White River, the CPR line followed the deep bays of the lake, through Schreiber and around Nipigon Bay down along Black Bay, past the Sleeping Giant and into the port city. The Sleeping Giant was twenty miles long, a human-shaped granite peninsula stretched out in the lake. Frank Archibald told them that an Ojibway legend had it that the Giant—the Indians called him Nanibijou—was turned to stone for revealing the secret location of peninsula silver to the greedy white man.

When the train came to a stop at the station they saw two big Castle Assads— Tony's name for Billy's house in Lowvert—with the same roof peaks, dormers and corner turrets, the same three storeys of dirty red bricks. Here the turrets were bookends on either side of a two-storey building housing the station's large waiting room. Big white squawking birds swooped around the station peaks. For some of them it was the first time they had seen seagulls.

The station faced the water and if you looked that way you could see railway tracks on jetties extending out into the lake, and to the left of the jetties a number of tall, concrete windowless structures they were told were grain elevators.

They formed up on the station platform and, after a word of welcome from the mayor and city dignitaries, the first wave of Algonquins in Port Arthur marched heads high past the city band, which was playing "The Maple Leaf Forever."

The Maple Leaf, our emblem dear,
The Maple Leaf, forever!
God save our King and heaven bless
The Maple Leaf forever!

Out on Water Street just down the hill from the Prince Arthur Hotel the proud column passed a building that reminded the little leaguers of the bridge over the narrows at Ames Lake. Crowds on both sides of the street clapped and cheered an enthusiastic welcome and in no time at all they found themselves standing at ease in front of what had once been a tourist resort. Now Current River Camp was their home away from home and would be for the next eight months.

Chapter Two

OCTOBER 20, 1940. Current River Camp. Our new home has a great view of Lake Superior. Can even see the Sleeping Giant on a clear day. The dance hall has been turned into our Mess Hut (2 sittings for each meal) and the tourist log cabins up on the hill behind the hall are now the officers' quarters (4 to a cabin). The rest of us are in H-huts grouped around a huge parade ground at the bottom of the hill, east of the Mess. We moved in just after the local Regiment, the Lake Superiors, moved out. They are known as the Lake Sups around here. We have been here three days now and are just getting to know the city. Should say "cities" as P.A. is right next door to Fort William. If I remember my Canadian history right, Fort William was established in the 1700s as a North West Company fur trading outpost and P.A. came later. Some of the gang have been downtown to check out the night life and report that it is pretty rough and tough. Lots of dock workers and sailors hanging around the beer parlours. And lots of Finlanders, Ukrainians and Italians, not to mention Poles. Popovich says he feels right at home. Says once they saw his uniform he didn't pay for a beer all night. Word is Fort William has a big red light district down around Pacific Avenue. That would explain the first day lecture from the padre about personal morality and loose women. Also the films shown by the MO about the dire consequences of the clap and the painful treatment methods thereof.

Excerpt from Barney's Diary

The first time their newly issued Lee Enfields were used for real was at the Mount McKay rifle range. An Ojibway settlement was nearby and both the settlement and the range were on the Fort William side of the McIntyre River dividing the two communities.

Bull's-eye targets were set up at the base of the mountain, a slope of shale running up to a cliff, the cliff straight up a thousand feet to what looked like a man's flat black cap sitting on the head of the mountain. Gillie told them they were firing at the mountain because it was a well-known fact that most of them couldn't hit the side of a barn door.

Firing began from a prone position at a range of two hundred yards, the spotters in the concrete dugouts underneath the targets using a red disc on a long pole to show them where on the concentric rings of the bull's eye they'd placed their shots. Most were on target, as Gillie well knew they would be, because Northern Ontario boys knew how to shoot, especially Frank Archibald, who hit the bull's eye dead centre eight times out of ten.

When each section was finished, the men were taken aside, and in another instance of "Carrying Coals to Newcastle," shown how to clean their weapons with the small bottle of gun oil and the weighted, flannel pull-through found in the spring-loaded clip in the butt of their rifles. They were strongly advised to make use of these cleaning materials every day and were taught a little action rhyme to hammer home the message that their rifles were to be treated with great respect: "This is my rifle, this is my gun. This is for business, this is for fun," the weapons instructor pointing to his rifle and then to his groin as he chanted the verse.

When not at the rifle range, officers, Gill among them, were dispatched to search out suitable sites for training manoeuvres. The *rumeur de jour* was that the regiment might be part of an invasion force to retake Norway and so the search was concentrated behind Boulevard Lake, a body of water man-made in the 1920s by damming the Current River upstream from the camp. Around the lake, on the hill behind the officers' cabins, was a vast park, mostly trees— evergreen, willow, birch and poplar—with scores of trails; a good place for cross-country ski training.

When the snow came they were issued long, white, hooded anoraks, presumably so they would blend in with Norway. They were also supplied with skis and bindings that fit over their army boots. Thus outfitted they were trucked over to Mount McKay to a ski school run by some local Finns. Downhill training was to come before cross-country and that's when Billy's fate was sealed.

When it came to downhill skiing it wasn't that the little leaguers were know-nothings, it was just that the runs on Mount McKay weren't the slopes down to Ames Lake. And army boots were made for marching.

After their instructors had demonstrated the fundamentals and they'd practised a bit on some slow, small adjacent hills, the platoon took T-bars up to the top of the mountain, where they turned to find themselves looking down at a slope suggesting the earth really was flat and they were perched on the edge of it.

"I can see it now," said Billy shaking his head. "The old man gets a telegram tomorrow saying, 'Regret to inform you that your son, Private William Assad, is reported missing in action after going ass-over-teakettle off a cliff on Mount McKay near Port Arthur.'"

"Or," said Barney, "your son, Private Assad, died bravely with a big spruce tree up his ass."

"Hey, yeah, that would be great for the holidays. With his white coat, our Billy could be the angel on top of the regimental Christmas tree."

"Fuck you, McDougal, and all your Irish ancestors."

They all laughed for a bit until, one by one, they sputtered off into silence, each one of them requiring serious time to thoroughly examine the profound significance of their foggy breath in the cold morning air. Finally Popovich posed the question they were all avoiding. "Okay, boys, who is the first man to go?"

Nobody said a word. Nobody moved. After a minute, Al looked at Barney. "Suppose we have to set an example, eh, Lance Corporal?"

"Certainly, Lance Corporal, but which lance corporal will set it?"

"Aha, Lance Corporal, that is the question. Tell ya what. I'll flip ya for it. Tails I win, heads you lose."

"Very funny, sir. Who's got a coin?"

Billy took off his gloves and dug in his pants pocket for a quarter. Thumbing it in the air, he caught it and covered it on his wrist. Al called heads. He always called heads. And heads it was. So Barney offered a mock salute and quickly shoved off, followed by Christensen, then Reggie, then Popovich, Ross and the rest. Al was the last to go, right behind Billy.

He tried to remember what they'd been told, to ski in winding sweeps from side to side and was getting a feel for it, leaning in and out of his wide turnings as he navigated between rocks and spruce trees and other wonders wrought by the hand of God. Curving past a number of soldiers heaped in a tangle of jutting skis and waving poles, casualties of inexperience or too much exuberance, he could see that they were grinning and laughing and none the worse for wear. However, farther down in front of him was Billy, his slow sweeps more like sharp zigs and fast zags.

Al had a premonition and snowplowed to a stop just as one of Private Assad's zags took him over a mogul and launched him out of sight, yelling, into a clump of spruce. Fearing the ensuing silence, Al bent down, quickly undid his bindings, and scrambled toward the last sighting of the Lebanese daredevil.

When Al found him at the base of a tree, Billy was unconscious, his forehead gashed and bleeding, his left leg bent at an angle Mother Nature had never intended.

Once their first casualty of the war was tobogganed down the hill, taken to hospital and patched up—eight stitches in his forehead and a cast from toe to thigh—Billy found out his accident was going to be an early Christmas present when the medical officer told him he would be shipped home to recover. There he knew he would be nursed back to health by a certain Mabel Reath, one of Beth's classmates Billy had begun courting just before Borden. Barney said there was a silver lining in every cloud.

The day Billy was bundled off, a few of the downhill survivors went into town after supper to see a double bill at the Lyceum featuring John Garfield in *Flowing Gold* and Wayne Morris and Rosemary Lane in *Ladies Must Live*. The lads were looking to be entertained but before the features, *Movietone News* showed them what the *Luftwaffe* had done to Coventry.

A city in the English Midlands, Coventry was famous for its timbered buildings hearkening back to medieval times, its fourteenth-century cathedral, and the legend of Lady Godiva who supposedly rode naked through the town on a dare. But on the night of November 14, 1940, Coventry became famous for another reason. Heinkel bombers, loaded with incendiary explosives, razed the cathedral to a Gothic ruin, burned the medieval timbered buildings to ashes, and charred hundreds of people to a crisp.

The Germans paid dearly for the raid. Or so they were told. A voice brimming with patriotic enthusiasm told the Algonquins slumped in their theatre seats that 100 enemy planes had been shot down in flames by the heroic RAF. Al shook his head, remembering the conversation with his father in Veterans Park and wondering if the Germans had any planes left, given that the RAF had shot down so many so often.

By the end of November they were playing hockey in the Lakehead Hockey League. Seven teams were in the LHL with the Algonquin Mooseheads quickly establishing themselves as one of the top three, so good that most of the boys from Lowvert, who hadn't really played since their boyhoods, saw little ice time.

In mid-December they went to their first dance, hosted by the YMCA at the local armouries, hanging out with a bunch of nurses from the Fort William Sanatorium. They talked, drank beer and jived in their army boots to music made popular by the Andrews Sisters.

In no time at all they were home on Christmas leave, Billy meeting them at the station in a walking cast, telling them he and Mabel were getting married on Boxing Day and that Tony was going to be his best man.

"Tony who?" asked Al with a grin.

"Hey, when I got home, Pietro came to see me. Gave me Tony's address. Said he wanted to hear from the gang. So I wrote to him."

"So when's he comin' in?"

"Next week. Day or two before Christmas. Said he'd send a telegram and let me know for sure. He's playin' hockey for an army team, outta Cornwall."

"So how's he gonna get off for Christmas?"

"Same way you guys did, I guess."

So Christmas 1940 was going to be a very special occasion. The little leaguers had been looking forward to spending some time in the old hometown celebrating the season with their families and friends. Now they had other reasons to lift a glass or two. Billy's wedding and Tony's visit.

But Tony never showed up. The telegram said he was sorry but he'd just found out that the team was travelling out West for a series of exhibition games over the holidays. When Al heard the news he went to Billy and told him to ask Barney to be his best man.

"But I was gonna ask you, Al."

"And I was hopin' ya would, Billy. But I know Barney would be tickled pink if ya asked him. I'll be an usher."

And so the wedding photo of the bridal party showed the happy couple flanked by Barney Berman as best man and Beth McDougal as matron of honour. Beside Beth were a number of nurses from the hospital, while beside Barney were Al, Reggie and Frank. All the men were in uniform and all of the women in hats and suits, there being no time and little money for the traditional wedding garb.

Leaving Billy behind to begin his married life and finish his convalescence, they returned to Current River for New Year's Eve so the rest of the regiment, the second shift, could get some holiday time. They had a party in their H-hut, toasting 1941 with poor man's champagne; but after a couple of beers Al drifted away to sit near the coal stove at the back of the hut and look at the pictures he'd brought from home: snapshots of his son splashing in his baby's bathtub; lying bare bum on his belly on a rug; being cuddled by his grandmother; proudly displayed for the camera by his grandfather and standing on unsteady legs holding his mother's hand.

Chapter Three

JANUARY 21, 1941. Current River Camp. Just found out what "red light district" means. Apparently in the First WW the whorehouses in France used to advertise their presence by lights, blue lights for officers and red lights for the common soldier. Amazing what you learn in the Army, isn't it? Wonder why "blue light" didn't survive? Not enuff real men in the Officer Corps to keep the blue light ladies in business? The rumour this week is we're not going to Norway, not right away anyway, but we are going to relieve the Home Guard at some of the POW camps in the North. Sounds like one Company will be going to Espanola, another to Gravenhurst and another to Monteith. Hope our Company goes. Give us a chance to see what the tough guys of Adolph's Master Race look like. I'll be tempted to walk up to the first one I see, point my rifle at him and say, "Ich bin ein Jude." Wonder what he'd do? Billy's back with us. Still walks with a bit of a limp but says his leg is fine.

Excerpt from Barney's Diary

Barney got his wish. The little league was among those chosen for Monteith, just down the T&NO line from Lowvert.

Just before leaving Current River Camp, Lieutenant Gill called Lance Corporal McDougal aside and told him he was recommending him for promotion to sergeant.

"I've been keepin' a eye on you, my boy. Seems to me, stripes or no stripes, doesn't matter, you're the leader of your gang. You've got one stripe now and the army might as well give you two more and make it official."

Al shifted his gaze from Gill to the ground at his feet. He didn't say anything. He was trying to contain his surprise and at the same time find a way of saying, "Are-you-out-of-your-goddamn-mind?" graciously.

"What's the matter, McDougal, cat got your tongue?" It was what Al's mother used to say to him when he had nothing to say for himself. He looked up.

"Sergeant? Ah, jeez, Gillie." He shook his head. "I dunno. I'm not sure. When push comes to shove I think I'd rather take orders than give them."

Gill was looking at him, his head cocked to one side, a sly grin on his face.

"Hey, Gillie, you gotta know. Ya musta thought of this. How can ya give an order to a buddy that might get him killed?" He was thinking of Billy and Crow, Reggie and Barney. And Ross. Yeah, Ross. A kid, for Pete's sake. "I'd feel like a murderer. How could I live with myself?"

His lieutenant sighed and nodded, "Yeah, I thought of it, all right. Thought about it for a long time when I was promoted. And the way I figured it out was this: Better me givin' an order, better you givin' an order, than some stupid shit who doesn't know his arse from his elbow."

He paused for a moment, reviewing his own argument, then shrugged and started to turn away. "Think about it, my friend. But don't take too long. I need to know right after breakfast tomorrow."

By breakfast Al still hadn't made up his mind. He'd thought about it most of the night, tossing and turning. He mulled it over sitting on the john, he pondered while shaving, deliberated while making his bed, and weighed the pros and cons over his porridge and scrambled eggs.

As he was putting on his greatcoat in the hallway of the mess, he looked up and saw the commanding officer's New Year's message still tacked on the bulletin board.

> Be truthful.
>
> Be patient with and considerate of all.
>
> Be respectful to your superiors; kind and generous to your equals; just and civil to your subordinates.
>
> Be clean and smart in your personal appearance.
>
> Obey lawful orders cheerfully and promptly.
>
> Be firm in doing what is right.
>
> Let your 'Yea' be yea and your 'Nay' be nay
>
> Remember your Creator in the days of your youth.
>
> Fear God, Honour the King.

Reading it again this morning Al's opinion of the message hadn't changed. It was still Boy Scout stuff. Yet something struck him about it. "Let your 'Yea' be yea and your 'Nay' be nay." Another way of saying fish or cut bait, shit or get off the pot.

He left the mess hut and picked his way up the hill using the packed snow path of the shortcut through the trees. He found Gill and told him he'd do it.

"On one condition."

"And that would be?"

"Make me acting sergeant and then . . ." His voice trailed off and he shrugged.

Gill thought for a minute, then nodded. "Okay, it's a deal. Acting sergeant it is. And if it doesn't work out we'll do what we have to do."

He stuck out his hand and the two men shook on the deal. Then Al stepped back, stood at attention, winked as he smartly saluted, and turned on his heel to make his way back down the hill on the road this time, the long way around, squinting in the brightness of the morning sun on the snow, hoping he'd done the right thing.

A few days before entraining for Monteith, the company was briefed on what to expect. The camp, designated Camp Q for security reasons, was situated south of the village and separated from it by the T&NO rail line and the gravel highway to Porquis Junction. The main gate was just across the highway from the railway siding. There prisoners were taken off the POW trains arriving from ports on the East Coast where Germans and Italians got their first introduction to Canada after disembarking from POW ships sailing from Liverpool and Greenock, Scotland. Their second introduction came as their twenty-five coach trains—two Home Guards in every coach, windows nailed shut and no doors on the toilets—trundled westward through the hamlets and towns of the Maritime Provinces and school kids standing beside the tracks stuck out their tongues and thumbed their noses at the enemies of their king and country, Wops and Jerries.

At Camp Q the rectangular prison compound was surrounded by an outer and an inner fence about fifteen feet high, both topped with barbed wire. On each corner of the wire and at the midpoint on all four sides was a guard tower manned by a sentry with a World War I Lewis machine gun. Inside the compound were a kitchen and mess hall along with four other buildings. The biggest of the four housed a barbershop, a tailor shop, a shoe repair shop, a post office, the POW administrative office and a canteen. The three smaller buildings included a recreation hall, chapel and infirmary.

Accommodation was provided by eighteen Canadian Army H-huts, so called because they were constructed in the form of the letter "H," the long sides for sleeping and the short connecting link in the middle for toilets and showers. Each hut had a capacity of eighty prisoners, forty in each wing. Not all of the huts were filled in January of 1941. There were still rooms to let.

The H-huts were built off the ground with a crawl space underneath. This, they were told, was so guards could duck down for a look-see to make sure nothing funny was going on, no tunnelling from beneath the huts out under the wire.

In the centre of the compound was a large parade square used primarily for roll call but also as a soccer pitch in summer and, when flooded, a hockey rink in winter. On the side of the square closest to the gate, a swimming pool was under construction.

"A swimming pool! Jesus H. Christ on a crutch! A swimming pool for fucking Nazis?"

Billy wasn't shouting but his loud whisper carried to almost every corner of the mess hut where their briefing was being held. He was quickly ordered to stand and identify himself to the briefing officer.

"Assad, sir, Private William, B55380, and this here soldier sitting beside me, sir, is my buddy, Lance Corporal Barney Berman, we grew up together. Sir, Lance

Corporal Berman is a Jew, sir, and he is too much of a gentleman to say anything so I am speaking on his behalf and I expect on behalf of all of us here, sir. That building a goddamn swimming pool for Nazi pigs who we know have killed Jews and Polish women and children, as my friend Private Popovich can tell you, sir, not to mention English civilians by the thousands in their bombing raids on London and Coventry—they should not have any fucking swimming pool, sir!"

It was the longest and most formal speech Billy had ever delivered in his life and it was greeted with a standing ovation. His listener, arms folded across his chest and the hint of a smile on his face, waited it out and when the men sat down, cleared his throat and growled, "Private Assad, you are an insubordinate son-of-a bitch!" There was silence as Billy prepared himself for a verbal shit kicking. "But I agree with you a hundred and ten percent."

The unexpected was interrupted by a swift and vigorous applause, which was immediately waved down. "Except . . ."—pause for emphasis—". . . except for one thing. Sometime soon, maybe next month, who knows, maybe next year, you boys will be on a battlefield somewhere in a shooting war with these Nazi pigs. Some of you will be killed. Some of you will be wounded. And some of you will be captured. Now, if we treat our German prisoners of war right, the thinking is that word will get back to Germany and if any of you boys get captured you'll be well treated over there."

There were more than a few hoots of disbelief at all this and the officer held up a hand. "Boys, what I've just told you is what I've been told on good authority. It's the reason why there's a swimming pool at Camp Q, and a canteen, and a lot of other things. It's not for them. It's for us. If we get captured."

He waited for the muttering to die down. "And there's one other thing. And it's important." He pointed a finger at them.

"If word gets back that being a POW is a pretty good thing over here, then when things start getting tough for Jerry over there he might think surrendering is a pretty damn good idea."

The officer was nodding with emphasis now. "Boys, the more of them we can get to throw down their arms the fewer of them we'll have to fight. There's more than one way to win a war, boys."

The Algonquins were then told what to expect in terms of camp inmates. When Monteith had opened it was filled with students, professors, labourers, businessmen, rabbis, priests in their black robes, and scores of Orthodox Jews with their beards, sidelocks, skullcaps and prayer shawls. Their crime was that they were German nationals caught in England when war broke out and all German nationals were seen as potential spies, saboteurs and fifth columnists. So they were rounded up and sent to the colonies where they could do no harm.

At camp Q they were joined by other German nationals rounded up in Canada—men deemed to have opportunities for espionage because of their business and industrial connections and recent immigrants who were members of suspect organizations such as the Canadian Society for German Culture or

Deutscherbund Kanada or Canadian-German groups associated with the National Socialist German Workers' Party, the Nazi Party itself.

As Barney sat and listened to all this he stared at the floor and slowly shook his head at the unbelievable idiocy of lumping rabbis and Orthodox Jews in the same POW camps as Canadian Nazis, self-professed followers of the Jew-hating *Führer*. He thought to himself that the Jews had left Germany because they were Jewish and now were imprisoned in Canada because they were Germans.

His musings were interrupted by a Billy elbow in the ribs. "Ya hear that?"

"What?"

"Listen."

The officer was talking about the present occupants of the camp. Barney heard him say, ". . . and these are proud and arrogant veterans, the conquerors of Europe who believe England will fall within the month and the war will be over by Easter."

Later Billy told him what had been said while Barney had been pondering the unfathomable stupidity of the bureaucratic mind. The inmates first in Monteith had now been shipped out to another camp in New Brunswick near a place called Ripples. Their replacements were German navy personnel, including some submariners captured when their U-boats were sunk in the North Atlantic. As well there were *Luftwaffe* pilots shot down over England and the veterans the major mentioned, soldiers from General Erwin Rommel's Seventh Panzer Division that had crushed Northern France in a matter of days.

"Now, gentlemen, you will be relieving the Home Guard at Camp Q. As you know, the Guard is composed of veterans of the last war and they've been on the job since the beginning. Not only do they need a rest but they also require some training to deal with the kinds of POWs now coming to Canada. But the vets will be around for a few days to help with orientation. Then you'll be on your own. Any questions?"

There were a number of how, what, where and when questions concerning their specific duties as prison guards. Would they be working around the clock in eight-hour shifts, one platoon per shift? Did they have to go inside the wire at any time or would they be strictly outside? If they had to go inside would they go with their weapons? How many men were in the towers with the Lewis Gun? They were supposed to be there for six weeks, would there be any time off? What was the food like? Billy wanted to know if they would eat as well as the Nazi pigs.

Some of their questions the major answered and others he promised would be answered once they got to Camp Q. But there was one question he didn't answer because no one thought to ask it. No one thought to ask what they were to do if the proud and arrogant conquerors of Europe attempted a mass escape.

Chapter Four

FEBRUARY 5, 1941. Camp Q. Been here a few weeks now and are well settled in. Home Guards left day before yesterday. Just the Camp CO and a few of their officers left. No chance yet to stick my rifle up a Nazi nose and tell him who I am, mostly because I'm stuck behind a desk doing the paperwork for PWD or Prisoner Work Details. Which also means I am in a different platoon now. Administrative. If they leave me here guess I'll end up with HQ Company back in PA. Big excitement the other day that I forgot to mention. Al's platoon was assigned to meet a trainload of POWs at 0300 hours, 40 below zero. Marched them into the Rec. Hall in the compound where they were searched and catalogued. Billy said a lot of them spoke really good English and were snotty as hell. Asked Al at breakfast who they were and he says more Seventh Panzer types and one SS officer. I believe the SS are the sick bastards who do their basic training with German Shepherds. Start out with them as puppies. Then, after a year, as part of their final vows to Hitler, a sign that they have but one supreme loyalty, they slit their dog's throat. Bright, sunny and cold today and we are still digging out. Tons of snow. Worst storm in 30 years. Or so they tell me. Trains going by with locomotives pushing big red snowplows to clear the tracks. Snowbanks on the highway are easily ten feet high. Billy got a note from Mabel today. He's going to be a father. Al asked me to speak to one of the POWs and get some cigars from their canteen in honour of the occasion. Will give me a chance to practise my German. Won't tell Billy where I got the stogies. He wouldn't appreciate it! Surprising what Jerry can get in his canteen—candy, gum, chocolate bars, ice cream and soft drinks, boot brushes, hairbrushes, shaving brushes, toothbrushes, clothing brushes, face cream, fruit salts and magazines including Look, The New Yorker *and* Reader's Digest. *Am told that fresh fruit is also available from time to time with apples selling for a penny and bananas at four cents apiece.*

Excerpt from Barney's Diary

While Barney was writing in his diary Al was up in the northwest guard tower checking in with Popovich and Christensen. He had Arnie's binoculars and was peering at a group of prisoners some three hundred yards away huddled together near the far end of the hockey rink up against the snow banked high against the perimeter fence.

Al could make out the uniforms, a half-dozen U-boat crew in their black berets, gray-green leather jackets and trousers; three or four airmen, *Luftwaffe* bomber crew, shivering in their tan-coloured summer flying suits; and a couple of Panzer types, black battle jackets belted tightly over black pants bloused over black boots.

These men were gathered around two other POWs who looked like they were having a lively exchange of views. The shorter one was dressed in a prison issue mackinaw with a big red circle sewn on the back to identify the wearer should he be so bold as to venture outside the wire without an escort. For the same reason, his pants had a red stripe down the right leg. Billy had scoffed at the red circle and stripe. "As if an escaped prisoner is gonna walk around out there with a big red circle on his coat and a red stripe down his pants."

Until it was worn out, POWs were allowed to wear the uniform they had when captured, and Al recognized the taller of the two debaters as being the SS officer he'd escorted from the train, a hard and mean looking man in black—a jacket with the double lightning flash insignia on the lapel and breeches tucked into jackboots.

"Take a look." He handed the binoculars to Arnie.

"At what?"

"See those prisoners over in the corner?" He pointed. "Take a look and tell me what you see."

Arnie planted his feet, adjusted the lens, waited a moment, then took a deep breath and spoke very slowly. "I see sea shells by the sea shore."

Popovich slapped his thigh and howled with laughter. Al just shook his head and grinned. Ever since they'd met the Pole and the Swede, both he and Barney were always getting them to do tongue twisters, being particularly fond of Popovich's version of "I'm not a fig plucker, nor a fig plucker's son but I'll pluck your figs till the fig plucker comes."

"Okay, Christensen, you're a real comedian, but it's 'She sells sea shells by the sea shore,' and ya still can't do 'Peter Piper picked a peck of pickled peppers,' but never mind. Just take a look at those guys, will ya?"

"Yes sir, Sergeant." Arnie gave Al a backhanded salute and then turned to focus on the corner of the compound. After a moment, still looking, he spoke out of the side of his mouth. "Well two of 'em are havin' a real argument, I can tell ya that."

"What else?"

"About the two guys?"

"Yeah."

"The little guy's been a POW for a while right? A civilian."

"'Cause he's not in uniform?"

"Right."

"Probably. What about the tall guy?"

Arnie took a moment to centre on the tall guy. He stared for a bit, then held the glasses aside in his left hand while he rubbed his eyes with the knuckles of his right. When he brought the glasses up again the tall Nazi turned his face toward the tower and Private Christensen remembered. The rec hut. Blond hair cut far above the ears, square jaw, thin lips, eyes, hard and cold and the officer's cap with the German eagle on the peak, the skull and crossbones just above the visor.

"That prick, the one who would not talk to us because we were not officers. Yes, I remember him. Said he was a Hauptmann."

"Yup, a captain, and he was only gonna talk to another captain until Gillie explained the facts of life to him."

Gill's explanation was to take the Hauptmann outside in the cold, stand him in the middle of the floodlit parade ground without a coat and tell him to wave to the guard towers when he'd decided he wanted to come in and talk to whoever asked him a question.

Al had the binoculars now and was observing the debate again when suddenly the SS officer looked up at the tower as if he knew they were watching. He turned his back and obviously said something because, very quickly, the group broke up and scattered to different H-huts. As best he could, Al made a mental note of who went where, especially the two principal debaters. Then he handed the binoculars to Popovich and beckoned Arnie to follow him. He wanted to take a closer look at things.

Once inside the compound he shuffled around the rink with Arnie in tow sniffing around for anything out of the ordinary. He had just crossed the blue line on his way to the spot where the POWs had had their powwow when he heard a shout behind him. "*Verdammter Kanuck!*"

Al slid to a stop. He wasn't sure what the words meant but he had a pretty good idea. Taking a slow deep breath and blowing it out, he pivoted on his heel and saw the SS Hauptmann heading toward him.

"Did you say something, Captain?" The tone of Al's question and its unspoken tag end was ". . . you snotty Nazi son-of-a-bitch."

The Hauptmann put on a solemn and puzzled face and shook his head as if he hadn't understood a word the Canadian had said. Al looked down at the ice for a second and then up at the now-smirking Nazi. He knew he was being taunted and had to fight the urge to bloody the Hauptmann's nose.

Then suddenly his face creased in a wide grin, surprising the German, who looked at his captor quizzically. He had no way of knowing that Al was remembering a hockey game, Billy taunting a kid from Iroquois Falls, shouting at him, "Your mother wears army boots," the kid swinging his stick, Billy ducking and skating away laughing when the kid got a penalty. Sometimes you looked pretty stupid when you got your Irish up.

He was trying to remember some German phrases Barney had been teaching him. Finally he nodded and pointed his finger at the SS officer. *"Für euch ist der Krieg zu Ende.* For you the war is over."

He couldn't remember all of the next phrase so he threw in a little English. "You," pointing again, "are a *Kriegsgefangener* and don't you forget it, chum. You are *kaputt.* You are Hauptmann Kaputt."

With that he turned and made his exit from the rink and the compound.

Two days later Al was awakened in the middle of the night by degrees, barely conscious of the first noise, a hockey referee's whistle, shrill, over and over again followed by distant sounds of slamming doors and shouting men. He grunted, pulled the blanket over his head and rolled over.

But he swore and came up, hard and fast, like a wooden marionette jerked on a string when he heard the sharp crack of a rifle shot, then two more. He sat there shaking his head and rubbing his eyes wondering if he'd been dreaming. But the wail of the camp siren said no.

Quickly now he swung his legs out of the bunk and stood, shivering but wide awake. The barrack lights came on and he glanced around at men still sleeping, men half out of their bunks and men standing trying to get their bearings. Al slept in his long johns and socks, the H-hut was damn cold at night, so it didn't take him long to get dressed, ducking into his sweater, pulling up his pants, hooking his suspenders over his shoulders and bending to lace up his boots. Grabbing his greatcoat and winter cap he ran to the door. Just as he reached for the latch, the door was pushed open from the outside. Gill stood there, eyes wide, chest heaving.

"Get the lads together," he stopped to catch his breath. "Get them together at Camp Security and wait for me there." He turned to go.

"What'll I tell 'em?"

"Tell 'em there's been an escape. Tell 'em they've got a job to do. Now get movin'."

Al shouted at Gill's back. "How many got out?"

"Jesus, Al, how the hell do I know! Go, go go!"

Al had the lads ready in ten minutes. Snowshoes, skis, white parkas and loaded Lee Enfields. Thirty minutes later Gillie came sauntering through the door, stamping the snow off his boots. He took off his greatcoat, threw it over a chair and went to the pot-bellied stove to warm his hands. After a minute he spoke over his shoulder.

"Okay, gather round the stove, boys." He rubbed his hands together for another few seconds and then turned to face them.

"There's been an escape."

They looked at him. He shrugged. "Ya already know that."

They nodded. "Okay, what ya don't know, what I don't know, what nobody knows is how many got out. They're doin' a hut-to-hut head count right now, so we should know pretty soon. Another thing we don't know is where Jerry's headed. So until we have some answers you stand down." *Hurry up and wait* was a venerable army adage.

There were no complaints. No one was keen on heading out into the thirty-five-below-zero cold. But they were curious.

"What exactly will we be doin,' Gillie?"

"We'll be goin' after 'em and when we find 'em, we'll be bringin' 'em in."

"Know how they got out?"

"Not sure yet."

"So, if ya don't know how many got out or how they got out, howdaya know there was even an escape?"

"Ya heard the shots, Private?" Billy nodded. "Well, the guard patrolling outside the wire by the rink just happened ta see something move in the snow on his side of the wire. When he went to investigate the something got up and started to run."

Gill chuckled. "Guess the poor bastard didn't know whether to shit or go blind. Said it was just as if a snowman was layin' on the ground and all of a sudden got up and skedaddled. Guard got off three shots but it was dark . . ." He raised his hands in a "what-can-you-say" gesture.

When there were no more questions, Gill motioned to Al. "Pick three or four men and get out there. Grab some of those big flashlights they have in the guard hut and nose around where the guard saw the big, running snowman."

He grinned at this as if he didn't really believe the story. "And take a look at the wire and see what ya can find."

Al pulled his sleeve back and glanced at his watch. The time was 0235. He was surprised. He thought it was later. He felt like he'd been up for hours. Looking around he caught Crow's eye, then Billy's and Reggie's and Arnie Christensen's. Once he'd briefed them he sent the Swede over to the guard hut to pick up the flashlights. Then he led the rest of them, their rifles clutched in one hand and snowshoes in the other, to the road that ringed the outer wire. There they swung left, double-timing it to the spot where the guard had shot at the snowman, boots crunching the hard-packed snow, breath fogging the frozen night air.

A half-dozen Algonquins were milling around by the light standard on the far side of the culvert, a square cap made of tarred railway ties that bridged the gully twisting beside the compound where the rink was. A soldier pointed to the top of the snowbank, where a private from Five Platoon was talking to Major Lapointe, the camp commandant, who looked like the British actor, Ronald Colman. Al climbed the bank and caught the tail end of an explanation.

". . . and then he just disappeared. Down the gully, I guess, sir."

Lapointe turned as Al stood at a precarious attention on top of the bank and saluted. "Ah, Sergeant, it is much too cold for such formalities. Private McGinn here has just been telling me what he saw and I would like you to listen and tell me what you think."

Lapointe nodded to McGinn and the private repeated his tale. He had been walking his beat back and forth between the tower at the corner and the one by the culvert. At about 0145, just after he'd turned around to head back to the corner tower, he heard something behind him. He said he remembered the time because his relief was scheduled for 0200 hours and, since he was freezing and couldn't wait to get in from the cold, he'd been looking at his watch a lot.

Wheeling around in the light of the perimeter lamps, he caught a glimpse of what looked like a big, bulky white bag sliding over the snowbank down into the gully. Unshouldering his rifle he ran back, climbed the bank and flashed his light into the darkness of the culvert opening, an opening almost covered by snow. He could see nothing but had the presence of mind to run to the other side and there he saw the bag squirm out and start to run. It was then that he blew his whistle.

"So there's a guy in the bag and he's running?" Al was wondering how anyone could run through the snow at the bottom of the gully.

"Well, yeah, Sarge, but come ta think 'bout it, ya know, it was a funny kind of runnin', like he had a load in his pants and two left feet."

"So ya took a shot at him and . . . ?"

"First of all I yelled, ya know, halt, and when he just kept goin' I fired a round above his head. Then when he didn't stop I tried to hit him. But he was just a shadow by then. It was too dark to see."

"What do you think, Sergeant?" Al had thanked McGinn and climbed down the snowbank with Lapointe. The two stood face to face, huddled in their greatcoats, the major stamping his feet to keep the blood circulating to his toes.

"Ever see a snowshoe race, sir?"

Lapointe shook his head.

"Neither have I, but we used ta fool around at it. When we were kids out getting our Christmas trees. Lots of fun. And when you race in snowshoes, sir, you look like you've got a load in your pants and two left feet."

"Ah," Lapointe was nodding his head, "then I take it you believe the man had snowshoes."

When Al nodded, Lapointe continued. "What about this snowman bit?"

"Camouflage, sir. Some sort of white covering."

"Yes, Sergeant, I was thinking the same thing. Anything else?"

"Yessir. If you and I are right then I think they've gone to a lot of trouble just to get one man out. So my hunch is that they've got a bunch of them out."

The major did not seem surprised, so Al continued. "With your permission, sir, I would like to take my men inside the compound now and see if we can find out where and how they got out."

The major nodded. "Take Scout McLean with you. He should be just about finished the head count by now." Scouts were unarmed Home Guards whose responsibilities were to patrol inside the wire and keep an eye on Jerry's comings and goings. From time to time they made surprise inspections of inmate quarters in search of homemade radios, escape paraphernalia or anything of a suspicious nature.

It took quite some time before Scout McLean was located and he was fuming. "I don't know how the fuckin' bastards are doin' it. But they are."

Al had seen no point standing around in the cold so they had trooped back to the guard hut to wait in the warm and it was there that the scout had come cursing through the door. "We done the count twice, and ya know what? There's no one missin'."

"Whataya mean there's no one missing?"

"Just what I said, Sarge. There's not one single Jerry gone. There are 489 prisoners in this camp. There were 489 prisoners at the lights-out check. And there are 489 prisoners in their bunks right now."

"That's bullshit."

"Oh, I know it's bullshit."

"Did ya make sure, did ya check that there was a real live body in a bunk and not just a rolled up palliasse under a blanket?"

"The second count we did. That's what took so long."

McLean took off his cap and sat down heavily in a chair, his hands rubbing down his face from his forehead over his eyes, the stubble on his cheeks and under his chin. He sat staring off into space for a minute, then looked up defiantly at Al.

"But we'll get the fuckers in the mornin' when we line 'em up outside and do a count in daylight." His head bobbed. "We'll get 'em then, Sergeant. Mark my words. We'll get 'em then."

Al nodded. "Okay, McLean, there's nothin' we can do about numbers now but that doesn't mean we have ta sit here like bumps on a log. Let's go look at the wire."

Back out in the cold, dark morning of the now quiet compound, they made their way around the rink until they were opposite the culvert where Private McGinn had seen his snowman. As they stood in the glare of the compound lamps looking at the snowbank up against the wire, a light flicked on inside Al's head.

"Hey, McLean, the prisoners clear the storm snow from the rink?"

"Hey, yeah. They clean the snow off the rink all the time. We feed 'em and clothe 'em, Sarge, but we don't wipe their arses for them."

"You sure, McLean?" Billy was off to one side with Reggie listening in. He turned to his Sergeant. "Whataya gettin' at, Al?"

"Look at that snow bank, Billy. All that snow. More at this end than the other, eh? What did we do with snowbanks like that when we were kids back home?"

There was a puzzled silence. But only for an instant. "*Tabernacle!* Tunnels!"

"Right, Reggie, tunnels. We dug tunnels in snowbanks like this. Dammit ta hell! I shoulda seen it yesterday. Billy, you and Arnie go get us some shovels."

The sky was beginning to lighten when they found the first tunnel and the tip of the sun was edging over the horizon when they found another two. Each one big enough for a crawling man, the three tunnels converged in a space like a little igloo up against the wire. It was roomy enough to easily hold McLean and the five Algonquins.

With their flashlights they could see where the wire had been neatly snipped and how. A pair of cutters made with sharpened skate blades had been left behind along with chocolate bar wrappers and the remains of burned candles, evidence that workers had been on the job for some time. And there were some homemade snowshoes, rope tightly strung around hand-carved wood, as well as camouflage clothing all in white—flour bags sewn together to make ponchos.

Al wasn't surprised at Jerry's ingenuity. He'd had a chance to read reports on foiled escapes, prisoners found to have on their persons everything but the kitchen sink—hand-drawn maps of the surrounding area and government maps of Ontario, of Canada and the United States; train schedules; food and civilian clothing (Billy was right about red circles on mackinaws and red stripes on pants); hand-made knives fashioned from scrap metal, slingshots with pellets cast from old toothpaste tubes, a fish spear made by straightening a large table fork and adding barbs to the tines.

He also remembered a bunch of them sitting around with McLean and Philion, two of the scouts who were breaking them in with tales from Q and other camps about the kinds of things discovered in prisoner mail—messages from Germany written on wax paper with indelible pencil, messages hidden in cigars, nutshells, tinned goods, sausages and loaves of bread.

"Hey, Jigger," McLean was talking to Philion, "remember that time we found a radio antenna threaded through a clothesline?"

Philion smiled and nodded his head. "Yeah, I remember." He looked at the rest of them around the table. "We checked it and thought the clothesline felt a little stiff."

"Where did the clothesline come from?" Al's question.

"From Eaton's."

"Eaton's!" Billy yelled.

"Oh yeah, they kin order stuff from Eaton's catalogue."

"Where do they get the money?"

"Some of 'em get money from home. German money. We change it for 'em. Some of 'em make things and sell them to people. Ya know, farmers they work for, people like that."

The room was silent for a moment as Billy shook his head in wonder, "Absolutely amazing. Absofuckinlutely amazing. So does Eaton's sell machine guns? Grenades? Tanks? Maybe we could start our own little war up here."

Al grinned, "We regret to inform you . . ."

Billy picked it up, ". . . that your son, Private William Assad, was seriously wounded today just down the road from you in Monteith, as a matter of fact . . ."

Barney jumped in, ". . . while engaged in combat with an enemy heavily armed with weapons they got in the mail from Eaton's . . ."

Gill added, "Reports from the front are sketchy but it is believed that Private Assad has been taken to a POW Camp for Canadians far, far away where there is no canteen, no rink and no swimming pool . . ."

". . . and no fucking Eaton's catalogues." As Billy thumped the table with his fist the whole room erupted.

Chapter Five

FEBRUARY 6, 1940. Gillie and Al are leading a ten-man section in pursuit of Jerry. There are nine of them including the SS Captain and a German national by the name of Braucks who was Secretary-General of Deutscherbund Kanada *when war was declared. The Scouts have figured out how they were able to get out of the huts, trap doors concealed under the potbellied stoves used for heating. In one of the huts they also found a saw, homemade by filing teeth in the metal strapping used to bind packing cases. We are trying to nose around here to see what we can find out about where the escapees might be headed. Not all prisoners are fanatical Nazis or "Blacks" as we designate them. Most are Gray and a few are Whites and these are the ones who might part with some information. But we have to watch out for* the Largergestapo. *These are Blacks selected to keep their fellow prisoners in line. And like the Gestapo in the Fatherland, they are pretty damn ruthless. There are reports from some camps in Alberta that the* Largergestapo *have killed other prisoners when they have suspected them of collaborating. Shit hit the fan this morning. A soldier in one of the towers was cleaning his Lewis Gun. He takes out the magazine but forgets to take out the round in the chamber. Then the stupid bastard pulls the trigger and fires a shot into the compound. Good thing all the POWs were confined to quarters. Never a dull moment here at good old Camp Q.*

Excerpt from Barney's Diary

The ten men in pursuit of the escaped POWs—Billy, Frank, Reggie, Arnie, Popovich and Ross among them—wore white anoraks and were loaded down with rifles, full packs and sleeping bags. Al and Gill both had binoculars, Gill a map and compass. They were marching on skis again just as they'd done before Christmas at Current River Camp when training for the invasion of Norway, but this time it was for real. This time the Lee Enfields were loaded.

With Crow leading and Al bringing up the rear, the patrol followed the snowshoe tracks in the gully until they disappeared on the snow-packed surface of the King's Highway. At that point the lieutenant and his sergeant conferred and decided it would be a waste of time searching for a trail on the other side of the road. Jerry wouldn't make it that easy. Their best bet, they decided, was to start checking abandoned barns and farmhouses, shacks and sheds on the theory that the escaped prisoners would be holed up for the day waiting for the cover of darkness before chancing open country again.

All abandoned buildings along the tracks and the highway heading south were marked on the map. It was one of the smart things Camp Security had done when they'd put together Q's just-in-case recapture plan.

The first building was about a mile from the camp between the tracks and the highway, just down the road from the turbine generator on the Driftwood River. The structure had once been a walled and roofed-over holding pen for cattle being transferred from railway to highway, and vice versa. The roof of the pen now sagged in the middle under the weight of snow and one of the side walls was splintered and caved in. Neither Gillie nor Al thought it likely that Jerry was inside—it was too close to the camp and too obvious a hideout. But still they didn't want to take any chances so they put their heads together and talked about how they would handle an approach. Because it was something they'd never done before, Gill grinned and called it "on-the-job-training."

Once the two of them were satisfied with their plan, Al summoned the rest of the patrol, telling them to take off their skis and approach with caution, fanning out in a pincer movement, rifles at the ready to cover all sides. They didn't know if their foe was armed with anything more than pepper, slingshots or primitive spears. But the officer and his sergeant weren't taking any chances.

It was tough going wading through the snow—up to their hips in places—but they were able to move quickly, low with heads down, where it was crusted hard enough to support a man's weight. Once they were about a hundred yards away Al pointed to Billy and Arnie, sending them, each with two men, crouching wide to opposite corners of the pen on the highway side. He placed Reggie, David Ross and the rest of the platoon prone in a semi-circle with their rifles trained on the caved-in side of the building, motioning Frank to the centre. Al wanted his best shot where he could be most effective.

Satisfied the men were all in place, he looked at Gill, who nodded, and the two of them along with Popovich crawled close enough for Al's shouted command to be heard by anybody hiding in the pen.

"*Achtung! Achtung!* You are surrounded. *Kommen sie heraus.*" Barney's German lessons were greeted by the sound of a broken-down building creaking in the cold. Al yelled again. More creaks. He could feel sweat forming on his forehead. It was what, thirty below zero, and he was sweating? He grunted and turned to Popovich.

"Stan, go take a look. And don't try ta be a hero!" The last words were said to the Pole's backside as he scuttled toward the building, Al and Gill watching him over the sights of their rifles.

Popovich ran low beside a drift and then dodged and weaved over a patch of bare frozen ground until he was crouching, his back up against the side of the pen. Once he'd caught his breath, he turned and poked his head through a gap in the grey, weathered wood. Al could see him leaning in, looking one way, then another before he crawled inside and disappeared.

"Where the hell did he learn that? That's right outta the book." Gill was shaking his head in wonder.

"It's all those Western movies he goes to. Thinks he's Tom Mix."

Al held his breath. He would give Popovich thirty seconds. He started to count, one-a-thousand, two-a-thousand, three-a-thousand. He was at twenty-three-a-thousand when he saw the Pole stick his head out of the same gap he'd entered.

"It is very all clear, Sarge," he shouted. "Nothing here except piles of old cow shit."

Al lowered his Lee Enfield and let out his breath as Gill stood up and called out to the rest of the platoon. He had decided it was time for a break and he motioned them into the shelter of the pen where they could build a fire, make some tea and have a bite to eat.

"What'll it be, boys, bully beef or bully beef, bully beef fried or bully beef boiled, bully beef roasted or bully beef toasted?"

"Save the bully and your poetry for supper, Mr. Assad. Chocolate bars and tea will do us for now. I wanna get goin' while we still have some daylight."

Gill was looking at the map, pointing with his finger. "There's a farm just down the highway about three, four miles from here. It's one with a 'phone and we're supposed to call in tonight. If we ski across country here," he traced a route for Al looking over his shoulder, "we should be there before it gets too dark. We can sleep in the barn. And the next three places we gotta check are right around this farm," he tapped the map with his finger, "here, here and here. Should be able to cover them in the morning easy."

February days were still short days in the North and the sun was beginning to set as they packed up to go. After tea and the warmth of the fire in the pen it was damn hard to get moving, all of them close to running on empty because they'd been up and at it since just after midnight.

Al sagged against a post just inside the dilapidated pen door hanging drunkenly on rusty hinges. He felt limp, like a deflated inner tube, the kind they used to fill with air and then float out into the middle of Ames Lake. Dragging on a cigarette he was thinking that it was more than just the physical energy. It was the energy you spent thinking and worrying and anticipating and then kicking yourself for not thinking and worrying and anticipating hard enough. And sometimes when you were spending that kind of energy you felt more drained than if you'd been digging ditches all day.

The first of the evening stars were sparkling diamonds in the blue-black sky when the patrol took off their skis in the farmyard and were shown into the barn. While his men played with the two farm dogs—both a mixture of collie and German shepherd—Gill went into the house to use the telephone. When he returned he had nothing to report. Hauptmann Kaputt and Braucks along with their pals were out there somewhere but nobody had seen hide nor hair of them. The only information was that Barney was checking with his Whites to see if there was any scuttlebutt as to where the escapees were headed.

Supper was on the house and bully beef wasn't on the menu. The farmer's wife and her two shy boys who looked to be about eleven and twelve brought in slabs of their own churned butter, and loaves of bread still warm from the oven. Then it was the farmer, with a hand from Arnie Christensen, lugging over a pot of beef and barley soup, the pot about the size of a milk can, so there was plenty to go around. As each man came forward with his mess tin there was a smile from the farmer who ladled out the soup and his wife who cut and buttered the bread. Billy was especially appreciative, but the farmer just shook his head, telling him it was the least his family could do for the boys in uniform.

When the serving was done and the family turned to leave, Billy called the young lads over and gave each of them a regimental hat badge, his own and another he'd grabbed from David Ross. The youngsters were thrilled and when Billy stepped back and saluted them, they smartly returned it, their very own boys' version, fingers splayed against their heads. Looking on, Al smiled with the hope the world would be rid of Hitlers when little boys grew up.

After a post-meal cigarette outside in the cold, the patrol bedded down in the hayloft. Most of them were asleep in minutes, but Gill told Al there was no rest for the wicked as he motioned him over beside the cream separator, where he had unfolded his map beside an oil lamp set on top of a barrel.

"We gonna find these guys, Gillie?"

"Ya don't think we'll ever catch up to em, eh?"

Al shrugged. "Well, number one, they got half a night's jump on us. Number two, while we're fartin' around checking abandoned buildings during the day, they're makin' a beeline at night to wherever they're goin'."

Gill sighed and nodded. "Yeah, that's the way I figure it, too." He rummaged in his breast pockets for his cigarettes and then remembered they'd been asked not to smoke in the barn.

"But maybe there's a bright side to this," he pointed a finger at his sergeant, "maybe we'll make better time on skis than they will on snowshoes. So who knows, eh? We could catch up to 'em after all."

He didn't sound too convincing even to himself, so he moved on to discuss how to handle the three buildings in the morning. To save time they would split up into three sections of four men, one abandoned building to each section. If any one of the three sections came up with something suspicious they were to send a runner back to the others and all twelve of them would then link up for a closer look.

Once a plan was in place both of them felt a little better about their prospects and went with some satisfaction to their hay beds, where they slept the sleep of the wearied just.

The next morning it was still dark when they were roused by Gill's traditional greeting. The farmer's sons brought toast and tea just before the pursuit patrol assembled in the yard, the dogs barking and dashing in and out among them. The plan was that Al along with Gill and Billy would each lead a section to one of the sites and if nothing turned up, the sections would rendezvous at mileage 104 on the T&NO line with representatives of the RCM Police, the provincial and railway police.

"The brass are getting a tad itchy about the situation. Want a little liaison between us and the coppers. Two heads are better than one. Et cetera. Et cetera. And be there at noon, gentlemen. No later." Gillie's words as he waved them off.

The morning search was fruitless. Gill's section found more mature cow shit in a rundown barn. Al's men skied down the roadbed of an old spur line and investigated a shack that had once kept watch over a gravel pit, but there was nothing there. Billy thought he was onto something when he kicked open the door of a broken-down log cabin on the river and found empty cans of pork and beans beside the remains of a fire. But once he'd had a closer look it was clear that the cans and ashes had been there for some time, probably from the summer when farm kids had used the cabin as a fishing camp.

At noon Gill, along with his sergeant and Private Assad, crowded into the section gang hut at mileage 104 where Highway 11 cut across the tracks. The three soldiers reported on their morning and then heard from the provincial police about roadblocks on the highway and from the railway police about thorough searches of freight trains, boxcars in particular. A corporal from the RCM Police told them the thinking was that Jerry was still in the area and produced new maps with more abandoned buildings to check.

"What about more men?" Gill asked the corporal, who seemed to be in charge.

"More coming in tomorrow afternoon. More T&NO police and more provincial police. And a guard company from Gravenhurst. We'll have to set up a briefing for them wherever you're bivouacking tomorrow night, Lieutenant."

Gill got out his map and showed the corporal. After sorting through the two maps and agreeing on which buildings looked more likely than others, the consensus was that those close to the tracks and the highway would be left to the railway and provincial police while the Algonquins on skis would head into the bush and check out derelict lumber camps.

"Looks like the closest one is right here," Gill tapped the map with a finger for Al's benefit, "about three miles south of this farm right here. Family by the name of Blackburn. I figure if we get moving right away we should be there," he looked at his watch, "by 1600 hours. What say you, Sergeant?"

Acting Sergeant McDougal thought for a moment. "Yeah, we could make it by then if we really push it, but we'd hafta camp there overnight because by the time we finished checking out the place it'd be too dark to get back to the farm."

He looked at Gill. "Why don't we head for the farm, drop off the platoon and I'll grab a couple of guys and take a look. If it's nothing I'll either stay there for the night or, if it's a full moon and we can see where we're going, we'll head back to the farm. What say you, Lieutenant?"

Gill stuck his head out the door of the hut and looked at the sky. His head came back in and turned grinning to Al. "It's clouded over. Guess you'll be sleepin' in the rough tonight, my boy. Who'll you take with you?

"How 'bout Crow and Billy? Christensen, too. He'll know what a shanty camp's supposed to look like."

"Sounds good to me."

So they all skied down the middle of the frozen river highway to the Blackburn farm, a yellow clapboard house, some outbuildings and a sturdy red barn on top of the hill that sloped up from the Driftwood. Gill had a quick chat with the young man who came out of the house to greet them and soon Al along with Billy, Crow and Christensen were inside the farmhouse sitting at the long dining room table wolfing down bread and cheese and wild strawberry jam chased with mugs of hot milk. It was their first meal since breakfast and there wasn't a single, solitary crumb on their plates when they rose from the table to go to work.

After stuffing some hardtack and tinned beans in his small pack and hanging snowshoes on his back in case skiing became impossible, Al checked the map with Gill one last time. Satisfied, he took a compass bearing, strapped on his skis and led the way along the fence on the north side of a long, narrow pasture behind the barn and then through the tag alders and into the woods following a trail that had once been a bush road but now, even with the snow, they could see was heavily overgrown. He figured they had about an hour of daylight left and would be at the site while there was still enough light to see—and here he mentally counted them off—if they skied hard, if they didn't have to resort to snowshoes, if the trail didn't get any worse or peter out.

After a mile or so through the spruce forest the bush road petered out on the ice of a beaver pond. Once across, it took them some time to find the trail again because it was off to the left behind a stand of birch trees. The industrious beavers had obviously covered a dogleg turn.

When Al estimated they were getting near the lumber camp he put Frank Archibald in the lead and brought up the rear, reminding Arnie and Billy as they passed him that sound carried in the cold so be quiet. And quiet it was, the only sound being the caw-cawing of distant crows and the occasional rat-a-tat-tat echo of a busy woodpecker oblivious to the temperature.

Frank led them onwards for another half mile or so and then stopped, motioning the rest of them to come up. When he pointed with his ski pole toward a clearing through a break in the spruce, Al could make out a structure of some kind but there were too many trees to get a good look so he nodded to Frank and Arnie to check it out. The two of them unstrapped their skis, tied on their snowshoes, and, with rifles in hand, moved out in single file only to stop dead when Al hissed at them and waved his hands apart telling them to spread out. In a minute more they were out of sight and in another few minutes Al heard the crows again, closer this time. He looked up to see if he could spot the birds when Billy nudged him, shaking his head. He looked at Billy quizzically for a second until he understood and grinned. The crows were Crow. His long, drawn-out caw was an all-clear signal.

When Billy and Al moved forward, Arnie whispered to them that the building with its log walls and roof had once been a stable for the lumber camp horses, the Clydesdales, Percherons and Belgians. The door to the stable was long gone and inside you could see that the stalls and mangers were rotting away; a fingernail digging into the wood would hook it out in chunks if it weren't frozen solid.

Following Arnie's lead they gathered around him at the back of the stable near the wide hinged flap where the horse manure was shovelled into the yard. He spoke in a low singsong voice, the one Al noticed he used whenever he talked about lumbering.

"Looks like we came in from the rear end of the camp. The camboose where the shanty men would be sleepin' and eatin' will be down the trail about a hundred yards, I make it."

Al nodded and was about to tell Frank to take the lead again when he froze and put a gloved finger to his lips. It was an unnecessary gesture. Each one of them had heard the same noise, a man-made sound that didn't belong in a bush where the four of them were supposed to be the only humans around.

Soundlessly in the gloom of the back of the stable they grabbed their rifles and moved apart, Al and Frank slipping quietly to either side of the big open door and Billy and Arnie easing open the back door to the manure pile. When it began to screech Al whispered a curse and they stopped. He pointed a message, telling them to stay where they were, and eased his head around the doorpost. Winter darkness was coming on fast and he couldn't see much of anything. But he could hear something. He ducked back in.

"Someone's comin' down the trail. The way we came." They looked at him, willing him to tell them what he didn't know. He shook his head and began directing traffic, pointing to himself and Frank to leave the stable and circle to the trail, one on either side, then to Arnie and Billy to take over at the stable door.

As he moved away from the door, Al was remembering how hard it was to see the stable from the trail. He was counting on that and the dark and their white anoraks to make them invisible.

And so they were to Popovich who didn't see a thing until two ghosts stepped out from spruce trees on either side of him, two ghosts with Lee Enfields cocked at his head. Later when the story was told, Al would laugh until the tears came when Frank solemnly described the look on the Pole's face.

Popovich was hustled into the stable where he handed Al a note, which he read with the aid of Billy's cigarette lighter. Printed in capital letters, the message, from Gill, said that one of Barney's Whites had reported that the escapers planned to hide out in an abandoned lumber camp until the snow was gone and the hunt had slackened. They'd taken plenty of food with them and planned to snare rabbits and slingshot partridge to extend their supply. The White wasn't sure but he thought the camp was supposed to be somewhere between Monteith and Shillington.

Before he read any further Al handed the message to Frank, gave the lighter back to Billy to hold, dug the map out of his breast pocket, unfolded it, and held it to the light.

"Only two abandoned camps around here, this one up ahead and another closer to Shillington."

He thought for a moment. "But this one here is more off by itself."

"Yeah, that's what Gillie says." Frank Archibald had taken in the rest of the note.

"He says it's closer to Monteith and more isolated and," Frank was reading out loud now, "of the two, more likely."

"Gimme that." Al quickly read the rest of Gill's print and then looked up at the men gathered around him. His men. It wasn't the first time he'd thought of that particular possessive pronoun. And every time he did, it bothered him.

"Questions. First of all, we gotta make sure they're here, so how do we do that? Second, if they're here we gotta make sure they stay here while we get word back to Gillie and the rest of the patrol."

He turned to Popovich. "Think ya can find your way back tonight?"

"*Ja*, I follow ski tracks. It is what I did coming here."

"Yeah, but its gonna be dark, really dark. No moon, no nothin'."

"Do not worry, I will make it."

Al inhaled and blew out, air through puffed cheeks. "Okay. Look, take the compass, that'll help. You know the heading?"

"*Ja, ja.*"

"Okay, you got a lighter, matches or somethin'?"

"*Ja, ja.*"

"Awright. Now how're we gonna do this?"

The answer took some time, but in the end a plan was devised that made sense to all of them. They would stay in the stable until midnight, when Crow would head out for the camboose, scout around, do his stealthy Indian stuff. If he came back with word the Jerries were there then the four of them would take up positions around the camboose shanty while Popovich skied like hell back to Gill to return with reinforcements at first light.

Midnight being seven hours away, they tried to make themselves comfortable while waiting. Not wanting to advertise their presence with a fire, they ate cold beans, hardtack and canned peaches and then as silently as possible cleared away debris, unrolled sleeping bags and stretched out. Sleep was only possible if you could block out the cold and in case anyone was able to do it—Al knew he couldn't—he set up two-hour watches with Popovich and Billy taking the first one. Then he laid himself down, promising himself he would take it easy for a minute and then get ready for what could be a long night.

The next thing he knew someone was shaking him awake and Frank Archibald was saying, "Al, it's time."

"Whataya mean, it's time?" Sitting up abruptly, he shook off the sleep and looked at his wrist. But it was pitch black in the stable and he couldn't see the time.

"Shit, Crow, what time is it?'"

"It's 2345."

"Dammit!"

"Ya needed the sleep, Sarg. We covered for ya. Anything ya wanna tell me before I go?"

Al looked at his friend. "Yeah, be careful, Crow. Be careful."

Then Frank was out the door saying he'd be back in an hour and Al was up, swinging his arms, getting the circulation going again. He wanted to clap his hands and stamp his feet, he wanted to run on the spot and do arm rolls, but settled for taking off his gloves and blowing warm breath through the cold hollow of his clasped hands. He didn't want to make any noise.

Frank was back in thirty minutes, a series of quick, short crow calls to let them know he was coming. He was breathing hard and had to wait to catch his breath.

"They're there! The bastards are there."

Al woke the sleepers and the five of them moved toward the door where the cloud cover had broken and there was now some light from the moon and stars. They spoke in whispers.

"I didn't take the trail. Figured if they *were* around they'd have it booby trapped with wire and tin cans or somethin' so I circled around through the bush and came in behind the camboose."

Frank described it to them: log walls and roof with a big wooden chimney in the centre. "No windows, so I bellied up closer and could see there was a track in the snow up the side of the buildin'."

He bobbed his head. "I knew then but just ta make sure I crawled along the track until I got to the corner and stuck my head around the front. Sentry was at the door and I watched him move out into the trail then back again and start to come around my side so I beat it back down the side and inta the bush."

Billy asked him, "Ya recognize the guy?"

"Nope. But I damn sure recognized what he was carryin'."

"The son-of-a-bitch had a weapon, right?"

"Sure did, a twelve-gauge."

"Probably got it from Eaton's catalogue."

"Okay, gents. What do we know?" Al interrupted Billy before he got going on Eaton's. "We know they're there. We know there are nine of 'em. We know they're armed. Be nice to know how well, but let's assume the worst. Let's assume they're well armed. Anything else?"

"Yeah. We know they're there but they don't know we're here."

"Good, Billy. You're right. And let's keep it that way."

He put his hand on Popovich's shoulder. "Okay, Stanislas, get yer ass in gear. Tell Gillie to bring the guys in quietly before sunup and I'll rendezvous with him here. Now go!"

When the Pole had disappeared down the trail, Al turned to Frank and asked him to draw a map in the snow of the camboose camp and the surrounding bush. Looking at it they picked the spots where the four of them could best keep the building under observation without themselves being seen.

"Sure there's only one door, Crow?

"Yeah, I'm sure."

"Arnie?"

"Never seen one with two."

"Awright, but just in case, I want you, Crow, to cover the back. The rest of us will take up positions here for me," he pointed with the toe of his boot, "and here for you, Arnie, and over here for you, Billy. Now, when do ya figure first light will be, about 0730?"

Heads nodded. "Okay, I'll head back here around 0600 hours. The rest of the patrol should be here by then. I'll brief them and we'll be back in strength by 0700 just in time to give Jerry a surprise wake-up call."

On their snowshoes and following Frank's back, single file into the bush, they moved off in the moonlight to the left of the trail and began a wide tramping loop designed to bring them to the rear of the camboose. It was tough going because they had to make their way in absolute quiet through a thick and tangled underbrush. Even in those places where it thinned out, the path was often blocked by cul-de-sacs of fallen trees and rotting stumps. Jerry had chosen well. What would have been a ten-minute snowshoe on the trail took them almost three-quarters of an hour through the bush before Frank halted the column and the other three peeled off to take up their positions among the trees with clear sight lines to the camboose door.

Arnie went one way, circling wide of the camboose, and Al followed Billy around the other side. The two of them were more than halfway along their loop when the night silence was shattered by a cacophonous parody of wind chimes loud enough to wake the dead.

"Jesus, what the hell was that?"

Crouching, Al waved Billy into silence beside him as he turned his head to listen. He didn't have time to get into any kind of explanation. He knew what it was. It was Arnie Christensen tripping one of Jerry's tin can alarms.

He had to think. What would Jerry do? Would he assume it was an animal, a moose, a deer, and roll over and go back to sleep? Or would he check it out?

The answer came from the camboose in a sequence of obvious commands and acknowledgments, all in guttural German. Jerry was going to check it out. Billy put his hand on Al's arm and whispered.

"Let's wait. If they don't find Arnie maybe they'll think it was an animal."

Billy's sergeant nodded, grateful for his pal's advice. But he wasn't going to follow it. Not entirely. He returned the whisper.

"I hear ya, Billy, but let's try and get a little closer just in case Arnie needs some help."

It proved to be a wise decision as they had moved only a few feet when the boom of a shotgun was answered by the familiar and rapid cracks of a Lee Enfield.

Al and Billy, rifles at the ready, came in from the bush, awkward in their snowshoes but moving quickly, side by side and bent over, just behind the tree line in front of the camboose. Suddenly their shoes caught a wire and tripped another tin-can alarm. Both of them belly-flopped in the snow as the night erupted. Tin cans clanging. Germans shouting. Germans shooting.

The two Algonquins twisted to free their boots and burrow into the snow, the pop and zing of bullets chopping the air around their heads, the quick thunk-thunk-thunk of rounds hitting the trees behind them.

Returning fire the three Algonquins heard a man scream. Al looked up to see a figure silhouetted in the moonlight slumped over, not moving, half out of the camboose wooden chimney.

Billy elbowed his way over, "Looks like the fuckers are shootin' from slits in the logs. There's no way we can hurt 'em."

"Yeah, and every time we fire we're showing 'em where we are." Al winced as a round hit the tree above his head.

"Look, Crow's got the chimney covered. Scoot behind me. Get Arnie. Bring him around. The only way out for Jerry is the door. The three of us can keep 'em cooped up till Gillie gets here. Go now. I'll cover you." Popovich wasn't the only fan of Tom Mix.

Billy rolled away in the snow to his left, bellied along for a bit and then got up and ran, dodging back through the trees, while Al fired rapidly at the camboose door, the smell of gunshot up his nose, and then quickly rolled to his right as the Germans zeroed in on his muzzle flashes.

Head-down behind a spruce tree, chest heaving, mind racing, he took in air and did his sums. Nine Jerries. No, eight now. Eight Jerries. Four Canadians. Eight Jerries with at least one shotgun and a bunch of rifles. If the Germans managed to pinpoint the Algonquin fire it wouldn't be long before they figured out the odds. Maybe with Crow on the roof and the rest of them moving around the camboose shooting from different positions Jerry would think he was surrounded by a superior force. But even then his instinct told him Hauptmann Kaputt was one mean Nazi bastard who would fight to the last man. He tried to get himself inside the Hauptmann's head. What was he thinking? What would he do?

It was quiet now as Al kept his eyes on the camboose door. He didn't want any of the enemy getting out and infiltrating behind his men, shuddering at the thought of trying to distinguish in the dark between white-clad friend and white-clad foe.

Just then Billy and Arnie rolled in beside him and he told them to stay put, eyes front, while he went back around through the bush to look for Crow. But it was Crow who found him hissing his name from behind a snow-covered stump.

Al jumped. "Shit Almighty, Crow. I went right by ya. Didn't even see ya."

"Weren't supposed to, Sergeant."

The two of them hunkered down in a little hollow by the stump and talked things over. "That guy in the chimney?"

"Yeah, Al."

"What's it like ta kill a man?"

"Ask me tomorrow."

Al sent Frank back to the other side of the camboose and sat on his haunches guessing at the time. Somewhere around 0200, he thought. In four or five hours the rest of the platoon would arrive and then Jerry would have no choice but to give up. In the meantime the Algonquins would keep their eyes peeled. If fired on, they would not return fire. If spoken to they would not respond. There would be nothing to give away their numbers or positions.

After a long, freezing hour of tense silence, Al heard the camboose door creak open. On his belly between two spruce trees close together, he levered himself up on his elbows, his eyes straining at the dark purple of the night, and felt his shoulders knot when a shadowy something was stuck through the partly opened door and fluttered in a gust of wind.

"Ve vould like a conference." The shape of a man was inching out the door of the camboose.

"Our officer vould like to speak mit your officer." The voice kept edging out the door slowly repeating the two phrases, "Ve vould like a conference," and "Our officer vould like to speak mit your officer."

Al knew he had to do something. He couldn't just let the German walk out the door and into the trees. Or could he? Maybe let the prisoner go by and then step out behind him and surprise him with a rifle in the ribs?

As the POW stepped out of the shadow of the building and into the moonlight Al relaxed when he saw what had fluttered in the wind. A white flag tied to the end of a tag alder branch. The men in the camboose were going to surrender.

Al pushed himself up until he was kneeling behind the two trees watching the flag approach. He was just about to stand and move out into the clearing where the German could see him when his Irish fey kicked in and he shivered. He shivered because it was damn cold, but mostly he shivered because he had a feeling something was wrong. Very wrong.

A split second later he saw what it was. The man with the flag was about ten yards from the tree line when he dropped to the frozen ground and the seasoned

Germans in the camboose, the proud and arrogant veterans of the conquest of Europe, proceeded to show the green Canadians, veterans of Camp Borden and Current River, how to execute a textbook combat manoeuvre.

While some fired from the slits in the walls, others jumped out of either side of the door and then, spacing themselves, knelt to take over the job of covering fire as their remaining comrades rushed outside, running for the bush on either side of the camboose.

Al didn't think. He reacted. But it was if he was in another dimension of time and space, a slow motion dimension where seconds took minutes and minutes hours, a dream state where the enemy moved languidly and he pulled the trigger of his Lee Enfield ever so slowly—five sluggish times at Jerry moving as if he were wading through chest-high water. Then, slow as molasses, Al rolled away from the counter fire he knew would be aimed at his rifle flashes. Now down behind a spruce stump he could hear Arnie and Billy shouting and shooting and could see Nazis down in the snow.

Back in real time he tried to count bodies but he couldn't distinguish piles of snow from humps of men. Something drew his attention to the top of the camboose. In the light of the moon he saw Frank Archibald bracing his feet on either side of the roof beam log and inching past the body of the German slumped out of the chimney. Al turned back to ground level and got off another clip to keep heads from turning and looking up while Crow was moving into place just over the camboose door. When he saw that Frank was ready, he crawled to another spot along the tree line and yelled into the moonlight.

"Kriegsgefangene. Für euch ist der Krieg zu Ende. You are *kaputt!"*

His effort was met with a burst of rifle fire and then screams as Crow fired from his prone position on the roof. Al yelled again. "Prisoners of war! For you the war is over! You are finished! You are surrounded!"

Mostly silence now. Al waited for a brief moment before calling out to Billy and Arnie telling them to move in carefully while he and Crow stayed put. He knelt on one knee, his Lee Enfield sighted on the camboose, watching carefully as his comrades came forward, rifles pointing at humps in the snow which they prodded with the toes of their boots. His heart skipped a beat when a hump moved off to Billy's right and skipped again when Frank fired and the hump flattened in the snow.

More silence. Then a shout. "They're all dead, Al." Arnie was kneeling beside the last body, turning it over.

"Okay, I'm comin' out. Crow, come on down and keep an eye on us."

The three of them moved about counting the dead. There were four bodies halfway between the tree line and the camboose including the man with the white flag. He was the hump that moved and Al could see a dark stain, black in the moonlight, spreading on the man's chest, oozing through his flour-bag poncho.

There were three more bodies at the door of the camboose. One of them was Braucks, his face permanently frozen in a grimace of pain. Al looked around. "Where's that fuckin' Hauptmann Kaputt?"

The reply was King's English perfect. "I am in here, Sergeant, and I am coming out now with my hands up. I remind you of the Geneva Convention as it applies to prisoners of war."

Later in the dawn's early light when Gill arrived with the rest of the patrol he was welcomed by the sight of the SS officer, hands tied behind his back, sitting in the snow beside the eight bodies of his comrades laid out neatly in a row. Inside the camboose he found four exhausted Algonquins, gaunt-faced and drinking tea from mugs held in shaking hands. They were slumped around a fire made in what was left of the old stone oven and looked up at him when he came through the door. But no one spoke. There was nothing to say.

Chapter Six

APRIL 12, 1941. Current River Camp. Tomorrow is Easter Sunday. Certainly could use a resurrection around here! Hasn't been the same since the incident at Camp Q. We're in the Army and we're being trained to kill but training and the real thing are two different things. Killing changes a man. Frank is even more quiet than usual. Billy has lost a lot of his edge and both he and Al are drinking too much. But not as much as Christensen. He gets "pissed to the eyeballs" (Billy's words) every night. I don't know how he gets up in the morning. Just heard yesterday how Jerry faked the head count. Used the trap doors to move from hut to hut. When the count was finished in one hut some of them would scuttle out and crawl to another where they were counted again. Smart bastards. Ruthless too. The White who told me where the Hauptmann and his fellow escapees might be hiding out was found hanging from a rafter in the Rec Hut. Hard to tell if he died from hanging or the beating he was given. The note from McLean said he was battered to a pulp.

Excerpt from Barney's Diary

Not even a visit from Tony Foligno got them up and going again. Tony had moved on from the army team in Cornwall to play for the Ottawa Commandos. His new teammates included Kenny Reardon up from the Montreal Canadiens, Neil Colville, Alex Shabicky and Sugar Jim Henry from the New York Rangers, and Bingo Kampman from the Toronto Maple Leafs. Tony was now playing hockey with the best the National Hockey League had to offer to Canada's war effort, not bad for a young man one generation removed from Foligno, a small town in Italy that Canadian soldiers calling themselves the "D-Day Dodgers" would come to know well in the summer of 1944 as they fought their way across the Lombardy Plains against the First Paratroop Division, the toughest soldiers in the *Wehrmacht*.

There was some grumbling in Algonquin ranks about men whose service to their country was playing hockey. Not guys like Tony who wore battledress during the day and shin pads and hockey pants at night. At least Tony had to do basic training. But as Barney pointed out, guys like the Montreal Canadiens' Rocket Richard, Toe Blake and Elmer Lach didn't have to go anywhere near the army because they were deemed to have "war-worker deferrals." That meant that in the summer, Richard worked in a munitions plant, Blake in a shipyard and Lach in an aircraft factory. Barney was pretty steamed about that.

But he was pooh-poohed by Matthew Gill, who seemed to know a thing or two about the business of professional hockey. Gill told Barney that the Toronto Maple Leafs were doing the same thing and so was every other team in the NHL. It all had to do with money. And money talked. Fans in Montreal wouldn't pay to watch the Canadiens if the Rocket was in the army, just as fans in Boston wouldn't pay to see the Bruins without their All-Star goalie, Frank Brimsek, who spent his summers serving with the U.S. Coast Guard. And, Gill added, if fans stayed away then teams would fold and there was no way rich and influential owners like Toronto's Conn Smythe would stand for that.

The Commandos were on their way out West to play for the Allan Cup and had stopped off in Port Arthur for an exhibition game with the LHL All-Stars. Afterwards the veterans of the Lowvert Maple Leafs congregated around a table and twenty-five-cent pitchers of beer at the Mariaggi Hotel, where the Commandos were staying, just across from the station. Tony was the centre of their attention and when he introduced them to Shabicky, Reardon and Kampman, all of the groaning about NHL players evading army service was forgotten in the scramble to get autographs. Al got Bingo's for his boy, Billy got Shabicky's for his son-to-be and Reggie got Reardon's for himself.

But the good mood only lasted until Tony asked them what they'd been doing lately and they told him about Camp Q. Wartime censorship made certain no news of the incident had ever been published so Tony was whistling with surprise as Al reluctantly passed on the story.

There wasn't much more talk after that. Just a lot more drinking until Tony said he had to go. They said goodbye to him in the hotel lobby and, with Reggie leaning on Crow and Barney bringing up the rear, staggered off to find a cab back to camp.

Cap's Taxi Stand was across the street and when Billy banged on the door it was opened by a husky Finlander. In Port Arthur the Finns had a reputation— they were all communists who didn't support the war. So what happened next was predictable.

When the Finlander stepped outside and saw what shape the Algonquins were in, he told them that as far as he was concerned they could walk back to the camp 'cause he wasn't having any more goddamn drunken soldiers puking in his cab.

As he was turning his back on them, Billy grabbed him by the shoulder and jerked him around. "Listen, you mean-faced son-of-a-bitch, if ya don't drive us we'll go back ta Current River and get the rest of our platoon, come back here and break every window in the stand and slash every tire in every taxi ya got. Then we'll all puke on you, ya commie bastard."

When the Finlander angrily pushed Billy away, Al stepped up and punched him, a right cross to the nose that staggered him. When his hand went to his face touching for blood, Reggie kicked him, hard, army boot, in the shins.

Before things got completely out of hand, Crow, who'd been drinking ginger ale all night, waded in and put a stop to it. He shoved the Finlander back into the taxi stand and then herded his drunken friends down the street to find other means of transportation.

The next day was a Sunday and when Al woke up his head felt like it housed a little man hammering out a relentless and garbled Morse code, the slow death of a thousand dashes. He forced himself to get up and get dressed.

Stumbling out of the barracks he made his way to the trail up the hill behind the barracks, past the officers' cabins and into the woods, where he leaned up against a tree, pulled out his smokes and had a long talk with himself.

Later in the sergeant's mess at breakfast he spotted his lieutenant making his way over to his table. Gill sat down and threw an arm around Al's shoulders.

"Listen, my boy, I've watched you for three or four months now and I'm convinced you've got what it takes. I'm gonna recommend those three sergeant's stripes be a permanent addition to your wardrobe."

Seeing the look on Al's face he smiled. "Hey, I'm a lieutenant and my job is easy. I get orders and I pass them on to my sergeant, I pass them on to you. You've got the tough job, you have to fit those orders into reality, you have to interpret those orders depending on what's happening in the field. Your job's more important than mine."

Al shook his head and started to say something but Gill shook his head stopping him. "Uh, uh. You listen to me. You did a hell of a job at Camp Q. Did what ya had to do and ya did it well."

"Not all by myself, Gillie. I talked to the guys and they helped."

"Of course they did. A good sergeant does that. He listens to his men. But the final decisions at the camboose were yours and they were good decisions. You've got solid common sense, McDougal, and that's what this army looks for in a sergeant. A guy with a head on his shoulders who can think in the heat of battle and make the right decisions when his men's lives depend on those decisions. And . . ."

Al cut him off, "Gillie, I wasn't thinking out there. I was praying."

Gill chuckled. "Well, whatever you were doin' it worked."

Gill stood. "Now don't give me any more guff. You're my sergeant and that's final. And, by the way, one of the reasons you are is that Frank and Billy spoke to me and said you should be. Arnie, too."

The next day they were out on a twenty-five-mile route march to Kakabeka Falls, a mini-Niagara in a spectacular rocky gorge west of Port Arthur. It was a bright day, warming with the first hint of spring, and they were sprawled on the shoulder of the road on a ten-minute break. There were a couple of new recruits in the platoon, still wet behind the ears, and the old-timers were planning on having a little fun.

"Maybe when we get back tonight we can send a couple of 'em out to paint the Last Post."

"And tomorrow we can send them over to Stores and get them to ask the quartermaster for ten feet of firing line."

Barney had picked up a rock embedded with what looked like shiny purple glass and Billy asked him what it was. "Amethyst," he said turning it over in his hand, the crystals catching the sunlight. "Lots of it around here."

He held it up to the sun. "It's important in our Jewish tradition. Also," and here he slyly looked up at Al, "there's another tradition saying that possession of amethyst prevents drunkenness."

Al took his cue. "Hey great, Barn. Gimme that and get another for Billy and Arnie."

Everyone chuckled. "Seriously, boys, we need to watch the booze. All of us." But Al was looking at Billy and Arnie when he said it. "And we need to put Camp Q and Hauptmann Kaputt behind us." He stood up and grinned. "And that's an order from your sergeant."

It was an order that produced a series of exaggerated salutes and a chorus of, "Yessir, Sergeant. Whatever ya say, Sergeant."

"And kiss my Royal Canadian Arse, Sergeant." Billy punched him on his stripes and nodded his assent.

At the Falls, where they had their noon meal, the Lowvert gang went looking for Doug Dobson, one of the new recruits. His mother had been their Grade Three and Four teacher at Victoria School, and his younger sister had just completed normal school in North Bay in 1938 and was now teaching Grade Five and Six at Victoria. Dobson's father, Earl, had a potato farm just outside of town about a mile beyond Frank Archibald's cabin on the North Road.

They found their teacher's son leaning on a wooden parapet overlooking the layered cliffs of the Falls, watching the water rushing down into a fine mist forming a rainbow near the bottom. He didn't hear them coming over the roar of the water and Billy grabbed him from behind, scaring him half to death.

"Hey, Dougie, how the hell are ya?"

"Hey, yourself, Assad. How the hell are *you?*"

A smiling Dobson shook hands with each one of his visitors in turn, greeting them by name. He was tall and angular, his face scarred by chickenpox. Older than they were, he hadn't signed up with them because his father argued he was needed on the farm.

"How's your mom?"

"She's fine. She sends her best. Said to tell all of you she hopes you're better behaved in the army then you were in Grade Three."

That got them laughing at "Remember When" stories—the time they'd put a garter snake in Mrs. Dobson's desk drawer; the time Greta Pawson had peed her pants at the blackboard. After a bit Al asked Dougie how he'd managed to get away from his old man, a crusty, hellfire-and-damnation Baptist who made Barney's father look like Mr. Congeniality.

"Gonna get harvest leave. Army promised I could go home for a week or so in September and help him get the potatoes in."

"Your dad happy with that?"

"Nope. But he didn't have a choice. I told him either that or I was goin' and not comin' back. Ever."

The rest of spring was mostly uneventful except for two significant events, the Stanley Cup playoffs and the attempted theft of Nanibijou.

Foster Hewitt kept them abreast of playoff hockey. For every game he broadcast there was always a crew of Algonquins huddled around a radio somewhere in Current River Camp waiting for the familiar, "Hello, Canada and hockey fans in Newfoundland and the United States . . ."

In 1941 it was the Boston Bruins versus the Leafs in the first round and despite the heroics of goalie Turk Broda and forward Syl Apps, the Leafs lost in seven games, three of them by scores of two to one. The U.S. Coast Guard's Frankie Brimsek was the story in the Leafs series and right through the rest of the playoffs as the Bruins won the Stanley Cup.

The excitement of the playoffs in April was supplanted in May with the thrill of the raid on the Ojibway settlement near the rifle range at Mount McKay, a Billy Assad-led expedition conceived after the lads learned they were soon to be off to Camp Shilo in Manitoba.

An eight-foot guardian statue kept watch at the entrance to the Indian camp. According to Billy this guardian, made of sheet metal he said, was the famous Ojibway warrior named Nanibijou and it would be a great idea to take the warrior to Shilo as a souvenir of their stay in Port Arthur.

Billy had formulated the plan of attack, a night mission, eight brave men and true, faces blackened with boot polish, courage fortified by a few beers. But it was a plan betrayed by SNAFU, the god of war. SNAFU, or Situation-Normal-All-Fucked-Up, decreed that the liberation of Nanibijou from the posts that held him up, the sound of bolts being driven from the warrior's body—steel, not sheet-metal—would be that of a resonating gong that could be heard for miles.

In the wink of an eye, dogs were barking and lights were coming on in the settlement. Some of the lights were flashlights, some were burning torches, and in no time at all both were bobbing down the road toward them. The Ojibway were coming after the Algonquin.

Frank Archibald told them later that Indians in the bush often kept oil-soaked rags handy to make torches to scare off marauding bears, but this was knowledge they didn't have when they most needed words of reassurance to banish fearful thoughts. *They were going to be scalped. They were going to be lynched. They were going to be burned at the stake like the Jesuit martyr, St. Jean de Brébeuf.*

Sizing up the situation in an instant Billy ordered a strategic withdrawal leaving Nanibijou behind them teetering on two bolts.

Ten days later they were boarding a colonist car for Shilo listening to the Port Arthur City Band playing Vera Lynn's, "Wish Me Luck As You Wave Me Good-Bye."

Shilo was quite a change and no one had a kind word about the place, Billy summing it up for all of them when he dubbed their new lodgings, "the arsehole of the world."

At Current River they could walk to downtown Port Arthur. At Shilo the nearest civilization was Brandon and it was miles away over a prairie flat as a pancake. Barney wrote in his diary that if a soldier got homesick and decided to go AWL you could see him going for two days.

Then there was the sand. Worse than Borden where it was only in their food from time to time. At Shilo it was in their food *all* the time. Also in their boots, in their underwear and, when a wind came up, in all their orifices including mouth, nose, ears and anus.

At Shilo the talk was that they were headed to the Far East. When they were issued short-sleeved shirts and short pants they figured it wasn't just talk.

Clothing wasn't the only change as the regiment went through its first major reorganization. Officers and men were going and coming, the goings mostly men invalided out because of flat feet, bad backs or bats in the belfry.

But there were also those who were tired of training and had asked for transfers to units next in line to join the two Canadian Divisions already in Britain.

Popovich is one of the first to get his wish. He hears rumours about the creation of a secret and elite force of commandos on the lookout for recruits who have been lumberjacks, forest rangers, prospectors, hard-rock miners and trappers, in short, men who eat nails for breakfast. The Pole figures this is right up his alley and he quickly volunteers along with a dozen or so of his comrades. But after tough medicals and even tougher IQ tests, Popovich is the only one chosen and bids adieu to the gang at the beginning of June.

Gillie is also one who goes. He goes because he is sent to Britain with a number of other officers to learn the lessons of modern warfare, bitter lessons learned at schools of hard knocks in Europe and North Africa.

New equipment and weapons were now arriving daily as Canadian factories finally began to churn out the materiel needs of a modern army. And even though the new equipment and weapons meant more training, at least it promised to be different, which was enough for the little league of nations who knew from Camp Q that they were not yet ready to go up against Jerry.

Since the beginning of the year, the news had been both good and bad. More than 23,000 people had been killed in England by *Luftwaffe* bombers. The Wops were on the run in North Africa but the supermen of the Third Reich were on their way to stiffen the Italian backbone. British forces in Greece had surrendered. The Canadian passenger ship *Nerissa* had been torpedoed off Ireland with the loss of seventy-three Canadian soldiers. The British battleship *Hood* was sunk by the German battleship *Bismark*, and then a week later— sweet and quick revenge—the *Bismark* was sunk by British planes and warships.

Then in June news came of the German invasion of Russia. The headline in the *Toronto Globe and Mail* was big and black and bold: **NAZIS INVADE RUSSIA**. And underneath in smaller type: **Claim Hun Repulsed with Big Losses; Churchill Pledges Help for Soviets; R.A.F. Downs 58 Planes in Two Days.**

Also in June the little league, along with their adopted brothers, are assigned to the Carrier Platoon with its eight lightly armoured tracked vehicles armed with the Bren gun, a twenty-two-pound light machine gun using the same .303 ammunition as the Lee Enfield but capable of delivering 500 rounds a minute on full automatic.

A carrier resembles a small tank with the top half peeled off like an opened tin of sardines. The vehicle can travel at thirty-five miles an hour and turn on a dime when the driver brakes one track and guns the other. In deference to its British origins, the carrier is a right-hand drive with the Bren gunner on the driver's left. When sitting, both driver and gunner are protected by a half-inch steel plate shield with slits for viewing.

Carriers are multi-purpose vehicles used for ferrying troops, ammunition and food to the front and the wounded back to the Regimental Aid Posts or RAPs in the rear echelons. But what excites Gill's replacement, Lieutenant Robbie Kendrick, is the possibility of carrier reconnaissance, rapid incursions behind enemy lines drawing fire, bringing back prisoners and intelligence—Kendrick's word is "Intel"—about the enemy's deployment and strength and the location of his heavy machine guns, his mortars, his tanks and artillery. Kendrick is a gung-ho warrior.

The Lowvert Algonquins, together with Ross and Christensen, spent a day climbing all over their new toys, taking turns driving out through the prairie grass in the flat gopher country yelling and laughing at each other over the bulldozer sounds of the carriers. That same evening they took turns moaning and groaning about Kendrick.

"Who is this guy? Some kinda a cowboy? Thinks the war's gonna be some kinda show right outta the wild West?"

"Yeah, and he's gonna be the good guy in the white Stetson who rides inta town and shoots the bad guy and gets the girl."

"I think he wants to be a hero awful bad. He's gonna be one of them guys lookin' for a Victoria Cross." Billy was shaking his head.

"Know what he said to me?" Ross looked around the outdoor table in front of their barracks where they were smoking and watching the red sun flatten into the shape of a fried egg, sunny side up, as it went to bed on the horizon. "Asked me, 'Where you from, Kid?' I told 'im. He sez, 'Where's that?' I told 'im it was in Northern Ontario. Then he sez, get this, he sez, 'Somewhere around Gravenhurst?' Not quite, I sez. It's about 300 miles northwest of Gravenhurst."

"What did he say then?"

"Nothin'. Just smiled and patted me on the back."

"What an arsehole."

"Nah, he's more than that. He's a perfect arsehole."

"What's a perfect arsehole?"

"An arsehole from Toronto."

"Toronto?"

"Yeah, that's where he's from."

Al was listening but saying nothing even though he agreed with the sentiments. Kendrick was definitely one of those guys who believed his shit didn't stink, who thought Toronto was the centre of the universe and didn't have a clue about the rest of the country, never mind the province.

But Al had to live with Kendrick and didn't want to take sides unless he had to. He had a feeling that time would come, but until it did . . . His thoughts were interrupted by Barney, who'd just sauntered over from Battalion.

"You're pretty quiet, Sergeant."

Before Al could reply, Billy interjected. "Hey, Barn! How's the rear echelon warrior?"

Ever since Barney had been assigned to Battalion HQ, Billy had kidded him about his safe and cushy job that would keep him far removed from the fighting units and the heat of battle. Barney was a little sensitive about the subject, but he knew that if he ever let on he was, he'd be hounded all the more.

"Got some good news for you boys."

"And that is?"

"Some two-week leaves coming up."

"Hey, Barn, you're a real *schmensk*. Tell us more."

"Well I just got a peek at the orders but it looks like all of ya are getting to go home the first week in July. Me, too. And the word is '*mensch*,' Billy."

"*Schmensk, mensch*, whatever. We love ya, Barn." Billy gave him a bear hug and Barney's glasses slid down his face.

"What's a *mensch*, Corporal Berman?"

Barney slid his glasses back over his ears. "A *mensch*, Mr. Ross, is an honourable man. It's a Yiddish word."

"And what's a Yiddish, Corporal Berman?"

"Fuck off, Private Assad."

Billy gave him another bear hug and they spent the rest of the evening swatting mosquitoes and planning the food they were going to eat and the parties they were going to have at home.

When they got off the morning train in Lowvert the only greeters were Joe Assad, Ben Berman and Gramps McDougal, because they were the only ones who knew about the leave, Al telegraphing his father that their arrival was to be a surprise. Hiding out in the baggage room, they found it plastered with war posters. One was a stylized drawing of a worker standing behind a soldier with a Tommy gun. The worker was handing ammunition to the soldier. Underneath the drawing, in big block letters, were the words, *BACK THEM UP!*

Another poster was a picture of a traffic light. The top red light said *Stop Waiting.* The middle yellow said *Get Ready to Beat Hitler,* and the bottom green, with marching men in the background, urged the reader to *Go and Enlist Now.*

The plan was to hike out to Slaughterhouse Lake and hang out in the old Assad cottage for the rest of the morning and then, in the early afternoon, march over to nearby Menard's Lake to the Assad's new and bigger cottage where their unsuspecting families would be gathered for a swim and picnic.

It all went like clockwork. Sandy McDougal had even hired a piper who led them smartly in with "Road to the Isles." As they marched into the long curve that led to the cottage, the picnickers on the beach could hear the bagpipes and were up and looking to see what was going on. What they saw in the distance coming out of the curve were soldiers in short pants, arms swinging in unison, chests out as if they were passing in review before King George and Queen Elizabeth at Buckingham Palace.

There was a lot of excited chattering at the lake and then, as the soldiers got closer, screams of recognition. Mothers and wives, sisters and brothers and friends, laughing and crying, rushed to hug and be hugged. With tears in his eyes, Sandy said it was a sight he'd never forget as long as he lived.

The boys from Shilo swam in their underwear, drank beer kept cool in buckets of ice and gorged themselves on potato salad, cheese, cold ham and chicken, homemade rolls and pickles and relish and apple pie and ice cream until, by the time the sun went down, they could barely move.

Because it was their first leave since Christmas, there was a lot of catching up to do, a lot of stories to be told and a lot of questions to be answered, and for the first time there were some subjects soldier sons and husbands didn't feel much like talking about.

"Just one of those things, ya know. It's a POW camp and prisoners try to escape and it was our job to go after them." Al shrugged and sighed. "Wish we coulda brought all of them back but we couldn't."

"You don't hate them, Son?" Sandy had heard something in the way his boy was speaking.

"I do and I don't. I hate the fanatics like my good friend, Hauptmann Kaputt. But the ordinary Jerry in the camp? He's just like me. Or Billy. Or Reggie. Or Frank. Just doin' his job."

They were sitting in the living room on a Sunday, in the early afternoon, having tea after church. Al had been able to steer clear of the shootings for close to a week but today when he could no longer avoid it, he'd given them a very condensed version of events, especially the firefight at the camboose.

He surprised himself with his response to his father's question. In basic training he'd just taken it for granted he would hate Jerry the moment he laid eyes on him. There would come a time when he would but now, in the summer of 1941, after living with the enemy for a month at Monteith, after seeing him in the flesh, after smelling his distinctive odour, whatever feeling he had, it wasn't hate.

"Did ya know that Germans smell?"

"Well, we all smell, Dear."

"Yes, Mother." Al nodded gravely and looked knowingly at Beth who was starting one of her shaking-with-laughter fits because she had a pretty good idea of what her husband was going to say. "And some of us smell very bad in bed at night after a day at Menard's Lake drinking beer."

"Yes, indeed," Beth choked. "Very, very bad."

"But we're not talking about that. We're talking about the smell of people. You know, Italians, Tony's dad, Pietro, smells of garlic. Babies smell of talcum and burp." He was holding his son in his lap and making a big show of sniffing him. "That's what I'm talking about." He handed Sandy Jr. to Beth.

Myra nodded. "And Germans, Dear?"

"Germans smell of sauerkraut."

"For the same reason Italians smell of garlic?" It was his father's bemused question.

Al threw up his hands, "Yeah, Dad. I suppose so. 'Cause they eat a lot of it. Sauerkraut and sausage."

"Where would they get the sauerkraut, Dear? We can't get any in our stores here."

"Oh, they have their own farm gardens at the camp. Grow their own cabbage and make their own sauerkraut. As for the sausage?" He gave his mother an "I haven't the foggiest" gesture, but then he stopped and caught himself, and after an instant started to shake with silent laughter. It was a laugh he had been holding inside for a long time and it was a laugh he couldn't stop. He put his head down until his forehead almost touched his knees and still he couldn't stop. He threw his head back and gasped for breath and it was of no use. Finally after a long struggle and a number of false starts he got it out. "The sausage," he took a deep, shuddering breath, "the sausage they get from Eaton's catalogue."

He couldn't figure out why they only laughed politely. He thought it was hilarious and was still laughing when he went to bed and made love to his wife for the second time that day.

Chapter Seven

JULY 14,1941. Shilo. Billy got off one of his better lines on the train back. Reggie had dug out his guitar and the boys were gathered round singing a few tunes to pass the time. Went through all of Arnie's camboose songs, then a few Andrews Sisters like "Roll Out the Barrel" and "Don't sit under the apple tree with anyone else but me." When it came to "Home, home on the Range, Where the deer and the antelope play" Billy gave us his discouraging word. He said if you show me a home on the range, I'll show you a house full of gopher shit. I should send it in to Reader's Digest for the <u>Quotable Quotes</u> section. Anyway the line cast a pall on the proceedings. Reminded all of us where we were going. Al tried to buck up the gang by talking about the fun they were going to have with the Carriers and the new weapons like the Bren. Said they would also be getting grenade training and that there was a good chance the rumour was true about Hong Kong now that the Japanese were flexing their muscles in the Far East. From what I hear at HQ I think he's right.

Excerpt from Barney's Diary

Al was one of the first to get his hands on the newest weapon in the Algonquin's ever-growing arsenal.

"Chicago piano" was the nickname for the American-made Thompson submachine gun, a weapon favoured by Prohibition era gangsters like Al Capone, John Dillinger, Pretty Boy Floyd, and Baby Face Nelson. The Thompson was fed from a drum magazine in front of the trigger guard and could fire 650 rounds a minute, about the same rate a good piano player in a speakeasy could tickle all the ivories with one sweep of his thumb.

Al wasted no time in getting Billy to take his picture in tin hat and battledress leaning forward with his Thompson in a "stick-em-up" stance *à la* Hollywood's Jimmy Cagney playing G-man up against Capone. Billy promised he'd send the snapshot direct to Hitler. He said once Adolph saw it he'd shit himself, go blind and surrender right away.

The summer months at Shilo were spent careening around the prairie learning what carriers could and could not do. One of the things they could do was tip over fairly easily. Fortunately Ross and Dobson got out from under without a scratch.

When not chasing each other's dust trails in the carriers, they tried out the Brens on the rifle range and found out what the army had told them was true. For once. The Bren was one of the finest light machine guns ever made.

Reggie took to the Bren like a duck to water and it was funny to see because when you looked at the weapon you just naturally assumed it would be best handled by a good-sized man, a man with the heft of a Frank Archibald, and willowy Reggie didn't fit the bill. Especially when firing from the hip. But he handled the Bren like it was just another guitar and after only a few days on the range he could stand sideways to a target and then on a signal turn and hit the bull's eye almost every time. What Crow was to the Lee Enfield, Reggie was to the Bren.

In their spare time they played softball, platoons against platoons, and they played for keeps as if all the energy dammed up waiting to be unleashed on Jerry were let go on each other. Softball was another name for war and the Carrier Platoon turned up with a secret weapon, a pitcher whose surname was Yates and whose father had baptized him William Butler.

William Butler Yates was an American whose father taught English literature in Boston, the home of some of America's greatest authors including Ralph Waldo Emerson, John Greenleaf Whittier and Henry Wadsworth Longfellow. When Yates showed up at practice and introduced himself to Al he winked and said he wasn't the Irish William Butler Yeats who wrote poetry and plays, he was the American William Butler Yates who could neither read nor write. Al wasn't sure what he was talking about and didn't care. All he was interested in was Yates's ability to throw a softball.

"Whattaya doin' in the Canadian Army, Yates?"

"Well, Sergeant, I got tired waiting on President Roosevelt to do the right thing so I hopped a train to Montreal." He pronounced the city's name with a strong accent on the first syllable. "From there I came over to Toronto," here he enunciated each and every syllable, "went to the nearest recruiting office, and you know the rest of the story."

Yates was chewing tobacco and punctuated the end of his explanation by skilfully whooshing expectorant at a clump of prairie grass behind the backstop, coating green with brown.

The rest of the story was that when he showed up as a replacement at Shilo and word got out he'd played semi-professional softball in New England, Barney went to work shuffling forms and forging signatures and in no time at all, the American was on his way to the Carrier Platoon.

Al looked around and saw that the practice field was not the sole domain of the Carriers, so he yelled for the team to come over, introduced Yates all around and then led his charges off behind an H-hut where he paced off the distance between home plate and pitching rubber, marking the spots by dragging his heel in the sand. Then he told Yates to show Billy his stuff.

The newcomer announced his first pitch would be a fastball and when Billy caught it he wished he hadn't. He let out a whoop, shook off his catcher's mitt and blew repeatedly on his burning palm. Yates grinned and spit and told Billy to get ready for a riser.

He was a tall man with extraordinarily long arms and when he threw the riser the ball seemed to come from just off the top of his boots and keep slanting all the way to the plate until Billy caught it about eye level, shaking his head in amazement.

Yates then said he would throw a drop and when the ball got to the plate it dipped about a foot and almost hit the befuddled Billy smack dab in the family jewels. At that point Al called a halt to the proceedings and swore everyone to secrecy. Yates would be kept under wraps until the first game.

Back at his H-hut Al found a message from Kendrick asking his sergeant to meet him at the officers' mess as soon as he got in. When he got to the appointed place, Al found Kendrick smoking a cigar, which he used to wave Al over.

"Hey, Sergeant McDougal, sit down and take a load off your feet." It was a hale-fellow-well-met greeting as phony as a three-dollar bill and Al stifled the urge to roll his eyes.

"Sergeant, I thought you and I should have a little chat." Kendrick stood, striking a pose, his cigar hand raised, the other behind his back.

"I thought we should get to know each other a bit better." An attempt to blow a smoke ring failed badly. Kendrick grimaced and started to pace up and down in front of his sergeant, collecting his thoughts for a speech of great import.

"Now I understand you have a wife and son and that you were working on the railroad before you signed up. In Lowvert, was it?"

"Yessir." Al looked at Kendrick and thought to himself, *What the hell are you doing talking to me like you're an old man and I'm a little kid. I'll bet you're younger than I am, arsehole.*

Al's "Yessir" was greeted with a curt nod. Gillie would have given him a look and asked what this "Yessir" business was all about.

"And just where is Lowvert, Sergeant?'

Al thought of Davie Ross and his conversation with Kendrick. "Just a little bit north of Gravenhurst, sir."

"Hmm. That's funny. Our family has a summer home north of Gravenhurst. On Lake Muskoka just east of Mortimer's Point, and I don't believe I've ever heard of Lowvert."

He frowned and shook his head. "Oh well, I don't suppose it really matters, does it?"

Oh but it does, sir. It matters a lot if you don't know that Lowvert is nowhere near Gravenhurst.

"Let me tell you a little bit about myself, Sergeant. I'll start with my father." Al shifted in his chair. *Probably a close relative of King George.*

"My father, Major Kendrick, is a veteran of the First War. Fought at Vimy Ridge under Arthur Currie." *Who the fuck's Arthur Currie?*

"Came home and got his law degree." *Better than the clap.* "Was made a QC in 1928." *So your father's a Queen's Counsel and mine is a baggageman. La-de-da.*

"To prepare me for a life of public service, my father sent me to Upper Canada College, probably the best preparatory school in Canada." *Yeah, and my father sent me to Victoria Public because it was the only school in town.*

"Then I went to Trinity College at the University of Toronto and graduated with an honour's degree in history last May. Two weeks later I got my commission and two weeks after that I was assigned to the Algonquins." *In other words your old man pulled some strings and here you are and we're stuck with you and you know sweet bugger all about soldiering.*

"Now, Sergeant, this is how I see our enterprise." Kendrick sat now and waved his cigar importantly.

"I see it from the perspective of history and throughout history mankind has fought to preserve civilization from the barbarian whether that barbarian be Genghis Khan or Adolph Hitler. And the fight always requires brave men, brave men like Nelson, Wellington, Kitchener, brave men who will do their duty for God and king. This war, Sergeant, is *our* chance to be brave men and do *our* duty for God and king. The torch has been passed to us. We must not fail."

Al thought he was listening to one of Reverend Manson Payne's sermons and when Kendrick finished was tempted to stand and belt out a hymn. He ran through the possibilities in his mind and settled on "Faith of Our Fathers! Living still in spite of dungeon, fire and sword."

There was a silence in the room and when Al looked up, he saw the lieutenant was staring at him and suddenly realized he'd been humming the hymn. He cleared his throat and smiled. "Yessir, I believe you're right, sir."

"Sergeant, I hope you are taking this seriously."

"Certainly, sir. Absolutely, sir."

"Very well, Sergeant." Kendrick took some papers from the briefcase at his feet. "As you know, the Carrier Platoon will be a recce platoon. Our job will be to probe and search for the enemy. It will require initiative, self-reliance and above all bravery." *Not to mention an officer with a brain in his head.*

"With that in mind I've laid out a training plan." He handed a file to his sergeant. "I want you to study the plan until it's second nature to you."

"Yessir."

"And I want you to drill the platoon on the plan until it's second nature to them. Is that clear?"

"Yessir." *Can I go now, sir?*

"Thank you, Sergeant. You may go now."

"Thank you, sir." *And kiss my arse, sir.*

"One last word, Sergeant."

"Yessir?"

"If there is anything in the plan you don't understand, don't guess at it. Come to me and I will explain it to you."

"Yessir. And thank you, sir."

Al saluted, turned on his heel, marched out the door to the first garbage can he saw, lifted the lid and tossed in the file.

If Hollywood had been making a movie of all this, the camera eye would have lingered on the garbage can and witnessed a cursing Sergeant McDougal stepping back into the frame a second later, reaching into the can and digging out the file he'd just dumped.

"Gentlemen, what you have in your hand is a type thirty-six grenade. Your grenade is not primed or loaded, so you have nothing to worry about."

It was the morning after Kendrick, and the platoon was gathered around an instructor about to demonstrate the fine art of throwing a grenade. Al was having a hard time paying attention because he was still steamed about yesterday and his mind was wandering, savouring stories he'd heard about officers whose men didn't care for them. In some less disciplined outfits, platoons went through lieutenants like a dose of salts and even among the Algonquins it was known that one or two officers had been threatened with bayonets at their throats. Smarten up, or else.

"Grenades were first used as weapons of war in the fifteenth century. They were shaped like pomegranates and that's how they got their name."

Billy raised his hand. "Sir, if they'd been shaped like bananas would they have been called 'banades'?"

"If they'd been shaped like your brain, Billy, they would have been called 'peas.'"

"Or softballs for the size of my balls."

"More like mothballs, ya mean."

The instructor just smiled and juggled the grenade in his hand patiently waiting out the banter.

"The type thirty-six is the smallest of any of the weapons you will use in combat but very effective with small concentrations of enemy forces because," he grinned as he flipped his grenade at Billy who caught it and grinned as he threw it back, "when it explodes it spews about eighty pieces of jagged metal in a tight little circle. So if one of these babies goes off in the middle of us today, the resulting shrapnel would kill or wound more than half of this platoon."

Al looked around at the thirty Algonquins listening to the instructor and caught the eye of Private William Butler Yates, who winked and spat tobacco juice.

"Now the first thing we are going to learn is how to throw a grenade." The instructor looked at them, his eyes twinkling. "Don't suppose any of you boys from Northern Ontario ever played cricket, eh?

"I say, old boy. Cricket eh, wha'!"

"Sir, I believe cricket is a game for gentlemen and, as you can see, sir, there are no gentlemen here."

"Speak for yourself, Yates. What does an American know about being a gentleman?"

"I believe our lieutenant might know how to play cricket, sir." Billy offered his opinion with a snide grin.

"Ah, yes. Kendrick is your man, isn't he?"

"Yessir."

The instructor nodded slowly, the expression on his face saying, *Yeah, you're probably right. Kendrick* would *know how to play cricket, wouldn't he?*

The rest of the morning was taken up with throwing unloaded grenades, the same way a "veddy propa" English gentleman would deliver a cricket ball, arm down then up and over. It would be another day or so before they'd get to lob the real McCoy.

That evening after supper, Al sat down to write some letters home. His father had recently begun typing his letters and his son couldn't resist. "I received your letter the other day and must say you are becoming quite a typist. I'll bet when you finished, your finger was really sore."

He went on to mention the new recruits, Yates in particular, and what a great pitcher he was. "He's a funny duck, chews tobacco and lets on he's a bit of a hayseed but I think he's just trying to hide his light under a bushel. Anyway, can't wait for the first game to see the look on the faces of the first batters who try to hit his pitches."

His letter to his mother said nothing about guns and grenades and a lot about Billy and Barney, the mosquitoes and the weather, the ball team and the food, "much worse than Borden." He didn't say that some of his comrades had taken matters into their own hands and gone deer hunting in the nearby game preserve. Venison was a welcome relief from mutton even when it brought the RCM Police to the camp looking for deerslayers.

His letter to Beth was mostly about Kendrick and the number of men who were fed up and going AWL. "You might remember a chap by the name of Braddock from Shillington. Walked out of camp and rode the rails to Port Arthur. Stayed with a girlfriend there and got somebody to buy him a ticket to North Bay, where the military police just happened to be checking up on boys who had left home without a note from Daddy. Braddock fessed up right away and the MP let him go when he promised to head back here after a few days at home. Something about his mother being sick. Only trouble is his mother died four years ago. Anyway Braddock's a lucky man. Could have been charged as a deserter. The problem is most of the lads are bored silly here, the food is lousy, the scenery is worse and there's nothing to do and nowhere to go at night. If something isn't done soon half the Regiment will be AWL and the other half will have transferred out to other units with a chance to go overseas."

Their first ball game with Yates on the mound was Sunday afternoon against the Engineers, who met their predictable fate in the bottom of the first—three batters, nine pitches, side retired. The same thing happened in the second inning as well as the third and fourth and all subsequent innings thereafter.

In September, as the German Army encircled Leningrad and Canadian Corvettes sank their first enemy U-boat in the Battle of the Atlantic, the Carrier Platoon strutted into the playoffs undefeated. Their opponents for the Regimental Championship was a team from one of Charlie Company's rifle platoons. The "Charlie Horses" also had a pitcher. Cary Cram from Sudbury.

Cary, whose nickname was "Creepy," wasn't as fast as Yates, nor did he have the American's repertoire of pitches. In fact he had only one pitch and it was downright . . . well, downright creepy. The ball came at you so slowly it looked like a watermelon. But when it got to the plate it started to jitter and jive, shiver and shake leaving the batter with two choices. Either he could leave the bat on his shoulder and watch a called strike or swing at thin air as the ball jitterbugged past him.

Going into the first game the Carriers were a tad overconfident and a combination of a throwing error and a couple of lucky hits off Yates in the sixth allowed the Horses to canter off the field with a one to zero victory.

The second game of the best of seven finals was no better. Yates had a bout of wildness late in the contest and walked in the winning run. The Horses gloated and the Carriers fumed.

The third game was all-out war. Yates took the first shot with his first pitch— high, hard and inside forcing the leadoff Horseman to hit the dirt. When he got up and dusted himself off, he glared at the American and yelled if he tried that again he'd get his Yankee arse kicked back across the border. Yates just grinned, spat tobacco juice and struck the indignant batter out on three straight pitches, a fastball, a riser and a strike three that left Al shaking his head. Yates had thrown a Creepy Cram special.

When his team came off the field and Al got up to take his coaching position along the third baseline, he grabbed Yates as he jogged off the field.

"Hey Willy, what the hell was that?"

"Ah shucks, Sarg. Just somethin' me and Billy cooked up. Easy pitch to throw but it's a junk pitch. Not fit for a real man."

"Ya mean you coulda thrown that pitch before?"

"Hell, yes!"

Yates winked and ambled off to take his spot on the player's bench. Al shook his head and then motioned Reggie over for a whispered chat before he stepped into the batter's box to lead off. Reggie, who could run like a deer, nodded to his coach, took his place at the plate and bunted Cram's first pitch along the third base line. He was safe by a mile.

Billy was next up and he did the same thing down the first base line. The first baseman fielded the ball and tried to get Reggie at second but his throw sailed into centre field. Reggie ended up at third and Billy at second.

Davey Ross was up next and he struck out. Crow was the clean-up hitter and he too had a quiet chat with Al before he stepped up to the plate and planted his feet as far forward in the box as the rules allowed. He would try to get his bat on one of Creepy's pitches before the ball began its St. Vitus's dance over the plate.

It worked. Crow looped the second pitch into right field, easily scoring Reggie. Urged on by a windmilling arm in the coach's box at third, Billy chugged around the hot corner and steamrolled into home, arriving at the same time as the throw from the outfield. If the catcher holds on to the ball, Billy is out by a country mile, but Billy slid, army boots high, kicking the ball out of the catcher's mitt.

When the catcher took exception to Billy's greeting, the two of them went at it fists flying, a signal for both player's benches to join the fray until there was hand-to-hand combat at home plate.

When cooler heads prevailed, both Billy and the Horse catcher were thrown out of the game but the Carriers had scored a couple of early runs and that together with a rejuvenated Yates brought victory in game three.

It got easier after that. Either Creepy lost some of his magic or the Carriers gained some confidence—maybe, Al thought, it was a little of both—but the Charlie Horses never won another game. Yates said it just like the battle of Shiloh in the American Civil War when the South under General Albert S. Johnston won the early skirmishes but the North under General Ulysses S. Grant regained lost ground and, in the end, won the fight.

By the last days of September it was clear they were not going to Hong Kong. Others had been tabbed for that job and all the Algonquins could do was slouch in the Rec Hall and grumble as they watched the *Movietone News*, the Royal Rifles of Canada waiting to board a train in Val Cartier, Quebec and the Winnipeg Grenadiers in short pants waving good-bye from a ship somewhere on the West Coast. Of course, the *News* didn't say where these soldiers were going—no sense in tipping off Tojo—but it was obvious to the frustrated among the ranks in Shilo.

Not that they wanted to fight the Japs—if the Japs went to war. Their fight was in Europe against Jerry, not in the Far East against bowlegged little fanatics waving swords and shouting "Banzai!" It was just that Hong Kong was an opportunity to finally *do* something and it was this that had galvanized men from the North, born and bred to think of themselves as doers. That was the reason they were grouchy at not being chosen to go, a grouchiness that turned to white-hot anger when the consequences of that decision became apparent. Not only did the Rifles and the Grenadiers get to go, they went with Algonquin equipment—Jeeps, trucks, motorcycles and more. The Carrier Platoon had to give up both their carriers and their Brens. Even Chicago pianos were requisitioned, as Al found out when Kendrick ordered him to turn his in. All they had left were their Lee Enfields.

So more and more men went AWL, more and more transferred out and scuttlebutt started making the rounds that the regiment was going to be disbanded, its men dispersed to other units in the Canadian Army.

"Goddammit! They beg us ta sign up. Tell us we're joinin' the best outfit there is. A Northern regiment for Northern boys. Finest boys on the face of the earth. That's what they tell us. And now they're gonna send us off to some namby-pamby outfit from who-knows-where. Probably somewhere in the South. Some Toronto outfit. The Toronto Tabby Cats. We'll be called the 'Pussy Boys.'"

Billy was on one of his rants and no one had the gumption to disagree with him on an Indian summer Sunday afternoon just inside the game preserve, where they were eating peanuts and drinking root beer under some trees on the edge of a pond that Westerners called a slough.

September had been a good month for Billy, the Regimental Softball Championship and fatherhood—Mabel had given birth to a son and Billy had promptly nicknamed him Shabicky in honour of his favourite New York Ranger. He told Al that someday Shabicky and Two-Ton Tony were going to play in the NHL and make their old men proud.

But now it was October and Hong Kong was no longer on the table, gone, along with their equipment, and the regiment was up for grabs and Billy was in a sour mood.

"All that's left is grenade training! Some stupid bastard probably drop a live one and get us all killed. To hell with root beer. Gimme a real beer, Yates."

Yates had managed to scrounge some beer for those who had not taken the pledge at Kakabeka Falls and he fished a bottle from his store in the cold waters of the slough. Al glanced at Billy as he reached for it and Billy looked back with a shrug as Yates reached for one himself, took the bottle opener from Billy to uncap it, swallowed a mouthful and started to sing the regimental song. The tune was "John Brown's Body." His voice was low and mocking.

Our Regimental number is one hundred and fifty-nine,
We come from New Ontario, the backwoods and the mine,
They dressed us up in khaki and we signed the dotted line,
As we go marching on.
Glory, glory to the Algonquins
Glory, glory to the Algonquins
Glory, glory to the Algonquins
As we go marching on.

When he finished there was a long silence of held breath broken by Billy taking a noisy swallow of beer, wiping his mouth with the back of his hand and then glaring at the bemused American.

"Fuck you, Yates. Who are you tryin' ta kid. Ya come up here ta join the Canadian Army pretending you're some kind of tobacco-chewin' hick. But you're not, are ya? You're just some nose-in-the-air bastard playin' around with your country bumpkin cousins up in Canada, the ones from the wrong side of the tracks. Fuck you!"

The two of them were standing now facing each other about a foot apart locked in eye contact until Yates broke into a grin and winked.

"You found me out, Billy. You found me out. Now if you would kindly excuse me, I'm going to have a swim."

And with that he bent down, pulled off his boots, peeled off his socks, stripped off his clothes and waded out into the slough where he turned and solemnly saluted his comrades before diving into the water.

As Al watched him go he laughed at the sight of a naked man, torso of ivory white bordered in your basic angry red and dark brown—the red circling the back of the neck, the brown on arms from elbows to wrists, on legs from knees to ankles.

"Geez, Crow, he's blacker than you are and you're not even close to being a white man."

"Me thankful for that, Kemosabe."

"Hey Crow, that Kemosabe stuff, that's what Tonto always says to the Lone Ranger. What's it mean, anyway?" The question came from young Ross and the Lowvert boys all hid their grins.

Frank put on his inscrutable Indian face and looked solemnly at Ross. "Kemosabe mean, 'Stupid fucking white man.'"

"Aw, come on. Yer kiddin' me, right?"

"Nah," said Billy putting his arm around Davey, "he's not kiddin' ya, Kemosabe."

It was Wednesday afternoon following a morning of parade ground drills when they finally got to throw live grenades, but not before their instructor spent a good hour reminding them of how it was done.

"Now gentlemen, watch carefully because this time it's for real."

His students were standing in a semi-circle in a wide trench behind a shoulder-high earth berm topped with sandbags. With a show-and-tell gesture, the instructor held up a grenade in his right hand with two fingers of his left hand hooked through the grenade's ring.

"This ring is the safety pin. You pull it when you're ready to throw. This arms the grenade. Is that clear?"

His question was answered by a series of attentive front row nods but kibitzing from the rear. The instructor turned to Al.

"Sergeant, I suggest you speak to the boys in the back of the class. Please explain that this is not a summer camp for Girl Guides."

Al acknowledged the rebuke and pushed his way through to the two offenders, youngsters he recognized as new arrivals, playful puppies no more than a week old. They were bright-eyed and bushy-tailed and grinning like the village idiot as their sergeant approached, reached out two hands, grabbed their shirt fronts and dragged them to the front where both he and the instructor could keep an eye on them.

"Now then, gentlemen and girls," nodding to the puppies, "once you pull the pin you hold the lever in place against the grenade like this." He demonstrated at eye level around the semi-circle. "The lever is like the trigger on your rifle. When you let go of the lever you're pulling the trigger and you have five seconds," he held up five fingers, "five seconds before she blows. You can hold this thing forever with the pin pulled but once the lever is released you get rid of it, PDQ. Understood?"

He looked at his class, his eyes asking the question of each man in turn. Satisfied that the telling of how it was done was clearly understood by all, he had one last word for them before he moved on to the showing of how it was done. "Watch."

Holding the grenade up for all to see, he brought it down, pulled the pin and waved it in front of them. "Okay? Nothing doing until I release the lever, right?" Heads nodded. "Now I'm going to pull the trigger and throw and as soon as I let it go, get your heads down. Duck!"

He lobbed the missile over the berm and began to count off as everyone but the two puppies hunkered down. They were on their tiptoes craning to see what was going to happen. The count had reached "three-a-hundred" when a flying tackle from Al knocked them to the ground.

The silence after the crump of the exploding grenade was broken by an irate instructor, hands on hips, his face about six inches from the two frightened gawkers. "Do you two fucking greenhorns understand the King's English? When I say 'duck' here, I am not talking about our web-footed, feathery friends. Do you have any idea what shrapnel does to flesh and bones. Jesus Christ Almighty!"

The rest of the day was spent in groups of five spaced out behind the berm, pulling pins, lobbing grenades and ducking. Over and over again, Al and the instructor watching like hawks whenever it was the turn of the puppies. At the end of the day the puppies were up for their last throw along with Dougie Dobson together with two other players from the softball team, Moose MacKenzie, the first baseman, and Hermanson, the centre fielder. Standing below the trench on the back side, Al heaved a sigh. It would soon be over.

Dobson had just returned from harvest leave and while waiting for the instructor to finish talking to the group last up, was joking with Hermanson about German grenades called "potato mashers" by Canadians because of a wooden handle and steel head with a flat end, a perfect tool to pulp spuds. "Promised to bring one back for the old man. He likes mashed potatoes."

Hermanson's reply was cut off by the instructor's query. "Ready, gentlemen?"

"Yessir!"

"Right! Now you know what to do. One last time, do it!"

Five pins were pulled as one and five grenades launched as one. But only four cleared the berm. One of them clipped a sandbag and dropped back down into the trench. The puppy whose missile it was cursed and scrambled to pick it up in the sand. The others froze until the instructor screamed at them to get out, jolting Dobson and MacKenzie to follow him as he grabbed the back lip of the trench and vaulted over to safety. In the trench one puppy was still digging frantically and the other was frozen on the spot. It was Hermanson who saved them by belly-flopping on the live grenade, smothering the explosion with his body.

When Al came running up he saw the instructor on his knees beside Hermanson pulling him over on his back. There wasn't a mark on his face but his battledress was torn to shreds, his chest dark with oozing blood and his intestines bulging a glistening blue-gray in the hole where his stomach had been. A sharp smell reminded Al of the stench that still lingered in the ruins of the abattoir at Slaughterhouse Lake. He turned away, leaned over and vomited.

That night he sat by himself at a table in the sergeants' mess, a letter from Beth open in front of him as he wrote to Hermanson's wife in Port Arthur. It wasn't his job, it was Kendrick's, but Kendrick didn't know Hermanson and even if he did Al didn't trust him to say what needed to be said without gucking it up with references to God and king and supreme sacrifice and "greater love hath no man than this" and other candy floss phrases not from the heart.

He told Hermanson's wife that her husband had given his life to save two young men and that as long as his comrades were alive they would never forget that they had been privileged to be friends with one of the bravest men they had ever known and that when her son was old enough she should show him this letter, which he and every member of the platoon had signed so the boy would know that his father was a true hero.

When he finished he was crying as he looked again at the picture Beth had sent, a picture she had taken when he'd been home in July, a picture of himself and his son beside him, both in uniform, his the short pants and short sleeves of Shilo, the young lad in a child's size version that Beth had sewn— wedge cap and tunic with sergeant stripes on the right sleeve. On the face of the photograph in the bottom right corner she had written, "My soldier boys."

PART
TWO

Chapter Eight

DECEMBER 7, 1941. Niagara-on-the-Lake. Sunday morning and all's quiet on the Welland Canal. Been here about two weeks now and all we have done is stand sentry duty at the Queenston Power Plant and patrol the banks of the Welland making sure we don't fall in when it's slippery from snow. The only excitement is when the boys get bored and shoot up some tin cans in the water. When challenged by their officers the excuse is that they are just following orders to destroy any suspicious objects floating down the power canals toward the generating plants. And that's our job here. To prevent sabotage. But isn't that supposed to be up to the Veteran's Guard? Anyway it's better than being in Shilo. Anything is better than Shilo. Being stuck on the Lowbush for six months would have been better than Shilo. The day before we left some of the officers at HQ were thinking of asking the Pioneers to get some dynamite and blow the camp to Kingdom Come so no other Regiment in the Canadian Army would have to put up with the place. Here in Niagara, most of the boys feel like they are at least back in Canada after a tour of duty in some foreign country. The song on the train east, it must have been sung a thousand times, was "Gee Ma, I want to go, Back to Ontario, Gee Ma, I want to go home." But the rumour is we won't be home for long so if we won't be here for a long time then we can at least be here for a good time and in our spare time, slip across the border to New York State and sample American beer and American girls. According to reports they really have a thing for boys in uniform, especially brave men whose task it is to guard Niagara Falls from saboteurs!

Excerpt from Barney's Diary

Barney capped his pen and stared off into space, thinking. Even though he didn't write in his diary every day, he was now into a second volume, this time a lined school scribbler. Part of him thought he should be writing in something more grand, something in a burgundy hard cover for example, but the other half, the more practical half, knew better. A scribbler could easily be folded and tucked away in the blouse of his battledress where he could quickly get at it during a lull in the fighting. Barney had vowed to himself that he wasn't going to be a rear-end warrior forever. For the time being he was more or less content but when the regiment finally went to war, if it ever did, he was going to be at the sharp end of things, preferably with Al and Billy and Reggie and Crow. And his diary.

He looked up, annoyed at the sound of a radio turned to full volume. He was about to shout, "Turn it down, will ya," when he caught some words.

". . . repeat. This report has just been received. The Japanese have attacked Hawaii. The American naval base at Pearl Harbor has been heavily bombed by carrier-based planes from the Japanese navy. Unconfirmed reports are that several hundred American sailors have been killed and at least two battleships, the *Arizona* and the *Oklahoma*, have been sunk. More reports will follow on the six o'clock news. We now return to our regular Sunday afternoon programming."

The next day the Japanese attacked Hong Kong. The Royal Rifles and the Winnipeg Grenadiers had to fight without any of the Algonquin equipment. Half the weapons and vehicles from Shilo, the Brens, the Jeeps, trucks, motorcycles and carriers got lost in the mail, and the rest were diverted to Manila and handed over to the Americans defending the Philippines.

The battle for the British colony lasted until December 25 and on that day, when Christians on both sides of the war in Europe were celebrating peace on earth, good will towards men, and Bing Crosby's song, "I'm Dreaming of a White Christmas" was a new and popular hit on the radio in North America, the Canadians in Hong Kong ran out of ammunition. On Boxing Day, they were forced to surrender. Their casualty lists were grim: 300 dead, another 493 wounded. Some taken prisoner were barbwired together and used for bayonet practice.

When weeks later the full extent of the disaster filtered down to the Algonquins on the Welland Canal there were many silent prayers of thanks along the lines of there-but-for-the-grace-of-God-go-I, especially among those who had itched to go. Had that itch been scratched many of them would still be in Hong Kong in makeshift graves or among the hundreds in POW camps where there were no swimming pools and no Eaton's catalogues and where prisoners were regularly beaten, starved and worked to death by their sadistic captors, among them the Kamloops Kid, a Japanese-Canadian born in British Columbia who made a point of seeking out his imprisoned countrymen for special treatment— beatings and torture. The Kid would be hanged for his treason in Hong Kong on August 25, 1947.

But in February 1942, thanks to a wink and a smile from Lady Luck, the Algonquins had nothing to do with the brutal Kamloops Kid in the Far East. They were off to the not-so-Far East, to another British colony, this one called "Newfoundland."

Barney's rumour had proved out. The regiment had been back in Ontario for only a little over two months before the lads were on the move again, heading by train for the East Coast, going back the way German prisoners for Monteith had come, through Rivière-du-Loup on the south shore of the St. Lawrence in Quebec, Campbellton and Moncton in New Brunswick, and finally down into Halifax where, except for a very few, their first ocean voyage awaited.

The Northern Ontario Regiment wasn't the first Canadian unit to garrison the British outpost across the Cabot Strait from Nova Scotia. The Royal Highland Regiment of Canada, the Black Watch, had been the first, crossing from Canada in June 1940. Then it was the Queen's Own from Toronto, followed by the Royal Rifles before they went to Hong Kong. The Algonquins were relieving the Prince Edward Island Highlanders, who had been in the colony since July 1941.

It wasn't hard to explain the Allied interest in Newfoundland. Known as "the Rock," the island was closer to Europe than any other part of North America. It was the Far East of the Western World. Only Britain and Newfoundland stood between Hitler and North America and if Britain fell then the North Atlantic would be a German highway, an *Autobahn*, to Canada and the United States. And so it was determined that the rocky island would be a roadblock on that highway and the Canadians, along with the Americans after Pearl Harbour, were making sure that the roadblock was armed and ready to deal with anything the enemy might have in mind to dismantle it, be it shelling from battleships, raiding parties put ashore from U-boats or bombing from aircraft launched from rumoured aircraft carriers.

It wasn't hard to sell Newfoundland to men who'd had their fill of training, training and more training. The prospect of putting that training to use was a welcome one and was the reason the Algonquins got off the train in Halifax with a spring in their step and grins on their faces. Unfortunately, no one had told them about seasickness.

Their transport to "Newfy-john," navy slang for St. John's, is the *Lady Nelson* and the lads spend a night on board in Halifax's Bedford Basin waiting for a convoy to form up. For most of the crossing the *Lady Nelson* will have some escorts, a Royal Canadian Navy destroyer and three corvettes, but once off Newfy-john, the *Lady* and the Algonquins are going to be on their own.

The purpose of a convoy is to protect against the German *Unterseeboot*, so vessels form a box with the destroyer leading the way, setting a zigzag course that makes it difficult for any U-boat lurking off the coast of Nova Scotia to get a bead on any of the vulnerable ships. One corvette is stationed on each flank of the convoy and there is a "tail-end Charlie" astern. All four of the escort ships sweep the ocean with undersea listening devices called "sonar" by the Americans and "asdic" by the Canadians. The asdic has a range of 1,500 yards and emits a pinging sound like the echo of a tuning fork. When the sound makes contact and the pinging becomes more rapid, the asdic operator signals the ship's bridge, the klaxon signals "battle stations" and the crew prepares for a depth charge attack.

The depth charge is a steel cylinder containing some 300 pounds of explosives preset to detonate at various depths. The charges are launched from the port and starboard sides of the ship or dropped from the stern in a diamond pattern. It is hardly ever a direct hit that kills a U-boat but rather the cumulative effect of several nearby explosions that eventually crack the submarine's hull and send boat and crew to a watery grave.

The *Lady Nelson* is a small ship, so small she can take only half the regiment in one trip. Designed to ply the relatively calm waters of the Mediterranean, she has a tough time in the rough-and-tumble of the Atlantic, where the waves are sometimes so high that the escorting corvettes momentarily disappear from view. Once out of Halifax Harbour, it isn't long before the Algonquins feel like they are riding on one of Creepy Cram's weaving and dipping pitches as the *Lady* bucks her way through the towering seas. When the bow goes up the stern comes down and when the stern goes up the bow comes down. It is a gigantic teeter-totter and it isn't much fun.

Soon the lads are beginning to sweat and feel dizzy. Then stomachs lurch and contents spew. The medical officers on board hand out peppermints and urge the afflicted to eat bread in an effort to settle their innards, but nothing works. Toilets overflow, the stench of vomit is everywhere, and, to make matters worse, the voyage lasts forever.

The convoy commander on the destroyer has had reports of U-boat sightings, and changes course, heading for the pack ice off Newfoundland. Pack ice is frozen sea water sometimes more than two feet thick, making it almost impossible for German submarines to hunt a convoy, but equally impossible for the *Lady* to make any real headway. Coming out of Halifax the convoy is at maximum speed—ten knots—but once in the ice that speed is cut by more than half and the convoy barely moves. But still the men are sick.

In the late afternoon of the fifth day of a crossing that in peacetime would have taken two days, Al and Billy stood on deck leaning over the rail on the *Lady Nelson*'s starboard side. The two friends were not supposed to be there but the gagging stench below decks had driven them up into the cold and freezing spray in search of air that didn't smell of vomit. Below decks, scores of their comrades were too ill to move and more than a few were in sick bay being fed intravenously.

On the rail, huddled in their greatcoats, they took in lungfuls of chill sea air, almost forgetting their stomachs churning on empty. Neither had eaten for four days now and it was open to question whether they would ever want to eat again.

"Ya know what I wish, Al?" Billy lurched as the ship shuddered through the ice. "I wish a German sub would put a couple of torpedoes in us right now, sink this goddamn tub and put me outta my misery."

Al turned and looked at his pal. Billy's face was gaunt. He had lost weight. He looked like hell. But then they all did.

"Wonder what it would be like ta be in the water." Billy looked over the rail. "Cold as Toby's arse, I'll bet. If ya don't drown right away ya probably just go ta sleep. Not a bad way ta go when ya think about it."

Al was thinking about food and desperately trying not to because it made him even more queasy. He liked to eat and his memory was being ornery, serving up a potpourri of home-cooked images: roast beef and Yorkshire pudding; apple pie and cheese; roast chicken and cranberry sauce; butter tarts, ham sandwiches, bacon and eggs. He retched and spat phlegm.

Billy was still musing about death. "Ya know, Al, I keep thinkin' about Hermanson. What was goin' through his head when he saw that grenade lyin' there. Was he thinkin' about his wife, was he thinkin' about his kid?"

"Yeah, two kids. The ones in the trench with him, Billy. Two dumb kids who happened to be his buddies."

On deck that night the two of them crawled under a rubber dinghy lashed near a vent from the engine room and tried to get some sleep. Despite the warm air from the vent, it was a cold, hard rest, their stomachs roiling with every roll of the ship. But the air was free of vomit and that was everything to them. In their troubled dreams they didn't notice the *Lady Nelson* changing course and speeding up.

When they awoke in the clear cold of the morning and stood to stretch stiff limbs they saw that the horizon was empty. Both the pack ice and the convoy were gone. With the exception of one escorting corvette, they were now on their own for the run into St. John's.

Just as they turned from the rail and were sucking up the will to report below, there was a sharp jar and grind as if a huge wave had pushed the ship against a concrete pier. The *Lady* immediately lost way and the ship klaxon began to sound the alarm. Both Al and Billy, still half asleep, stood rooted like trees as half-dressed men came rushing and shouting on deck, struggling into life jackets and taking up stations around the lifeboats as they had been taught to do the first day out in "abandon ship" drills.

No one really knew what had happened but it could only be one of two things.

Either they had hit an iceberg, which was unlikely, since it was not yet iceberg season and there were none in sight; or they had been torpedoed. But if they had been torpedoed there were no signs of it. No explosion. No smoke. No list.

Neither one of them had thought to bring a life jacket when they'd come up on deck the afternoon before and they felt a little stupid, half-baked and half-naked moving with their comrades to their assigned station. Kendrick was there, pacing up and down, being officious, and when they spotted him they knew what to expect.

"See here, you two, where are your life jackets? Sergeant, you know better than that!"

He was striding in their direction when Frank Archibald came up behind them and handed each a jacket behind their backs.

"Right here, sir," said Billy as he shrugged into his and Al followed suit.

Kendrick stopped and frowned. Al could see that he was wondering if his eyes had played tricks on him. Then he shrugged.

"Well, get them on, get them on, this isn't a picnic, you know."

"Yessir!" It was a struggle not to grin.

When Kendrick had withdrawn to berate others milling around the lifeboat station, both Al and Billy turned to thank Crow, who nodded solemnly. "Happy to be of help, Kemosabe."

Billy was about to sass back when they heard explosions and looked up to see the corvette in the distance racing across their bow dropping a pattern of depth charges. Discipline was forgotten in the rush to watch. Even Kendrick momentarily forgot himself in the excitement and gaped with the rest at the boiling sea where the charges had detonated.

The Algonquins hoped to see debris or an oil slick telling them the U-boat had been killed, but nothing appeared and after another thirty minutes of depth charges the corvette heeled and returned to station in front of the *Lady*, signalling the show was over.

Talking about it afterwards, the consensus was that they had been hit by a torpedo but it was a dud. Lady Luck had winked again.

A day later on a calm sea but still on roiling stomachs, the Algonquins were told they were coming in to Newfy-john. On deck Al could see nothing but an unbroken coastline of cliffs and small mountains of rock. When he asked one of the crew he was told the harbour entrance was so narrow it was invisible at a distance—probably the reason it was chosen by the first explorers. A harbour entrance not easily seen reduced the likelihood of unwelcome visitors.

Just how narrow the entrance was became clear as the ship slowed to come into it. The passage between two terraced rocky cliffs was like a fjord and looked to be about three hundred yards wide. High up, cut into the rock on either side, were artillery emplacements housing menacing seventy-five-mm naval guns trained on the opening between the guardian cliffs. Once past the guns Al could see two smaller ships ahead of the *Lady*, tugboats turning slowly away from each other as if taking different forks in a trail and towing what looked like a series of red barrels opening two halves of a gate. When he asked what he was seeing he was told the red barrels were buoys and the ships were opening the submarine net, heavy wire cables from surface to bottom forming a barrier to any U-boats trying to sneak in underwater to get at ships inside the harbour.

Once through the gate, as the *Lady Nelson* slowly turns away to port from the Cabot Tower high on Signal Hill where the first transatlantic radio message was received in 1901, Al can easily see what the sailor is talking about. There are scores of ships in Newfy-john, scores of U-boat targets. Some are anchored in the middle of the harbour and others lined up beside jetties like the tankers secured alongside the Imperial Oil wharf. Besides tankers and tugboats there are merchant ships, destroyers and Royal Canadian Navy corvettes from the NEF, or Newfoundland Escort Service, whose job it is to convey eastbound convoys to a pencil mark on a chart called MOMP, or Mid-Ocean Meeting Point, where they are handed over to the Royal Navy. There is no love lost between the two services. The older, more experienced British navy nicknames the younger, upstart RCN the "Royal Collision Navy" while the Canadians dub the Royal Navy "the Barnacle Brits."

Counting the many different country flags on the ships in the harbour, Al comes up with a little league of nations numbering sixteen. He sees that some of the ships are being repaired and takes note of what a German torpedo can do when the *Lady* inches by a tanker with a hole in the bow at the water line— jagged as if a giant shark had come up from underneath and clamped its teeth into the ship, twisting and tearing until a huge chunk of steel plate had been ripped out of the hull.

On the other side of the harbour across from the naval wharf is the city itself, the business buildings of Water and Duckworth Streets giving way to clapboard houses painted in reds and greens and blues and whites all rising steeply from the water to the colonial government buildings on the hilltop. It is something out of a boy's adventure storybook.

The *Lady Nelson* is tied up to the wharf at the east end of the harbour and the Algonquins disembark, woozy and wobbly, down the gangplank, grateful to be on terra firma once again. They expect to be trucked to barracks at Lester Fields where John Alcock and Arthur Brown set off on the first non-stop transatlantic flight in 1919, but no such luck. It's shank's mare with full pack and it is all they can do in their weakened state to straggle down Water Street from one end of the city to the other and then up the steep hill to their new home in the west end.

On Water Street there are posters in store windows reminding the Canadians they are now in a war zone where you need to be wary of spies and saboteurs. One poster shows a torpedoed tanker burning and sinking. The caption reads, "Loose Lips Sink Ships." Another is a cartoon of three creatures with the tails and fangs of rats and the faces of Hitler, Tojo and Mussolini. The warning about these rodents is, "Look Who's Listening!"

A third is a series of panels telling a story in the fashion of the action comic books of the day. The first panel shows a soldier on the telephone telling his sweetheart about a troop train. In succeeding panels the sweetheart tells her father and the father tells his friends at his club, where a spy overhears the conversation and telephones the saboteur. The last panel shows a train wreck and the admonition, "Careless Talk Brings Tragedy in Wartime."

The bright sky of early morning has given way to clouds and a Newfoundland winter mist is a sheen on their faces as the Algonquins straggle up the hill to Lester Fields. When people come out of their coloured homes to wave and clap them on, weak legs get a little stronger, weary backs a little straighter and drooping heads a little higher.

A horse drawn coal cart comes clopping down the hill toward them, the driver tipping his hat and speaking to each group of soldiers he passes. When the cart gets to Frank and Billy they see the name "C.F. Lester" painted on the side panel and wonder if the Lester on the coal cart is the same man who gave his name to their destination. The driver speaks to them and says what sounds like, "Aye bys, bit of a whisky rain fallin'."

The two soldiers smile and nod and when the cart has gone completely past them Billy turns to Crow. "What the hell did he say?"

"Beats me."

"Thought I heard him say somethin' about a whisky rain."

"Me too. Wonder what that is?"

Billy chuckled, "A real cheap drunk."

Their conversation with the driver of the coal cart marks their introduction to the King's English as spoken in Newfoundland and it would be a good number of months and dozens of conversations later before they understood the language well enough to know that in Newfoundland there is no such thing as "whisky rain" and the word for "misty" is "misky."

When they finally made it to the barracks, dumped their sodden packs and flopped in exhaustion, an old friend stopped by with a word of welcome. In an instant, Lieutenant Matthew Gill was enveloped by suddenly energized well-wishers, delighted to see him and eager to hear of his time in England. But Gill wanted to hear about their adventures on the *Lady Nelson*.

"I am given to understand, gentlemen, that you were hit by a defective torpedo—or at least that's what you've been told."

"How the hell ya know that, Gillie?"

"Ah, Private Assad. Lieutenant Gill listens to Lord Haw-Haw."

None of them had ever heard of the gentleman in question so Gill had to explain that he was a treasonous Brit, a Limey Nazi whose broadcasts from a powerful transmitter somewhere in German-occupied Europe were beamed nightly to England and now via short wave to Newfoundland. Haw-Haw wasn't really a lord nor was Haw-Haw his name. His real name was William Joyce but the Brits called him Haw-Haw because of his raucous laugh.

"So this Lord Haw-Haw knew about the torpedo?"

Gill nodded. "Yup. The broadcast we picked up here was all about welcoming the Algonquin Regiment to Newfy-john. Haw-Haw said he hoped the little scare you had on the *Lady Nelson* wouldn't put you off your feed. Then he laughed that laugh of his and said you chaps probably didn't have much of an appetite anyway after your voyage across the Gulf in the vomitorium."

"Vomit what?"

"Vomitorium. It's a room the ancient Romans built in their villas. On feast days honouring their gods they would eat like pigs, go to the vomitorium, stick a finger down their throats, puke and then go back and eat some more."

"Son-of-a-bitch! How'd he know that?" It was Al's question.

"About vomitoriums?"

"Yeah sure, Billy." Al turned back to Gill "How did he know about us puking our way across from Halifax?"

"The bastard knows everything. When I was in England with the rest of the Canadians on course there, he knew where we were going and what we were going to do before we did. The German propaganda machine obviously has him connected to a network of well-placed spies all over the world who feed him information all the time."

"So what you're saying is that the Germans have spies here?"

"Yesiree, Al my boy. Especially here, with all the information floating around about convoys. And not only that." Gillie was nodding vigorously. "The army's here, the navy's here, the air force is here, the Yanks are here. You bet Jerry has spies here. And probably had one on the *Lady Nelson* itself."

"Well," Billy chimed in, "if there was a spy on board he didn't pass on any military secrets. We did puke our way over here, Gillie. And because of that we're gonna stay here. We're gonna spend the rest of our lives here. We're never gonna leave."

Everybody laughed because Billy had put into words what everybody was thinking. Their clothes, their underwear, their skin still stank of vomit and not one of them relished the prospect of any more rough seas. They all knew the time would come when they would again have to go down to the sea in ships but as far as they were concerned the later the better.

When the Algonquins were given a couple of days off to recuperate—Billy dubbed it "compassionate leave"—they used their time to reconnoitre new surroundings. Yates went off to watch his countrymen at work transforming farm fields into the American base at Fort Pepperell on the banks of Quidi Vidi Pond not too far from the Mount Cashel Orphanage for homeless boys. Al, Barney and Billy along with Reggie, Frank, Arnie and Dougie Dobson formed up as a reconnaissance patrol and headed down to the waterfront.

The skies had cleared somewhat so they took their time and a circuitous route, strolling by 200-year-old homes built by eighteenth-century merchants on spacious lots on Kingsbridge Road, stately stone structures with peaks and dormers and turrets reminding them a bit of Castle Assad in Lowvert. Then their tour took them to the centre of town where wooden houses were raffishly coloured and cheek to jowl and where there was no running water and the honey wagons came round at night to collect the day's human waste. The fringes of blackout curtains in house windows and the shaded headlights of cars parked on Water Street were a reminder that no lights were allowed in St. John's from sundown to sunup, nothing to guide German naval guns or *Luftwaffe* bomb aimers.

As they made their way along the crowded waterfront, the men from Northern Ontario marvelled at the sights and sounds—the many different uniforms and different languages—sailors, soldiers, airmen and merchant seamen from all corners of the world.

Tired after their cook's tour, the patrol followed directions to the Knights of Columbus Hostel on Harvey Road. The hostel was brand spanking new, built the year before by the Knights for military personnel flooding into the city. It had an auditorium where variety shows were staged and bands played for dances. There was a cafeteria where you could get a bite to eat, reading rooms where you could put your feet up, recreation rooms where you could play pool and table tennis, and dormitories where you could rest your weary bones.

After a lunch of fish and chips in the cafeteria, the patrol split up to check out the facilities. Al went to one of the reading rooms and sat at a desk where there was stationery embossed with the K of C crest. He penned letters to his wife, his parents, Tony Foligno, and Stanislas Popovich, who was well into his commando training, apparently somewhere in the wilds of Montana.

Al wrote for most of the afternoon because there was much to tell and the telling of it was enjoyable. At one point Barney joined him with his diary and the two of them wrote quietly together for about an hour.

Finally Al put down his pen and looked over at the diarist. Nodding to Barney's scribbler he asked, "Whattaya gonna do with all that, Barn, sell it to *The Reader's Digest*?"

Barney looked up. "Nah, I'm going to write a book, gonna call it *War and Peace*."

"Seriously, Barn."

Barney leaned back in his chair and thought for a minute. "Someday Al, when this is all over, people will want to know what it was all about, what it was really like for lads like you and me. Not for the politicians. Not for the generals. But for the ordinary Canadian soldier, the PBI, the Poor Bloody Infantry."

"And your diary will tell them?"

Barney shrugged and laughed. "Hey, you want to know the real reason I'm writing this? I'm writing it for my sons."

"Your sons! Barn, you're not even married. You don't even have a girlfriend."

"But I will, Sergeant. I will."

That evening, back at the barracks, Yates sauntered in bearing gifts from Fort Pepperell—two cartons of Camel cigarettes and a bottle of screech.

Screech was a by-product of trade with the Caribbean. For 200 years before the war, Newfoundland ships carried salt fish to the West Indies and returned with fruit, molasses, salt and rum. The rum was shipped in wooden barrels and enterprising islanders discovered that empty rum barrels still contained strong drink if you filled the barrels with water and swished it around. After a few days the rum in the wood seeped into the water and when the resulting liquid was bottled it was dubbed "swish." Swish became "screech" when American servicemen first sampled this potent concoction and let out a godawful scream, a scream the natives named a "screech."

At least that was the story Yates told them as he offered round the bottle, one swallow apiece, as medication for upset stomachs. It turned out to be just what the doctor ordered even for those like Al and Billy who had sworn off strong drink.

The next day new equipment arrived—replacements for what had been taken from them in Shilo—trucks, Jeeps, motorcycles, carriers and Brens. But no new

Chicago Piano for Al. Gill explained that the Brits had developed a new submachine gun called a "Sten" to be issued to the Canadian Army, as the American Thompson was phased out. In the meantime, Al would have to make do with a Lee Enfield.

With the new equipment came new duties. Rumours that German U-boats were entering out-of-the-way bays to recharge batteries and take on fresh water brought orders for a recon patrol to visit the bays, talk to the people and gather intelligence. Gill was told to take Kendrick and the Carrier Platoon, and Kendrick was told Gill would be the officer in command.

Studying the map in preparation for the patrol, the two officers along with Sergeant McDougal were fascinated by the place names. Motion Head. Bull Head. Bald Head. Black Head. Then Witless Bay, Pouch (pronounced Pooch) Cove and Blow Me Down, Heart's Delight and Heart's Desire. Gill laughed out loud as he pointed Al to a name on the west shore of the Avalon Peninsula.

"We have to check out this place, Al. We just have to."

Al looked at the map and saw that Dildo was just north of South Dildo. He thought of Northern Ontario's South Porcupine just south of Porcupine and felt right at home.

The patrol set out at 0500 hours, three carriers and a truck containing supplies and a radio, a number nineteen wireless. The men were armed, just in case, with rifles, Brens and grenades. The weather was foul, a driving rain that soon turned to snow, making for treacherous going. By the time they stopped for a bite to eat near a place called Seal Cove, the soldiers in the open carriers were wet and cold and miserable and not quite so fond of Newfoundland.

The vehicles were parked to form a tight triangle in the lee of a rock overhang and inside the triangle they put up a makeshift roof using their groundsheets. There they had their tea and some canned salmon sandwiches.

Al was drinking the last of his tea when Gill and Kendrick approached. "Care to go for a walk, Sergeant?"

"Sure, Gillie. Where to?"

Al noticed Kendrick frowning and guessed why. In Kendrick's army you didn't speak to an officer as Al McDougal did with Matthew Gill. Knowing this, Al resolved to be even more familiar with Gillie whenever the opportunity presented itself.

Gill inclined his head toward the water. "Thought we'd go down to the wharf there, see if anyone's around and find out what's going on."

He didn't add "if anything." He didn't have to. Al knew that Gill didn't really believe the stories going around about German U-boats using Newfoundland as a home away from home. Gill believed there were spies, that made sense to him, but he privately scoffed at tales of U-boat crews mingling with the crowds at K of C dances in Newfy-john.

But Al wasn't so sure. He remembered Monteith and Hauptmann Kaputt and didn't find it far-fetched at all that crews would be putting into shore or dancing the night away on the same floor as Canadian and American soldiers. The Germans he'd met were smart enough and certainly cocky enough.

The wharf was built of wooden planking spanning a series of ballast beds extending out from the shore. A ballast bed was a square wooden crib made of logs. Inside the crib were rocks piled up from the ocean bottom holding the crib in place and providing a foundation for the wharf.

At the end of the wharf was a shingled shed with smoke curling from a tin chimney and blowing with the rain-swept wind into shore. When Gill knocked on the closed door, it was opened by an older man, creased, leathery face, pipe in his mouth, and a twill captain's cap perched on the back of his head. The shack and the man smelled of fish.

"Aye?"

"Sir," said Gill, "we are from the Canadian Army on patrol in this area and we are sorry to disturb you but we are wondering if you've seen anything suspicious around here in the last little while."

The man's eyes twinkled, "If yer meanin' one of them Jarman subs pullin' up to me wharf 'ere an' offrin' to barter me black bread and sausage fer cods' tongues . . ."

Kendrick sternly cut him off. "Yes, sir, that's precisely what we mean. German U-boats coming into shore and taking on supplies. When did this incident happen?"

Gill rolled his eyes and Al winked broadly at the old fisherman who nodded in quick understanding. Turning to Gill he said, "Yer friend 'ere isn't too bright, now is he. Matter a fact, oid say he's 'bout as stupid as Tom's dog who put his arse in the well ta git a drink."

Both Al and Gill immediately had a violent coughing fit that went on for an embarrassing period of time. When it was over they saw that the old man had closed the shack door and Kendrick was moving to yank it open again. Gill reached out, and taking Kendrick by the arm, turned him away, guiding the Toronto lieutenant and a grinning Lowvert sergeant back up the hill to the carriers.

Their experience at the fisherman's hut in Seal Cove, which Al gleefully recounted to the rest of the patrol, was repeated over and over again in the following days with some of the people in the isolated outports of the Bay having even less to say than the fisherman at Seal Cove.

It wasn't until the morning of the third day that Gill was forced to reconsider his scepticism about visiting U-boats. The place name on the map was Gallows Cove.

The weather had cleared and for the first time in two days Billy said he could see past his nose. He was driving the lead carrier with Al and Gillie, Yates and Arnie Christensen, his passengers taking in the passing scenery on the jarring trail—stunted junipers and spruce trees, called "tuckamores," scattered among the rocks of a blasted terrain that reminded some of them of Sudbury. Every mile, or so it seemed, there were frozen ponds scooped out of the rock. Once they saw a moose and they all saluted their regimental emblem.

Soon the trail petered out completely at the top of a rise that slanted down to the boulder-strewn floor of the Cove. The Algonquins dismounted from the carriers, scrambled down the slope and started poking around the flotsam and jetsam of the shore. A strong sea was beating in and a cold, salt spray showered soldiers who got too close to the water. It was this more than curiosity that made Doug Dobson and Frank Archibald head for a stream off to their right, a stream that meandered inland from the ocean through shore boulders and into a cleft in the rocky face of the slope about a hundred yards from where the carriers were parked.

Al saw them go but paid little attention. He was more interested in the coloured glass and seashells he had gathered and was smiling to himself, thinking of calling Christensen over and getting him to try the "she sells seashells" tongue twister one more time when he heard a shout from the direction Crow and Dougie had taken. It was a shout that brought all of them scrabbling over the pebbles and rocks to the gloom of the cleft where a layer of sand deposited by the stream as it curved farther into the rock extended like a shelf into a hollow carved by years of high tides. Both Frank and Doug were crouched there pointing. Al, his chest heaving, hunkered down beside them and saw what they had partially uncovered. It was a rubber dinghy.

Once they'd cleared away the driftwood, seaweed and bits of canvas laid with obvious care to hide the dinghy, they dragged it out of the cleft into the light of day, where they saw that it was far from empty. Oars were lying on the bottom and in one corner wrapped in oilskins were two suitcases piled one on top of the other. The first one was filled with clothes. A civilian suit with an Eaton's label on the inside jacket pocket was folded carefully on top, and underneath, an Algonquin Regiment battledress with two pips on the epaulette signifying it was the uniform of a lieutenant. When the bottom suitcase was opened it was found to contain a heavy-duty flashlight, batteries, antenna wire and a short-wave radio.

Al was on his knees in the dinghy examining the radio when he heard a voice behind him. "Don't touch a thing, Sergeant!"

He ignored Kendrick and turned grinning to Gill. "Well, Gillie, whattaya say? A young lieutenant's hideaway? Come down here for a paddle in the moonlight with his best girl? Or maybe just a quiet place ta listen to some jazz, Guy Lombardo and his Royal Canadians? Whattaya think?"

Gillie was forced to acknowledge that the dinghy had come from a submarine. There was no other plausible explanation. Especially when Al pointed out the German markings on the radio. The question then was what to do with their find.

After talking it over, the decision was made to put everything back exactly the way it was found and leave a two-man guard, Al and Frank Archibald, with an insistent Lieutenant Kendrick nominally in charge. Meantime the rest the patrol would head back in the direction of St. John's. As soon as they were within the ten-mile range of the number nineteen wireless they would radio into Lester Field and ask for instructions.

All this took the rest of the day and, because night travel was out of the question, it wasn't until mid-afternoon of the next day that Billy roared into the Cove with a relief force consisting of an Intelligence officer and a section of men from the homegrown Newfoundland Regiment. Their orders were to lie in wait for whoever came by to visit the dinghy.

The Canadians never did find out if the Newfoundlanders nabbed a spy in Gallows Cove. Or a saboteur. They weren't around long enough to find out.

Chapter Nine

MARCH 1, 1942. On the Newfy Bullet. To help pass the time Reggie and Arnie have been working on a song to the tune of "The Wabash Cannonball." Once they finish a verse they go through the train teaching it to the rest of us. I think they're up to number eight by now but the best one so far in terms of describing our present condition has to be the verse that goes,

> *A soldier he decided*
> *That to heaven he would go,*
> *So he tied himself to the railroad track,*
> *When he heard the whistle blow,*
> *He must have been there a long time,*
> *For he had starved to death,*
> *Waiting on the railroad track,*
> *For the Newfoundland Express.*

A big part of the problem is the snow drifting over the tracks. Sometimes it's too much for the plows and the lads have had to get off the train and help the crew shovel a cut through the drift and that takes time. But I suspect that even in the middle of the summer this train is as slow as molasses. So naturally the Algonquin wits have decided to call it the Express. When we left St. John's somebody said that the tender on the locomotive had a sign on it, "Britain delivers the Goods." When we get to Botwood, if we ever get to Botwood, the suggestion is that we add a line so the sign will read, "Britain delivers the Goods too late to do any good."

Excerpt from Barney's Diary

About 300 miles northwest of St. John's on the Bay of Exploits, Botwood had been both a seaport and a seaplane base before the war. At the seaport on one side of town, ships were loaded with ore for English steel mills and newsprint for London dailies. On the other side of town the seaplane base was a fuelling stop on the transatlantic run between America and the British Isles.

The site for the seaplane base had been selected by the first man to fly solo across the Atlantic. In 1933, six years after his historic flight and a year after the body of his kidnapped baby son was found buried in a shallow grave, Charles Lindbergh landed in Botwood on another of his cross-ocean jaunts, this time with his wife Anne. At the time Lindbergh was a technical advisor to Pan American Airways and evidently was impressed by the possibilities of Botwood because two years later the town's harbour was selected by Pan Am and British Imperial Airways as a base for their transatlantic flying boats. The new service was welcomed to Botwood on July 5, 1937 with the arrival of the *Pan American Clipper III*, outbound from New York via Shediac, New Brunswick, for Foynes, Ireland.

The flying boats of the day were four-star airborne hotels. For example the pride of Pam Am's fleet, the *Yankee Clipper*, was fitted out like a plush suite of rooms complete with spiral staircase, separate dining facilities for men and women, and a well-stocked bar. Drinks and meals were served by waiters in double-breasted white jackets, and white linen tablecloths were *de rigueur*. Built to carry seventy-four passengers, the *Clipper* had sleeping accommodations for forty and a crew of eight.

When Britain declared war on Germany, Botwood became a Royal Air Force base for PBY-5A Canso Amphibians charged with the responsibility of coastal defence and anti-submarine patrol. In April 1941 control of the base was transferred to Canada and this brought Canadian troops to guard the planes and artillery guarding the base.

The artillery at nearby Philip's Head consisted of American ten-inch guns weighing thirty tons apiece and capable of firing a 600-pound shell more than eight miles out to sea in the event any German battleships steamed into the outer Notre Dame Bay. Closer to shore, underwater incursions were blocked by a submarine net across the entrance to Botwood Harbour.

In case of attack by long-range shore-based planes or shipborne aircraft, anti-aircraft batteries ringed both the seaplane base and the port. Many doubted the Germans had the capability to launch such attacks but the prevailing attitude was better to be safe than sorry, and this was the reason Canadian soldiers were also warned to be on the lookout for a surprise drop of enemy paratroopers, which had been so effective in the German conquest of Norway, Greece and Crete.

When the Algonquins finally arrived in Botwood, their transport, a narrow-gauge, Toonerville Trolly train with its gas lamps and wooden slat seats—in the opinion of the little league, a poor excuse for the real thing—was at verse nineteen of *The Newfoundland Express*: *We left St. John's on Monday,/ The day was bleeding cold,/ The engineer was roaring drunk/ So some of us were told./ He said if you're not anxious/ To answer a request,/ We'll get there sometime next month/ On the Newfoundland Express.*

Living quarters and parade ground were up the hill just above the Masonic lodge on Botwood's Water Street. Al decided that there must be a Water Street in every city, town and village east of Montreal. Halifax had one, St. John's had one, and now Botwood had one. But then so did Port Arthur. Must be every city, town and village anywhere near a large body of water.

Down the hill, just to the east of their quarters, was the base hospital called into service soon after the Algonquins arrived when a good number of soldiers came down with the mumps and "to avoid contagion" had to be quarantined in the hospital's isolation ward.

The regiment spent the first few weeks at Botwood getting to know the place and their duties, which they were advised to take very seriously because Botwood was well known to the enemy. Before the war German merchant ships had been frequent visitors and there was no question that enemy knowledge of the bay, its shoreline, inlets and coves was extensive. Therefore, in addition to providing round-the-clock infantry protection for the anti-aircraft and coastal batteries and patrolling the coastline around the town, there was also the matter of security at the base and the port, where the Algonquins were required to inspect crew and longshoremen's identification passes and assist the navy's coast guard cutters in boarding and inspecting ships entering the harbour. All in all it was a hectic time compounded by a manpower shortage thanks to the mumps.

It wasn't until a Sunday morning in early April that Al had a chance for a breather. He was up at dawn and wandered down to the seaplane base in the quiet of the early morning, a warm spring sun just over the horizon slanting on the water and reflecting off the cockpit windows of a PBY Amphibian sitting on its wheels on a ramp up from its mooring in the water. Looking at its squat fuselage head-on made him think of a big frog hunkered down, balancing a wing and two engines on top of its head.

Once he was cleared by the sentry at the gate, Al walked out onto number one slipway and sat on the end, his feet dangling over the water, a navy blue almost black in colour and smooth as glass. His mind drifted to other waters of a different colour—the weathered copper of Ames Lake in the setting sun, the dark, early morning brown of the pickerel stream into Slaughterhouse Lake, where you could lose yourself in the fishing and before you knew it, the sun was at high noon.

He sighed and took a deep breath, scenting the tang of the salt air, watching the squawking gulls diving at the water and swooping up to settle on the buoys. Farther out just off Killick Island he could see what looked like a black ball bobbing in the water. The ball would bob up for a moment and then bob down for longer periods as it swam closer and closer to shore. His mind lazily registered beaver but then he chuckled to himself and said out loud, "Seal, ya dummy, it's a seal."

There were no beavers in the salt waters of a Newfoundland bay of seaplanes and patrol boats and oil slicks. And now in the gaps of the gull cries he could hear the seal snorting. Beavers slapped the water with their tails. Beavers didn't snort.

The sounds of seal and seagulls in the stillness of the morning were silenced by the roar of a PBY engine starting up as the first of the morning air patrols got set to take off. It was the end of his reverie and Al levered himself up to slowly retrace his steps on the slipway. At the end he turned right and walked along the causeway toward the ammunition dumps on Killick Island, which took its name from the rocks on the island's shore, rocks that were used to make "killicks" or anchors for boats and fishing nets.

Cut into the side of the island was a series of cave-like rooms reinforced top and bottom by thick slabs of concrete. Access to the rooms was through heavy steel doors about twelve feet high and four feet thick. Behind the doors inside the cave rooms were stacks of wooden boxes containing artillery and anti-aircraft shells, mortar shells, dynamite, bombs, depth charges and belts of .303 ammunition for the PBYs. All in all, enough to blow up the island, the base and half the town. Another Halifax explosion.

Al had been told that part of their training in Botwood would involve the storage and handling of live ammunition and as he stood there on the gravel road in front of the steel doors he thought of Hermanson and shivered.

Continuing along the road, he climbed the hill above the dumps and wandered through the poplar trees past hollows of snow not yet melted by the spring sun. When he got to the head of the island he stood to watch the PBY taxi out into the bay for takeoff. Once the plane had lumbered off the water, he reached into his tunic, pulled out a pen and a Knights of Columbus writing pad he'd "borrowed" from the hostel in St. John's, sat on a stump facing the water, and began composing letters home.

For the first time since Monteith, when they had been under orders not to talk about the escape and the casualties, he had to be careful what he wrote. Newfoundland was a security zone, so personal mail had to be censored and censorship was a pain in the arse. It wasn't that soldiers were inclined to write home about troop movements, convoy sailings, artillery locations or the hundred and one other things the enemy might want to know and could find out by reading the letters. No man wrote about these things, mostly because it was stuff that would bore their readers to tears. And besides, even if someone did by chance mention the not-to-be mentioned, it was never explained exactly how the enemy would get their hands on this sensitive material. The answer offered by the cynics in the ranks was that it would have to be spies in the post office, hundreds of eager beavers hiding in basements and steaming open envelopes, poring over contents and then getting on the wireless to Lord Haw-Haw.

So it wasn't what they wrote that concerned them, it was that someone was reading what they wrote especially to wives and girlfriends. Not only that but the censor reading their letters was always one of their officers, always someone they knew, someone like Kendrick.

The solution was not to say anything personal beyond the usual Xs and Os and to devise a code for the rest. Each man had his own personal code. For Al, Ames Lake was the ocean. Canoeing across Ames Lake to what he called "the Memorial Rock" in Veterans' Park was crossing to Newfoundland. The people of Monteith were the Germans and the people of Monteith in their boats were U-boats.

But there was one code word the men from Lowvert had in common and it came up time and time again when they wrote about Kendrick. Their letters home to Canada from Newfoundland were laudatory when it came to their lieutenant. He was praised as an officer uncommonly close to his men, an officer with outstanding leadership qualities. He was, they said, a real Kemosabe.

David Ross had expressed some concern about Kendrick reading the word over and over again and eventually asking what it meant but he was told to say it was James Bay Cree for "trusted friend."

"He's not gonna believe that."

"Sure he is. Probably thinks he is our trusted friend."

Once Al finished his letters he sealed and addressed the envelopes, tucked them in his jacket pocket, and set out for the fisherman's wharf, where Yates had promised to introduce them to a real delicacy. Lobster.

When he arrived, Yates and Billy were chewing the fat with a few of the locals, all of them standing by a steaming cast iron pot set over a fire burning in an oil barrel cut in half. Yates pointed to the pot and when Al peered over the edge he could see green lobster cooking to red.

In a few minutes hungry buyers were huddled around the lobsterman who dug into the pot with a small wooden bucket attached to a long handle—Newfoundlanders called it a "spudgel"—and doled out the fresh-cooked crustaceans. The one-pound lobsters went for the equivalent of thirty-five cents Canadian, the two-pounders for fifty cents, and anything bigger than that sold for seventy-five cents. Once Al had turned out his pockets and produced the required coin for the Algonquin purchase the lobsterman who took his money grinned at the three of them.

"You Canadians look hungry enough ta eat the leg o' the lamb o' God."

With a look of wide-eyed innocence, Billy said, "Oh no, sir, we Canadians don't eat sheep. Not since Camp Borden where we ate mutton with the wool still on it. Keeps yer stomach warm in the wintertime, I'll tell ya."

They lugged the lobster in a couple of haversacks over to a nearby cove where Barney and the rest of the gang were waiting and where Yates showed them how to crack shells and pick out the succulent meat from tails and claws. All this was accomplished with the tools at hand—rocks and bayonets. Afterwards, sitting around smoking and nursing their beers and iced tea, it was agreed this was the best meal they had ever had in all the time they'd been in the army.

Billy lifted his bottle of Alexander Keith's India Pale Ale to Yates. "I propose a toast to our American pal here. Sometimes he's a world-class prick. And sometimes he's a world-class genius. Today, Yates, yer a genius. Here's to ya."

Yates was drinking Moosehead Ale and gestured with his bottle, "Stick with me boys, and we'll have a good war. Lotsa booze, lotsa smokes, lotsa good food and lotsa good women."

His promise was greeted with shouts of "Hear, hear!" a chorus Billy interrupted with a wink. "Just make sure, Yates, when yer talkin' about lotsa good women yer not talkin' about another Quarter Guard Anny."

This brought a second chorus of "Hear hear!" Quarter Guard Anny was the nickname they had bestowed on a certain St. John's prostitute, a very plain Jane in appearance but more than generous when it came to oral sex, a favour which she nightly bestowed on the sentries posted at the four quarters of the wire around Lester Field Barracks. Sometimes she did it for money and sometimes for nothing more than a souvenir. When Anny came down to the station to see them off for Botwood, many of the Algonquins who bade her a fond farewell did so waving hats bereft of badges.

The day after their lobster feast the Algonquins went back to school, their classroom being one of the empty hangars at the PBY base and their teachers Matthew Gill and other officers, all recent graduates of England's Camp Aldershot, where they had been instructed in what the British army called, "Training in Fieldcraft and Elementary Tactics," otherwise known as "battle drill." Supposedly it was the brainchild of Lieutenant Colonel Bernard Montgomery, but the man had borrowed many of the concepts from the *Wehrmacht* whose name for battle drill was *Indianerkrieg*, which prompted Frank Archibald to mutter something about how smart Jerry was.

Battle drill was training for combat conditions, and the rumour was it was all done with live ammunition. This was one of the first things Gill said to them when he stood to speak from a raised platform at the end of the hangar opposite the doors. He held up a booklet.

"Gentlemen! I have here our Canadian Army training manual on the subject of battle drill. Let me read to you what it says. 'The object of battle drill is to inculcate into a fighting body a system of battle discipline and team spirit and to give every man a knowledge of certain basic team plays that will guide him in any operation he may undertake in battle.'"

Gill went on to explain the four principles of battle drill. The first one was to train soldiers to act instinctively. This involved repetitive drills of certain tactics; for example, tactics to defend against an ambush would be practised, over and over again, always under fire, until the men were sick of it. But when they were finished practising, it would be second nature to them, they would be able to react immediately and without thinking, and that, Gill said, would save lives.

Another principle of battle drill was its focus, and that would be on the platoon and on training each and every man in the platoon to act as leader if necessary. Gill said this was very important because of what the British had learned from Jerry in France. Jerry, he said, targeted officers because in the German Army the officer was the only one who knew what was going on. So if a *Wehrmacht* officer was lost so was the rest of the platoon.

"Jerry figures it's the same with us and that's why his snipers are always on the lookout for officers, especially lieutenants," and here Gill grinned and shrugged. "But thanks to battle drill, gentlemen, we are going to put one over on the Germans. If one of us goes down," he gestured at the officers in the front row, "our training will ensure that the platoon sergeant will be able to take over and if a sergeant goes down then a corporal will be able to take over and if a corporal gets it in the neck then any mother's son-of-a private will be able to do the job, which I'm sure you privates out there already believe you can do anyway without battle drill."

At this there was scattered laughter in the hangar and a shout from the Carrier Platoon, a voice with a mock British accent, "Right you are, old chap. Right you are. Tally Ho! Pip, pip!"

Gill nodded toward Billy. "The third principle of the drill is to toughen you up." This was greeted with knowing groans, but Gill held up a hand. "It's not what you're thinking, lads. I'm not talking about route marches and PT. You've all had enough of all that. I'm talking about drills that will, as closely as possible, approximate what you'll come up against in the field. In the field you might well have to cross a river hand over hand on a cable stretched over the water. You might have to crawl through barbed wire under fire, toting your field packs into the bargain. You might have to carry mortars and ammunition as you belly through a culvert. We are gonna set things up here in Botwood so you'll be able to get some idea of what all that's like.

"Okay. Last point. What's going to be the one big difference between Borden, Shilo, Newfoundland and occupied Europe?"

"Outdoor plumbing?"

"French cuisine?"

"Quarter Guard Antoinette?"

The hangar exploded in guffaws. Gill held up both hands in supplication. "I knew I shouldn't have asked that question. So let me give you the answer. The one big difference, besides the ones you with your vast wisdom have already mentioned, is that an enemy will be gunning for you with everything he's got. Artillery, mortars, tank rounds and machine guns. Bullets will be zipping by your ears and the ground will be exploding under your feet. There will be smoke and dust and so much noise you won't be able to hear yourselves think. It will be, gentlemen, hell on earth.

"So what we will be doing these next few months in Newfoundland is getting you ready for all that. We will be trying to inoculate you against the sounds of battle, against the feel of battle. From now on, with every drill you do, stun grenades will go off in front of you, artillery flashes will blind you, flares will explode in the middle of your section. There will be machine-gun fire beside you, behind you and above you. So make no mistake. If you stick your head up you'll get it shot off. Same goes for your arse.

"Mark my words, gentlemen, it will be so close to the real thing that you will swear it is the real thing."

Battle drill began the next day in an inlet that reminded Al of Seal Cove, with its pebbled beach merging into bigger rocks and then boulders at the foot of an escarpment dotted with tuckamores clinging to patches of sandy soil nestled in stony crevices. The men were dressed in fatigues or coveralls because they had been warned they were going to get wet and dirty practising a beach assault.

"Not to mention rotten and stinky." Al was gagging as he lay half in water and half on the beach using the butt of his rifle to push slimy pebbles aside as "enemy fire" crackled just over his head. He was face down in a putrid bed of fish offal strewn all over their section of beach. It was too much for too many. Shouted orders to advance were ignored as men stood, oblivious to the shooting, cursing and swiping at the guck clinging to their fronts only to be quickly dragged back down to safety by their comrades. Others simply rolled back into the water to wash it off. The sounds of retching mingled with swearing, the chattering of the Brens and the noise of exploding flares and stun grenades. Chaos was the order of the day and the exercise had to be called off as vomit and fish guts overwhelmed it.

The men were trucked back to the barracks, where they stumbled into the showers, clothes and all. Afterwards when fatigues were hanging out to dry on the barbed wire behind the H-huts and the men, washed and freshly clothed, had been called to order, Gill had a chat with them. He was not a happy man.

"I take your point, Sergeant McDougal. Fish guts was probably overdoing it. But when you hit the beach you never know what you will find. Someday there will be an invasion of Europe and if we're the lucky ones to be in on it and there are fish guts on the beach or more likely Canadian guts, your buddies' guts, you won't be able to say hey, this is too much, let's call it off and go back to barracks for a shower. You'll have to fight through it, you'll have to get your asses off the beach and move inland. Because if you don't somebody else on some other sector of the beach is going to pay a helluva price."

The message was delivered and the message was received. What no one knew, because Gill told no one, was that the fish guts were Kendrick's idea. He'd taken it upon himself to inject what he thought would be a little realism into the first battle drill and Gill only found out about it after it was all over.

Standing behind the gunners and watching the platoon wade onto the beach and belly down under fire, Gillie couldn't fathom the scene which then unfolded, men jerking upright, men thrashing back into the water as if they'd been stung by hornets. His first terrified thought was that the Bren gunners had misjudged their aim and were shooting their comrades-in-arms, so he'd screamed, "Cease fire! Cease fire!"

It wasn't until he'd scrambled in panic down the escarpment and skidded on the slime himself that he made sense of what he'd witnessed. And it wasn't until the slimy men had left the cove that he started asking around and found out who the culprit was.

"Listen, you dumb tub of shit!" He'd taken Kendrick off down the beach out of earshot of the Bren gunners, who were packing up. "First of all, I'm running the show here. Not you. Me. Understand?"

"It's my outfit." Kendrick looked at Gill defiantly.

Gill ignored him. "Secondly, as far as battle drill is concerned you don't do anything, you don't even fart without checking with me. Do you understand that?"

Kendrick stared out to sea and said nothing.

"Look at me, soldier!" Kendrick looked at him. Gill wanted to punch the snotty bastard but took a deep breath instead. "Right now, this is between you and me. I'll say nothing to the captain. I'll say nothing to your men. Especially not your men. But if anything like this happens ever again I will. So help me Jesus, I will."

Kendrick shrugged. "The captain is a friend of the family, Gill. How do you think I got here in the first place?"

"I don't give a shit how you got here, Kendrick. It's what you do here that counts. And let me tell you something. The captain may be a friend of your family and your father's nose might be so far up his ass that all you can see is the back of your old man's head. But if I were you I wouldn't count on that. If your men ever turn on you, then your father will be no help to you. The captain will be no help to you. You, sir, will be completely and utterly fucked."

The next day they went to another beach and this time it was a little better. When they came off the beach, the centre section gave covering fire for the flanking sections, who ran doubled over to take up positions on either side of the enemy Brens. But still there were problems. Buried bundles of gun cotton set off electronically simulated an artillery and mortar attack, which "killed" most of the section giving covering fire, while the "enemy" on the rise threw thunder flash grenades on the flanking sections "wiping most of them out" before they could mount an attack.

The next day on the same beach they did it again after Gill explained their casualties of the day before. He told them that most of them had been "killed" because they had failed to follow a basic rule of combat.

"I know you boys are buddies and love each other's company and would like nothing better than to go through this war all kissy face and arm in arm like a bunch of Limey poofters. But on the battlefield that'll get ya killed and that's why, yesterday, the umpires ruled so many of you *hors de combat*."

"What kinda horse, Gillie?"

"The kind of horse you look at in the mirror every morning, Private."

"Yeah, Billy, a horse's ass."

"That you I smell, Dobson?" Billy turned around. "Guess you haven't changed yer underwear since yesterday when that gun cotton went off right below yer balls and ya shit yer pants."

Once Gill managed to stop the bantering, he explained that in combat bunching up would get them killed as quick as a wink. In combat you had to spread out. He told them the officers acting as umpires and whose job it was to decide who lived and who died would be watching them closely this time around to make sure they got it right.

So this time when the whistle blew they remembered to spread out, the flanking manoeuvre worked, and the "enemy" machine gunners—grinning soldiers from the Newfoundland Regiment—were either killed or taken prisoner. It was their turn to be horses de combat, as Billy put it.

Still Gill wasn't satisfied, telling them the umpires were too generous. It was his opinion that too many of them had been "killed and wounded" putting one enemy machine-gun nest out of action; their casualty ratio was too high, too many Algonquins for too few Germans. He told them the reason was that they had not taken advantage of ground cover and reminded them of their last days in Borden when they'd risen up from the ground like ghosts and scared the shit out of a visiting member of Parliament.

When Billy protested there were no trees to hide behind on the beaches of the Rock, Gillie said there were rocks. And high tide lines. And driftwood. And boulders. And next time to use them.

After nine consecutive days doing beach landings, ten if you counted the fish gut beach, the time scheduled for this part of battle drill was finally up and they were rotated back on patrol, a two-week stint at Point Leamington. The men came away from the beach assaults tired but feeling good about themselves and what they had accomplished, the best of which was getting a pat on the back from Gillie on the last day for a job well done.

Point Leamington was a village about halfway between Botwood and Leading Tickles, which came by its name from the days when "tickle" meant "uncertain." A tickle summer was a summer of unreliable weather and tickle water was water with winds and tides that made for tricky sailing.

The road to the village was a road in name only, no more than a track up a long hill through a forest of fir and ponds still patched with slabs of ice. Used mostly in the winter to cut and haul pulpwood, it was tough going in May when the ground had softened. More than a few times trucks had to be winched through boggy spots by the tracked carriers, two to a truck.

A crow's eye view of Point Leamington would put the village on the bottom right corner of a triangle of land, with the point of the triangle jutting out into the water. One side of the triangle was called West Arm and the other, South West Arm. A stream flowed into the South West Arm and the carriers drove slowly into the village over a rickety wooden bridge spanning the water, fast flowing with the spring runoff.

From his perch in the lead carrier, Al could see the water twisting and rolling down a fair-sized falls of jagged rocks and then roiling through a set of rapids before it ran on under the bridge. Villagers were out on the omnipresent Water Street waving Union Jacks and shouting words of welcome. The Canadians grinned and waved in return as their caravan of vehicles passed fishing boats and dories and cordwood on the water side, and headed toward a point of land on the far side of the settlement where they were to set up camp.

A young, dark-haired woman with a child clutching her skirt stood outside the General Store and shyly handed up a bouquet of daisies to Reggie, who reached down and took them with a smile and a thank you: "*Merci, Madame.*"

The woman's hand went to her mouth in surprise and Reggie heard her cry, "*Bienvenue, Monsieur.*"

He turned in amazement and blew her a kiss as the carrier trundled him away. It was the last thing he expected. A Newfoundlander who spoke French.

The camp had been left in good repair by the boys from Charlie Company who had moved out the day before, leaving just a corporal's guard in case Jerry launched a full-scale invasion between company rotations. Creepy Cram was there waving them in and when he saw who was coming he reached down into his pack at his feet, pulled out a softball and lobbed it underhand to Al who caught it and threw it back. "Ball four, Creepy. Ya still can't throw a strike." Creepy chuckled and thumbed his nose.

Once the vehicles were parked, Al supervised some of the unloading, keeping an eye on things as packs and supplies were carried to quarters, Bell tents pitched on a rise above the water. Then when most of the unloading was done, he went walking down toward the water through birch trees and tuckamores, winding his way past the green and yellow lichen clinging to the rocks leading down to the shore. He almost slipped twice, once on a moss-covered stone slab running like one of Nanibijou's fingers into the water and then on the shore itself covered in loose shale. At the water's edge, he stood and gazed at the far shore bordered by dense stands of spruce, and below the trees, more layers of shale still covered here and there by patches of snow. Then he bent and picked up a piece of the flat, thin shale and skipped it over the water, dark and icy cold when he went down on his haunches to twirl his fingers in it. He thought it might be good fishing water, it had that look and feel and he wondered what kind of fish he could catch if he had a hook and a line.

When he heard his name being called he stood and turned to see Kendrick striding down the slope towards him. "Sergeant, I want you to look after the unloading of the ordnance. It goes in the sandbagged tent up behind the cookhouse, the one off by itself in the shade. Step lively now."

"Yessir, Lieutenant." *And I hope you step lively on some moss and fall flat on your arse, sir.*

When he got to the sandbagged tent that served as the camp ammunition dump he saw to his horror that there was a line of men from the trucks working like a bucket brigade at a fire heaving boxes one to another, boxes of ammunition, mortar bombs, grenades and dynamite.

He roared, "Jesus, Mary and Joseph!" An expression he'd picked up from the locals. "Are you guys outta yer minds? That stuff's not bully beef. That stuff's dangerous. Ya hand it over, ya don't throw it over!"

He stood there shaking his head as the men complied. After watching for a minute he trudged back to the carrier to get his pack and look for his Bell tent— accommodations for eight sleeping feet toward the centre pole.

Their time at Point Leamington was a combination of more battle drill and rotating sections out to the tip of the triangle where there was an observation post with a clear view of the waters beyond the West and South West Arms. Here their orders were to keep a binocular eye toward the sea on the lookout for enemy shipping, particularly U-boats, which the local fishermen insisted were frequent visitors to the isolated coves dotting the Arms. But the only dangers Charlie Company had reported were icebergs, huge sculpted chunks hived off Greenland glaciers drifting their way south toward the convoy lanes between Canada and England and the ocean grave of the *Titanic*.

Battle drill in Point Leamington was a lesson on how to take a small town, the kind they would encounter in any invasion of Europe. The villagers were used to it now, having been "liberated" several times in the last little while by each succeeding company of Algonquins up from Botwood.

The village wasn't ideal for the exercise because the drill was based on flanking manoeuvres, which were a little hard to do when one of your flanks was in the water. The objective was to learn how to drive an enemy, holed up in buildings and houses, out into the open where the Brens firing down the street would take care of them.

For obvious reasons this was a drill without live ammunition and every time they did it Reggie came running down the street at the end of the drill making Bren gun noises as he "shot" from the hip. It wasn't long before he got what he was hoping for, an audience of one, the smiling dark-haired woman who had welcomed him *en français*.

Two or three evenings later when the Lowvert gang was sitting on the shale beach after supper smoking and shooting the breeze, Al asked where Reggie was and Billy winked.

"Our Reggie has a girlfriend, Al. In the village. He goes down there every night now to parley-vous the ding dong."

"Takes his guitar with him, too," said Ross.

"Well, well." Al grinned. "Maybe we should go down there and offer to sing along. A few verses of the 'Newfoundland Express.'"

A few days later, on a Sunday, they were invited down, Al and Billy and Frank Archibald. The house, set back behind Water Street, was a two-storey, ramshackle affair of weathered clapboard, stairs leading up from a dirt path to a veranda above, which had a peaked roof and stone chimneys on each end. When they knocked, Reggie greeted them at the door and ushered them in to meet the Noseworthy family.

The Noseworthys were Protestants in a Protestant town. The Irish Catholics of St. John's were nowhere in sight in Point Leamington. Only Pentecostals and Salvation Army, and a Methodist Church on Water Street.

First Reggie introduced the dark-haired woman. Her name was Charity. Al was impressed. He said later he thought she was as cute as a button, another one of his mother's expressions. Then he shook hands with Charity's brother, Goody, her father, Christian, and her mother, Evangeline. The Algonquins didn't know it but father, mother and children were all named after characters in John Bunyan's *Pilgrim's Progress*.

An older lady, toothless and hard of hearing, was wrapped in a crocheted shawl and sitting in a rocking chair near the fireplace. She was introduced as Charity's grandmother and the reason Charity spoke a bit of French. The grandmother traced her family roots to some early French fishermen who had settled in the area "a long time ago"—as Reggie put it, "when Jacques Cartier discovered Newfoundland." The maternal tongue was almost gone now but enough had been handed down to Charity that she could dredge up traditional expressions at appropriate times.

They sat for Sunday dinner at a long table made from salvaged shipping crates and ate fish cakes and boiled potatoes with strong tea and johnnycake for dessert. Christian Noseworthy spoke fondly of Reggie, who'd brought them bacon and butter he'd liberated from Algonquin stores.

"Why, when I first sees de by, when Char first brought 'im home, I takes one look at 'im and sez to de wife, 'Evangeline, dis by's so scrawny dat if de door opens and no one comes in, den we knows it's him.'"

Reggie laughed. He was sitting beside Charity, who had a boy sitting shyly in her lap. His name was Martin and he was dressed in a grey wool sweater, short blue pants and long brown stockings. He was dark and petite like his mother and Charity fed him from her plate with help from Reggie, who acted as if the boy were his long-lost son as he tickled him under the chin and tousled his hair while the adults finished their tea.

Afterwards Reggie told them that Martin was a love child born to Charity six months after her man had been lost in the seal hunt when the ice shifted and he drifted off out to sea and a frozen death. His name was Martin and he and Charity were to be married when he returned with enough money from the hunt to build his bride a home.

Charity's brother, Goodwill, wanted to know about soldiering and Billy gave him a short, funny history of the subject, which had them all in stitches, even the little leaguers, who'd heard all of Billy's lines a thousand times.

Sitting beside Goody, Billy put his arm around him. "It's not a bad life, young fella. Ya might want ta think about joinin' us. That way we could look after ya while Reggie here looks after yer sister."

Both Reggie and Charity blushed and Al, out of the corner of his eye, caught Christian Noseworthy shaking his head at his son. Al had the feeling that the subject of joining up was one the two of them had discussed before and that there was a difference of opinion between them.

Chapter Ten

SEPTEMBER 1, 1942. Botwood. Still think of the first of September as the beginning of Fall. Guess it has to do with it always being the month school started up again, bringing with it the end of freedom. Al and the lads are off to Lewisporte in a couple of days. It's just up the Bay of Exploits and is a fuel dump for Ferry Command flying out of Gander. Good target for Jerry so the arty and ack ack boys are there in force and Support Company is going up to baby-sit them. Bob Hope and the singer, Frances Langford, along with Edgar Bergen, Charlie McCarthy and Charlie's lamebrain pal, Mortimer Snerd, were storm stayed here the other day and kindly offered their evening to entertain the troops. Real thrill to see them in person after listening to them on radio for so long. Especially enjoyed Bergen and McCarthy. Charlie in his top hat, monocle and tuxedo. "I'll clip ya, Bergen. So help me I'll mow-w-w-w ya down!" But Hope got off the best line of the night when he stood on stage and put his arm around Langford and asked her what was the matter. She said, "I don't know, Bob. I just feel funny." Hope grinned and replied, "Well, Franny, put your hand in my pocket and you'll feel nuts." Got a long letter from Tony today. Says he asked last June to be released from playing Army hockey so he could catch up with the rest of us but didn't pass the physical. Wrenched his knee in the playoffs. Is going to try again now that the knee is healed up. Says after Dieppe it's about time he did his bit.

Excerpt from Barney's Diary

On August 19, 1942 more than 3,800 of Tony's fellow Canadians were wounded, captured or killed on a French beach, a place called Dieppe.

At first the newspapers reported that the surprise raid across the Channel was a daring and triumphant success, but then the telegrams began to arrive in Calgary; the prairie towns of Saskatchewan; the Ontario cities of Windsor, Hamilton, Toronto and Ottawa; and in Quebec, Montreal. *We regret to inform you . . .*

The same newspapers that first hailed the landings soon began to publish casualty lists. Entire regiments had been all but wiped out—the South Saskatchewans, the Calgary Regiment, the Essex Scottish, the Royal Hamilton Light Infantry, the Royal Regiment of Canada, the Queen's Own Cameron

Highlanders, and Les Fusiliers Mont-Royal. After the lists came the rationalizations, all of them summed up in the phrase of a British colonel, "Valuable lessons have been learned." Reading about all this in Lewisporte, the Algonquins thought Canada had paid a hell of a price so that some armchair, rear-end warrior, some lisping Limey, could learn valuable lessons.

Some of the men killed had once been Algonquins who had been straining at the leash for action when the regiment was stationed at Shilo. They'd asked for and been given transfers to regiments going overseas. But they were still seen as family and many of them had kept in touch and now they were dead and letters from Lowvert mentioned their names and the grief of their loved ones. *Dear Allan, You will remember young Alward from Haileybury. . . . Dear Barney, When you first went to Camp Borden you mentioned meeting a young Jewish boy from Kirkland Lake. . . . Dear William, We have just heard from Mrs. Thomas Smythe of Iroquois Falls who thanked us for our letter of sympathy regarding the death of her boy at Dieppe. We can only imagine what she is going through . . .*

Lewisporte, with one exception, was a reprise of Point Leamington, the same guard duty, the same patrols and the same battle drill, involving yet another daily liberation of yet another Newfoundland village. The one exception was submarine lookout duty at Burnt Bay, a camouflaged log tower fronting a stand of spruce on a point of land northwest of Lewisporte near the village of Brown's Arm. In three weeks of scanning the waters, binoculars pressed to sore eyes, the lookouts report a good number of whales but only one U-boat, essentials noted, deck and tower guns, number on the conning tower—a large "69" scripted in a Germanic hand—and one peculiar feature. Painted on the conning tower was a picture of a laughing cow. It was the U-boat's nickname, chosen by its whimsical commander when the vessel was berthed in the occupied French port of St. Nazaire in October of 1941. *La vâche qui rit* is the logo for a French dairy.

"You and me got a break comin' up." Billy and Al were out for a noon-hour stroll down from the camp toward the water and Billy was spilling the beans despite his promise to Barney.

"A break?"

Billy shook his head in mock sorrow. "You sergeants don't know nothin', eh? A bunch of us got leave in a week. You and me included."

"Don't bullshit me, Billy."

"No bullshit, Al. It's the truth. Talked to Barney this morning. Said the orders been cut yesterday. Said not ta tell anybody till it's official." Billy grinned. "So I didn't, did I?"

"You gonna go?" Al remembered Billy's post-*Lady Nelson* vow.

"Damn right I'm gonna go." Billy put his arm around his friend. "And you are, too. But not by any puking ship."

"How else we gonna get out of this place? We gonna be the second coming and walk on water?

"Nope. Gonna fly over it. The PBI is gonna travel PBY."

Al threw a questioning look at his pal, who explained. "Yates is buddy-buddy with some o' the fly boys and they go into Halifax once a week for maintenance, supplies or something. I dunno. But you and I and our Yankee pal are hitchin' a ride. Trust me, it's in the bag. We fly to Halifax, hop a train there, we'll be home in three days. Four tops. Now get yer arse over to the telegraph office and send a wire to yer wife. Tell her ta drop all her boyfriends real quick 'cause her old man is comin' home and he is, as they say in Newfoundland, right some horny."

Al felt like a kid at a birthday party who'd made a wish, blown out all the candles and had his fondest dream come true. Right then and there.

He reached to wrap his arms around his pal to give him a hug and Billy was backing off in feigned homophobic horror when the world exploded and the two of them were bowled over by a shock wave rolling up from the water, shattering windows, blowing away tents and splintering wooden barracks into matchsticks.

Both of them scrabbled at the ground trying to dig in with their fingernails as rocks and flying glass and pieces of wood tore the air above their heads. They were each thinking the same thing. The *Laughing Cow* was shelling the base.

After what seemed like half an hour, Al opened his eyes and raised his nose out of the gravel where he had tried so hard to bury it. As he slowly raised his head and looked around he was reminded of pictures he'd seen of the London Blitz.

"Jesus, will ya look at that!" He was on his knees and turning to Billy. "Billy?" There was no answer. "Billy!" Nothing. Billy, face down, wasn't moving. Al felt like the bottom was falling out of his stomach. He knelt by his friend and shook him. Again nothing. "Billy!" Now it was a cry. He reached to turn his boyhood friend over on his back and as he did so the corpse spoke.

"Time ta get up, Sarge?"

Al blew air. He felt his ears pop. "Listen, you fuckin' Lebanese prick. That was not funny. Not funny at all."

Billy puckered his lips and made kissing noises as he sat up and looked around.

"What the hell happened?"

"Dunno, but let's go find out."

They stumbled down the hill toward the sounds of cries and shouts. Sirens had started up and soldiers were converging from every direction, some of them with rents in their battle dress, others with face cuts from flying glass but paying no attention because of their fear that others were worse off.

As soon as Al saw where everyone was headed, as soon as he took in the pall of brown smoke rising from the spruce trees in the distance, he knew what it was. It was the dynamite tent.

The dynamite tent was a Bell tent sitting on a rise just above the water. It was filled with blasting caps and fourteen boxes of dynamite to be used to tunnel ammunition bunkers out of the rock. The dynamite wasn't supposed to be in the Bell tent, wasn't supposed to be anywhere near the village or the base. It was supposed to be stored at the Killick dumps and brought up by Duty Boat as needed. But some officer at Company HQ had ordered up "a shipload" because he was tired of the logistics of bringing in a box or two every time a box or two was needed. He thought it would be much more efficient to bring in the dynamite all at once and store it closer to hand in a Bell tent that just happened to be a few feet from another Bell tent, this one housing Algonquin sentries.

Civilians were now joining the rush, some with white bedsheets, others with blankets; an older man, puffing with exertion, came by carrying a brace of two-by-fours on his shoulder. Al stopped him with an offer to help.

"Tanks, bye. Need deese for stretchers."

Where the dynamite and sentry tents had been was now a huge smoking scoop in the earth ringed by split and ragged spruce trees and bodies, some of them dead and covered by blankets, others alive but unconscious, still others moaning and writhing as soldiers and civilians knelt beside them tearing bedsheets into bandages, staunching blood and binding wounds.

Al stood rooted to the spot by the carnage in front of him until Billy called out and he shook himself to grab one end of a stretcher made from blankets wrapped around two-by-fours. Grunting with the effort, the two of them lifted a soldier, blood oozing from his bandaged head, his face contorted, calling for his mother. Following pointing arms they lugged their casualty to a waiting Jeep that would take him back into town where a makeshift hospital was being set up at the Knights of Columbus Hall.

Billy and Al spent a frenzied hour, sometimes on stretcher duty and sometimes helping the walking wounded. Then they slumped exhausted beside the trail leading to what was now a gravesite. As Al tried to find a comfortable spot in the spruce needles he felt something underneath his leaning elbow and sat up to find out what it was.

"Jesus, Billy. Jesus!"

A startled Billy looked up to see his friend grasping a uniformed arm severed at the shoulder. "Shit!" Billy stood up grimacing.

Al stood there holding the arm not knowing what to do when he heard a cough behind him. It was the older man he'd helped with the two-by-fours.

"Give dat ta me, lad. Ilse takes care of it fer ye." He smiled at Al, took the arm and carried it like an offering to God, a solemn procession back down the trail to the blanketed bodies still beside the hole.

It seemed like he was only gone for a minute when they saw him again, trudging back up, motioning for them to follow, leading them to his home up the hill on the other side of the road.

His name was Mickey Cahill, he pronounced it "Cal," and he introduced them to his wife, Bridie. "Mother," he said, "deese byes 'ave been trew 'ell and gone. Dey needs a drink. Big uns."

The big uns turned out to be tumblers of screech with a dash of water. The grateful Algonquins sat on the front room sofa and murmured their thanks before gulping down their drinks as if they'd just come in from a desert trek without a drop for days.

Bridie took their empty glasses into the kitchen and filled them to the brim a second time. As she brought them back in on a tray and Billy reached for his tumbler her husband held up his hand.

"Now lad, dis would be powerful drink ye have. If ye swallows dis one like t'other, ye'll be flat on yer arse lickity split."

Billy smiled and nodded, held up his glass in a silent toast and then quickly drank it down. The old man laughed and winked at Al, who was following Cahill's advice and sipping, as a silence settled among them, the old man with a faraway look in his eyes.

After a bit, he spoke. To no one in particular. "'Tis a sorry business, war. Sorry business. Saw some terrible tings meself in de First War. Aye, terrible tings."

He nodded his head. Slowly. Then he glanced at his guests. "Worse den today, byes, worse den today, if ye ken believe it. In France it was. Place called Beaumont-Hamel."

There was another silence and then Cahill stood up. "Now you byes rest a wee while. Then mother will cook us a bite o' supper."

Al was about to protest, about to say no-thanks-we-should-be-reporting-back-to-base when a tired voice in his head said, "Piss on it."

So he smiled and nodded to his host, who smiled in return. Then Cahill went over to Billy, who was already fast asleep, his chin on his chest. He bent and lifted Billy's legs on to the sofa, unlaced and took off his boots, and put a cushion under his head.

When Al awoke it was dark and he was in a bed in his underwear. He sat up rubbing his eyes and wincing with a pounding headache. Where was he? He had no idea.

He sat for a minute with his head in his hands and then swung his legs to the floor to stand at the window next to his bed. Drawing aside the curtains, he drew up the sash, leaned out and took a deep breath of the cool night air.

It was then that he started to get his bearings. He was in the Cahill house. He'd had a drink with Billy, who'd fallen asleep. But how did he get upstairs to bed? And Billy? Snoring in the bed next to his.

He didn't know. But what he did know all of a sudden was that he had to take a leak. Badly. He thought about what to do. Sneak downstairs and go outside? He rejected that idea. Stumbling around in the dark in a strange house and waking the dead in the process wasn't a good idea. He supposed he could piss out the window but . . .

Then he remembered something Reggie had told him and he knelt beside his bed and reached around under until he found the chamber pot.

When he woke again it was light. His Bulova registered 5:45 a.m. He felt something heavy on his feet and looked down to see his battledress cleaned and pressed lying across the foot of his bed. He got up and almost tripped over his boots, polished to a spit-shine, lined up beside his bed.

Dressing quietly so as not to wake Billy, he reached under the bed for the chamber pot, vowing he would do one thing for himself. At the foot of the stairs he followed the smell of cooking bacon to the kitchen, where Bridie Cahill was scrambling eggs. When she saw what Al was carrying she reached to take it from him but he shook his head and she told him where to dump it.

When he came back in from the outdoor privy, Mickey was in the kitchen, hitching his suspenders over his undershirt. "Did ye sleep well, lad?"

"Yes, Mr. Cahill. I did. Like a log."

Cahill grinned. "Screech'll do dat fer ye, Sergeant. And call me Mick."

"Only if you call me Al. And by the way, I have a question for you, ah, Mick."

"Yes, bye."

When Al had emptied the chamber pot in the outdoor privy he had chuckled at what he saw on the inside bottom of the pot—the face of a man with nasty, glittering eyes.   "So who's the angry guy in the chamber pot? I think I know why he's mad but just who is he?"

Cahill grinned black teeth. "Ah, bye, dat's de Butcher o' Ireland. Dat's Oliver Cromwell. Our family's been pissin' and shittin' on 'im fer 'undreds o' years, da bastard."

Al laughed and nodded his head. "Good for you."

Billy came down the stairs then in his fresh pressed uniform and shiny boots. He went over to Bridie Cahill, kissed her on the cheek and thanked her for his spiffy look.

Bridie blushed. "Ah, 'twasn't me, lad. 'Twas a leprechaun that did it." Billy winked at her and she winked back.

Over breakfast she had the two soldiers in stitches telling them stories of her childhood on the Rock. "Me brother and me was off ta Mass this Sunday, see. Me brother Charlie is chief steward now. On de *Caribou*. It's a ship, a ferry sails between Port aux Basques and Sydney in Canada where you byes is from. Anyways, way back den Charlie was about ten years old. I was eight. We was crossin' a meadow, see, on our way ta Mass and along comes dis big auld bull and starts in chasin' de two of us, eh. And Charlie, well, Charlie, he takes ta runnin' like de divil and leaves me to dat auld bull. Now dat auld ting was some saucy. Came right up ta me and I falls down in a pile o' rocks. And da bull, dere he was, his auld eyes lookin' straight at me. I was some scared, believe you me. But den I closed me eyes and said a wee prayer. 'Jaysus, Mary and Joseph, 'elp me.' Den I opened me eyes, closed me fist as tight as I could and gives 'im a smack in de nose as 'ard as I could. Musta hurt 'im 'cause he went runnin' away. Got ta Mass on time, too. Tanks be ta God. And did I ever let Charlie forget it? Leavin' his wee sister to da big, auld bull? Not on yer life. Not on yer life."

When they left the Cahill's the two Canadians wanted to offer something to this generous and caring couple, something tangible to express how much they appreciated their kindness, but they couldn't think of anything that would not be insulting. So they stood awkwardly on the doorstep to hug Bridie and shake hands with Mickey.

Back at the barracks they found they had not been missed in the aftermath of the disaster. They could have been AWL for days and not been missed. Five men had been killed and about a dozen wounded. Already fingers were pointing, and pointing predictably at the lower ranks on duty at the dynamite tent. It was said that a corporal had accidentally discharged his weapon and set off the explosion. It was said that a spent cartridge was found in the breech of his rifle. Billy scoffed.

"Listen, Al. There were trees and rocks and body parts blown to hell and gone around that hole. And they managed ta find a rifle with a spent cartridge in it? All in one piece? Sure they did. And pigs fly. It's arse covering time, Al. Time to blame the PBI. And it's all horseshit. That fuckin' dynamite shouldn't have been there in the first place and whoever the brainless brass twit was ordered it there is the one who's responsible, that's fer sure."

Billy was still pontificating on the flight to Halifax and on the train home. By the time the T&NO pulled into Lowvert, Al had a pain in his stomach and he didn't know if it was from listening to Billy for three straight days or heartburn.

Wives and sons were at the station to greet them. Two-Ton Tony and Shabicky were swept up into their fathers' arms. After hugging his wife fiercely, Al headed for the baggage room, where his father was waiting with a tail-wagging, barking Tippy lunging on a leash. The two men shook hands, the dog pawed and licked, and then the four of them walked home with an excited dog leading them around the lake and up the steps to the house, where Myra was standing at the open door waiting to embrace her son, thinking all the while of young Alward from Haileybury who would never again come home to his mother.

At table that evening, a table of roast beef again, Yorkshire pudding again, apple pie and cheese again, Al picked at his food, feeding bits of meat to the dog at his feet under the table.

His father smiled at him. "That dog is eating more than you are, son."

"Yeah." Al looked up from the dog. "Ya know, I've had a stomach ache for two days now and I'm just not hungry. Dunno what it is. My favourite meal," he looked at his mother apologetically, "and I can't eat a bite."

"Well, this is serious. Allan McDougal sitting with a plate of roast beef and not hungry!" Myra was jocular but there was concern in her eyes. She turned to Beth. "Nurse, maybe you'd better have a look at the patient and see what's ailing him."

What was ailing him was acute appendicitis and Al McDougal spent the first week of his leave in hospital recovering from emergency surgery. Doc Evans told him it was a close call. Recuperating at home he played with his son during the day and when play was done, he read to him, *Chicken Little, Little Red Riding Hood, Hansel and Gretel,* and repeatedly the boy's favourite, *Jack and the*

Beanstalk. Every once in a while with *Jack*, Al would skip a line or two of the story only to be told in no uncertain baby English to quit farting around.

At night Al listened to the radio. Wayne and Shuster and their zany songs like "When the Swallows Come Back from Kapuskasing," or Sunday nights and *The Jell-O Program*, Jack Benny opening with "Jell-O, everybody!" just in case his listeners needed to be reminded of who sponsored the show. Al also tuned in to *The Fred Allen Show, The George Burns and Gracie Allen Show* and *Fibber McGee and Molly*, from which he adopted the line: "My sister married an Irishman." "Oh, really?" "No, O'Reilly." For the rest of his time at home, anyone, family or friends, foolish enough to say "Oh really" in the presence of Allan McDougal got a quick "No, O'Reilly!" in reply.

By the time he was ready to head back to Newfoundland, Billy was long gone and Al had to travel solo. His telegraphed orders stated that he had to be in Halifax the night of Thanksgiving Day to board a ship called *The Lady Rodney*.

Beth had the evening shift at the hospital so it was Sandy who walked with his son to the station and shook his hand as he boarded the train. Each wanted to hug the other but each felt it was something that just wasn't done. At the junction, Al transferred to the Toronto train and asked the porter to make up his berth right away. He was still not quite up to snuff and tired easily.

In Toronto he boarded the train to Montreal and there transferred again, this time to the overnight passenger to Moncton which was supposed to arrive the next morning but a freak October snowstorm near Rivière-du-Loup slowed them down enough that Allan McDougal knew then and there that he wasn't going to catch *The Lady Rodney* in Halifax.

He used the time in Moncton to telegraph his predicament and was told to report to the military police at the Halifax station, where he would be given new travel orders, which turned out to be a ticket for the morning train to North Sydney where passage had been booked for him on the *Caribou* sailing to Newfoundland's Port aux Basques. From there it was the Newfoundland Express to Botwood.

After he'd had a Thanksgiving Day turkey sandwich and a cup of tea at the Red Cross kiosk set up for servicemen in the station waiting room, Al curled up on a bench to catch forty winks thinking that it could well be Christmas before he got to Botwood on the Express. He hummed a few bars of the song and just before he dropped off to sleep remembered that Bridie Cahill's brother Charlie was chief steward on the *Caribou*. He made a mental note to look him up once he was on board.

It was Tuesday, October 13 just after seven o'clock Newfoundland time when he boarded the *Caribou* along with other military personnel, army, navy and air force. As was the custom in wartime, members of the armed forces boarded first and as was the custom with ships bound for Newfoundland they were on Newfy time.

Once up the gangplank he dumped his kit bag and stood leaning on the rails watching other passengers boarding in the light of the wharf lamps high on poles stretching the length of the dock. The last of the military came up, Newfoundlanders shouting and laughing, Royal Navy tars in their bellbottoms. Then it was the turn of the civilians, men in suits and men in overalls, mothers with babes in arms, two nursing sisters in their blue uniforms, and a blushing couple holding hands, the man carrying a suitcase, hastily scrawled but clearly marked in white paint: "Just Married."

Cargo was also being winched on board including mail and bag after bag of Prince Edward Island potatoes. Fifty head of cattle, beef on the hoof, were already tied down in the hold.

After a bit of taking it all in, Al began to shiver in the damp chill of the sea air and made his way to his cabin below deck, picked out a bunk and left his kit bag on it to stake out his claim. Then he set out to explore the ship, walking the deck amid the to and fro of busy crewmen and chattering passengers, sticking his nose into nooks and crannies, noting the lifeboats up on their davits behind the single funnel from which wispy grey smoke was trailing up into the sky toward the early stars of night. He passed the dining salon and stepped inside, thinking this might be the place to find a chief steward, but seeing no one and nothing except tables and chairs of polished hardwood, he made his way back out on deck and headed toward the sound of music coming from the main lounge. As he stepped through the door he saw a soldier at the piano, a soldier he knew, singing in a familiar voice, "K-K-K-Katy, my beautiful Katy, You're the only g-g-g-girl that I adore . . ."

"Willy Yates, what the hell are you doin' here?"

"Ah, Sergeant McDougal, I am about to sail the ocean blue, evidently along with you." And Yates pounded the keys with a few bars of "You Are my Sunshine, my only Sunshine," and then segued into a haunting rendition of "The Whiffenpoof Song," sounding to Al just like the crooner Rudy Vallee.

"Yup, Sergeant, that's what we are, you and me. Poor little lambs who have gone astray. Little lambs of God. *Agnus Dei.*"

Al could see now that Yates had had a snootful and when he sat down on the piano bench beside him he could smell it. Beer.

As if he was reading his sergeant's mind, Yates asked, "Wanna beer, Al? Got some Budweiser in my kit bag. Top of the piano up there. Some Keith's too if ya'd like that."

Al stood and took a Bud from the bag, he liked American beer, popped the cap with the opener Yates handed him, took a long, thirsty swallow, and then sat down again beside the pianist who was now playing "My Bonnie Lies over the Ocean," but singing

> *My father's an apple pie vendor,*
> *My mother makes synthetic gin.*
> *My sister sells love for a living,*
> *My God, how the money rolls in.*

When Yates got to the chorus, other voices joined in and Al turned to see the Royal Navy circling around.

Rolls in, rolls in,
My God, how the money rolls in, rolls in.
Rolls in, rolls in.
My God, how the money rolls in.

My brother's a slum missionary,
Wot saves poor young women from sin.
He'll save you a blonde for five dollars,
My God, how the money rolls in.

Yates went through a half-dozen more ditties before he grandly offered the piano to one of the sailors, who proceeded to carry on with the excellent program of evening entertainment his American comrade had initiated. Yates sang along for a few more minutes, then, bowing to his successor, grabbed his kit bag and motioned Al to follow him out on to the deck.

"Fresh air, Sergeant. Need fresh air." Yates dropped his kit bag by the seaside rail, took one deep breath and then another, shook his head and reached into his blouse for his chewing tobacco and pocket knife. He cut off a plug and fingered it into a bulge in his cheek while Al lit a cigarette.

Yates pointed out to sea. "See that?"

"Can't see a damn thing, Yates."

"Look to your left, over there." Willy pointed again and Al made out a shape moving through the water near the harbour mouth. "Our escort for the trip over. A fuckin, dinky little minesweeper, for Chrissakes. Really gonna scare the shit of any U-boat out there." Yates spat brown into the water.

Just then the two Algonquins feel a lurch as the *Caribou* begins to get underway, swinging slowly to starboard away from the ferry terminal and then pointing for the harbour mouth. Once through, the *Caribou* will take the lead and the minesweeper will take the tail-end Charlie position using its asdic to sweep astern of the *Caribou* for any lurking submarines.

There is no question U-boats are out there. Just two days before in the Cabot Strait, the freighter *Waterton* was torpedoed in broad daylight; and on the run over from Port aux Basques, the *Caribou's* escort depth-charged a suspected sub.

The minesweeper Yates has just disparaged is the Royal Canadian Navy's *Grandmere*, named after a small town in Quebec just north of Shawinigan Falls. A Bangor class vessel, she has a top speed of sixteen knots and is not designed for escort duty. The reason she is pressed into service tonight is because other ships that are designed for escort duty—the much faster corvettes and destroyers—are all assigned to the lifeline to England, a priority more important than shepherding vessels in coastal waters. That is left to makeshift arrangements, and accounts for *Grandmere* being assigned to the *Caribou.*

The captain of *Grandmere* is not happy with his orders, which are by the book, the gospel according to the British doctrine of anti-submarine patrol. Captain James Cuthbert firmly believes it would make much more sense to be zigging and zagging with his asdic out in front of *Caribou.* But, as the Germans put it, *"Befehl ist Befehl"*—orders are orders—and tail-end Charlie it is.

"Didn't know you could play the piano, Yates."

Yates grinned and spat another stream of tobacco juice over the side. "Hey, Sergeant, Private W.B. Yates is your basic Renaissance man. No doubt about it. No doubt at all."

"So, Private, how come yer late gettin' back?"

Ah, Sarge, I met this blonde, see, back in Boston and she just led me astray." Yates sang. "Baa baa baa."

"So you're AWL? Kendrick will have yer balls fer bookends."

"Ah, you haven't heard! Kendrick is no more. Kendrick has gone bye-bye. To where, nobody knows. But then nobody cares."

Al told the American about his appendix, pleasant days playing with his boy and recuperative nights listening to the radio.

"So what's your favourite show?"

Al shrugged.

"Ah come on. Ya gotta have a favourite. Who's your favourite character? How about Throckmorton P. Gildersleeve. Ya know, from *Fibber McGee and Molly?*"

Al chuckled, remembering.

"Then there's Dr. Rancid Squirm from *The Fred Allen Show.* And Judge Nullen Void." They were both laughing now. "But the best, the best, Sarg, has gotta be the characters on *Vic and Sade.*"

"Never heard of it."

"Best characters on radio. Jake Gumpox. Dottie Brainfeeble. And my personal all-time, super-dooper favourite, Ishigan Fishigan from Shisigan Michigan."

Al exploded with laughter.

"Hey, Sarge. It's funny. But it's not *that* funny."

When Al finally caught his breath, he solemnly nodded his head. "Oh yes it is, Yates. Oh yeah. Just wait til ya hear Arnie Christensen do it. Then you'll see how funny it really is."

When Al looked at his watch, he made a face. It was close to eleven and he was damn tired. "Still don't have all my energy back. Gonna take forever, I suppose."

"Nah, you'll be fit as a fiddle in no time, Sarge. Anyway, see ya in the morning. I'm gonna hang around a bit before I turn in."

Al waved adieu to Yates and headed down to his cabin. From the light cast when he gently eased open the door, he could see two of the lower bunks were occupied by soldiers sleeping fully dressed while on the floor beside each was a lifebelt draped over a pair of boots. Al thought the caution was admirable and followed suit. He was not going to be caught a second time without a life preserver.

In no time at all he was fast asleep, lulled into dreamland by the thrumming of *Caribou's* engines. His last waking thought was one of surprise that he'd been at sea now for more than three hours and hadn't even thought of being seasick.

Chapter Eleven

OCTOBER 13, 1942. Botwood. After months and months of bad news there's finally some good news in the war news. The Yanks have given the Japs a kick in the arse in the Solomon Islands, Montgomery is proving that Rommel is human in North Africa and Ivan is putting up a hell of a fight against Jerry at Stalingrad. Have a feeling Hitler's going to rue the day he invaded Russia. Word is that Jerry is handcuffing our POWs taken at Dieppe in retaliation for us tying the hands of the few German prisoners we captured on the raid. Lord Haw Haw says it's regrettable but a necessary reminder to us that we must follow the Geneva Convention which is pretty rich coming from a bunch of thugs and butchers the likes of which the world hasn't seen since the Middle Ages. Billy says Al should be back any day now. Just in time to hear about the latest caper, the Algonquin hijacking of train number 9. Word is the engine bell is still AWL.

Excerpt from Barney's Diary

In the early hours of the morning following Barney's late-night diary entry, a restless Willy Yates was prowling the deck of the *Caribou* in his continuing quest for fresh air, which was getting more fresh by the minute, he figured the temperature had dropped to damn near freezing. Striding past the hanging lifeboats, he reached up to touch one of them as if to assure himself they were real.

He blew on his hands and then ambled on his long legs to the stern, the ship's flag flapping above his head at the rail where he squinted into the darkness trying to see if he could make out *Grandmere*. Seeing nothing but the dark of the night he heaved a sigh and turned to look up at *Caribou's* smokestack, shaking his head and cursing at the thick, billowing smoke, a beacon of invitation to any U-boat lurking on the surface searching for prey.

Then shrugging what-the-hell, Yates moved on to the other side of the ship, past an open hatch, fresh air for the cattle below, restless, bawling and pulling against the ropes holding them in place. Nodding his head in sympathy he kept going until he found himself at the bow in front of the wheelhouse where the ship's captain, Ben Tavernor, tall and husky, was silhouetted staring hard into the night as if willing land to appear. It is ninety-six miles across the strait to Port aux Basques and Yates believes they are about halfway there.

Once around the wheelhouse, AWL Willy headed back to the stern, where he took a deep breath and blew it out as he brought his watch close to his face, checking the time. It was 0325.

At that very instant the night explodes and the *Caribou* rears like a bucking horse, throwing Yates over the rail into the freezing Cabot Strait. Stunned by the cold of the sea, his heart hammering his ribs, he claws his frantic way to the surface and finally comes up spitting salt water, heavy with boots and uniform. Manoeuvring onto his back, he reaches to unlace and kick off the deadweight on his feet. It is only then, treading water, that he looks at the *Caribou* wallowing with a broken back. He sees smoke and steam and hears screams.

By now his uniform is waterlogged and he has to fight to stay afloat. He tries to swim to where he thinks there might be lifeboats but makes no headway. Twisting his head this way and that his eyes seize on something drifting on a swell to his left. He kicks hard and comes upon a hatch cover evidently torn from the sinking ship. Wrapping his arms around it, he pulls himself half out of the water and thanks his lucky star.

To this point the sea has been calm, but now Yates feels it beginning to roll as he registers a sound behind and to his right. Ship's engines. He cranes his neck. It is *Grandmere*. He rages. *Too late, ya stupid shit. Too late to save* Caribou. *Too late to save the cattle. Poor dumb beasts. But at least you'll save me. And anybody else who doesn't go down with the ship.*

But *Grandmere* isn't coming to save him or anybody else. It is veering away and it is the wake from this turning that has bobbed Yates up and down on his hatch cover. At the crest of one of these waves in the light of a starshell from *Grandmere* he sees a U-boat, a laughing cow painted on the conning tower.

At this moment on the *Caribou,* Al is bracing himself on the slanting deck, helping women and children into useable lifeboats. A good number of boats are hopelessly tangled in the davit rigging while others on the starboard deck were smashed and holed when the torpedo hit. The Algonquin sergeant has a goose egg on his forehead and is favouring his right hip, injuries sustained when he was thrown out of his bunk by the force of an explosion that split the mahogany beams in the cabin's ceiling and rained chunks of wood down on top bunks and sleeping soldiers. When he gathered his wits enough to pick himself off the floor already awash in seawater, the night lights in the cabin flickered and went out.

His cabin mates and boots were nowhere to be found but he did manage to feel out his lifebelt, and strapping it on, hurried out into the tilted corridor in his sock feet. Then it was up the stairs, water rushing down in a torrent, and out on the tilted deck, where he saw a madhouse of hollering crewmen, husbands clutching their wives, mothers calling for their children, children crying for their mothers. It was a scene he had witnessed before in the mind's eye of his boyhood, reading stories of the sinking of *The Titanic,* the ship's orchestra playing "Nearer My God To Thee."

A woman is suddenly beside him with a baby in her arms, a boy wrapped in a knitted blue shawl. She is without a lifebelt and rooted to the spot begging with fearful eyes. He shrugs out of his lifebelt and holds her baby while she fastens the belt around her waist following his shouted instructions. Then with the boy in one arm, he uses the other to help her down into a lifeboat, handing her the child as he hollers encouragement in her ear.

When he looks around and sees there is no one left, there is nothing more he can do, he turns to get into the boat after the mother and child but it is already swinging its way out and down to the water. If he doesn't make it into this one he will have to jump into the water and if he does that he risks being sucked under when the ship goes down. Decision made, he leaps into mid-air, grabs one of the lines lowering the lifeboat and slides down, the rope searing his hands. When the boat hits the water, Al hits the boat, wincing as his hip collides with the inside of a gunwale.

The men in the boat grab oars and begin to row away as fast and as hard as they can. Suddenly there is a shout and the oarsmen rest at the terrible sight of *Caribou* rearing up with a raging roar of exploding boilers. In the afterglow Sergeant Allan McDougal also rises up and sees something he will never forget. He sees it as the human eye takes in a flash of chain lightning, fleetingly, starkly and clearly. He sees the forward part of the dying vessel canted and sliding backwards into the roiling sea, and in the wheelhouse, the tall figure of Ben Tavernor going down with his ship.

Something makes him look at his watch. It is 0330. He shakes his head and almost loses his balance as the oarsmen suddenly go back to work putting more distance between the lifeboat and the suction of the sinking ship. But then there is a scream. The lifeboat is filling with water. The seacocks!

Seacocks are the plugs in lifeboat hulls pulled when the boats are in their davits to allow rain or sea water to drain through. In the bedlam of getting this lifeboat launched no one has remembered to put the seacocks back in.

Now there is a frenzied attempt to do so. But with panicked people shouting and jostling it is hopeless. With a lurching roll the boat tips and Al goes over the side, down into black, swirling water so cold it takes his breath away. When his lungs are just about to burst his head finally breaks the surface and he sees he is some fifty feet from the shadowy hull of the lifeboat. What energy he had, fuelled by adrenaline, is almost gone now and he has to force himself to swim, a laboured breaststroke, back to the overturned boat. He hears voices around him, people crying for help, but he can barely help himself. Something floats by in front of him, a square shape, and he reaches to grab it but it is leathery and slips from his fingers. As it rolls over and away from him he catches a glimpse of white lettering: "Just married."

At the last minute, just before he gives up hope, he is carried by a saving wave to the side of the overturned lifeboat. But his relief is short lived. There is no purchase, there is nothing to hold on to, and when his fingers slide on the hull he begins to think that this is it, this is the end. He remembers Billy on *The Lady Nelson* looking down at the water. "Cold as Toby's arse, that water. If ya don't drown right away ya probably just go ta sleep. Not a bad way ta go when ya think about it."

And then he sees a lifebelt dangling in front of his face and a voice urging him to grab on and when he does, he is pulled up the hull until hands reach down under his arms and drag him to lay spread-eagled and hyperventilating on the upturned bottom.

There are only a dozen or so survivors on the hull and they are all men. There is no sign of the mother and her baby son in a blue shawl.

But there is no time to weep, as the boat is suddenly rocked by explosions in the sea around it. The blasts hit like a kick in the stomach. At first Al thinks it is the U-boat firing at them and a white-hot blaze of anger gives him a surge of energy. Fucking Ratzis. Walter Winchell's word for Hitler's boys. But it is not the U-boat. It is *Grandmere* dropping depth charges.

Captain Cuthbert reckons *The Laughing Cow* is submerged nearby, hiding from his asdic underneath the lifeboats and the noise of *Caribou* breaking up as she goes down. Cuthbert wants to make sure the submarine stays down, far down, too far to surface and machine-gun survivors. He has heard stories of U-boat atrocities and is not in the mood to take any chances with people in the water this night, people who are now his responsibility, as is his ship and crew, which is another reason he wants to force the submarine to stay down where it hasn't got a hope in hell of launching torpedoes at *Grandmere*. So he takes a calculated risk and orders his crew to drop charges as close to the lifeboats as they dare.

One of the men on Al's capsized boat has rigged a rope from a bowline back through and tied to the shaft of the rudder aft, and each man has an arm hooked around the rope, holding on for dear life as the boat wallows in the waves from the exploding charges. But it is not enough. One of the charges detonates almost below them and a volcano of water erupts, lifting the lifeboat and rolling it on to its side. Clinging to the rope with both hands, Al has a vision of the tormented in Hell. For one horrific instant, he catches sight of those who didn't surface when the lifeboat first tipped, their bodies caught in rigging, their eyes open and bulging in death. As quickly as they appear they disappear, in the blink of an eye, and the boat falls back in the water hull up and he drags himself up and over the keel.

Of the dozen men hanging on the rope a moment before there are now only seven left. Seven shivering and exhausted men. There is a cry from the water, a bobbing head and hands reaching up to the lifeboat. One of the seven, a pilot officer from the Royal Canadian Air Force, lets go of his hold on the rope and leans down, stretching to grasp beseeching hands. He gets a grip on those hands but hasn't the strength to pull and is himself dragged into the sea, going under with the man he has tried to save. Neither surfaces. Both are gone.

When the first streaks of dawn crease the sky there are only four men left on the hull and Al is weaving in and out of consciousness. There is a moment when he thinks he is home in Lowvert and at church, because he can hear his mother

and the choir singing, "Rock of ages, cleft for me, Let me hide myself in thee."
Then the ancient Irish hymn, "Be thou my Vision, O Lord of my heart; Naught
be all else to me, save that thou art, Thou my best thought, by day or by night,
Waking or sleeping, thy presence my light."

He drifts out and then back in, his hands almost frozen to the rope. The light
in the sky is brighter now and the choir is still singing, not in church this time
but in some boisterous music hall. "Roll out the barrel, we'll have a barrel of fun.
Roll out the barrel, we've got the blues on the run." And then, even in his
delirium, an unmistakable voice.

> My father's an apple pie vendor,
>
> My mother makes synthetic gin.
>
> My sister sells love for a living.
>
> My God, how the money rolls in.

Al is head down draped over the hull so has to raise himself to see the choir.
It is in another lifeboat drifting close by, right side up and full, with Willy Yates
in the bow conducting the chorus.

"You all right over there?" A voice from the choir. But Al is too weak to reply
and the question is not repeated because of the deafening roar of low-flying
aircraft. Two PBYs sweep over the lifeboats, the scattered bits and pieces of
wreckage, carley floats, planks and hatch covers supporting a few here and one
or two there.

The planes waggle their wings and the human wrecks in the water respond
with a ragged cheer. Al lifts a limp hand trying to wave. Then his eyes flutter
shut.

When they next flutter open he is wrapped in heavy blankets on the deck of
Grandmere. A kneeling sailor is beside him with one arm under his head and a
cup of hot coffee laced with rum to his lips. Al coughs with the first sip but the
second goes down without a hitch and in no time at all the cup is empty. He
smiles his thanks to the sailor, who looks at him with awe.

"Soldier, you are one tough son-of-a-bitch. We had to pry your hands off that
rope. One fucking finger at a time."

Al swallows and begins to cry. No sound. Just tears. The sailor is still holding
his head and when he sees the tears he hugs this survivor to his chest and holds
him until his ragged breathing takes on a deeper and measured rhythm and he is
fast asleep.

"How's the sarge?" A voice above the sailor. It is Yates dressed in borrowed
navy fatigues, two sizes too big for him. He has a blanket around his shoulders.

"Doc says he's in shock but should pull through. Ya know him?"

"Sure do." Yates, bloodshot eyes, grinned. "He's my platoon sergeant. My
best buddy."

The sailor nodded. "Anything I can do for you, soldier?"

Yates winked. "Yeah, Commander, ya can. Some more of that medicine you were giving the sergeant. Enough for both of us?"

The sailor smiled. "Coming right up."

Yates took over from the sailor and drew his blanket around Al. His lifeboat of choristers had been the first to be shepherded by *Grandmere*'s whaler to the scramble net thrown over the minesweeper's side and the American had been the last up the net to be embraced by Captain Cuthbert, waiting on deck. Taken below and stripped of his uniform he was given scalding hot coffee, a Hudson's Bay blanket, heavy wool socks and new duds.

After a second dose of java he'd dragged himself up and gone looking for footwear, which turned out to be a pair of rubber boots, a gift from the Government of Canada. Shod now, he made his way above to watch the rest of the rescue, leaning on the rail and peering at the human cargo coming up the net, the dead roped in blankets and carried over the shoulders of grunting sailors, the barely living hollow-cheeked, some hand over hand on their own but most with a sailor on either side, half lifting, half carrying, the same sailors time after time, down and up, a pat on the back from their captain and then down and up again. Over and over. Yates wanted to applaud.

After an hour or so of not seeing the face he was looking for, Yates nodded smartly to himself and went with a happy whistling to search the ship. He did not and would not believe his sergeant had been lost. Al was on *Grandmere* somewhere and William Butler Yates was going to find him.

He first stuck his head in the forward mess deck where most of the ratings ate and slept. Not a soul there. Then he wandered past the open door to the captain's cabin, maple furniture, bunk and desk and cabinet above a sink. Next he went past the canteen, tins of cigarettes, flat fifties, on a shelf. Sweet Caporals, Black Cats, Buckingham's, Turrets, British Consols—prices of other goods listed on a blackboard—chocolate bars 5¢. Lifesavers 5¢. Coke 5¢. Shoelaces 5¢. Razor blades 5¢. Shaving soap 15¢. Shoe polish 15¢.

Into the latrine—stainless steel sinks, shower stalls and toilets—he nudged open green doors with the toe of his boot. Nobody. Turning he looked at himself in the long mirror above the sinks and laughed, remembering the old joke about the not-too-bright sailor writing home to his mother telling her he'd been promised a promotion to captain of the head.

Still whistling he went out on deck checking stretchers and people huddled in blankets. He didn't bother with the dead because he was dead certain Allan McDougal wasn't among them. *Faith is the substance of things hoped for, the evidence of things not seen.* He was around on the port side when he finally saw the face he knew he would.

Now several hours later when the sun was late afternoon in the sky and the two of them had finished a third thermos of coffee heavy on the rum, *Grandmere* was turning for the run into North Sydney harbour.

With a stomach full of grog, Yates figured he should be pissed to the gills but he was stone cold sober. He glanced down at Al, who was fast asleep. He thought about waking him but decided to let him rest a little longer. If it were up to him he wouldn't wake him at all but he's been told. "Yates, there is no goddamn way they are carrying me off this ship, understand?"

When *Grandmere* finally docked and her lines were secured, Yates shook Al gently by the shoulder. "Time to meet the press, Sergeant."

Groaning, Al looked up. "Huh?"

Yates reached out a hand, pulled his friend to his feet and with one arm around his waist pointed with the other down to the wharf. The area around the foot of *Grandmere's* gangplank had been cordoned off with both city and military police out in force. But behind the roped-off area were men with cameras and men with notebooks. The word was out.

The two Algonquins made their way, slowly and deliberately, step by step, Al leaning on Yates, down the gangplank, where they were told they would have to wait their turn for an ambulance. Reporters shouted questions at them, their names, their status, civilian or military, where they were from. Yates shouted back.

One of the reporters ducked under the rope and approached. He looked to be no more than fifteen years old, fresh-faced and very eager.

"So, boys, did you save anyone?"

"Sure did," said Yates.

The reporter with notebook open was writing furiously. "Who then?"

"Mrs. Yates' little boy. Name's William. Ya know. Like the Irish poet."

The reporter's eyes widened. "Oh, really?"

"No," croaked Al. "O'Reilly."

Yates hugged his sergeant as they stood and grinned at the reporter being hauled away by a burly MP.

When a returning ambulance pulled up, bell clanging, lights flashing, the two survivors were directed towards it together with a woman, a baby in her arms. As the woman was being helped into the ambulance she turned to stare at one of the men behind her. Then she shook her head at the attendant, stepped down and went over to Al. She looked at him but said nothing, she just smiled and handed him her baby wrapped in a blue shawl, a boy who started to fuss at the sight of the gaunt-faced man with tears coursing down his cheeks.

Al spent a week in the hospital in Sydney. His first task when his strength began to return was to write home and say he was all right. It wasn't an urgent letter because no one at home knew he had been on the *Caribou*, it was just a short breezy note to his wife on Canadian Legion War Services stationery, six cents, Air Mail.

After inquiring about everyone's health including Tippy's, he wrote, "By now you probably have read about the sinking of the *Caribou*. Guess what? Your loving husband was on it and survived. Tell Gramps the water in the Cabot Strait is damn cold. The Lowbush is like a bath in comparison. More on all this later but would you please ask your mother-in-law to start knitting another scarf, another sweater, socks, gloves. I lost every stitch of clothing and everything I had. Seems careless of me, eh? Anyway, I am well and having a good rest. As a reward for surviving they may let me come home for a bit. Just when you thought you were rid of me for a good long while, eh?"

It wasn't until Saturday, October 17, that the censors allowed the story of the *Caribou* to be published, and a day or so later Al had all the newspapers he could get his hands on scattered over his bed when Yates came by to say he was off to Halifax to hitch a ride to Newfoundland on one of the PBYs.

Together they sat and scanned the headlines.

16 WOMEN 14 CHILDREN AMONG 137 LOST ON CARIBOU. DYING WOMAN CLUNG DESPERATELY TO BACK SAYS SURVIVOR. SHIP SINKS IN FOUR MINUTES AFTER TORPEDO HITS. THRILLING RESCUE ON HIGH SEAS. SINKING OF *CARIBOU* 'JUST PLAIN MURDER' OF WOMEN, CHILDREN.

"Hey, Al, that's me." Yates pointed to the "Just Plain Murder" headline from the *Toronto Daily Star.*

"When did ya say that?"

"On the wharf. When we were yelling back and forth with the reporters."

Al smiled and shrugged. "I don't remember much from that day." Then with a faraway look, "Just holding the baby. Just that. Damn, that felt good."

Yates looked up and smiled and then buried his head to the papers again. After a minute, "Aw shit, look at this."

His exclamation jolted Al, who had been staring at nothing and remembering everything. His eyes followed Yates's pointing finger. "When the *Caribou* went down it took three Tavernors with it, the Master, Benjamin Tavernor, and his two sons, First Officer Stanley Tavernor and his brother, Third Officer Harold Tavernor."

"Gimme that." Al reached for the article Yates was reading, **Known Dead, Missing in Sinking of *Caribou*.** He scanned the various lists of those "missing, believed lost," under various headings, Civilians first, then Crew, followed by RCAF Personnel, RCN, Canadian Army, and finally U.S. Service Personnel. When he found the Tavernors his mind clicked on the last picture he had of Captain Ben and he began to stare at nothing once again.

"What was Charlie's last name?" Yates was reading over Al's shoulder.

"What?"

"Charlie, the chief steward. Remember? Brother of what's-her-name. Your friend. Bridie from Lewisporte."

Al slowly shook his head. "Ya know, I never asked."

"Well, I think he's gone, too. Look at the bottom of the list there. See? "Harry Hann, chief steward, Port aux Basques."

Al looked and sat back. "But the guy's name was Charlie."

"But there's only one chief steward, Sarge."

"Where's this guy, Harry, from again?"

"Says Port aux Basques."

Al sighed. "Yeah, that's him, then. I remember Bridie said he lived in Port aux Basques. Charlie musta been a nickname. Shit!"

He was staring again, wondering about the Cahills and all the other families in Newfoundland who had lost a loved one and was only vaguely aware that Yates had taken his leave to catch the train to Halifax. He looked at his watch for the time, forgetting it wasn't working, forgetting it was rusted, its corroded hands forever fixed when his lifeboat capsized and he was thrown into the frigid waters of the Cabot Strait at thirty-eight minutes after three in the morning of the fourteenth of October, nineteen hundred and forty-two. A lifetime ago.

Chapter Twelve

JUNE 10, 1943. Halifax. Tomorrow we're off to England, off to whatever the future holds and I'm sitting here thinking about the past, thinking about good old Newfoundland. Especially the people, God's gift to the human race. Even Quarter Guard Anny. Al told me the other day that Reggie's sent Charity and her boy to live with his mother and brother in Louvert. And Charity's brother, Goody, has signed on with us and will be on board the Empress of Scotland *tomorrow as an Algonquin. Billy was so impressed by the Rock that he's thinking of naming his second son (who Billy insists is on the way) after Botwood but Al told him Botwood Assad sounded a bit too aristocratic or a little stupid if it got shortened to Botty. Al suggested Billy call his boy Dildo instead. Billy pretended to laugh.*

Excerpt from Barney's Diary

Five of them, along with Goody Noseworthy, stood on the dock at Pier 21, kit bags at their feet, staring up at a huge ship painted a wartime grey, three smokestacks and eight decks. Yates, the fount of all knowledge, told them the vessel had been launched in December 1929 and christened *Empress of Japan*. It was then put into regular trans-Pacific passenger service between Vancouver and the Far East. In 1931 the *Empress* set the record for the fastest sailing time between Yokohama and Victoria, seven days, twenty hours and sixteen minutes. In 1939 it was requisitioned for duty as a troopship and, with Japan's entry into the war, renamed the *Empress of Scotland*.

Goody Noseworthy looked at Yates, starstruck by his encyclopaedic knowledge. The rest of them, Frank, Billy, Reggie and Al, reacted with mental yawns, figuring rightly that their favourite Yank had deliberately found out all he could about the vessel just so he could do to somebody what he'd just done with a wink and a grin to Goody.

The Algonquins had come down to Halifax that morning from Debert, an army base near Truro where they'd been training since leaving Newfoundland in January, battle drill in the tidewater flats of Cobequid Bay, where the stink of decaying fish brought back memories, not fond.

Shouted orders to form up got them up the gangway and directed to their quarters, officers to the upper decks and the PBI to E Deck, five decks from the sun and two decks below the water line, so far down you could hear the racket of the ship's screws and feel the rumble of the ocean underneath your feet. Al found himself somewhere in between with the rest of the three-stripers and whispered a prayer of thanks. He would not have been able to do the crossing below the water line. Below the water line he would have lost it, he would have gone mad.

His fear of drowning in the bowels of a broken, sinking ship wasn't the only way *Caribou* had changed him. It had also made him think a lot about luck and he had come to the conclusion that it was something like Edison's definition of genius—one percent inspiration and ninety-nine percent perspiration. Al figured he had survived the icy waters of the Cabot Strait through that kind of luck. He remembered the sailor on *Grandmere* telling him how his fingers had to be pried off the lifeline on the upturned lifeboat.

But he was also quick to acknowledge that he had more often been blessed with the other kind of luck, the kind that had nothing to do with how much you subscribed to the philosophy that God helps those who help themselves. The Algonquins hadn't gone to Hong Kong. He could have been—but wasn't—anywhere near the dynamite tent in Lewisporte when it blew, nor had he been in St. John's last December when the Knights of Columbus Hostel on Harvey Road had burned to the ground, killing ninety-nine people, servicemen and civilians.

There were close to 500 in the hostel that night and more than 300 of them were in the auditorium watching the stage broadcast of the Saturday night *Uncle Tim Barndance Show* when the building went up like a tinderbox. Afterwards some said it was arson, the work of German agents. But whatever the cause it was a staggering shock to the people of Newfy-john. There was no ventilation in the hostel, because windows were covered with blackout shutters, and the auditorium was soon filled with thick smoke, black and blinding. Exit doors opened inward and the panicked crush to get out had them blocked with bodies in no time. The roof was made of asphalt, which the fire quickly melted, and hot, burning tar fell on the trapped revellers, turning many of them into human torches.

"You, Allan George McDougal, could well have been there," he was talking to himself, "if not in the auditorium then writing letters in the reading room or asleep in the dormitory. You could have been one of those human torches."

But he wasn't. He was alive in a tourist-class cabin on the *Empress of Scotland* staring out a porthole into the fog of Halifax harbour, about to be on his way to England, which was that much closer to Jerry and that much closer to a further testing of his relationship with Lady Luck.

He sighed and looked at his watch, a new one, a Gruen this time, a gift from his father along with a copy of an old Irish blessing, typed with one finger, "the hunt and peck system," Gramps had called it.

> *May the road rise up to meet you,*
> *May the wind be always at your back,*
> *May the sun shine warm upon your face,*

And the rains fall soft upon your fields,
And until we meet again, may God hold you
In the hollow of His hand.

Al was reciting the blessing to himself from memory when there was a knock on the cabin door and Gill stepped in.

"Didn't catch ya playing with yourself, did I?"

Al grinned. "Nah, nothin' there ta play with. So cold in the Cabot Strait it fell off."

Gill sat on one of the cabin beds, leaned and rested his chin on his fingertips. "We got a bit of a problem."

"Which is?"

"Routine Order Number 37."

Al shrugged. "Okay, Gillie. I give up. What the hell is Routine Order Number 37?"

"You have to be nineteen for overseas service."

Al nodded slowly. "Ross."

"Yup. And Goody Noseworthy."

"Goody?"

"He's only fifteen."

"What the hell! Billy said he was nineteen."

"Billy's full of shit."

"I thought Ross was all right. Faked a baptismal certificate or something."

"Somebody squealed. One of his sisters, I think."

"Who squealed on Noseworthy?"

"His old man."

"So whatawe do?"

"Whatever it is it's got to be fast, 'cause we sail in another two hours and if we don't figure out something PDQ they'll both be taken off the ship."

And that, to make a long story short, is how it came to pass that privates Ross and Noseworthy became stowaways on their own troopship.

Gill was told nothing of the scheme. For his own protection. Al got hold of Billy and Barney—Billy to find a place to squirrel the two youngsters away and Barney to do some creative paperwork with passable forged signatures showing that Routine Order Number 37 had been followed to the letter and the two minors had indeed been taken ashore to wait until they were old enough to cross the pond.

It wasn't all that hard to hide them on board. The *Empress* had a peacetime capacity of some 700 souls, but there were close to 4,000 soldiers on the ship along with a cargo of flour, fish, aircraft parts and thousands of mailbags, letters from home to the boys overseas as well as parcels containing cookies and chocolate bars and cigarettes, socks and sweaters and tins of salmon, canned peaches, pears, and vegetables.

The *Empress* sailed for Liverpool without escorts. No destroyers. No corvettes. None needed. The ship was too fast for the U-boats, a great comfort to Al, who was further reassured by the weather. For the first few days of the quick voyage the fog was pea soup thick, you could barely see your hand in front of your face, let alone a ship from a periscope.

Days were spent playing cards, shooting the breeze and exploring the crowded vessel—the grand staterooms, ballrooms, lounges and cafeterias, where they were served in shifts, two meals a day, mostly fish with a tomato sauce. They walked the swarming deck past Lewis guns in turrets looking like giant steel washtubs, and stood by the anti-aircraft guns at the stern trying to see the serpentine wake of the ship through the fog. They took turns helping to feed the multitudes by peeling potatoes and washing dishes; and faithfully turned out for the endless abandon ship drills announced by the ship's klaxon. *Arougah! Arougah!*

Nights were hard for Al. Since the *Caribou*, the hours after midnight had been a time of restless, tormented sleep. On the third night out after watching Deanna Durbin in *Three Smart Girls Grow Up* and listening to Lord Haw Haw tell the world the *Empress* had been torpedoed, all hands lost, he fell asleep in his cabin, the close air smelling of body odour and stale farts, the porthole closed and blacked out. But it wasn't long before he was awake, sweating, the echo of his moaning cries mingling with the muffled swearing of his bunkmates threatening him with bodily harm. He mumbled an apology to those he'd disturbed, reached for his lifebelt, stepped over the sleepers on the floor and sneaked up on deck for a breath of fresh air.

He was surprised to find that the fog had lifted and the night was day. They were obviously sailing a far north route to England on the ocean of the midnight sun.

On the morning of the fifth day, a day when, long ago, God had reportedly created the great creatures of the sea and every living and moving thing with which the water teems, the sun broke through the fog and two Sunderland flying boats from RAF Coastal Command out of the American Navy base in Londonderry took up position over the great creature of the *Empress of Scotland*.

On the same day, upon entering the Irish Sea in the early evening, the flying escorts were replaced by a destroyer, the USS *Nelson*. The Emerald Isle was visible off to starboard, and watching from the rail through the setting sun, Al felt a stirring in the blood, some atavistic feeling that raised goose pimples along his arms and brought the family story to mind—United Irishmen, Protestants, mostly Presbyterians, crossing the sea from Scotland with a passion for the radical politics of the French Revolution and the wild democracy of the new United States of America, a passion transfused with a raw emotion they shared with the Irish Catholics, a loathing for all things British. With their rebellion crushed and their leaders hanged, Great Grandfather McDougal fled to the countryside and turned to farming, an enterprise that was to fan the fires of his hatred because the principal crop of his small holding was potatoes.

The next day, just after midnight, the *Empress* edged into the Mersey estuary, anti-aircraft guns set on pilings far from shore. Then, pushed by tugs, she finally docked at dawn and the boys from the little league of nations saw a familiar sight—one they had come to recognize courtesy of *Movietone News*—a bomb-blitzed English city.

A band on the wharf was playing "O Canada" and stevedores along with workers repairing the damaged docks cheered and waved their caps as the "Caneyedians" disembarked—men and boys from the true North, strong and free, feeling like conquering heroes as they smartly shouldered their kit bags across a set of railway tracks to board the strange-looking train puffing in wait for them.

"Well, will ya look at this!"

Billy was shaking his head in wonder and bending over to inspect the spidery undercarriage of the passenger cars. "Looks like some sort of sewing machine to me."

"Nah, it's the bottom half of a baby carriage."

"And just about as wide."

"How do ya get on this thing?" Ross was asking.

Yates nodded at the passenger car closest to them. "Pick a door."

"Huh?"

"Look." Yates was pointing. "On English trains, each passenger car has several doors and each door opens to your own little compartment, Davey me boy."

"Lord liftin' Jesus, you're a smart man, Mr. Yates."

"Thank you, Mr. Assad. You're not too bad yourself. For a Caneyedian."

"Fuck you, Mr. Yates."

"And the same to you, Mr. Assad."

The railroads of the old country were not the same as the new, not the same as the T&NO, the CNR and the CPR, but they served the same purpose. They got you where you needed to go and for the Algonquins in England in June of 1943 that was Hayward's Heath, a small hamlet in Sussex, south of London.

But first they had to get through Liverpool and that was slow going, not much faster than a double-time march, past the bomb-damaged docks and surrounding area, tenements, four and five storeys high, perched on both sides of the track, washing hanging from balconies that were suddenly and magically crowded with people, men in their undershirts, women with babies in their arms, laughing children, all of them shouting and waving scarves and handkerchiefs and little Union Jacks. After the tenements it was people in the streets, mothers with prams, people in two-decker buses, men in trucks, women on bicycles with one hand on the handlebars and the other blowing kisses.

Once through the city, the train picked up speed, heading south very fast with a whistle like a high-pitched car horn to which the sheep dotting the green fields and hills paid no attention. Billy and Frank along with Reggie, Arnie and Goody Noseworthy took turns at the window watching the countryside go by. Join the army and see the world.

They had no idea where they were, station names had been blacked out to confuse the Germans when an invasion was thought to be imminent in the summer of 1940, and now in the summer of 1943 they were blacked out still. The train tracks stretched through villages with horse-drawn carts in lanes and Victory Gardens planted behind thatch-roofed homes, through industrial cities of dirty brick buildings still standing beside skeletons of other buildings ravaged by incendiary bombs. But mostly the scenery was field upon field of green as far as the eye could see broken only by hedgerows and, here and there, little stands of forest. Robin Hood and his merry men.

At one point Billy groaned. "You see what I see?"

They looked at him. "In those fields?" They looked at him again. "Sheep, goddammit. Sheep and more sheep. No cattle, no beef. No pigs, no pork. Just mutton. Mutton, mutton and more mutton. Guess what army meals in England are gonna be, boys. Just guess."

It wasn't long after that Billy had to eat his words when the train stopped on the outskirts of a village to be boarded by members of the British Home Guard with dinner, tubs of bully beef hash and pots of sweet tea. The hash was ladled into mess tins and the tea poured from big enamel pots with spouts. When the ladle came to Billy he shook his head in sorrow. If mutton was at the top of his shitty food list then bully beef was a close second.

Coming into London was much worse than anything they'd seen on *Movietone News*. The entire east end of the city was a skyline bereft of tall buildings, a landscape that could only be described as a junk yard, streets ploughed through and around piles of trash and rubble. The gang from Lowvert stood stock-still, silent at the train windows as if they had just happened upon a funeral procession, hushed and grieving relatives shuffling soundlessly behind the coffin.

The train station was relatively undamaged and its cavernous, high-ceilinged concourse reminded them of the Grand Hall of Toronto's Union Station. But there was little time to gawk as they were quickly and efficiently hustled from one train to another, and on their way again in minutes, arriving after midnight at their final destination in total darkness, no stars and the blackout so effective it was almost impossible to make out the ground beneath their feet.

Stumbling from the train, bumping into things and each other, cursing and swearing, they were loaded on lorries, headlights fitted with blackout shields. No beacons for the *Luftwaffe*.

The Algonquins, bleary-eyed after an eighteen-hour train ride, were on the trucks for about two hours before they reached their bivouac of Bell tents in a field, accommodations they embraced with the enthusiasm of the exhausted who don't give a damn where they sleep as long as there's something above their heads to keep off the rain.

When they awakened and stepped out from their tents in the morning sun they found themselves in a countryside of green fields, dew sparkling on the grass, stretching down a gentle slope toward a stand of trees. Behind them, across the road, stood a manor house of red clay tiles, roof and walls, chimney pots and dormers, a house they later learned was built in the sixteenth century when Elizabeth was queen of England. Now when George VI is king the house is home to the commanding officer of the Algonquin Regiment of Canada, his senior staff, and about a dozen cats, evidently different generations of the same pater and materfamilias for they are all, more or less, fluffy black with white around the nose and short socks of the same colour on their feet.

While the higher-ups were busy planning training exercises, "schemes" they were called, the men in the field below were getting spruced up to explore their new surroundings: cities, villages and other points of interest, pubs close by. They had forty-eight hours of disembarkation leave.

Al, along with Barney, Billy, Crow and W.B. Yates, determined to see as much as they can in the time available, smartly hop a two-decker bus and head first for Brighton, about twelve miles south on the Channel across from Dieppe. Before the war Brighton was a popular coastal resort, but now the famous Brighton Pier with its carousels and penny arcades is cordoned off and there are warning signs along the white sand beaches: "Keep Off! Mines!" Parts of the city, entire streets, are also badly damaged by German aircraft returning from inland raids and dumping leftover bombs before crossing the Channel to their home bases in France.

That night they stay at a bed and breakfast where they meet the son of their hosts, a British soldier by the name of Ancaster who takes them off to his local where he explains the intricacies of English money and German mines.

Ancaster is a pioneer or engineer from the army camp at Aldershot. A veteran of Dunkirk, he now instructs recruits on the forty different types of anti-tank and anti-personnel weapons employed by the enemy. He has a "Bouncing Betty" with him in the pub, and an audience, uniforms and civilians, including a good number of women the Canadians aren't used to seeing mixing with men in drinking establishments.

"Our Jerry calls this 'ere a *Schützenmine*. We call it a Bouncing Betty or daisy cutter. It's full of ball bearings, 350 of 'em. 'Ere's how it works."

Ancaster put the mine on the floor and asked Barney to step on it. When Barney's boot came down the device bounced up, about three feet. Barney yelled and jumped sideways and the Brits in the audience almost killed themselves laughing.

Al looked at his countrymen and exchanged "yeah-okay you-got-us" looks. It was obvious that Bouncing Betty at the Pub was a form of entertainment the locals had all seen before, probably every time Ancaster came along with a new bunch of fresh-faced, gullible Caneyedians.

When the laughter sputtered out Ancaster explained that when Betty bounced she exploded, spraying ball bearings in a vicious circle, cutting off daisies. And legs.

"That's how your brother got his blighty, Kathleen. At El Alamein."

A blighty was a war-ending wound, often highly prized if not too serious, and Ancaster's remark was directed at a woman on the edge of the group gathered around the table in the corner where the pioneer from Aldershot was holding court. Kathleen had shoulder-length hair, raven black, a glass of beer in one hand and a cigarette in the other.

"I'm sure he'd rather still have his leg, Andy."

She was squinting at Ancaster through the haze of her cigarette but Al could read the expression on her face. It was very clear. Andy Ancaster was a horse's arse.

"Aye, you're dead right there, Kathleen. And let's hope our friends from Canada here keep that in mind when they head over across the moat to chase Jerry back to Bocheland."

Ancaster turned back to the Algonquins. "Now lads, you will also want to watch out for this 'ere mine."

He showed them a small wooden box. "Clever bugger, our Jerry. This 'ere is almost impossible to find with our metal detectors. Just a small explosive in the box, not enough to kill and they plant 'em on the verges where the infantry are likely to go."

"Verges?" Billy's question.

"Shoulder of the road." Yates answered.

Ancaster nodded. "This one's designed to injure one man and tie up a couple of comrades helping him. This way Jerry gets three men out of action."

Al got to his feet to get another round of beer, counting on the barmaid to give him the correct change because he just couldn't get his mind around pounds, half-crowns, shillings and thrupenny bits, no matter how hard he listened to Ancaster's explanations.

When he returned with a loaded tray there was an argument in full swing among the uniforms as to what you were supposed to do if you stepped on a Bouncing Betty. One group argued that, if you kept your foot on it, Betty wouldn't bounce up, she would explode underground. You would lose a foot that way but a foot was better than a leg or your bollocks. The other side insisted you could get away without a scratch if, when you released your foot, you fast flopped to the ground, flattening yourself like a pancake. Then when Betty bounced, the ball bearings would spray above your head and you would be A-okay, shipshape and hunky dory.

The Canadians listened for a bit and then at a signal from Al swallowed the last of their beers and drifted toward the door. Kathleen was the only one who noticed them leaving. She smiled and wiggled fingers at them.

The next morning at breakfast they discussed where to go next, Barney and W.B. wanting to go up to London, with the rest of them, taken by the English countryside, voting to spend what little time they had left roaming East Sussex.

"Look, let's save London for when we get more time, when we have five or six days instead of one or two." Al's argument won the day.

So the five of them spent the next two days wandering the highways and byways, most of the time by bus but sometimes on foot, up hill and down dale, fascinated by the flora and fauna, strange to them, of southern England—the tall hornbeam and holly hedges, leafy chestnut trees and towering Sussex oaks that furnished the timber for Nelson's fleet—grouse and the ubiquitous rabbit, the funny-looking magpies and the English version of the Canadian crow, which they were told were rooks who lived in colonies called rookeries. Whatever they were called and wherever they hung out, Frank Archibald was still able to talk to them. Apparently rooks and crows spoke the same language, the former, according to Frank, with a bit of an English accent.

There were the ruins of the odd castle to explore and musty, ancient churches smelling of mouse droppings near quaint villages with privet hedges and rose gardens and the royal borough of Tunbridge Wells, a spa where upper-class Victorians had come for generations to take their ease.

On their way back from Tunbridge they found themselves just a stone's throw from Hayward's Heath in the village of Lindfield, where they meandered past a pond full of carp and then up the High Street to duck under a hanging sign featuring a harnessed Clydesdale and announcing the White Horse Publick House, just the thing for a tired and thirsty lot.

It was Yates's turn to buy and while they waited for him to return with their refreshments, Billy pulled out the English cigarettes he had purchased at their last port of call and offered them round.

"Are you kidding, Billy? Those Woodbines taste like shit. Here, have a Sweet Cap." Al shoved his package across to his friend who shook his head.

"When in Rome, do as the Romans do, eh, Billy?" Barney was grinning. "We drink English beer, we smoke English cigs. That the way it is?"

"Hey, they're not that bad. You should try Yates's chewing tobacco. Now that really does taste like shit."

Al was only half listening, looking around at the pub, low ceilings, axe-hewn beams, plaster walls, tables along the right wall where they were sitting, the bar on the other side and, and under his feet, a wood floor the colour of tar. Centuries of use.

When Yates came back with the beer he asked Barney about Ross and Goody Noseworthy. Barney sucked in air, blew it out and nodded.

"Ross is okay. Doesn't matter what his sister says. He's got that baptismal certificate. Phony or not it says he's nineteen as of last March."

"And Goody?"

"Could go either way. I've written to his father telling him I've got him assigned to Headquarters Company with me. Told him we were rear-end warriors, chairborne troops," he winked at Billy, "and there was no danger. No answer yet so we shall see what we shall see."

Frank wanted to know if the rest of them were as hungry as he was and when there was agreement he went off in search of food. A minute later he was back. "How 'bout eggs and chips?"

Barney took off his glasses and looked at Crow while Billy voiced the question they all had. "Eggs and what?"

"Eggs and chips. French fries."

"That all they got?"

"'Fraid so. Lady at the bar says there's a war on. In case we hadn't noticed. And says we're bloody lucky to get eggs."

When the food came Billy asked for catsup and was handed a bottle of Worcestershire sauce. He sighed and held it over his plate, seeking instructions.

"On the eggs, I would think," offered Yates.

"On the eggs it is."

Back at camp Al learned they were going to have the opportunity to revisit many of the places they had been in the last two days, entirely on foot this time, for the officers in the manor house had laid on some good, old-fashioned Camp Borden route marches, so that the iron in their blood wouldn't settle in their behinds.

The route marches were followed by mines and weapons training with the PIAT and Sten. Thanks to Andy Ancaster a certain few Algonquins were able to impress their comrades with informed comments about a certain few mines, informed comments that did not however extend to Projector, Infantry, Anti-Tank.

The American version of the PIAT was called a "bazooka." Both weapons were designed to serve as one-man tank destroyers, with the Canadian PIAT weighing in at thirty-two pounds and firing a $2^{1}/_{2}$-pound projectile capable of burning through a tank's armour to explode and spray shrapnel around inside. Splattered Jerry.

But the PIAT didn't live up to its billing. It was supposed to be effective at 100 yards, but if the training was any indication you would have to be a lot closer than that to be certain of hitting anything.

The Sten, first promised in Newfoundland, was more to their liking. It was uncomplicated and light—Al figured it didn't weigh much more than a six-pack of pop—had a range of about 200 yards and could be fired in automatic bursts or single shots.

First used by Canadians on the Dieppe raid it was about the only good news coming out of that fiasco. Those who managed to make it back in one piece praised the weapon's use of nine-mm ammunition, the same as Jerry's, which came in handy if you ran out of your own.

The Algonquins were just about finished with weapons training when news came of the Allied invasion of Sicily on July 10. Seven assault divisions, including the First Canadian under the command of Major-General Guy Simonds, landed on beaches south of Pachino. The Italians surrendered in droves and within a week Mussolini was driven from power.

With the invasion of Sicily some optimists in England were talking about the beginning of the end—if Italy was the back door to victory in Europe then it was only a matter of months before the Allies came knocking on the front door.

Al had an idea that Popovich was in the thick of things in Sicily. For some time there had been rumours floating around about a special unit, an international brigade, trained in the U.S. to be a spearhead force, and the Pole's letters had hinted he was involved, nothing specific to rile the censors, but enough to read between the lines.

Chapter Thirteen

JULY 21, 1943. Trafalgar Square. I am writing this sitting cross-legged at the foot of Nelson's monument just below the immortal words, "England expects every man will do his duty" and coming to understand why they call Trafalgar Square "Little Canada." Because every Canadian soldier in the country tends to congregate here. Looking up I can see them all around me. Just like the damn pigeons. Canada House is across the way, very nice, very comfortable, quiet reading room, leather couches where you can catch up on month old magazines from home and hear a readily understood version of the King's English. It will take us a bit of time, as it did in Nfld, before we won't have to say "pardon me, would you mind repeating that" every time someone here speaks to us. We (Billy, Yates and me) have been to Buckingham Palace (Buckhouse to the locals) and seen the bomb damage, checked out the Tower of London (closed for the duration), Westminster Abbey, St. Paul's Cathedral and the Houses of Parliament. Even spent an hour or two in Hyde Park listening to the ranters and ravers, including a mumbling monk, a screeching socialist and a woman extolling the mystic virtues of Rosicrucianism. The Cockney newsmen on the street corners are a pretty funny bunch. They all have blackboards at their stands and are forever chalking up little messages like "Startling News! Hitler Has Hives!" or "Goering Collapses Under Weight of Own Medals." Went down to Piccadilly Circus last night after blackout. Not a soul in the streets on the way but once there, crowds of people, laughing and shouting, having a ball. Wouldn't know there's a war on. Lots of prostitutes (the Yanks call them "Piccadilly Commandos") and they all carry little flashlights, flicking them off and on to advertise the presence of their wares. Yates insisted we have a meal at the Piccadilly Hotel where the menu was surprisingly varied. Billy's favourite of course but also roast loin of pork and apple sauce, something called "jugged hare" with red wine sauce, cold roast turkey with sausages and salad, stewed tripe with peas and onion sauce, and sweetbreads, which Billy was thinking of having for dessert until W. B. told him what they were.

Excerpt from Barney's Diary

Al hadn't gone up to London with them because he wanted to go off to be by himself in a quiet hamlet where he could stroll around, peer into shop windows and, if it struck his fancy, lie on his back on the village green and watch the world go by. He would find a room, sleep until noon, and then sit in a quiet pub with a beer and his book, *For Whom the Bell Tolls*.

He'd taken an instant liking to Lindfield during his first visit with the gang and had promised himself then that he would return because he saw the village as an oasis of tranquillity with its cottage homes and immaculately trimmed privet hedges sheltering green lawns, lime trees and flower gardens—roses, snapdragons, carnations.

Getting off the bus with small kit bag in hand, he wandered over to check the village pets, peering into the pond at the lazy carp, hardly moving, brown on the bottom and white on top as if bleached by the sun. The ducks, brands he'd never seen at home, kept an eye on him just in case he was the bearer of bread crumbs. After a bit he made his way up the hill on the High Street past the White Horse to another hostelry, a yellow brick building, on the wall a knight's shield with a lion resting on top and a motto lettered in a half-circle on the bottom of the shield. He had to shade his eyes to read the motto. *Nec Timere. Nec Timide.* He knew it was Latin but had no idea what it meant. He thought of *Ne-Kah-Ne-Tah.*

Turning he looked across at a stone church sitting framed on either side by clusters of Elizabethan houses. Once there was a break in the traffic, once the boy and the girl on the bicycle—the boy standing on the pedals and the girl on the seat, her arms around the boy's waist—and an old man pushing a cart of summer vegetables had passed in front of him, he crossed the street craning his neck at a church spire that reminded him of an inverted ice-cream cone clad in oak shingles.

Opening the gate to the churchyard he saw that that there was a low wall of grey stone just inside. Chipped in some places, leached in some places, the wall footings were covered with lichen. On the wall to the right of a weathered wooden bench with armrests and room enough for two was a chiselled inscription and a series of etched names. He bent to read. "Christ died for all men, these for their country."

These were men from All Saints' Parish, killed in the First World War. He counted. There were forty-five names. More than a few the same. Brothers. He shook his head.

Behind the memorial wall was the church graveyard, leafy trees shading leaning tombstones that to Al looked like rows of elderly veterans assembled for one last sick parade, barely able to stand by themselves.

Stepping carefully between the burial plots—he was once told it was bad luck to walk on a grave—Al stooped to try and read some of the dedications worn almost illegible by the passage of weather and time. He was struck by how young people were when they died of old age and by the number of children, mostly in the late nineteenth century, who hadn't made it past their third birthdays.

He sighed and went back to the bench by the wall, where he sat and dug in his kit bag for a chocolate bar. When he'd finished eating he rolled the bar wrapper in a ball and dropped it in his bag. Then he stretched out his feet, extended his arms along the back of the bench and closed his eyes hoping for forty winks devoid of bad dreams.

He didn't know how long he had slept, five minutes, ten minutes, half an hour, but when he opened his eyes there was a woman standing in front of him, smiling down at him. "Hello, Sergeant."

He squinted up at her with a questioning grin. She cocked her head, her smile widening.

"You don't remember me, do you, Sergeant?" She had a flowered scarf tied round her head and was dressed in a yellow summer frock, sensible brown walking shoes on her feet, and carrying a string bag of groceries.

Al sat up and scanned the woman's face, dark hair curling out from beneath the scarf, sparkling blue eyes set in an oval face, cupid's-bow lips. He had a feeling he'd seen those eyes before but he couldn't remember where or when. He stood up and took off his wedge cap. "Please sit down, Miss . . . ?"

"O'Halloran. Kathleen O'Halloran."

As she sat, Al stood straighter and snapped his fingers. It was the eyes and the name that made the connection for him. He smiled down at her.

"Ah, you wouldn't be, by any chance, the very same Kathleen from Brighton who thinks Bouncing Betty Ancaster is the cat's meow, now would you?"

Kathleen O'Halloran laughed. "I could think of a better description of Andy Ancaster, Sergeant. And I'm not from Brighton."

Al sat down on the bench beside her. "You're not?"

"No, I'm from here actually. From Lindfield. I was visiting my brother in Brighton."

"The one who . . ."

"Yes, the one who lost his leg at El Alamein."

They sat in silence staring at the afternoon sun slanting through the shade trees on the tombstones but seeing something else. Kathleen O'Halloran saw her brother in hospital grimacing with pain in a leg he no longer had, a nasty trick the nerve ends played on amputees, while Allan McDougal's flat eyes saw drowned women and children, caught in the rigging of an overturned lifeboat. Bulging eyes.

"It's very peaceful here, isn't it?"

Al shook himself and nodded.

More silence.

"You know, there's been a church here since the twelfth century. Not this building, of course," Kathleen inclined her head toward the spire, "but a building."

"Long time." A mumbled reply.

"Yes, Sergeant. A very long time." Kathleen took a deep breath and shifted the string bag from her lap to the seat beside her. She looked at him.

"Tell me, Sergeant, what are you doing here?"

"In the churchyard?"

She felt like saying, *No, on the planet Earth*, but instead she said, "Yes, in the churchyard. And in sleepy little Lindfield. Don't all you Canadian boys want to go up to London, see the sights and chat up the girls?"

Al, lost in his thoughts, didn't reply.

Kathleen sighed, stood with her string bag and turned to go. Al didn't look up, didn't move. It was as if Kathleen O'Halloran had suddenly ceased to exist.

She started to walk away but then her step faltered and she half turned to look back at the soldier on the bench. What she saw made her retrace her steps to sit beside him and reach out a hand, soft upon his face, turning his head toward her.

"You've seen it, haven't you."

He shook himself, his eyes wide, looking at her. "What?"

"You've seen it."

"Seen what?"

"Death. You've seen death."

Al drew a shuddering breath, blinked and blinked again, looking straight ahead. Then he nodded. Kathleen said nothing but took his hand and held it and they sat that way for a long time, both of them comfortable with the quiet and each other. They might have sat together until dark had not the church vicar come through the gate. An elderly man in a frayed, black cassock, he was balding with tufts of gray sprouting about his ears and he greeted Kathleen warmly.

"Ah, Kathleen. Thought that was your cycle out there."

Kathleen disengaged her hand from Al's and stood smiling. "Yes, Vicar. As usual."

The vicar was obviously waiting to be introduced to the soldier who now stood up beside Kathleen. The soldier, quickly sensing the difficulty, said, "McDougal, sir. Allan McDougal."

"You're an American, then." Only in England a little over a month Al had run into the assumption before. The English sometimes had trouble distinguishing an American accent from a Canadian.

"No, sir. Canadian. Algonquin Regiment."

The old man visibly brightened. "Ah, very good. Very good indeed." And he reached out to shake the Canadian's hand.

After he'd gone, Al turned to Kathleen. "I had the funny feeling that he wouldn't have shaken my hand if I'd been a Yank."

Kathleen chuckled. "Oh, he's like a lot of us."

They were walking together toward the churchyard gate. "You know the saying about the Americans, don't you?"

Al shook his head.

Kathleen posed as if she were delivering an important speech and with a dramatic declamatory gesture proclaimed, "The trouble with Americans is that they are overpaid, oversexed, and over here."

Al chuckled.

"Nice to hear you laugh, Sergeant."

He took a deep breath. "Oh, I'm pretty good at that, Miss O'Halloran." He lowered his eyes. "Most of the time, anyway." Then looking at her, "And by the way, now that you know my name, feel free to use it."

When they got to her bicycle leaning against a tree Kathleen asked him where he was staying and he shrugged. "Don't know. Thought I'd try one of the pubs. They have rooms, don't they?"

She turned to look at him, a hand raised to shade her blue eyes from the sun and said quietly, "You could stay with us."

"Us?"

"Yes. My father lives up the street. He'd be glad of some company. And we have plenty of room."

Al shook his head. "I wouldn't want to put you out."

"Nonsense."

"Well . . ."

"Good, it's settled then. Come along."

Al didn't move. He'd come away to get away, to be alone and, as much as part of him was attracted to the idea of a home away from home if even for a few days, another part of him didn't want the bother of having to make conversation with another human being.

Kathleen, sensing his hesitation, turned from the handlebars of her bicycle, and read his mind. Again.

"Look," she was smiling at him, "I know you probably came here by yourself on purpose. You want to be like one of those carp in the village pond content with floating on the surface all by yourself in the weeds for a few days and now you have this pushy woman, a right harpy, telling you to flip your fish tail and get moving. Have I got that right?"

Al smiled. Then he laughed. "How about—"

She interrupted. "How about you come along for tea and get a sense of the lay of the land. Then if you want to stay you will be welcome. If, on the other hand, you want to go to some tick-infested pub and sleep on some smelly, lumpy mattress and eat their rancid food and have them give you the cold shoulder because they think you're a Yank and steal your money because you don't know the difference between a penny and a pound and—"

This time it was Al who broke in. "Okay, okay. I give up." He laced his fingers behind his head in a gesture of surrender. "I am your prisoner, Hauptmann O'Halloran. I am *kaputt.*"

The house was on the far side of the pond, a front lawn sloping up from the water, a cobblestone path lined with rose bushes up to a front door recessed into a whitewashed entrance, outside drain pipes and leaded windows on either side. Looking up, Al could see three dormers with the same leaded windows, a steep wood-shingled roof with chimneys on either end.

Inside the house it looked like the Women's Auxiliary were using the front room as a storage depot for the used book table at the next All Saints' Church fete. Books were everywhere, piled on sofas and chairs, on the fireplace lintel, on the floor, and stuffed higgledy-piggledy into bookcases.

"Da," Kathleen said, "this is Sergeant Allan McDougal from Canada. Picked me up in the churchyard. Insisted I bring him home with me. Sergeant, this is my father, Patrick O'Halloran from County Clare." She pronounced "Patrick" in the Irish way. Pawd-rig.

If the W.A. had a table at the fete for rumpled old men, the man from county Clare who stood to greet the sergeant from Canada would have been there, reasonably priced for a quick sale. He had a full head of hair, snow-white and wavy, and was wearing a ratty holed sweater over a wrinkled shirt, frayed at the collar and cuffs, baggy pants and scuffed slippers, with a pipe stuck upside down in his mouth. But then there were his eyes, sparkling blue and impish like his daughter's, eyes that once he'd removed his pipe were joined with a grin as wide as the ocean. Al took to him instantly.

"Ah Sergeant, it's all right. I don't believe a word this child of mine says. Kissed the Blarney Stone too many times, she has. Welcome to ye and sit ye down."

There was nowhere to sit unless he sat on some books, and Kathleen's father, realizing Al's predicament, moved to clear a space.

"'Ere, let me move Charles for ye."

"Dickens," said Kathleen moving to help her Da. "This is Charles Dickens's chair." She mimicked her father as she gathered up books. "'Ere's *Oliver Twist*. And 'ere's *David Copperfield*. And 'ere's *Great Expectations*."

"And 'ere's the back of me hand if ye don't git yourself off into the kitchen and fetch us some tea." The grin was even wider.

"Kathleen laughed. "You see, Sergeant—"

Al looked at her.

She started again. "You see, Allan, where I get my bossy nature."

She wiggled her fingers at him and stuck her tongue out at her father as she retreated from the room. Her father fondly watched her go and then sat beside the fireplace across from Al and began stuffing his pipe with tobacco. Once done, he struck a wooden match on the fireplace stone and lit his pipe. Then he puffed. Then he looked at his guest.

"You are the spitting image of my son, Sergeant."

Al looked up. "Your son who—"

"—lost his leg at El Alamein. Yes. But he lost more than that, Sergeant. Shell shock. He's lost his mind. Doesn't recognize his sister. Nor me."

"I'm sorry, sir."

"Ah, don't be sorry, Sergeant. He's alive and he'll come home to us one of these fine days, the Lord willing."

He shifted in his chair. "You know in the First War he would have been shot? That's what they did to shell-shocked lads in those days."

"I didn't know that."

The old man grunted. "Oh, yes. Said they were cowards, you see. Blindfolded them, put them up against a wall and shot them. Their own comrades shot them. Ordered to do it, mind you."

Al looked away and said nothing. Patrick O'Halloran studied the soldier across from him, sighed and laid aside his pipe. He spoke quietly "You've had a bit of a shock, haven't you, son."

Startled, Al looked at the man in wonderment and shook his head. "Is everyone in your family a mind reader?"

O'Halloran laughed. "Some of us. And some of us, some of the women, have the gift of second sight."

"Kathleen?"

This time it was O'Halloran who didn't answer. Instead he heaved himself out of his chair, shuffled over to the bookcase behind Al and stood there, finger to his lips, thinking. Then he reached up, pulled out a book, blew dust off the cover and returned to his seat.

"Stories of the Irish people from Cuchulain to the Easter Rebellion." He held up the book. "Full of people who could read minds and tell the future, Sergeant McDougal."

Then he looked squarely at Al. "These are stories a man with the name of McDougal should know. Being that you're Ulster Irish yourself." There was a twinkle in the old man's Irish eyes.

Al didn't want to ask how O'Halloran knew the McDougal family history. Instead he just grinned, "Tell me some stories, Mr. O'Halloran."

"Not until we've had our tea." It was Kathleen, coming from the kitchen announcing the table had been set. Al got up and followed father and daughter into the dining room, where he stopped dead when he saw that what the O'Hallorans called tea, the McDougals called supper.

He had been expecting a cuppa and a cookie but what he got was a feast, beginning with tinned peaches topped with whipped evaporated milk and then a main course of cold roast chicken, slices of smoked ham, hard-boiled eggs, lettuce and tomatoes, thick-cut brown bread with butter, and tipsy cake for dessert.

He thought it was one of the best meals he had ever had anywhere, let alone in England on wartime rationing. He had no idea where or how Kathleen had managed to find it all—perhaps like his mother she knew people who knew people—and he had no idea whether or not this was standard fare in the O'Halloran home and he wasn't about to be impolite and ask. He was content to feast, and his evident enthusiasm in devouring the food on his plate prompted an observation.

"And you, silly boy, were going to eat in one of our local establishments."

Kathleen's father joined in. "And he seems such an intelligent lad, daughter. It is hard to imagine how he could think such a meal could be found in one of our local establishments."

"Indeed."

Al raised his teacup. "A toast to the cook."

"Not in this house ye don't."

Al looked confused. "I'm sorry. I . . ."

"He means the O'Hallorans from County Clare don't toast with tea," said Kathleen. "If you'll hang on a minute I'll get the whisky."

"Aye and we'll have a proper toast to the cook. And a few other people as well."

And so they did. They raised a glass to Ireland and to Canada. They toasted ancestors, McDougal and O'Halloran. Patrick toasted his son Ned in Brighton, and Kathleen toasted her mother in heaven, and Al toasted Hermanson and the Cahills of Newfoundland, Captain Tavernor and Charlie Hann, Captain Cuthbert, and the crew of *Grandmere*.

And then they raised their glasses to all the boys in uniform, even the overpaid and oversexed Americans. And after the toasts, they sang songs. And after they sang songs Patrick O'Halloran told stories of Irish heroes and English villains.

The next few days went by in a blur, the nights spent listening to Patrick's Irish tales and then sleeping like a baby, the days with Kathleen on a bicycle built for two riding the narrow country roads from early morning to late afternoon, picnicking beside brooks where they fed bread crumbs to the water fowl and then, stretching out on a blanket, listening in the quiet to the birds, naming the shifting shapes of the clouds in the sky and the aircraft that flew through them, bombers bound for Germany, American Flying Fortresses with escorts of RAF Spitfire fighters.

All too soon Al's leave was over and it was time to return to camp. But camp wasn't far away, in England nothing was far away, and he was made to swear a solemn oath by the great Irish warrior of pagan times, the son of the Sun God, Lugh, the legendary Cuchulain, that he would return by the next weekend, if not before, don't-bother-calling-just-show-up-at-the-door-potluck-on-the-table.

It wasn't an oath that was hard for him to take. But it turned out to be an oath he could not keep because no sooner was he back in camp than the regiment was packing up for their first big scheme in England.

Training to date had been largely on their own but now that the Allies were in Sicily on their way to Italy it was time to train for the Big Show and the Big Show, the invasion of France, would involve fighting with other regiments at brigade strength and brigades at division strength, thousands and thousands of men. For this they would have to know how to fight with tanks and with artillery, and how to fight as one unit among many, each with a specific role. And the invasion was coming, some said it would be as soon as Christmas, catch Jerry singing *Stille Nacht,* so they had to learn large-scale operations quickly.

Their first lesson was with the arty boys, finding out how to advance under a barrage. It was raining and they were somewhere near the Channel in an isolated part of East Sussex where there was no danger shellfire would be hitting anything human, Billy hoping for some sheep.

An officer with the Fifteenth Field Regiment of the Royal Canadian Artillery was explaining how it was done, Al and Yates listening as they huddled together under a poncho along with Billy, Reggie and Davey Ross. Frank Archibald had been sent off the day before to Aldershot to take sniper training. Gillie hadn't forgotten what Crow had done to the bull's eyes on the rifle range at the foot of Mount McKay.

While the officer was talking, Billy was whispering to Al about all the fun he'd missed in London, telling him lies about how much beer they'd drunk and how all three of them, but especially Barney, had been mobbed by the Piccadilly commandos.

"They wanted ta pay Barney! Pay him to take 'em down an alley and put it to 'em up against the wall! Can ya believe that, Al? Can't ya just see him humpin' away, glasses fallin' down his nose?"

Billy was nudging Yates in the ribs and Yates was shaking with silent laughter. Al wanted desperately to laugh along with them but, conscious of his responsibilities, affected a we-are-not-amused tone of voice.

"Will you guys shut the fuck up and listen. Ya might learn something. Might save your life someday." He spat on the ground to cover the grin on his face.

"Let me repeat, gentlemen," the officer's voice drifted over, "because I can see that some of you are plainly sceptical. There is no danger here. The Fifteenth Field has done this kind of shoot many times. You have nothing to worry about."

But there was plenty to worry about as far as the Algonquins were concerned. Live shells from twenty-five-pounder guns were to be fired over their heads as they advanced on the double in the rain and in the muck to take advantage of an enemy "stunned and demoralized" by the artillery.

There is supposed to be a 300-yard gap between shells exploding and infantry advancing, but then as somebody said, the camel was supposed to be a horse only something went badly wrong on the assembly line.

What if—in the confusion of noise, the crumping sound of shells being fired, the sizzling crackle of shells overhead and the flashing concussions of shells hitting the ground and exploding—what if, in all this, the gap narrows and lads get too close?

Or what if rounds fall short? It has been known to happen. The guns are miles behind the advancing infantry and one tiny mistake in calibrations, one wrong turn of a dial and a shell that is supposed to land in the middle of the foe lands in the middle of friends. Friendly fire.

And even if there are no mistakes, guns heat up and with the heat there is less compression behind the shell and with less compression the shell falls short. The PBI.

This is what they talk about waiting at the start line for the "creeping barrage" to begin, shifting from one foot to another, cupping a last cigarette from the wet, adjusting the straps on their tin hats. Restless.

With the first crump of arty rounds echoing behind them the whistle blows and they begin a slow run to their objective, the top of a rise in the distance, hard to see in the rain, driving now.

Suddenly there is a monstrous roar of orange and black flashes erupting just ahead and the ground quakes beneath their running feet. The soldiers in the first wave hesitate, instinct telling them if they keep going they will run right into the barrage. But officers urge them on toward the rolling thunder of exploding shells until it seems that one more step and they will be in the middle of hell.

But then another piercing whistle and down they go, flat on their bellies, in the grass and mud, hands over their ears, waiting for the barrage to lift and move on and when it does they do too, vaulting gashes in the ground still smoking from the shells that made them, following the advancing thunder, down on their bellies, up on their feet, on and on up the hill until, chests heaving, they reach their objective.

Rumour has it they will have to do it again in the afternoon, but after sitting around for hours waiting, they are ordered back to their temporary camp, tents pitched about a mile away on the grounds of some estate, a baronial mansion below a crumbling castle up on a hill. They are exhausted, hungry and filthy dirty but feel better after a wash-up, dry clothes, and a hot meal brought up on trucks, even if it is mutton stew.

After supper the sun came out and Al wrote his first letters home since leaving Canada for England, telling his father about the voyage to Liverpool, Patrick O'Halloran's Irish stories and the fun of a creeping barrage. Then he got going on the food, mostly quoting Billy on the subject: "Mutton! Mutton! Mutton! Who has got the Mutton? Yes, quite decidedly we have got the Mutton. For breakfast we have a ground-up mixture of 90% bread, 8% water, 1% Mutton and 1% saltpeter squeezed into some sheep guts and labelled sausage. For dinner we have roast Mutton and sheep's gravy. For supper, Scotch broth and shepherd's pie both made from a sheep long since dead. If you are fortunate enough to get any pastry then it too is made of Mutton fat instead of lard and even the potatoes are fried in Mutton grease. As Billy keeps saying, army food over here is really baaaaad."

He wrote to his mother about the beauty of the English countryside and what Billy and Barney had told him of their visit to London.

He wrote to his wife and told her about the food, about the English countryside, and London, about Patrick O'Halloran and a few passing comments about his daughter Kathleen, nothing more, because he didn't want to worry his wife, who had no doubt heard more than a few stories of overseas romances and that wasn't what he and Kathleen were all about. He thanked Beth for the pictures of their son. "Yes I got the snaps and they were all very good but I too liked the one in the sand pile best and have it in my wallet. Young Sandy is getting better looking every day and soon will be as handsome as his father."

The next day the word came down that the Algonquins were now part of the 10th Canadian Infantry Brigade of the 4th Canadian Armoured Division. The brigade was comprised of themselves along with the Lincoln and Welland Regiment, the Argyll and Sutherland Highlanders of Canada, the tanks of the South Alberta Regiment and the artillery of the 15th Field.

This news was quickly followed by orders to get ready to move, north this time to Norfolk, for manoeuvres on a divisional level. Most of the troops went by train to King's Lynn, but the Carrier Platoon went by road along with the regiment's trucks and Jeeps, the guns of the 15th Field towed by lorries, followed by the South Alberta tanks.

Getting to their destination was itself a training manoeuvre, a time and endurance test to see how well they could do, moving a great distance with all their vehicles, weapons and gear on unfamiliar roads that snaked their way through a foreign land, foreign in more ways than one.

First, the secondary roads, typical of England, and Northern Ontario, for that matter, were winding and narrow, built to follow cow paths. The difference here in the old country was whole stretches of road bounded on both sides by hedgerows, so that in places it was like driving through an open-air tunnel.

Then, there were no signs—neither direction nor location—for the same reason railway station signs were blacked out. No point in telling invading Germans how to get where they needed to go.

Finally, to make matters more difficult for a Canadian, one had to drive on the left and keep a sharp eye out for oncoming traffic when one came up to the brow of a hill or were halfway through a blind curve and there was no room to pass, and right in front of you a flock of sheep was being herded from one field to another. Billy drove his carrier with his eyes on the road, a prayer on his lips and his heart in his mouth.

At Thetford, on the morning of the third travel day, they stopped by the ruins of Holy Sepulchre Priory to wait for stragglers, the hopelessly lost and the mechanically maimed. Al lit a cigarette and wandered off to look, stepping around the curious little mounds of dirt on the close-cropped lawn leading up to the ruins, piles of loose stone and falling down walls covered in ivy.

"Moles."

"Huh?"

"Moles." It was Yates coming up beside him. "The little piles of dirt? Dug up by moles. You know. Like the gophers at Shilo."

"Jesus, I'm getting tired of people reading my mind."

"Huh?"

"Never mind."

"So you happy with the arty exercise?"

Al shrugged. "Guess so. What do you hear?"

Yates took on a conspiratorial air and leaned closer to his sergeant. "Agent Yates hears the brass are pretty happy. They're thinking not bad for the first go-round. But the word is we'll have to do it a few more times until it gets to be second nature to us. You know, like goin' for a crap."

Al grinned. "I think a few of the lads went for a crap in their pants when those first rounds came in." He shook his head. "What a helluva noise."

Yates thought for a moment. "Know what I think, Sarg?"

Al flicked his cigarette, but to his feet and ground it into the dirt. Then he turned to Yates with a smile. "What do you think, Private?"

"I think war is primarily an aural experience."

"Know what I think, Willy?"

"What?"

"I think you should be having this conversation with Barney. He might understand what the hell you're talking about."

"Oh yeah, I forgot. You're just poor white trash from New Ontario, the backwoods and the mine. Don't know nothin' 'bout them there big words."

Al snickered. "Yup, just like you, Yates. Good old boy from the Boston States. Playin' softball. Chewin' tobacco. Don't know nuthin' neither."

Now it was the American's turn to chortle. When he spoke it was with the deep voice of a radio announcer: "The Shadow, Lamont Cranston—a man of wealth, a student of science, and a master of other peoples' minds—devotes his life to righting wrongs, protecting the innocent and punishing the guilty. Cranston is known to the underworld as the Shadow—never seen, only heard, his true identity known only to his constant friend and companion, Margot Lane."

Al smiled, remembering his radio nights convalescing in Lowvert. "Margot Lane. Yeah." Nodding his head. "Margot. That the name of your blonde in Boston? She an aural experience?"

"Yeah, as a matter of fact." Yates mimicked the sounds of a woman in orgasm before turning serious.

"But the sounds of war, Al. Think about it. It's all sounds. The sound of the marching bands when off you go to fight for king and country, the sounds of the trains, the sounds of basic training, that first rifle shot on the range, that first live grenade exploding. The sound of a Bren, a carrier going full throttle, artillery, a ship's klaxon, an air-raid siren, those tanks behind us in the convoy."

Just then Ross wandered over with a furry little black and white ball in his arms. Al looked at the furry ball, then at Ross. "A cat, Ross?"

Ross looked at Yates who looked at Al. "You didn't know?"

Al's expression said no.

Yates explained. "It's one of the cats from Regimental HQ at the Heath. Our new mascot. Name is Max. Maximillian Algonquin of the RCFF, the Royal Canadian Fur Force."

Max cast a wary look at Al and with the help of Ross delivered a paw salute.

Al walked over and scratched behind the cat's ears. Then he straightened and shook his head. "Okay, Ross. But be careful. There's probably some army regulation somewhere, Regulation 1234567$\frac{1}{2}$, that says fraternizing with cats is forbidden."

"Oh, there is such a regulation, Sergeant." Yates was nodding his head vigorously and Al was staring at him quizzically. "Saw it just the other day when I was boning up on the rules. It's Regulation 1234567$\frac{3}{4}$ actually and it says that it is forbidden to fraternize with felines *and* fräuleins."

"Thank you kindly, Private Yates, for that information. I presume that's one of them there aural regulations."

"Absolutely, Sergeant, absolutely."

Chapter Fourteen

NOVEMBER 5, 1943. Thetford Training area. This is the day the Brits celebrate the discovery of a plot—1605 it was—to blow up the King and Parliament. Tradition being a big thing in this country there's to be a party tonight to celebrate at the Golden Lion up the road in Hunstanton. It's called Guy Fawkes Night and the publican who has family in Toronto has issued us a special invitation. After about two months of schemes it's about time we had some fun. First there was TAKEX I, a simulated withdrawal movement in the fenlands with the South Alberta tanks. Next it was TAKEX II, more infantry/artillery stuff with Charlie Co. acting as the enemy, all decked out in German uniforms, Creepy Cram complete with a Hitler moustache. After that it was OBSEX, a joint exercise with the Lincs & Winks, and the Ashcans, the Argyll and Sutherland Highlanders. OBSEX was followed by GRIZZLY, a scheme to practise frontal assaults on a firmed-up enemy position across the River Wensum. And now we've just finished BRIDOON, a tactical advance pitting the 4th Canadian Armoured Division against "enemy attacks" led by the 9th British Armoured Division. There seems to a difference of opinion as to the worth of these schemes. Officers and higher ups think they're grand because they get to play God and run things, ordering units here and there, moving them around like checkers on a great big board. The Signal Platoon gets to play with their radios and figure out the communication bugs that come with any large operation so they're as happy as the proverbial pig in the proverbial stuff. But the ranks by and large think the schemes are pretty useless and boring as all get out because most of the time no one, below the rank of lieutenant, has the faintest idea what is going on. And then there's all that time spent standing around waiting for something to happen. Add that to the weather—rain, fog and cold, and it all makes for a lot of grumbling. Anyway tonight we'll have a few beers and convince ourselves it was all worthwhile.

Excerpt from Barney's Diary

A hotel built with reddish-brown stones, the Golden Lion faced the Hunstanton village green, the ocean—the Wash—only a hop, skip and a jump away down a gentle slope dropping off sharply in a jumble of more stones, the same colour as the Lion.

Al and Barney, fresh from a stroll to the end of Hunstanton Pier, were late arrivals and when they stuck their heads into the Sandringham Pub at the Lion it was wall-to-wall people wreathed in cigarette smoke. It took them some time to find what corner of the establishment the gang had commandeered, with Al finally pointing through the haze to an effigy of Guy Fawkes hanging from a ceiling beam, a straw-stuffed leg dangling over the head of W.B. Yates, who was leaning over talking to a woman whose back was toward the new arrivals.

When they neared the table Yates saw them and stood up, arms waving enthusiastically. "Boys, boys, come over here and meet Maud Gonne."

Al heard the woman laugh and had barely registered its familiarity when Maud Gonne stood, turned round, and extended her hand. "Hello, Sergeant."

It was Kathleen O'Halloran.

Yates first looked at the expression on Al's face, then at Kathleen's. "Hey, you two know each other?"

Al was too stupefied to say anything. It was Kathleen who replied, blue eyes dancing. "Oh yes, we go back a long ways, your sergeant and I."

"You do?" Yates couldn't keep the astonishment from his voice.

"Ah yes indeed, Mr. William Butler Yates. We met in a previous life when I really was Maud Gonne and Sergeant McDougal here was my lover and we were both active in the Irish Order of Mysteries."

Catching on, Yates nodded with a grin. Then, affecting an understanding but questioning tone, said, "But I thought Lucien Millevoye was your lover, Maud?"

To which Kathleen replied, "Ah, but that's what I wanted people to think, Mr. Yates. I wanted them to think Lucien was my lover, far away in France so I would be free to pursue my passion for Sergeant McDougal in Ireland. His name was Joseph Mary Plunkett then." Over to you, Yates.

"Plunkett." Yates was frowning. "Joe Plunkett." He nodded his head slowly, then sharply.

"Shot by the Brits for his part in the Rising. Stonebreakers' Yard. May 4, 1916."

"*Very* good, Mr. Yates," said Kathleen laughing and fluttering her eyelids at the American. "And to think what we say about you Yanks 'ere in our England, this 'sweet and blessed country, the home of God's elect.' "

Al felt that he'd just been parachuted into the middle of a sectarian conversation in which the initiates spoke a language only they understood. As he looked around the table at the others, he saw he wasn't the only one thinking this way.

Barney brought them all back to reality by introducing himself to Kathleen, and Al fell all over himself apologizing for neglecting his friend. Then, while the rest of the Algonquins at the table welcomed Barney to their spirited discussion about the value of schemes, Al drew up a chair and sat between Kathleen and Yates, looking from one to the other.

"Okay, you two. Time to report in. And if you can bring yourselves to do so, speak in English."

Kathleen put on her best yes-daddy-face and told him she was visiting an aunt in Hunstanton and had come in for a pint to mourn Guy Fawkes and his failure to blow up the king, when lo and behold she saw a few familiar faces from Brighton.

"Fine," said Al, not believing a word of it. "So far so good, but who's Maud Gonne and Lucien what's-his-name?"

Yates picked up the tale. "Maud Gonne was William Butler Yeats's girlfriend. You know, the Irish writer."

"The one you're sorta named after."

"Yeah, sort of."

"And the guy?"

"He really was Maud's lover."

"So let me get this straight, Willy. Your namesake was Maud's boyfriend but Lucien whatever was her lover?"

"Yeah, well, it was of them there Irish things, Al." Yates grinned. "In the army we'd probably call it a snafu."

Al nodded. "And Kathleen as Maud?"

"Oh boy! Maud Gonne was a looker, Al. A real beauty. Like Helen of Troy, 'a face that launched a thousand ships/ And burnt the topless towers of Ilium.' And eyes! Eyes 'as stars of twilight fair.' Like Miss O'Halloran here."

"And that's why he's been calling me Maud Gonne all evening."

Kathleen sat up a little straighter, tilting her head, her nose in the air and winked at Al, who was sitting there trying to sort fact from fiction, poetry from prose and, if need be, Kathleen from Willy.

"All right, my turn," said Yates. "How come you two know each other. And none of this blarney about a previous life, Maudie old girl."

"Well, we did meet among those who have gone to a better life," said Kathleen.

"What she means, Willy, is that we met in the cemetery at the church in Lindfield."

And Al told him the story. In very general terms. When he finished, Yates slapped him on the back, stood and delivered a mock-formal bow to Kathleen, and excused himself saying there were some RAF buddies of his around somewhere and that he'd promised he would let them buy him a pint or two. Al didn't believe a word of that, either. Yates was ceding Maud Gonne to Joe Plunkett.

Once the American had left the table Al smiled at Kathleen. "Ever been to the end of Hunstanton Pier?"

She shook her head and smiled back.

"Aunt never took you?"

She shook her head again. Wider smile this time.

Outside and bundled up against the night they picked their way down to the pier in the moonlight. Kathleen took his arm and snuggled close looking up at the sky. "Good clear night for the *Luftwaffe*."

"They don't come up this far, do they?"

"Not any more. My aunt says—"

"Kathleen O'Halloran. You don't have an aunt."

"I most certainly do, Sergeant McDougal!" Then she giggled. "It's just that I don't have one in Hunstanton."

"So what are you doing here?"

"Pawd-rig sent me up. To see how you were."

"How did you know where we were?"

"Lord Haw Haw?"

Al gave up and they walked on in silence, the only sound the ocean slapping the pier, the waves heading in to break on the shore of reddish-brown stones. It was Kathleen who spoke first, a different subject, a safer subject.

"Your Private Yates is an interesting man."

"Aye, lass. That he is," replied Al affecting a local accent.

Kathleen ignored him. "He's very well educated."

"Yeah, but with us he pretends he isn't. Obviously not with you, though."

"Oh, I don't think he was trying to impress me, if that's what you mean. I think he was delighted to find someone who had a mind for his game and could return his volleys."

"His game?"

"His knowledge. He seems to know a fair bit of Irish history and is well versed in . . . well, English verse."

Kathleen had her head down, thinking out loud. "Tonight he was quoting Marlowe, I think, and certainly Wordsworth. And he's a student of Yeats in particular."

She stopped and turned to look at Al. "William Butler Yates of Boston, America, knows a lot about William Butler Yeats of Sligo, Ireland."

They were at the end of the pier now and Al asked her if she was cold. She wasn't but she said she was and got what she wanted. His arm around her. They stood like that for a bit, awkwardly, hip to hip, looking down at the dark water, both of them on the edge of something.

Finally Kathleen turned and nestled herself against him. At first he just stood there frozen, then he took a deep breath and wrapped her even closer. When she looked up at him he kissed her, tentatively at first and then harder.

After a moment Kathleen pulled back, searching his face. "I've wanted you to do that for a long time, Allan McDougal."

Al exhaled. "Guess I've wanted to do it for a long time."

"You weren't sure?"

"Not till now."

"You're married, aren't you."

In all the time they'd spent together this was a question she had never asked and even now it wasn't a query, it was a statement. Another of her mind reads.

"Yes."

And he told her about his wife and son as they retraced their steps to the Golden Lion. When they got to the entrance door she reached out and took his hand, leading him up the stairs to her room. As they undressed shyly, their backs to each other on opposite sides of the bed, Al could hear the celebrations in the pub below, soldiers shouting, a piano being played. Yates?

Kathleen was already under the covers when Al turned around. He smiled at her and then stood to pull the cord to switch off the room's only light, a bare bulb hanging from the ceiling.

"Don't," she said. "I want to be able to see you."

He turned and leaned his arms on the foot of the mattress and started to crawl up to her, pulling the covers from her as he moved, first her shoulders, skin ivory-white, then down and over her small but perfect breasts, her belly, the dark of her pubic hair. As he came up beside her and turned, Kathleen kicked the covers off her legs and rolled to meet him and before he knew it he was hard inside her and she was thrusting beside him and then over on top of him, breathing hard, pumping faster and faster, her long hair flying, moaning, crying out and then shuddering.

Catching her breath she leaned over, kissed him and told him it was his turn. This time she was slower, deliciously slower until his back began to arch and then she moved on him faster, until he yelled as he jerked and jerked again and again until he was spent.

Kathleen stayed where she was, breathing hard and looking down at him, a mischievous smile on her face. "In England we call this a leg-over."

"I can see why," he said glancing at her bare legs astride him. "Two legs over."

"Was I too bold?"

He shook his head. "I didn't know it before but I like bold."

"Do you like me?"

Al smiling nodded.

"Say it then." Blue eyes laughing.

He looked up at her with a huge grin. "I, Allan George McDougal, Sergeant, Algonquin Regiment, B55379 do hereby swear that I like you Kathleen—" he paused until she filled in with "Máire," and continued, "—that I like you, Kathleen Máire O'Halloran."

Just before midnight he dressed and kissed Kathleen good-bye, telling her the regiment was moving back down to Sussex right after the next scheme and he would see her and Pawd-rig at Christmas.

Downstairs the party was still in full swing and he had the devil of a time rounding up the gang for the long ride home. Billy was dressed as Guy Fawkes and Fawkes as a private in the Algonquin Regiment. Yates had Reggie and Arnie along with a crowd of locals gathered round the piano and a young woman, a laughing blonde, was almost in his lap. Barney, pushing up his glasses, was deep in conversation with an older man dressed in tweeds and Ross was asleep in a far corner.

There was no sign of Dougie Dobson, who didn't show up until the last moment, rushing out from the cobblestone alley between the hotel and the borough hall pulling one of the local beauties behind him who in turn was trying to pull down her coat and dress high up her hips. At the Jeep he kissed the woman—hoots and hollers from his mates—and jumped in the back just as Billy gunned the motor and they fishtailed down the hill to the highway out of town.

Their last scheme in Norfolk was a go-round with the South Alberta Tanks, a Brigade exercise based on enemy battle tactics learned at the School of Hard Knocks in France and North Africa.

Jerry would often give up ground without too much of a fight and then, just when you thought he was well on the run, would counterattack in force. So the plan was for the Ash Cans and the Lincs and Winks, along with A and C Squadrons of the South Alberta tanks, to play the role of a counterattacking enemy while the Algonquins with B Squadron backed by the 15th Field Artillery would be the good guys defending hard-earned territory.

The Albertans had the newest tank off the assembly lines, the American-made Sherman, named after William Tecumseh Sherman, a general of the Union Army in the American Civil War, a man famous, or infamous, depending on your point of view, for the torching of Georgia in 1864, the only thing left standing being blackened chimneys, a.k.a. Sherman monuments. *"Hurrah! Hurrah! We bring the Jubilee!/ Hurrah! Hurrah! The flag that makes you free!/ So we sang the chorus from Atlanta to the sea,/ As we were marching through Georgia."*

As soon as the 10th Infantry Brigade had been formed Al had been in and out of the South Alberta tanks, a space not much larger than a four-passenger automobile, housing a crew of five, a crew commander, a gunner, a loader operator, a driver and a co-driver. Every time he lowered himself down through the commander's hatch, Al was reminded of the limerick Yates had taught him. *There was a young man from Boston/ Who had a baby Austin/ There was room for his ass and a gallon of gas/ But his balls hung out and he lost them.*

A friendly rivalry livened the relationship between tank crews and the PBI. Tankers looked down on the infantry literally and pretended to do so figuratively, razzing the men in full pack, the flat footers plodding along beside them on the schemes, carrying their weapons, heavier with each weary mile. The tankers rode in their weapon, sheltered from the elements and enemy fire, no blisters on their feet, no shin splints from double timing in rapid deployment.

But there was little envy among the flat feet for the knights in shining armour because the infantry knew what the knights also knew but wouldn't let on. Tanks were dangerous. Five men inside a ten-foot-high, slow-moving tin can were an inviting target. If the Canadians had their PIATs, the Germans had their *Panzerfausts*, which could do just as much damage. A soldier could run, a soldier could jump into a slit trench and hide. A tank was too slow to run, there was nowhere to hide, and if a *Panzerfaust* round pierced the tank's armour, igniting the ammunition and gas tank, then the crew had only a few seconds to bail before they were fried to a crisp.

The Algonquins learned a lot about tanks during the last scheme in Norfolk and the South Albertas learned a lot about the importance of their flat-footed friends. Without the infantry, their tanks were not all that effective. Tanks could not "see" the battle, they had to depend on the infantry for their eyes on the ground, soldiers reporting on the wireless from the various smaller battles in the big battle.

Tanks could take ground but they could not hold it. Only the infantry could do that. The key to winning any battle was the infantry.

The Algonquins learned some valuable lessons as well—how to fight *with* tanks and how to fight against them. Most of them got to ride in a Sherman to get some idea of what a tank's blind spots were—when infantry on the ground could be spotted and when they could not—knowledge that would come in handy when facing a German tank. They also learned to dig their slit trenches four feet deep and eight feet long but not so wide that a tank track would slide into it and crush them to death. A tank would go right over a properly dug slit trench.

When the scheme was finished near the end of November the Algonquins had handily defeated the counterattacking enemy, thanks both to their stubborn resistance in the face of a superior force and the timely intervention of their supporting artillery. When the arty's alert FOO, or Forward Observation Officer, spotted the enemy's tanks in the open he called in a Mike target and all twenty-four guns opened up. Game over.

Once packed up in Norfolk, the Algonquins headed south, not to Hayward's Heath as they had been told, but to the country about twenty miles to the northeast, near Tunbridge Wells. This time Regimental HQ was in Wadhurst Castle, square-cut greystone sheltered from the road by tall trees, oak, chestnut and what Yates insisted were Pacific redwoods.

The small castle, with its towers and pillars looking like rooks in the game of chess, had large mullioned windows overlooking a gently sloping lawn that ran into a treed pasture, which in turn rolled into a green valley bisected by a fast flowing stream. It was easy to imagine some lord of the manor in bygone days standing on his front entrance stone steps, lined on either side with ferns and rhododendron bushes, gazing with pride at the vista he saw before him. Had he returned by a trick of time in late November 1943 he would have been dismayed to see his view marred by trucks, Jeeps, carriers and Norton motorcycles for the Don Rs, or dispatch riders, parked every which way on the lawn and in the pasture below, most under trees for anti-aircraft protection, Bell tents as far as the eye could see.

Not much was laid on in the days leading up to Christmas, just a few route marches, some instructional films and church parades. After months of hectic schemes there was plenty of time to relax, time Al used to make frequent trips down to Lindfield.

He tried not to think too much about what he was doing, he wasn't sure he knew what he was doing, what his relationship with Kathleen was all about. It was just something that had happened, not something he'd gone looking for, not like some of his comrades who also had wives at home in Canada but had set out on girlfriend hunts as soon as they'd set foot in England and now had women tucked away in every corner of the land, women they fed with honeyed stories of vast cattle ranches in Ontario just a mile or so from Bay Street. The girls thought they'd found the pot of gold at the end of the rainbow. What was more likely was an outhouse at the end of a backyard.

But there were a lot of women in England for whom any old story would do, lonely women and woman coming of age when most of the eligible men were serving the Empire in far-flung outposts. Or women whose husbands were in prison camps or missing in action or never coming home. Soldiers, sailors, Spitfire pilots in the Battle of Britain, bomber crews over Germany whose tail gunners measured their lives in weeks. There were all sorts and conditions of women looking for a little comfort, a little kindness, a little loving, so that even with the competition from the Americans, girlfriends in England weren't all that hard to come by.

And there were lonely women in Canada, too, women whose men were in England where the regimental padres had their hands full counselling distraught soldiers whose mail consisted of "Dear John" letters, wives and girlfriends writing to say they were truly sorry but they had met someone else. Such were the wages of war.

When he thought of Kathleen, Al didn't think she was one of those lonely women craving the company of a man. She didn't strike him as being that kind at all. On the contrary she was one of the most self-sufficient women he had ever met. So if not lonely, then what? Maybe it was his resemblance to her brother, shell-shocked in Brighton. Al was with it. Ned was not. Maybe.

With Christmas coming, Billy got the idea of a party for the children of Lindfield and their families. He enlisted the Pioneer Platoon to make toys— wagons, fire engines, trucks, dolls, rocking horses and hand-carved wooden animals on wooden wheels pulled by a string, clicking and clacking along the floor.

The cooks were brought on side to beg, borrow and steal all the sugar rations in sight to make cookies and doughnuts and sweet cocoa. Both officers and men were solicited and they willingly gave up the contents of Christmas parcels. In 1943 food that was not directly rationed in England was on a points system with each person allowed twenty-four points a month. When a tin of pears cost you sixteen points, a gift of a tin from Canada, wrapped up as a present from Father Christmas, was a gift to be cherished by Mom and Dad.

But before the gifts there were movies courtesy of Barney and HQ Company— Mickey Mouse and Popeye the Sailor Man followed by a treasure hunt for the sweets from the Christmas parcels and afterwards a lunch also from the parcels—sandwiches from the tinned meats and dessert of cookies and doughnuts. This was wolfed down in no time flat while the cocoa was politely declined. The children would rather have tea.

The day after the party for the children, Al headed over to Maresfield at the invitation of his friends in the South Albertas. The knights in shining armour had decided to mark the festive season with a variety show of skits and songs and what the program billed as "a mystery guest from Canada."

The evening's entertainment got underway with the singing of "O Canada," smartly rendered by the regiment's brass band and vigorously sung by the khaki-dressed in the audience. Al always thought it was funny that a song he hardly ever remembered singing in Canada was sung so often and with so much enthusiasm here in England.

Once the crowd of soldiers and invited guests from the surrounding hamlets had settled down, the Alberta's CO strode to the platform with a word of welcome. He was Lieutenant-Colonel Gordon Dorward de Salaberry Wotherspoon. His family called him "Swatty" and the Albertans called him "Sir."

The show's first number was a can-can line bursting on stage and the audience roared at the sight of high-kicking men in rope wigs and straw-filled breasts, bare hairy legs and oversize army boots.

Next up was a young Albertan singing a medley of Irish songs in a voice that would put Bing Crosby's to shame. "The Minstrel Boy." "The Rose of Tralee." "The Last Rose of Summer." When he finished singing "Danny Boy" unaccompanied there wasn't a dry eye in the house.

Then came the skits, the best one featuring a sick parade featuring an MO who walked, talked, and looked like Groucho Marx. For a second Al thought it *was* Groucho Marx.

Doctor Marx was surrounded by ill and wounded men, many of them on crutches, and all of whom wore nothing but a towel around their waists. They stood there in obvious pain as the MO, smoking a foot-long cigar, slouched around lifting towels and peering at what was underneath, all the while asking rapid-fire questions. "Do you have VD? Are you an alcoholic? Do you like girls? Do you like horses? Do you want to get out of the army? Do you like cows? Do you want to go home? Do you like sheep?"

Various diagnoses were offered as the towel was lifted: "Son, you have a cute appendicitis there." The eyebrows jerking. Or, "Son, you are suffering from lackanookie." A leer to the audience. Or, "Son, you have psoriases of the liver, real bad." The maniacal grin.

There were other offerings, including the can-canners singing, "We'll Hang Out Our Washing on the Siegfried Line," and a skit of a Piccadilly Commando highly indignant to find that an Algonquin sergeant by the name of McDougal had taken advantage of blackout conditions to pay her with Toronto streetcar tickets.

At the conclusion of the show the master of ceremonies came to centre stage and in the voice of a carnival barker yelled, "And now, fair ladies and handsome gentlemen, now is the moment you've been waiting for."

There was a roll of drums and the audience grew quiet. "It is my pleasure to introduce our mystery guests. Yes there are two of them, ladies and gentlemen, and here they are," the band struck up a fanfare, "here they are direct from the Canadian Army Show, Wayne and Shuster!"

The audience stood, clapping and cheering, whistling and shouting, even the bewildered Brits who didn't have the faintest idea who Wayne and Shuster were.

The two comics came bounding on stage dressed as *Wehrmacht* privates, greatcoats, and German helmets looking like coal scuttles. The privates, Fritz and Schitz, were dumb as posts as the ensuing conversation between them soon revealed. The more they talked the more the audience laughed, side-splitting-rolling-in-the-aisles laughter. Wayne and Shuster laughter.

After Fritz and Schitz, whose first name was Ima, Johnny and Frank sang some of their patented zany songs starting off to Al's delight with "When the swallows come back to Kapuskasing." Then to the tune of "You Are My Sunshine," it was "My only Woodbine, my Willie Woodbine,/ I cannot smoke them, my throat gets sore./ When I awake dear, the next morning,/ I cannot smoke the Woodbines anymore."

But it was their finale that brought the house down. They were back to Fritz and Schitz, goose-stepping back and forth across the stage singing to the tune of Colonel Bogey, "Hitler, / Has only got one ball. / Goering, / Has two but they are small. / Himmler, / Has something sim'lar, / But poor old Goebbels, / Has no balls at all."

The audience was invited to sing along and they did, and Al figured everybody, on stage and off, sang the same verse about twenty times; and then Wayne and Shuster said good night and the show was over.

It was time to go back to work.

Chapter Fifteen

JANUARY 17, 1944. Wadhurst Castle. After spending week after week trying to work at my desk in this cold, damp building I now know why Herr Hitler did not invade England. No central heating. The only thing that keeps me going, keeps us all going, is the sense of expectancy in the air. You could feel it over New Year's in London. I understand there's been a place called London since long before the birth of Christ but I suspect that never has the city in all its 2000 year history been as crowded as it was during the festive season this year. They say there are over two million troops in Southern England now, two million men between Plymouth and Dover getting ready to invade the Continent and it seems to me that 1,999,000 of them were on leave in London over the holidays. They will not be in London next New Year's. They will be in Berlin. Hell what am I talking about? We will be in Berlin. Wouldn't miss that for the world! When you look back on it, 1943 was a good year. Africa and Sicily were conquered, Italy surrendered and air raids in England dwindled to almost none. These days the sky traffic is all one-way, wave after wave of bombers heading for the Third Reich, the USAF by day and the RAF and RCAF by night. Billy has decided to call son number two (born last Tuesday) "Lewis" after Lewisporte. We are all greatly relieved. Crow's back with us after his time at Aldershot. Has his very own Lee Enfield No. 4 Sniper's Rifle with telescopic sight and cheek rest. Said the sniper instructor was a little crazy. Veteran of the Italian campaign. Had a bunch of medals. When Crow said to him, "You must like killing them," he replied, "Nope, just wounding them, then when the stretcher bearers come out I get a couple more." Sometimes I wonder if we are going to be any better than Jerry when we get over there and the shooting is for real but then I guess you have to do what you have to do. If you box according to Marquess of Queensberry rules while the other guy has brass knuckles and kicks you in the nuts with steel toe boots then you're just a schmuck. You have to fight fire with fire. Have to get going now and let the lads in on the latest news. We're off to do a little sightseeing. Scotland this time. For invasion training.

Excerpt from Barney's Diary

For the Algonquins, Scotland was Shira Camp near Inveraray on Loch Fyne, the rugged, desolate scenery reminding them of Newfoundland. As the crow flies, Inveraray is about forty miles northwest of Glasgow, where there are people. In Inveraray there are only sheep, hundreds of white specks on the hills that rise up into the mountains where the clouds drift down to meet the fog coming off the loch to form a soupy brume that fills crevice and glen below.

But there was no fog when training actually began. It didn't even rain. The sun shone brightly on new toys—memorials to young men who gave their lives on the beaches of Dieppe in August 1942—so that others who came after might know that assaulting a heavily fortified beach would require more than young men, it would require novel, specialized landing craft and it was these that were waiting for the Algonquins in Inveraray.

The Algonquins got to play mostly with the LCAs and LCMs—Landing Craft Assault and Landing Craft Mechanized—practising timed debarkations on steep beaches, flat beaches, and even beaches where they stepped off into knee-deep water and started wading ashore only to find that the beach defied all expectations by slanting down instead of up and before they knew it they were swimming with rifles high, desperate to keep their weapons out of the wet. The more inventive among them used a common form of birth control, slipping condoms over the ends of their rifle barrels. "This is my rifle, this is my gun. This is for fighting, this is for fun."

Once on shore they battle-drilled on beach organization, similar to what they'd done in Newfoundland, finding cover under enemy fire and establishing their own lines of fire to support comrades coming in after them. They also practised the quick identification of safe exits so they could move rapidly inland away from Jerry's guns zeroed in on landing sites.

At night they went back to Shira Camp to dry out and on weekends into Inveraray to quaff a few and relax. But on their first few Saturdays in Scotland Al had stayed in camp. He knew it would be quiet with most everyone gone and every once in a while he craved quiet, every once in a while he needed the aural experience of silence.

When Barney and Billy had gone to London to see in the New Year, Al had spent the holiday at the O'Halloran's along with Yates, whom Kathleen had invited only after promising Al she would find a woman for Willy, a woman who could give as well as she got when it came to William Butler's grand and eclectic forays among his favourite literati. The woman Kathleen "found" was her aunt, her da's youngest sister Margaret, unmarried and down from Liverpool, in her words, "the capital of Ireland."

Al guessed Margaret O'Halloran had to be in her early forties but she looked to be in her early thirties. She had the O'Halloran eyes and Yates thought she looked a lot like Rosalind Russell. When he told her so she tossed her head and said she rather thought she looked like Vivien Leigh. Her brother rolled his eyes but Yates just smiled and nodded. Point.

Patrick served the whisky and Kathleen the food: raised pork pie, Scotch eggs and Christmas pudding. In front of the fire, logs crackling, the five of them spent New Year's Eve eating, drinking, talking and listening to music on the BBC, the Andrews Sisters and "I'll Be with You in Apple Blossom Time"; Lena Horne and "Stormy Weather"; Judy Garland and "Over The Rainbow."

When Elsie Carlisle crooned "A Nightingale Sang in Berkeley Square" and got to the words about the whole world being upside down they looked at each other as if to say "I'll drink to that" and did.

When Vera Lynn sang "The White Cliffs of Dover," they joined in.

> There'll be blue birds over, the White Cliffs of Dover
> Tomorrow, just you wait and see.
> There'll be love and laughter and peace ever after
> Tomorrow when the world is free.

When midnight came they stood, joined hands, and sang "Auld Lang Syne."

Al smiled to himself, remembering. Patrick had gone to bed right after toasting the New Year and Al, curled up on the sofa with Kathleen, had fallen asleep. When he awoke the fire had gone out and he was all alone. There was a note pinned to his sleeve. "Come to bed when you wake, Sergeant." And so he did.

Now, weeks later, he was thinking that's what he should be doing in Shira Camp, he should be hitting the hay, so he quickly finished a letter to the Bermans and turned in. He didn't sleep alone, for as soon as he lay down he had an officer from the Royal Canadian Fur Force curled up in the crook of his leg. Ross had left Max in Al's keeping and the sergeant fell asleep listening to the captain purring.

Beach assault drills were followed by obstacle training to give them some idea what they might encounter once they'd made it off the beach. With weapons slung over their backs, tin hats on their heads and bearing forty pounds of weight in their packs—rocks to simulate the ammunition, grenades and other odds and ends they would be carrying on D-Day—they climbed up and over ten-foot-high log barriers under fire, and they traversed streams, tank ditches and deep man-made gorges on rope bridges strung tautly across and far above the water and rocks below, pulling themselves along, their boots hooked over the rope behind them, one platoon at a time, while comrades watched from the safety of terra firma, not hesitating to offer loud and caustic observations as to the quality of the high-wire act above.

These were days of tough, hard work and Al didn't need much persuasion to join the next weekly Saturday night pub excursion. They were on their second pub and third pint when they were interrupted by a voice bellowing in broken English, an ear assault they hadn't been forced to endure since Shilo. Stanislas Popovich.

The big Pole went around slapping backs with his massive hands, bear hugging the breath out of Al and Billy. "You boys miss me, ja? You miss the big Polish prick from South Porcupine, ja?" He banged his chest. Tarzan of the Apes.

When he finally sat down he asked what they were doing in Scotland and they told him about the trials and tribulations of their training, how tough it was and how tough they were.

Popovich listened for a bit, his eyes amused, darting from one to the other and then suddenly he slapped the table and started to laugh—loud, raucous laughter that went on and on until it squelched all conversation in the pub. Heads turned and the Algonquins looked at him as he wiped spittle from his chin. Then he took a deep breath, held up a hand and ordered a round for the table.

"Listen, you boys," and he hunched forward speaking quietly now, "listen to what I am saying, ja? See this?" He fingered the red, white and blue braided cord looped over his shoulder above an insignia of a spearhead under crossed arrows. "Special Service Force. Black Devils." And then he told them where he had been and what he had done and what he was preparing to do.

As Al had suspected, Popovich had been in Montana, where an elite force of Canadians and Americans under American command had trained as commandos for special operations, their first one being against the Japanese in the Aleutians, a chain of volcanic islands stretching from the Alaska Peninsula west across the Bering Sea toward Russia.

After the Aleutians it was back to Montana and then in October to Italy on the *Empress of Scotland*, a ship "captured from the Japanese."

When Yates started to interrupt, Al kicked him hard under the table. The American cried out and Popovich raised bushy eyebrows.

"Nothing, old man, nothing. Just banged my shin on the table leg. Carry on."

Italy was mountains and rivers and the Hermann Goering Division, the best Jerry had to offer.

Italy was mines, especially mines that bounced up in the air when you stepped on them and then exploded, shredding guts.

The Pole's audience, more solemn now, nodded. They remembered being told about Bouncing Betties but not so chillingly.

Italy was "Moaning Minnies," a German weapon that fired rockets, six of them, one right after the other, rockets that made a long, drawn-out moaning sound before landing and exploding with a tremendous blast, spewing jagged shrapnel in a wide, vicious arc.

Italy was German mortars and German artillery—high explosives, armour-piercing air bursts and searing white phosphorus that fried flesh.

Italy was the dreaded eighty-eight, no warning, just a wham and a metallic screech when it was far too late to take cover, a wham and a screech over and over again, sometimes killing by concussion alone.

Italy was German potato mashers and German machine guns, Spandau tracers, stitching the water around them as they waded swollen rivers.

Italy was fighting in dense fog with Stens and grenades and hand-to-hand combat with knives in the dark.

Italy was slogging it out in the mud and the rain and the cold, fighting when they were bone tired, no food in their bellies and barely enough energy to keep their eyes open.

Italy was a bitch.

There was silence at the table as Popovich paused, took a long swallow of beer, and then wiped his mouth with the back of his hand. "And now we are here in Scotland, what is left of us. To get ready to go after those cocksnuckers again."

"Cocksuckers, Stan."

"Ja! It is what I said. Cocksnuckers!"

Then Corporal Popovich told them what the Black Devils were doing in Scotland, about their training in the Highlands and the moors with Lord Lovat's Commandos. Tough speed marches, cliff climbing straight up, boat drills, obstacle courses and finding their way on the desolate moors with nothing but a map and a compass, umpires, hard-nosed bastards grading their every move as life-size targets popped up in front of them to test quick reactions. Popovich said you had a split second to decide. Shoot the target or bayonet it. If the umpire thought you'd made the wrong decision then your whole squad had to run "the black mile."

"What's that?"

Popovich grinned. "You must do the whole course again. On Sunday. Only day off."

He shifted in his chair. "But we do not do black miles. This training is a wind for us."

He drained the last of his beer and stood up. "So you see boys that your old friend Stanislas Popovich who is lately from South Porcupine is not to be impressed by how hard it is, your training." He thumped his chest. "When you have done what I have been doing and seen what I have been seeing we will talk again and this time you will buy the beer, ja?"

With that he turned and lumbered out of the pub, his audience watching him go, not knowing that they wouldn't see the big Pole again for another seven months and when they did it would be in Normandy and there would be no time and no place to buy beer.

Easter 1944 came early in April, about a week after Sandy Jr.'s fourth birthday. His father had sent him a card and pictures of Scotland. "You must be a big boy now. Before you know it you will be off to school. Mommy tells me you can already read a little bit. Good for you! Give Mommy a hug for me and tell Gramps not to plant any Brussels sprouts in his garden this year. Brussels sprouts are boring. Don't eat too much birthday cake and remember always check for nickels and dimes which have a habit of showing up in birthday cakes. Sometimes they are wrapped in wax paper inside the slice that goes to the birthday boy so keep an eye out."

By Easter the Algonquins had been back at Wadhurst Castle for more than a month devoting their days to training and their nights to listening to Foster Hewitt broadcasting the Stanley Cup playoffs on the BBC, the corporation's kindly nod to the thousands of Canadians in their listening audience.

There wasn't much disagreement among the Algonquins as to who was likely to win the Cup. Montreal, Toronto, Detroit and Chicago were in the playoffs but the Canadiens had won the regular season with eighty-three points, far ahead of the Wings, Leafs and Blackhawks. Also Montreal's Bill Durnan had won the Vezina trophy and Maurice "The Rocket" Richard was playing sensational hockey. Even diehard Leaf fans like Allan McDougal figured Montreal wasn't going to have any problems in the playoffs.

And they didn't, although in the first game of the first round the Leafs outshot the Canadiens by a margin of 61 to 23 and outscored them three to one. But then Richard took over. In the second game he scored all five goals as Montreal won 5-1 and the Canadiens never looked back, winning the final game of the series 11-0, the most lopsided score in the history of Lord Stanley's playoffs.

Reggie was tempted to tap Al on the shoulder and rub it in but he didn't. You never knew how Al would react when it came to his beloved Maple Leafs.

Because the Canadiens were playing Chicago in the finals, Al became a temporary Montreal fan. He couldn't bear to cheer for an American team and he was glad he couldn't because the Canadiens swept the Hawks in four straight games with the Rocket setting a Stanley Cup scoring record.

Al and Willy spent the Easter weekend in Lindfield with Kathleen and Margaret, who insisted they all go to Mass on Easter Sunday morning. *In nomine Patris et Filii et Spiritus Sancti. Amen.*

It was the first time Al had ever been inside a Roman Catholic Church and he was intrigued by everything: the vestments; the incense—the odour of sweetness—the language; and the decor—stations of the cross and statues, blue and red paint peeling from the saints in plaster. *Dominus vobiscum. Et cum spiritus tuo.*

He wasn't completely lost, there being many similarities between the Church of England's Holy Communion and the Catholic Mass, the same order of ritual reflecting a common ancestry of sorts. The differences had to do with a lot more bowing and scraping in the Catholic Church if what Patrick, Kathleen and Margaret were doing beside him was any indication, Yates as well, for that matter. Willy seemed to know his way around.

The other big difference besides the Latin was a lot more talk of holy men with strange sounding names like "Chrysogonus," and many, many more reverential references to the mother of Jesus, who was called "the Blessed" Virgin Mary. *Communicantes, et memoriam venerantes, in primis gloriosae semper Virginis Mariae, Genitricis Dei et Domini nostri Jesu Christi.*

When it was all over, *Ite, missa est, Deo gratias*, and they were walking back to the house down the hill past the cemetery of All Saint's Church, Kathleen took his arm.

She didn't say anything, she just squeezed.

At the house, Patrick and Margaret quickly gathered together food and drink and went off to Brighton for an Easter Sunday visit to Ned while Willy and Al ambled into the kitchen with an offer to help Kathleen prepare the evening meal while they helped themselves to her da's whisky.

"One drink is all, you two. There'll be no falling asleep at my table this night."

"*Pax vobiscum,*" said Yates as he surreptitiously poured one more into both his and Al's glass. "Smells good." He nodded to one of the pots on the stove.

"Leek and potato soup. Tonight's first course."

"What's in this pot?" Al reached for the lid of a pot simmering on the back of the stove and didn't see the twinkle in Kathleen's eyes.

"Oh, that's the main course. Go ahead. Have a look."

Al lifted the lid, peered in and then quickly jerked back. "What in hell is that?"

"Begging your pardon, sir, but that would be a terrible thing to say about my cooking!"

Yates, curious, stepped up for a look, grimaced, and said, "Looks like a—"

"Sheep's head," said Kathleen. "Yes, Mr. William Butler Yates, that's what it is. And a very delicious one it will be when it's all cooked and laid on a platter on the table this evening. Especially the brains. Very tasty but very delicate. That's why we wrap the head in cloth when we cook it. To keep the brains with the head."

Al was retreating from the stove, the back of his hand to his mouth, his eyes wide. Yates looked at him, then at Kathleen, who was humming as she scraped diced carrots and turnips from a cutting board into the pot with the wrapped sheep's head.

"Guess we'll go into the front room," coughed Yates. "You seem to have things well under control in here."

"Oh yes, I'll be fine. I promise to call you if need be."

When the two men turned to go, Kathleen bowed her head, gulping down her laughter. But she wasn't about to say anything. She would let them stew a while. She winced at the pun.

In the front room Al made a face as Yates sat across from him. "Jesus, Willy. I can't eat that. I think the eyes are still in the head."

"Nah," said Yates. "I didn't see any eyes"

He looked at his sergeant with some sympathy. "Look, I don't like the thought of it any more than you but there's a trick to it, see? When it's served just take a little and when you're eating it pretend it's roast beef. I tell you, it works."

Al shook his head. He was sure it wouldn't work for him. But he didn't want to think about it anymore, so he asked Yates the question he'd been wanting to ask since the end of Easter Mass.

"Are you a Catholic?

"Nope."

"Then how come you knew what to do this morning?"

The question got them going on a discussion of religion, propelled mostly by the pressing need to drive away all thoughts of the fate waiting for them at the supper table. Yates explained that he was a "High Episcopalian," which was very close to Catholicism in the way things were done on Sunday mornings; and Al said that was probably the reason Billy attended the Church of England in Lowvert, because it was closer to what the family was used to in Lebanon, which Billy had once confided was Syrian Orthodox or something.

At Yates's suggestion they went for a walk down by the pond and into the countryside. When they got back an hour or so later, Margaret and Patrick had returned and Kathleen told them to clean up for supper. The two soldiers were the last to wash up and the last to the table. Not their usual *modus operandi* when food was waiting.

The soup was delicious and everyone said so. They ate it with wheatmeal bread and margarine. Al and Willy took their time, eating slowly, and finally, when they were finished, asked for seconds, more soup and more bread, all part of the strategy they had devised on their walk, the-soup-was-so-good-and-we-ate-so-much-we-can-hardly-eat-another-bite strategy.

It didn't work. Kathleen said there wasn't any more soup and gathered up the empty bowls, humming "Lili Marlene." She offered Al a winning smile as he handed over his bowl and then disappeared into the kitchen. In a minute she reappeared with a covered serving bowl, the sight of which caused Al to stretch a hand over his eyes and lower his head toward his lap.

Patrick rubbed his hands. "Ah, Sheep's Head Roll," he said, "my favourite dish."

"And mine as well," said Margaret enthusiastically.

"Allan, would you do the honours?"

Patrick started to hand over the carving knife but then stopped. "I'm sorry, lad, you won't need a knife. Just use the large spoon there. The meat just sloughs off the head. And mind the brains, that's a good lad."

Al swallowed as he stood and watched Kathleen remove the cloth covering the platter. Then he sagged back down into his chair holding the spoon at port arms. He turned and looked at Yates with the hint of a smile. Yates nodded slowly and then the two of them turned to watch their tormentors who were so convulsed with laughter they were barely able to maintain their equilibrium at table. There was nothing the two soldiers could do but grin and bear it and wait for the laughter to peter out. But just when it seemed it would, Yates's grin turned to a chuckle and the chuckle to a belly laugh. In an instant Al was laughing too, and that got the O'Hallorans going again and it was some time before order was restored and a gasping Kathleen was able to serve what was on the platter—a delicious ham and beef roll with gravy and vegetables.

Later, over trifle and tea, Al asked about Sheep's Head Roll and Patrick told him it was indeed one of his favourite dishes and he *would* eat it with relish during the week. He said fondness for sheep's head and other meats like heart and tongue were bred in the Irish poor, who often had no other choice if there was to be any meat at all on the table to go with their potatoes, which were always on the table. Except when the Great Famine came. He shook his head in sorrow.

"Now, Pawd-rig. Don't be getting maudlin on us. Especially on the subject of the Irish poor because, if truth be told, ye wouldn't know a poor son of the Gael if one were to fall dead at your feet."

Margaret was shaking a finger at her brother, who gave her a sly wink.

"How was our Ned today?"

Patrick brightened at Kathleen's query and told them all how well Ned was doing; he was sitting up from time to time and taking more of an interest in his surroundings. And his appetite was coming back.

The evening took its customary course, with Patrick soon off to bed, the sherry-drenched trifle and after-dinner whisky having the usual effect. Also as usual, Yates and Margaret excused themselves, leaving Al and Kathleen alone by the fire.

"Where do those two get off to?"

"Beats me," said Al.

"Do you suppose—"

"I started to ask him that today but decided it was none of my business."

"Nor mine," sighed Kathleen. She reached for Al's hand and standing drew him up. "Will you come to bed with me, Sergeant?"

He smiled at her and followed her lead up the stairs to her bedroom, down the hall from her father's, where she undressed him. When he was naked and shivering she pressed against him and took him in her hand and began to stroke him with the tips of her fingers. He groaned and worked at her clothes, undoing the buttons of her blouse and rubbing her hardening nipples with his thumbs. Then he reached and lifting her skirt, a finger over her knickers, hooked them down over her hips. She wiggled out of them and pulled him over with her to her dresser where he lifted her and she guided him inside her, gasping in his ear as she wrapped her legs around him.

All sense of time and place and identity was lost in their lovemaking. He was another man in another world in another age. He was a king. And Kathleen was his queen. She was his food, his drink, his Body of Christ. *Corpus Domini, nostri Jesu Christi custodiat animam tuam in vitam aeternam. Amen.*

Training in the weeks after Easter was smaller in scale than the exercises in the North. In the South, training was on a company level, which meant that the Carrier Platoon was assigned one week to go off and work with Able Coy, and then another week with Baker, and so on with Charlie and Dog. But it was hard to work up much enthusiasm for anything when the word came down they would not be going over on invasion day. Their division, the 4th Armoured, was to be held in reserve.

"Whattaya expect," said Billy. We're the Algonquins. Our motto should be, 'Others lead. We follow.'"

Slouched in their carrier parked in the driveway of Wadhurst Castle, they were having a cuppa with Barney. Corporal Berman, recently promoted, was trying to talk sense into Private Assad.

"Don't be daft, Billy." Barney had picked up some of the local idiom. "Dieppe was bad and this one won't be any better. The Germans know we're coming. Sooner or later. They might not know exactly where but they know. So you can bet your bottom dollar that they've spent the last two years getting ready for us all along the coast of France. Oh sure, we'll bomb the hell out of the invasion beaches, and the navy offshore will lob enough shells on Jerry that he'll think it's the end of the world. But when the bombers are gone and the shelling lifts and the lads go in, the Germans will crawl out of their bunkers just like they did in the First War. And once out they'll do their best to throw us back into the Channel. And their best will be pretty bad for the PBI on the beaches. So thank your lucky stars you won't be there. Some other poor sods will be but it won't be you, and your mom and dad and your wife and boys will be grateful it isn't."

The little league was accustomed to Barney making speeches but this was one of the longest and most impassioned they had heard for quite some time and they were a bit taken aback. No one said anything for a minute and then Billy looked up grinning and punched Barney playfully on the shoulder. But even a playful punch from Billy packed a bit of a wallop, enough that Barney spilled his tea and his glasses slid down his nose.

"Yeah, okay, Barn. You got a point. It's just that . . ." Billy's words trailed off.

Barney brushed tea drops off his battledress with the tips of his fingers and then peered over the top of his glasses at his boyhood pal. "You'll get your chance, Billy. We'll all get our chance. As soon as those beaches are secured Eisenhower will pour in the troops to hammer the shit out of Jerry before he catches his breath. That's where we'll come in."

Waiting for the balloon to go up seemed to be their chief occupation in the next few weeks, that and running errands and putting in time going through the motions of training. While the rest of them did the local pubs on Saturday nights, Al spent his in Lindfield and, if Margaret was there, so did Yates. And so the weeks went by.

One day in early May returning from a trip to a nearby farm where they'd been sent to tow back a wagonload of hay for palliasses they found out that things were getting serious. New Orders had been posted under the heading "Until Further Notice."

Until Further Notice no mail would be sent from England. You could write all you wanted to but nothing was going out of the country. Loose lips sink ships.

Until Further Notice the Regiment was on one-hour notice to defend against any enemy threats to southern England. The lads assumed that meant a pre-emptive German air strike or para drop against suspected troop buildups.

Until Further Notice the use of binoculars was forbidden within ten miles of the coast. That one they could not, for the life of them, figure out.

Until Further Notice there would be parades to check their paybooks to see that their medical shots were up-to-date; parades to check their "dog tags"; parades to see the chaplain to make sure of the name and address of next of kin where their personal effects could be sent in case "something happened."

They were also issued new kit bags, white ones, and told to stencil their names, numbers and company identification on them PDQ.

"Shit for brains," said Billy when he finished lettering his bag. "White kit bags!" He spat. "Perfect target for the *Luftwaffe*!"

The words were barely out of his mouth when the white kit bags were taken away and replaced with black ones that had to be lettered all over again.

Until Further Notice they were to be confined to base where security was so tight that if you were caught throwing away an empty package of cigarettes you'd be up on a charge. Canadian cigarettes indicated Canadian soldiers and presumably that knowledge was of inestimable value to the enemy.

"Now let me get this straight," Billy was sitting down, his feet tucked under his legs but he was on his high horse, "we can't go inta town for a beer 'cause Gerald might find out there's soldiers around. And we can't throw away empty packs of cigs because Gerald might find out there's Canadian soldiers around."

He threw out his arms. "Does anybody really think the Germans don't already know all this?" He slapped his forehead. "Huh, does anybody? Anybody?"

Barney tried to pacify him. "Well, Billy, I suppose Jerry does but I think what the brass is afraid of is somebody with a few beers in him letting something slip that Jerry doesn't know."

"Barn, Barn. No one knows a goddamn, fucking thing. So if ya don't know anything how can ya let somethin' slip?"

Barney looked around at them, one by one, and then up at Billy. He spoke quietly. "You know, and each and every one of us sitting here knows, we're not goin' over on the big day, Billy. The Algonquins are staying put."

Billy had his mouth open all primed for an argumentative reply but when Barney's words sank in he pursed his lips, nodded slowly and sat down. He had to admit that Corporal Berman, the rear-end warrior, the little league of nations' representative with the chairborne troops at Regimental HQ, had a point.

Chapter Sixteen

JUNE 6, 1944. Early this morning, while still dark, we heard the roar of bombers overhead. At first we thought nothing of it. Just another raid across the Channel. So we rolled over and tried to go back to sleep. But the roar didn't stop. The planes kept coming. Wave after wave after wave and soon the whole camp was wide awake, men stumbling out of their tents, officers and staff out of the Castle. Besides the aircraft—which we quickly figured out weren't only going, they were also coming back—we could also hear the thunder of artillery from the Channel coast. And then we knew! You can't imagine what it was like! The lads were thrusting fists in the air and cheering. Some were even crying and a few praying. At last, at long last, we were taking it to Jerry, we who had waited so long in England, we who were tired of waiting so long, we who were part of the greatest army ever assembled, the Brits, the Americans and us. We were going to give those sadistic Nazi bastards a kick in the arse that the world would never forget. What a day! After breakfast somebody had the presence of mind to put up a map in the Great Hall of the Castle so that we could all follow the progress of the D-Day invasion, particularly Juno Beach where our Canadians had gone in. All day long we stood in front of the map listening to the wireless reporting on "the most noble armada the world has ever seen," Churchill telling us there were more than 4,000 ships and 11,000 aircraft and everything was going to plan. We charted the progress of the landings and heard the official announcements made by Eisenhower, Montgomery and General Harry Crerar, Commander of First Canadian Army. Eisenhower spoke to the people of France telling them to take action against the enemy only if they received a definite order to do so and he assured the people of other occupied countries that their day of liberation was soon to come. Then his earlier words to the invasion forces were rebroadcast. "Soldiers, sailors and airmen of the Allied Expeditionary Forces! You are about to embark upon the great crusade toward which we have striven these many months. The eyes of the world are upon you, the hopes and prayers of liberty-loving people everywhere march with you. In company with our brave Allies and brothers in arms on other fronts you will bring about the destruction of the German war

*machine, the elimination of Nazi tyranny over the oppressed peoples
of Europe, and security for ourselves in a free world. Your task will
not be an easy one. Your enemy is well trained, well equipped and
battle hardened. He will fight savagely. But I have full confidence in
your courage, devotion to duty and skill in battle. Good luck! And
let us all beseech the blessings of Almighty God upon this great and
noble undertaking."*

Excerpt from Barney's Diary

The euphoria of the first hours of the invasion didn't last long as days
lengthened into weeks and the Algonquins and the Lincs & Winks, the Ash Cans
and the South Albertas, the entire 10th Infantry Brigade, became more and more
bored, more and more frustrated, more and more restless. While they were still
in England twiddling their thumbs, their countrymen—among them the North
Shores from New Brunswick, the Queen's Own from Ontario, the Chaudières
from Quebec, the Royal Winnipeg Rifles and the Regina Rifle Regiment—were
in combat with the enemy, not in faraway Africa, not in the Far East, but just
ninety miles across the water. It didn't help that Lord Haw Haw taunted them,
the country gentlemen of the 4th Division letting the nursing sisters get to the
beaches of Normandy before them.

The brass were aware of the mood so it wasn't long before Major General
George Kitching, the division's CO, came round with a pep talk. He stood in the
morning sun on the front steps of the Castle and they stood smartly at ease on
the lawn facing him, their Bell tents behind them and the valley and stream down
behind the tents. He told them the reason they had not been in on the assault was
that they had been chosen for an important task. Once a beachhead had been
firmly established, and he anticipated that would be in ten days or so, 4th
Canadian Armoured was going to lead the inland attack against two of the
enemy's strongest Panzer divisions, the Adolf Hitler and Hitler Youth. Kitching
told them it would be Canadian armour against German armour, the best against
the best. He said he knew who would come out on top when it was all over.

Most of the lads felt a lot better when Kitching was finished. But not all. As
they broke formation after being dismissed, Billy scoffed, "He's just sayin' that,
ya know. Pattin' us on the back. 'There, there, everything's gonna be all right,
little boys.' He's full of shit. Just like the rest of them."

Yates was getting tired of Billy's cynical and jaundiced view of the world and
said so and before anybody could stop them they were throwing punches. Fast
and Furious.

Dougie Dobson and Arnie Christensen broke it up before any real damage
was done, the combatants breathing hard and glaring, each wrapped in a pair of
restraining arms. When Billy pulled one arm free, he wiped at his nose and
examined the blood on his fingers before running his tongue around his top front
teeth, spitting and walking away.

Yates watched him go for a minute and then turned and jogged over to catch up with his sergeant, who had headed down the hill to get away from it all. The two of them walked together in silence past the tents and down into the valley to the banks of the stream, where they sat on an outcrop of rock and stared at the water, now a sluggish flow following the spring runoff.

After a bit Yates took a deep breath and blew it out slowly. "My mother died when I was seven years old. One day she was alive and smiling and the next day she was dead. Just like that." He snapped his fingers. "Brain aneurysm." He reached down, picked up a handful of pebbles and threw them into the water. "I can hardly remember her."

Al waited. He could tell there was more coming. Yates spoke haltingly, pausing as he picked out pictures from his memory.

"But what I do remember . . . little things, you know, her laughter, the way she looked at me when she took care of me that summer I had the measles . . . helping her make my favourite cookies . . . oatmeal . . . she used to pat my face with flour, laughing and telling me I looked like her precious little ghost . . . well . . ."

He threw more pebbles, listening to the sound they made when they hit the water, the quick splatter of heavy raindrops. He glanced up at the sky. Then he turned to look at Al and sighed. "Well, Margaret reminds me of her, Al. Margaret reminds me of my mother. The mother I can barely remember. Crazy, isn't it?"

Yates wiped at his eyes and chuckled. "You know all those times we disappeared and you were thinking . . . ? We just went for walks. A couple of times we stayed out until the sun was coming up. Walking and talking. Sometimes we came back to the house after you all had gone to bed and sat up and talked some more. I could talk to that woman forever and not get tired. Not get bored."

"What did ya talk about? Poetry and stuff?"

Yates laughed. "Nah, none of that horseshit. That's just me screwing around, having fun. We talked about life." And here Yates grinned. "'Know then thyself, presume not God to scan,/ The proper study of mankind is man.' We talked about life, Al. We talked about life."

Neither one of them said anything for quite a while as they stared at the water breaking over the stones in the shallows, the sun turning it into flecks of gold.

"Sometimes we talked about you and Kathleen."

Al shifted position on the rock but didn't look at Yates when he asked him what was said.

"Nothing much. Just that you two were good for each other."

Al turned to Yates now and smiled. "Well, I knew she was good for me—but me for her?"

"Oh, yeah." Yates glanced at his sergeant to make sure he was serious. "Yeah. You're her brother. You're her Ned."

Al nodded. "I wondered about that."

"Margaret said Kathleen was really close with Ned and when he came back wounded and shell-shocked it was as if he were dead; and then you came along and he was alive again."

"Me Jesus, him Lazarus, eh?"

Yates frowned at him. "Yeah, why not?

It was a rebuke for his sarcasm and he took it because he deserved it. He waited for a bit before he asked. "What do you think, Willy?"

Yates shrugged. "I think there's some truth in it. Hey, if Margaret's my mother ..."

He stood and stretched, shading his eyes, looking downstream, then fingers moving to explore the swelling around his left eye where Billy had nailed him.

"But it cuts both ways," he squatted down again. "You stitched up a tear in her soul and she did the same for you. For me that's a wonderful thing when two people can do that for each other."

Two days later just before midnight, the Algonquins suffered their first casualties since Newfoundland.

A week or so after D-Day the Germans had launched an offensive of their own—rocket bombs propelled from ramps in France and Holland against London and the troop buildups in southern England. The rockets were tipped with one-ton warheads and Hitler called them *Vergeltungswaffen*, or "reprisal weapons." The official Allied designation was V-1s but thanks to Cockney newsmen, the V-1s came quickly to be known as "buzz bombs" or "doodlebugs."

You could hear a V-1 coming, a put-put-put sound like a cheap outboard motor, and in the daylight hours you could see them, big, black, gliding crows usually pursued by RAF fighters, which often seemed to be too far behind to shoot them down. At night you could make out the yellow spout of flame from the jet engine on the tail end, a marker for pursuing anti-aircraft fire.

The Canadians at Wadhurst Castle saw their first V-1 late in the evening of Friday, June 16, and assumed it to be an enemy aircraft with its tail on fire. But the next morning the BBC disabused them of this notion by reporting an "attack on London by flying bombs of tremendous destructive power."

Following this first sighting, more and more of the scary *Vergeltungswaffen* swept over East Sussex, night and day, one of them put-putting right up the valley behind the Castle, following the stream bed as if it were a route marked out on a map.

And it was as the experts discovered, once they'd had a chance to examine the wreckage of a few downed V-1s. The doodlebugs flew preset courses on automatic pilot. Jerry wasn't guessing there were troops in the area. He knew.

In a matter of hours orders came down from the Castle to excavate tent floors so that all ranks could sleep safely below ground level. Slit trenches were dug around the Castle itself for the nightly accommodation of HQ staff.

After the fist fight with Yates, Billy had made a point of avoiding both Al and Willy for the rest of the day and throughout the next, because neither of them saw hide nor hair of him. They turned in on the evening of the second day, curling up in their underground berths, both wondering what to say to him when he finally did appear.

Al was in a deep sleep but came out of it suddenly, shaking his head, trying to get his bearings, trying to figure out what it was that had wakened him. It took only a second to come up with the answer that snapped him to attention. It was the silence.

In his sleep he had registered the put-put-put of an incoming V-1 but it was no longer an unusual sound so his brain hadn't issued a warning. It was the *absence* of sound that had screamed at him.

When ordered to dig down beneath their tents they had been told over and over again that as long as they could hear the doodlebug's motor they were safe. But when the bomb's motor cut out, when there was silence, they had ten seconds to take cover.

Al yelled to wake his tentmates and counted off the seconds, four-a thousand, three-a-thousand, two-a-thousand, one-a-thousand. Nothing. He held his breath. Still nothing.

Some were lifting their heads for a look when the buzz bomb exploded. The ground beneath them shimmied, the concussion like a physical assault, a fist to the stomach knocking the wind out of them and a hard slap to the head leaving a ringing in their ears.

But it was a welcome assault. It meant they were still alive.

Al had been sleeping close to the tent's entrance flap and scrambled to his feet outside in an instant. What he saw jolted him as if he'd grabbed a live wire. Up on the hill one end of the Castle looked like a *Movietone News* picture of buildings in Warsaw or London, hacked off by a frenzied giant with a very dull gargantuan axe.

Al could see it all quite clearly because some of the wooden outbuildings had burst into flame. He could hear shouts and the faint ringing of bells as fire trucks began to make their way over from nearby villages. He ran up the hill. Barney and Goody Noseworthy were up there somewhere.

When he got to the Castle's front lawn he could hear officers shouting orders, trying to get things organized, trying to keep men like Al, up from the Bell tents below, from overrunning the site and hampering rescue operations.

Al felt a hand grabbing his arm and a shout to stay where he was. He swore and jerked away from the restraint, pushing his way around to the severed side of the Castle, where he stopped when he sensed men behind him. He turned to see that he was leading a section. In the flickering light he recognized Crow and Reggie, Dougie Dobson, Davy Ross and Arnie Christensen. He nodded and pointed ahead to a pile of rubble that had cascaded down on a row of slit trenches. In a minute they were scrabbling through the choking dust, moving timbered beams and lifting stones. Then they were on their knees digging with their hands.

"Hey, move over!"

"Give us some room here!"

Two rough, male voices on either side of Al, one belonging to Willy Yates, the other to Billy Assad, kneeling, digging in silence until Billy cursed and held up his hand. He'd sliced open a couple of knuckles on a sharp piece of stone. Yates reached into his pocket and pulled out a handkerchief that he quickly wrapped around the wound. Billy grunted his thanks and went back to work.

About halfway down into the slit trench Billy uncovered an arm and yelled for a torch. Digging more quickly now and at the same time more carefully, they uncovered what used to be a face. Now it was a bludgeoned mass of gristle, skin and bone, just enough recognizable features left to know it wasn't Barney or Goody.

Al stood and called for others to take over, motioning Yates and Billy to follow him as he made his way over to another trench. There he grabbed Billy's torch and shone it into the hole as another body was uncovered, this one alive and gasping for air.

He did this over and over again at trench after trench, Yates and Billy on his heels, all three of them dreading what they might find.

When they came to the last trench and saw that its excavation had produced nothing, no soldiers in it, dead or alive, their dread turned to hope. Maybe Barney and Goody had decided they didn't have time to hit the trenches. Maybe they'd hunkered down safe inside the Castle.

This was Billy's idea and the other two followed him toward the driveway entrance. It was harder to see now, the fires in the outbuildings had been doused by the village firemen and the dark had once more come upon them, so it wasn't until the last moment that Al's torch picked out a stretcher being carried out the door. On the stretcher was a body shrouded in a blanket and Al felt something go inside him. He knew even before he drew back the blanket and shone his light on the dead man's face. Goody's face.

"Fuck!" Both of Billy's fists were clenched above his head. He was screaming at the stars and the moon and the gods of war. Goody Noseworthy had just turned sixteen.

One of the bearers swung his head back toward the Castle behind him. "There's another one in there. Found him lyin' on top of this guy. Looked like he was tryin' ta protect him or somethin'."

Al and Yates ran stumbling into the Castle, turning right as they entered, toward the side hacked off by the V-1. It didn't take them long to find Barney. He was propped up in a corner, covered in dust, his eyes closed, his breathing ragged, an MO kneeling beside him taking his pulse. When he saw Willy and Al, the MO shook his head.

Just then Barney's eyes fluttered open, his mouth working. He was trying to say something and Al dropped to his knees, leaning closer to hear the hoarse whisper.

"What did he say?" Yates was kneeling on Barney's other side.

"Wants to know how Goody is." Al could barely get the words out.

Yates moved in and spoke into Barney's ear. "Goody's fine, Barney. Fit as a fiddle. Thanks to you. You saved his life."

Barney smiled. And then he died.

PART THREE

Chapter Seventeen

JULY 23, 1944. Portsmouth Harbour. Here we are stuffed on board an LSI waiting for a convoy to form up to take us over to Juno Beach and I'm using the time to make my first entry in Barney's Dairy. I should have done this sooner but I just didn't have it in me. Hard for a zombie to do anything and that's exactly what I was in the days after the V-1 hit the Castle. Even had to force myself to write to Ben and Sadie. Billy wrote to Goody's folks. Of course he feels guilty as hell but Reggie told him that Goody wanted to join up and would have even if Billy had said nothing to encourage him. That made Billy feel a bit better but he still has a look about him that worries me. Anyway I've read everything Barney's written so far and now its up to me to finish what he started. I owe it to him and the people who someday will want to read it. So here goes. We left Sussex on 18 July by truck for Camp T, our marshalling area northeast of London. Went through the city with a Metropolitan Police escort at daybreak on 19 July and the early-rising Londoners cheered us all along the way. Just the way it was in Liverpool. When we got to the camp we were told to pay close attention to whistles. If we heard one it meant a buzz bomb was on its way. The night was not too restful as the whistle blew 52 times. Fortunately none of the rocket bombs landed anywhere near the camp. Maybe Lady Luck was giving us a break after Wadhurst. On the morning of 20 July we boarded our ships and off we went down the Thames but not too far as a storm in the Channel brought a halt to our progress. We didn't get to Dover until last evening and that was a night to remember, a real fireworks display. It seemed like all the anti-aircraft guns in Southern England were shooting at the buzz bombs and every time one was knocked down a great cheer went up from the spectators in the front row seats. Got to Portsmouth early this morning and word is we are to set out tonight under cover of darkness for Normandy and the rest of German occupied Europe! So Barney, here we go!

Excerpt from the Diary

On the morning of July 24 the men of the 4th Canadian Armoured Division woke up to find themselves in a traffic jam in the middle of the English Channel. Ships were everywhere—big ones, little ones and ones in between—

battleships, cruisers and destroyers, corvettes and minesweepers, but mostly now supply ships and Liberty ships, landing craft like the ones in Inveraray and landing craft they'd never seen before. Below the barrage balloons glistening like fresh-caught fish in the sky, the green waters of the Channel were choppy, not because of bad weather but because of wave-churning traffic all around them.

The Algonquins jostled for position on their LSI, shading their eyes from the bright morning sun, trying to make out the coast of France, trying to decide what was land and what was fog bank, as cormorants dive-bombed in front of their bow and cold spray splashed in their faces, a bracing aftershave lotion of salt water.

A shout and a pointing to the horizon. A black pencil line on a white sheet of paper, a line that grew thicker and darker as the LSI got closer and closer. Normandy! Al could see it now, Juno Beach, a strip of sand that forty-eight days ago had been held by Jerry and now looked to be populated by scurrying ants.

The ants turned out to be Jeeps and trucks and carriers and tanks, landing craft off-loading men and materiel. Now they could see landmarks they'd seen on film clips, the church steeple in the town of Courseulles, the lone house on the shore at Bernières-sur-Mer where the 9th Canadian Infantry Brigade had landed, the peaked roof and latticed siding, the balcony around the second floor.

Then two landing craft were coming toward them, one on either side of their LSI, and they heard the *arougah, arougah* of the craft's klaxon and the order over the Tannoy: "Attention! Attention! All hands. Prepare to disembark. Prepare to disembark."

Soon they were over the side climbing down the scramble net to the landing craft wallowing in the sea below, and in no time at all the craft was heading to shore and edging up to the beach where the nose ramp went down with a creak and a clang on the sand and the Canadians of 4th Armoured Division scrambled into Nazi-occupied France with not even the tips of their boots in water. So much for Inveraray.

The flat beach stretched as far as the eye could see and the sand beneath their boots was fine and white, the kind you could scoop under your toes and drag out in little furrows; but this was neither the time nor the place for bare feet in the sand.

As soon as they were all off the landing craft, they were formed up and quick-marched off the beach, boots slipping on the sand and then digging in for purchase up past dunes crowned with tufts of thick beach grass. Al reached down and ran a blade of the grass between his fingers. It felt like the palm fronds given out at church on the Sunday before Easter.

When he reached the top of the dunes he saw that the terrain levelled out again to more sand, this time with poppies. *In Flanders fields the poppies blow* . . . He stopped and used the back of his hand to wipe sweat from his forehead.

Once through the poppies, on another rise, the column passed the blackened remains of a German gun emplacement. Or maybe a pillbox. It was hard to tell because, whatever it had been, it was now crushed beneath what looked like a carelessly flipped, thick pancake of concrete that had landed half on a hotplate and half hanging over.

Beyond the concrete pancake, trucks were waiting to take them to their holding area, a farmer's field between the villages of Banville and Tierceville about three miles from the beach. Al jumped in a Jeep the better to see the scenery along the way.

Through the narrow, shattered streets of Courseulles and past a cemetery sheltered by red brick walls breached here and there by stray shelling, the convoy turned southwest through gently rolling countryside and cultivated farm fields dotted by thickets of trees and burned-out Sherman tanks.

It was here in the fields off the Normandy beaches and later in the fighting inland that the Shermans gained their nicknames, not based on glorious and daring exploits but on what happened to them when hit by enemy fire: flashing into flame so fast that their own crews called them Ronsons after the popular cigarette lighter of the day, so dependable it was advertised as lighting up "first time, every time." The Germans were more cruel. They used the popular word for British soldiers and called the Shermans "Tommy Cookers."

Banville was the next settlement on their route, its outskirts marked by a huge crucifix looming by the side of the road, the agony of the crucified Messiah compounded by more recent events. The village, not a soul in sight, was just a cluster of mostly intact cobblestone houses with slate roofs, built so close to the cobblestone street that Al was sure he could reach out and touch both sides at the same time if he could just extend his arms another inch.

Past Banville they trucked on for about a mile until waved off the road into a field ringed by tanks and the regiment's carriers, which had arrived the day before. Officers bustled about issuing orders, the first of which was to dig in, a not-so-easy task given that a foot under the soil was a layer of chalk, part of the same rocky piece of God's creation as Vera Lynn's white cliffs of Dover and just as hard.

For supper they dug into their Composite or Compo-rations for a sumptuous repast of meat and vegetables, M. and V. for short, which, after one bite, Billy christened Muck and Vomit. Then it was off to bed in their shallow, chalk-lined trenches reminding some of them of coffins lined in white.

The next morning, groaning from an aching night, Allan McDougal looked up to see Billy bearing a cup of tea and a copy of the Northwest Europe version of *The Maple Leaf News*.

First published in January 1944 for Canadians fighting in Italy, the *News* was a four-page tabloid written for soldiers by soldiers with some help from Canadian war correspondents like Ross Munro, Doug How and Charles Lynch.

The paper featured reports from the front lines—reprints from Reuters and Canadian Press—news from England dubbed "Mild and Bitter" and news from Canada, a regular feature called "Home Brew," sports scores, soldier poetry, letters to the editor, pin-ups, comic strips, *Blondie* and *Li'l Abner*, and cartoons featuring the voluptuous Jane, who wound up almost nude in every issue. Finally there was Bing Coughlin's *Herbie*, the weary and bedraggled, hapless and chinless Canadian soldier with the big nose, flat feet and no illusions about life in the PBI. Herbie was the first Canadian casualty on D-Day, stubbing his toe on Juno Beach.

The issue of *The Maple Leaf News* that Billy handed his sergeant that first morning on the field of battle was bordered in black, headlined in bold type. **Murder of Soldiers Stirs Canada's Hatred.**

The story was about a gruesome discovery on the grounds of L'Abbaye Ardenne, a crumbling medieval monastery just outside of Caen, the last resting place for seven North Nova Scotia Highlanders, each one shot in the back of the head.

Piecing together bits and pieces of information gleaned from French civilians and Canadian military sources, the reporter told how the North Novas had been captured the day after D-Day and brought to L'Abbaye Ardenne on June 8. L'Abbaye was then the headquarters of the 25th SS Panzer Grenadier Regiment of the 12th SS Panzer Division, or Hitler *Jugend*. The division's commander was *Standartenführer* Kurt Meyer.

For those who knew little of the 12th SS, there was another story on the front page, a backgrounder under the heading, **Hitler Jugend: The Führer's Teenage Fanatics.**

The Hitler *Jugend*, or Hitler Youth, was a Nazi version of Canada's Boy Scouts with one crucial difference. In Canada, the Boy Scouts were taught the precepts of Lord Baden-Powell, stressing knowledge of the outdoors and good citizenship. In Germany the Hitler Youth were indoctrinated with Nazi ideology stressing racial superiority, reverence for, and unquestioning obedience to, *Der Führer.*

Following the German defeat at Stalingrad in February of 1943 and the loss of the 6th Army, some three hundred thousand men, the Nazi regime was forced to turn to the *Jugend*, a huge reserve of youthful fanaticism, nine million strong. The teenagers were trained and led by SS officers, sadistic veterans of Nazi extermination camps and the slaughter of millions of innocents in Eastern Europe. The bloodstained leading the bloodthirsty. As the North Novas found out.

One of the French civilians, a woman who had been conscripted to cook for Meyer and his officers, saw the Canadians being herded inside L'Abbaye's courtyard. Their captors led them to a horse stall where they were forced to kneel, their hands tied together in front. When Meyer was told of their presence he was angry and turned to one of his officers, speaking in a low voice. Then the officer went over to the Canadians and began to question them. When it was obvious he wasn't getting the answers he wanted, he searched each of the seven and took all of their identification papers.

A few minutes later the woman, watching from a window in her quarters, heard a name called and saw one of the North Novas in the open stall dragged to his feet by a kid in a camouflage uniform spotted green and brown. The Canadian was pushed stumbling across the courtyard of L'Abbaye, past the sullen officer who had questioned him, past a duck pond and then up five stone steps into a tiny walled and shaded garden where monks once prayed to Mary, *in primus gloriosae semper Virginis Mariae, Genitricus Dei et Domini nostri Jesu Christi*. Almost the instant the Canadian was out of the Frenchwoman's sight a shot rang out.

The woman watched this happen six more times. It was all over, she said, in ten minutes. Seven Canadians. Nine shots. Because twice the first was not enough.

She said that after the first *exécution*, the remaining Canadians knew what was happening and before each one was then taken from the stall, he turned and shook tied hands with the comrades he was leaving behind. Forever.

She finished by telling Canadian military authorities that the last shot was still echoing from the garden when an SS sergeant came out and down the steps, smiling as he reloaded his pistol.

When Al finished reading, Billy spat out his question. "When do we get a shot at these bastards, Al?"

It was a good question because on the day it was asked the battle for Normandy was at a stalemate. By D-Day +90, Allied forces were supposed to be on the Seine, about sixty-five miles straight across northern France from Caen. But here it was D-Day +50, and they were barely on the far side of Caen. Instead of sixty-five miles they'd done about ten. At this rate it would take them almost a full year to get to the Seine and another six months to Paris and it would be 1946 before they got to Berlin.

The problem was *Feldmarschall* Erwin Rommel, the Desert Fox, who had given the British fits in North Africa. Now in Normandy, he was staging a repeat performance as his "well-trained, well-equipped and battle-hardened" army inflicted heavy casualties on the advancing Anglo-Canadian forces. The *Feldmarschall* ceded ground in yards only, grudging, bloody yards littered with bodies and the blackened hulls of hundreds of Tommy Cookers, both British and Canadian.

When the commander of the Anglo-Canadian forces, a frustrated General Bernard Montgomery, finally called upon the services of Bomber Command and Caen was virtually blown to bits, the Germans simply withdrew to positions on the high ground overlooking the city. After spending more than a month trying to get into Caen, Montgomery now had to find a way to get out. His way was lambs to the slaughter.

First it was an attack, code-named GOODWOOD, on July 18, with three armoured divisions, the biggest British tank assault in history. Two hundred of these tanks were destroyed by the *Wehrmacht*.

Next, on July 25, it was the turn of the Canadians in operation SPRING. The attack began the night before, using "Monty's Moonlight," bouncing searchlight beams off the cloud cover so that advancing forces could see in the dark.

But the ability to see in the dark could not overcome poor intelligence, a bad battle plan and a tough enemy. Operation SPRING was a disaster, more than 450 killed and another thousand wounded or captured, the worst mauling of a Canadian force since Dieppe.

It was not until the end of the month that Billy was to get an answer to his angry question and it came at a hamlet by the name of Hubert-Folie, which the Algonquins called "Hubert's Folly."

Chapter Eighteen

JULY 31, 1944. Hubert's Folly. Here in relief of the Stormont, Dundas & Glengarry Highlanders who can't stop grinning at our shiny Carriers, fresh uniforms and clean faces. They are a dirty, filthy, tired bunch and tell us that in a week or so we'll be just like them. Drove through Caen. Could smell it before we could see it, the stench of Slaughterhouse Lake. Unburied bodies everywhere, swollen and black. Too far gone to tell if they were German Army or French civilians. This used to be the capital of Normandy, a port city, a transportation and communications hub, five rail lines out of here and eleven major roads but when we saw the place it looked like Sudbury after an earthquake. Where buildings were still standing all the windows had been blown out and there were whole blocks with no buildings at all. Just pile after pile of snapped roof beams, splintered timber and heaps of stone. Our position at the Folly is about three miles southeast of Caen with the Ash Cans in Bras just northwest of us and the Lincs in Burgerbus about half a mile down the road south and east of us. Jerry is right in front of us, less than a mile away on top of a rise which we are told is Tilly-la-Campagne. Perfect spot for him. He can see everything we do down here and any little movement gets the attention of his mortars.

Excerpt from the Diary

Al heard his name being called and looked up from his writing to see Billy beckoning him over to Gill's carrier. All of the regiment's vehicles in Hubert-Folie were parked in an apple orchard to give them some privacy from the prying eyes at Tilly-la-Campagne. For added protection all trucks and Jeeps were nestled in dugouts to keep tires and radiators safe from flying shrapnel.

Al put pen and scribbler aside, set his tin hat on his head and made his way over to see Billy lifting the corner of a tarp covering some boxes tied down just above the name Gill had chosen for his vehicle, the lettering, *Gillie's Cruiser*, in white paint courtesy of Crow, who evidently had a hidden talent with a brush, a talent now in great demand. This meant they had seen more of Crow in the past few days than they had in some time because he was always around with his paintbrush satisfying the sudden need to name the carriers, a fad imported from the South Albertas, whose Shermans were all labelled. So far Al was resisting Billy's pressure to get with it.

"Yeah, so, *Gillie's Cruiser*. I'm supposed to get all excited and pee my pants."

"No, no. Not the name. Look what's under the tarp."

Al looked and whistled. "So that's where he got the stuff. The dirty bugger, he brought us what, two bottles, and he's got four boxes of it? I'll be damned."

The stuff was Calvados, the national drink of Normandy. Distilled from hard apple cider, it tasted like a bad cognac and at seventy percent proof packed a wallop even more powerful than Newfy screech, so potent that some of the lads with Ronsons used it for lighter fluid and it worked just like the original, "first time, every time."

"Aw, shit!"

Billy had clambered up on the *Cruiser* and was pointing down the row of apple trees toward the road, a Jeep and a truck heading for the orchard and trailing a plume of dust, a marker for Jerry.

This time his mortars were almost close enough for the men in the orchard to hear the *chug* of shells being launched, certainly close enough to register the *whir-a-whir-a* of their flight through the air.

The first explosions straddled the road about fifty yards in front of the oncoming vehicles. Then the road itself was hit dead centre. Jerry had it zeroed in and he was a damn good shot and the Jeep and the truck drove right into the barrage.

The Jeep flipped over and skidded on its back into the ditch, the driver and passengers crushed to death in the slide. The truck made it through but drew Jerry's fire into the orchard, where all hell broke loose as the mortars were now joined by eighty-eights, the first indication the explosion, the black puff of the airburst, the noise coming after, the wham and screech of metal grinding against metal, shells bursting in the treetops, showering shrapnel, tree limbs and green apples on the cowering Algonquins.

It was all over in five minutes and when the casualties were added up, six men were dead, eleven wounded, and Billy and Al were flammable. Shrapnel had punctured the bottles of Calvados on the back of the *Cruiser* and the two emerged from shelter drizzled in a sweet stickiness.

Grumbling about the food at supper that evening kept the minds of the newly initiated off the dead and wounded. Besides Muck and Vomit, Compo-rations offered a wide variety of other tasty dishes including Snake and Kidney (steak and kidney pudding), Stewed Snake (stewed steak), and Sewer Trout (salmon or sardines).

Al looked around at familiar faces, shaking his head and thinking how they were all turning into strangers, especially to themselves. He had always talked to himself, but now was cursing out loud, usually when nothing at all was happening, so that others looked at him and when they did he would grin and shake his head as if to say, "It's nothing, guys." And the night sweats were back along with the nightmares, drowned babies wrapped in shawls, floating, eyes open.

Billy had developed a head snap, a quick pecking movement like a robin at a worm. It too came, not when he was busy, but when he wasn't.

Yates had dropped all of his masks and seemed a little less confident about the world, the flesh and the devil. Reggie hadn't touched his guitar in weeks. Ross spent more time with Max than he did with his comrades. He'd built a bed for the cat in his carrier, a Compo-rations box lined with an assortment of used army issue—socks, underwear, and bits and pieces of blanket.

Arnie was more talkative than he'd ever been and Crow was more quiet. Dougie Dobson had taken to reading the New Testament, a leather-bound copy about the size of his hand and an inch thick. He kept it in his breast pocket over his heart because he'd remembered Sunday School stories from the Great War of how the Word of God miraculously stopped bullets.

Billy laughed at him, but Gill spoke for the majority when he told Dobson, "What the hell, Dougie, if it helps you get through this shit, then more power to you."

After they'd eaten and long after the casualties of the afternoon had been taken care of, Gill came by to examine the shattered remains of his Calvados and to announce that he had a job for them that night.

"Those mortar rounds this afternoon. Had to come from somewhere close by. Captain wants some men to poke around down there. See what else is going on. Maybe bring back a couple of prisoners for interrogation. Asked me if I knew a few good men who could do the job."

Al noticed that Gillie had taken to speaking in short, clipped sentences and thought of asking him about it, but instead posed a different question with a grin.

"So whataya doin' here? No good men around here."

"Good enough to find Jerry in the bush."

"Oh, that kinda good."

"Yup. That's the kind."

When his proposal elicited grunts of approval Gill pointed at Billy and Al, "You two. Wash out your battledress. Don't want Jerry to smell you coming a mile away tonight."

After dark they formed up in running shoes and blackface—Al, Billy, Arnie, Reggie, Crow, and Yates in place of Popovich. To guard against moonlight reflecting off headgear, tin hats were exchanged for berets. Weapons consisted of combat knives along with grenades and Stens wrapped in cloth to cushion any noise.

Their own artillery spotters figured the German mortars were between themselves at Hubert-Folie and the Lincoln and Wellands at Bourguébus, or Burgerbus, as Al insisted on calling it, the most likely location being a copse in the middle of a grain field south of the highway and west of the railway tracks.

The Lincs and Winks had cleared mines from both sides of the track the night before and laid down white tape indicating where it was safe to go, so the Algonquins moved quickly down to a point just opposite the woods and then slithered up and over the tracks and across the open space between the grain and the copse in no time flat, hitting the ground on their bellies at the tree line, noses inches from the ground covered in twigs and smelling of loam. No one moved a muscle, not even when swarms of man-eating bugs found them ripe for the taking. Except for their own muffled breathing, there wasn't a sound except for the night breeze and its whispering caress of the leaves in the trees.

After a couple of minutes Gill pointed to Frank Archibald and then at the woods. Quickly the Indian was on his feet and into the copse, disappearing without a sound. Now you see him, now you don't.

In twenty minutes he was back and whispering a Popovich, one of the Pole's more famous assaults on the King's English: "Looks like they flayed the coop. Left behind a few shell casings and a latrine pit, but that's about it."

Twisting his wrist to catch the moonlight, Gill looked at the time. "Early yet, boys. What say you? A little more exploring? Up that path there," he was pointing with his head to a narrow trail that snaked up the edge of the grain field towards Tilly. "Unless I miss my guess, Jerry's using that path. Mortars back and forth. Should be okay."

So off they went, slowly with Crow on point stopping every few yards to check the trail and to listen with an ear that could pick up the footfall of a rabbit.

About a hundred yards up the track, Al, who was bringing up the rear, saw shadows fast-dodging back down toward him, shadows taking on the shape of his comrades led by their lieutenant, who put a finger to his lips and motioned him along with the others off the trail for a quick squat-down conference. He spoke in a low voice.

"Jerry patrol coming down the track. We split up. Both sides. Let 'em pass. We'll follow. See what they're up to."

Al pointed to Arnie and Billy to go left with Gill into the grain. He would burrow into the hedgerow on the right with Crow and Yates. But it was an impossible mass of hawthorn and brambles, thick, impenetrable trunks, branches and vines, and at the last moment the three of them scurried back across into the grain to join the others.

No sooner had the parted stocks of grain swayed back into place than the first of the Germans appeared, a nonchalant *Waffen SS Scharführer,* both Al and Yates close enough to see the white lightning flashes on the collar of his tiger jacket, the camouflage windbreaker that draped over his camouflage pants, both jacket and pants spotted to blend with the colours of summer foliage, different shades of green and yellow and brown.

The *Scharführer* carried a Schmeisser submachine gun at his hip on a shoulder harness with two potato mashers jammed in the leather belt around his waist. Behind him at regularly spaced intervals came the rest of the patrol, nine soldiers in all, each tiger-jacketed, each with grenades, and most with Schmeissers except for the two who carried *Maschinengewehrs* or MG 42s, the German equivalent of the Bren.

As the Germans passed by close enough to spit on, Al's sensory memory kicked in when the warm night breeze caught the scent of sweat mixed with sauerkraut.

Was the SS patrol like their patrol, he wondered as he wrinkled his nose, sent to find out what the Algonquins were up to and maybe grab a prisoner or two for interrogation? Or was it a fighting patrol sent out to kill?

Gill was also weighing the same possibilities and, as soon as the last of the Germans disappeared down the trail, called an immediate council of war.

The Canadians were outnumbered but they had the element of surprise. Should they use it to wipe out the patrol or should they just try to grab a couple of the tail-end Jerries and sneak away with two prisoners?

In the end they decided to do what Gill's first instinct told him to do. Follow and see what Jerry was up to.

The Germans headed for the copse and disappeared among the trees. The Algonquins waited and watched. After about fifteen minutes, two sections— three men each—came out, one with an MG 42 and led by the *Scharführer* heading for the railway tracks, the other setting up on the trail as it came around the other side of the copse leading toward the Canadian forward line.

This deployment of the sections made Gill's decision for him. He would follow the one that was splitting the farthest from the others, the one with the MG headed for the tracks. He would surprise the Germans and take them prisoner.

Once again Crow was point and was told to stay as close to the enemy as he could, which wasn't hard as the enemy didn't bother much with silence until they got to the tracks. There, at a point where the rails came out of a long curve much like the T& NO line outside of Lowvert, the Germans set up the MG on a bipod in the depression on the same white-taped path the Algonquin patrol had used a few hours before.

When the machine gun was ready the *Scharführer* patted his comrades on the back and made his way quietly up the track ditch toward the Algonquin lines. His job was to pick a spot off the path where he would hide and watch the *Kanucks* pass by. Then he would follow, waiting until he heard the MG firing before moving forward to deal with any frightened stragglers his comrades had missed.

The Algonquins saw all this in the moonlight and planned accordingly. After a whispered conversation with Crow, Gill sent him to follow the *Scharführer* while he and Al, along with Billy, Arnie and Yates, took care of the MG crew.

Carefully and quietly, knives in their hands, they inched up behind the two SS at the MG. When they were close enough Al spoke in a low voice. "*Achtung. Für euch ist der Krieg zu Ende.*"

The two Germans jumped, their last movement as free men because Billy and Arnie rushed them and, pummelling them hard, shoved them face down to the ground before they could cry out. Quickly they were tied up, hands behind their backs, rolled over, frisked, dragged to their feet and pushed up over the rails to the other side of the track.

Leaving Billy to guard them with orders to shoot if they made a move, Gill gestured to the other three to follow him. As they left, Al looked over his shoulder at Billy, wondering if he was the right man to be left with his finger on the trigger of a Sten pointed at the two prisoners.

The four of them took their time navigating up the ditch on the side opposite the *Scharführer*, where Crow was keeping a watchful eye.

Once back to the junction of road and track where Reggie had been left to cover their rear, Arnie whistled and in a minute Reggie was beside them and in another minute after listening to Gill, followed them back down the rail line, this time on the side where the *Scharführer* was lying in wait. The plan was to make believe they were a patrol and get the German to do exactly what Gillie figured he was going to do.

Al thought it was all pretty risky. What if what Gillie thought was Jerry's intention wasn't? He shook his head and blew air. But Gillie seemed to know what he was doing and he *had* studied German tactics, so his sergeant swallowed his doubts and went along.

Having no real idea where the German was hiding off the trail, they kept going, kept up the pretense of an ordinary patrol, with Al sweating buckets and jumping at every sound the night made. When they reached the spot where the Germans had set up the MG, they hunkered down in ambush.

Their wait was brief. Crow's distant warning caw was almost immediately followed by the *Scharführer* looming out of the darkness, softly calling out names and asking questions in guttural German. Reggie's response was to let loose a burst from his Bren at the feet of the German, who cursed and danced away, right into the arms of Arnie, who grabbed him in a choke hold with a knife at his throat. The captive struggled briefly but stopped when Arnie's knife nicked flesh and Al and Yates appeared with their Stens aimed at his belly.

Gillie was euphoric, his fist pumping the air as he stepped out to take in the scene, the German face down, his hands being tied behind his back by Al, grunting as he twisted rope into tight knots. When Crow appeared to stand beside him, Gillie hugged him and then sent him over the tracks to get Billy and his charges.

The first faint lines of dawn were streaking the sky red, illuminating Canadian faces creased with huge grins as they shook hands all round, just like the old days in Lowvert after winning a hard-fought softball game.

Their prisoners sneered at this display. Not for them the cowed expression of the captured and defeated. They were professionals, their captors hillbillies. When Billy glanced over and saw the looks he felt a surge of anger, hurts old and new welling up.

"You frisk this guy?" Billy kicked out a foot indicating the *Scharführer*, a tough-looking representative of Hitler's finest.

"Jesus, no. We forgot," whispered Gill. "Just took his Schmeisser and grenades."

"Let me do the honours, then."

Billy laid down his weapon and walked over to the sitting prisoner. Squatting in front of him he beamed his best Sunday-go-to-Meeting smile and then backhanded the Nazi across the face, snapping his head to the side.

"For Chrissakes, Billy!" Al rushed over and put a hand on his friend's shoulder.

Billy shook it off. "It's okay, Al. Everything's okay. Everything's copacetic. Take a look, if you don't believe me."

Billy was nodding at the German who was smirking at both of them, a trickle of blood on the side of his mouth.

"Hey Yates, come over here." Billy kept his voice low. No point in making any more noise than was necessary.

Yates ambled over and Billy asked him if he knew Jerry's rank. The American shifted his Sten to his left hand and reached down with his right to pluck at the prisoner's jacket arm. "Looks like he's a *Scharführer*, a sergeant."

"Hear that, Al? Gerald here is a sergeant. Just like you. But he's a lot tougher, aren't ya, Gerald? You're a big shot. You're SS. My sergeant here's just a pussy compared to you, eh, sport?"

Billy was still squatting in front of his captive when the Nazi spat. Right on target. But Billy just grinned and flicked expectorant, phlegm and blood, from his forehead and cheek.

"Hey, I don't like you either, sport, but I got a job ta do and that's ta see what ya got in your pockets."

Billy gestured the sergeant to his feet. The German stood about a head taller than the Canadian, who set to work emptying every pocket the Nazi had. Then he stood and kicked the prisoner's feet out from under him as he pushed him tumbling to the ground.

"Little unsteady on yer feet, eh Gerald? You wanna do somethin' about that. Clumsy doesn't look good for the Master Race."

While Yates casually pointed his Sten to discourage any reaction, Billy squatted and pulled the sergeant's boots off, all the while keeping up his running, one-sided conversation, solemnly shaking his head at the German, who'd used a helping hand from Yates to push himself up into a sitting position

"Jesus, Gerald. Your feet really stink. You ever take a bath? Must have had one or two, eh? To wash the blood off."

Finished with the boots, Billy threw them aside. "How many Jews have you killed, Gerald? Not the whole fuckin' SS. But you personally? Ten? Twenty? We had a buddy was a Jew. You understand what I'm talkin about? *Jude?*"

The German's eyes flickered. "Yeah, you understand, don'tcha. Too bad he's not here right now. Used to tell us he couldn't wait to stick his Lee Enfield in a Nazi face and say, *Ich bin ein Jude*. Did I get that right, Gerald? I'm not very good at German. Can say a few things in Lebanese but German's too tough for me. Just a dumb Canuck hick, eh, Gerald."

Billy walked around behind the now bootless prisoner to check his tied hands and when he reached to test the knots he saw a glint of gold on the German's right wrist. For some reason he couldn't explain, then or later when he asked himself about it, he unclasped the watch and stuck it in his pants pocket.

The sneer returned to the *Scharführer's* face as he straightened his shoulders. Watching him Al had the feeling he was putting on a show for his comrades, who both looked younger than Ross, and it occurred to him with a start that he was face to face with the Hitler *Jugend*.

Billy reached down and grabbed the rope around the German's wrists, jerking him to his feet just as Gill came over.

"Okay, lads, time to get this show on the road. Let's march these bastards out of here. Let the Intelligence boys have a go at them at HQ."

Headquarters was located above the orchard in a chateau surrounded by trees and high hedges. The building had been badly damaged by heavy shelling, the grey concrete facade pitted and gouged, the windows on each of its three storeys and the two dormers on the roof shattered. But its four walls were standing and there was still serviceable space inside for all the paraphernalia of an army's nerve centre: field telephones and radios, number nineteen wireless A sets; maps tacked to boards resting on easels lit by shaded bulbs hanging above them and illuminating scores of coloured dots and arrows; portable stoves to brew a cuppa; folding tables and benches and assorted chairs and sofas culled from what original furniture had survived.

Going through the orchard on their way to HQ they attracted a crowd, comrades at breakfast leaving their Compo-ration baked beans, greasy bacon and hardtack biscuits with plum jam to congratulate patrol members and have a gander at the three Jerries who stood for inspection with the same look of disdain they had maintained since their capture.

While the lads gawked at the Germans, much as they used to stare at the carnival freaks featured in the shows that toured Northern Ontario every summer, Gill hurried off for a conference with his superiors. By the time he returned the excitement was over and the crowd dispersed.

He took his sergeant aside and Billy could see Al shaking his head vigorously as Gill spoke to him. As he watched the argument unfold, Billy remembered the timepiece he'd taken from Gerald and reached to take it out of his pocket.

The first thing he noticed was that it was a Bulova, just like the one Al had when the *Caribou* was torpedoed. Billy frowned, wondering what a German soldier was doing with a Bulova. Then he turned it over and saw the engraving on the back. Holding it to the light of the morning sun he read, "Walter Doherty. Graduation 1938."

Billy frowned again, thinking this time, picking at something stuck in a corner of his memory, and suddenly felt a cold shiver run across his shoulder blades. Pocketing the watch he went in search of Willy Yates, who was slumped against Al's carrier, sipping from a bottle of Calvados and smoking a cigarette.

Billy sat beside him and asked if he still had a copy of *The Maple Leaf News*, the one he'd given him, the one with the story of the killings at L'Abbaye Ardenne. Yates looked puzzled and shook his head.

"What do you want that for, Billy?" Yates passed him the bottle and Billy took a long drink that burned down his throat. His reply was a gasping wheeze.

"Tryin' to remember some names. The North Novas Jerry shot. I remember readin' their names in the paper, lots of mackerelsnappers, but damned if I can remember any of them."

While Billy coughed from the Calvados, Yates looked off in the distance searching through the storehouse of his mind. Then he nodded slowly. "I seem to recall a lot of Macs and Micks, you know, like McDougal. Which makes sense. Highlanders after all."

Yates pushed himself upright as if standing might jog his memory. He began a to and fro pacing thinking out loud, "Mac, Mac . . ." He shook his head in frustration. Then he stopped short.

"Wait a sec. There was an Irish name, I remember thinking about it, wondering how this Irish guy got mixed up with all those Scots."

He gave a satisfied nod. "Doherty. Yup, the name was Doherty."

He was grinning when he turned to glance at Billy. But the grin froze when he saw Billy lurching to his feet with an expression that started out as horror then segued into grief and just as quickly set in rage.

"Walter Doherty, Willy. His first name was Walter and he got a watch for graduating from high school."

This all came out in a growl and then Billy was gone, leaving Yates to wonder how his comrade knew so much about Walter Doherty. He stood for a minute, staring at the ground, his mind working. Then he stuffed the cork back in the Calvados bottle, stuck it in a corner of the carrier, and set off in pursuit, catching up to Billy just as he was in the middle of a heated discussion with Gill.

As Yates joined them Billy turned to him. "Yates and I'll take 'em up to HQ, Gillie. It'll be all right. You and Al got things ta do."

"Take who up?" Yates looked at Billy.

"The three Jerries."

Gill looked doubtful. His conversation with Al, the one Billy had witnessed, had been about this very subject, Al telling him that under no circumstances was Billy to have anything more to do with the prisoners.

But when Gill thought about it, Billy was right. Both he and Al did have other things to do. Something was up and he had been summoned to an O Group for 0900 hours and he wanted Al along to help him brief the Orders Group on what they'd seen on their patrol. Not much, but every little bit helped.

It was Billy's suggestion that Yates go with him that made up his mind. "Okay, take 'em up. The two of you. No shenanigans." He looked directly at Billy, who nodded.

Once the two of them had picked up their weapons, they went to gather their charges, who had been fed and watered by Reggie and Arnie, who were glad to get rid of the cocky bastards.

With their hands clasped above their heads, the three Hitler *Jugend* were herded off through the orchard up toward the chateau, Yates leading and Billy bringing up the rear right behind the *Scharführer* in his stocking feet.

Once beyond the eyes and ears of the orchard encampment, Billy called to Yates, who circled back to hear what his buddy wanted. After a short conversation the American shrugged and went back to the two kids, gesturing with his Sten. The three of them moved on, leaving Billy with the Nazi NCO.

Billy glanced around till he saw what he was looking for. Then jabbing his Lee Enfield in the German's ribs, he pushed him toward an opening in a circular hedgerow he had remembered seeing from the road the day they had come down from the holding area. He'd wondered then if it had been a play area for the children from the chateau or a little pen for keeping cattle. Once inside he saw it was the latter, the ground littered with old cow pies, and bare where cattle had eaten away the grass.

Billy jabbed the Nazi through the crumbling and dusty pies up against the far side of the hedgerow, where he turned him around. Stepping back a few paces and cradling his rifle in one arm, he reached with his free hand into the pocket of his blouse, pulling out Walter Doherty's graduation gift.

"Recognize this, ya fucker?"

He held the watch up by its band. The *Scharführer*, hands on his head, looked but his eyes said nothing.

"Sure ya do. Belonged to a kid, a Canadian kid ya shot in the back of the head."

Billy made a pistol with his thumb and forefinger and pointed it at his own head. "Bang! You shot him and took his watch, you gutless prick!"

Again the Nazi gave away nothing. Billy spat on the ground. "So you and I, Gerald, are gonna have a little trial here, see, and I'm gonna be the judge, the jury and the executioner. Get it?"

Billy put the watch back in his pocket and raised his rifle, pointing it at the German's head.

"The charge, Gerald, is murder. You shot and killed Canadian prisoners of war in cold blood. That's against the Geneva Convention, see. So I find you guilty of murder and I hereby sentence you to death by a firing squad of one. Me. Do you understand what I'm sayin', you son of a bitch?"

Billy was shouting now, shouting and crying, the tears wetting the stubble on his cheeks, the rifle twitching in his outstretched arms. He lowered it and held it in one hand, wiping tears with the other. Then quickly, resolutely, he raised his weapon and aimed again. Calmer now.

"I also find you guilty in the deaths of Barney Berman and Goody Noseworthy and a lot of other guys who died tryin' ta save this world from the likes of you and your kind, you SS bastard!"

With that Billy took a deep breath, steadied his aim, and pulled the trigger.

Chapter Nineteen

AUGUST 12, 1944. Cintheaux. Operation TOTALIZE is finally over and we are licking our wounds. Word is that the Algonquins alone suffered more than 150 casualties, including about 50 killed and another 50 taken prisoner. Moose MacKenzie who was with Billy on the Nanibijou caper in Port Arthur and who played first base for us in Shilo was cut to pieces by shrapnel at Quesnay. Creepy Cram will never throw another softball. He was wounded and run over by a Tiger Tank at St. Hilaire Farm. The Farm is our new front line. It is about 9 miles down the Falaise highway from Tilly so by my calculations we lost 16 men for every mile we took from Jerry. At this rate in another 45 to 50 miles the Regiment will be completely wiped out. TOTALIZE was supposed to be the big break-out attack and take us all the way to Falaise. We got about half-way there before we were forced to withdraw and now, at last, we look just like the Sand, Dust and Gravel Boys. A dirty, filthy, tired bunch. Mail call this morning. A pile of letters from Louvert finally catching up. Gramps McDougal got an advance call from the telegraph operator so he and Myra along with Billy's parents went over to the Berman's a few minutes after the telegram boy. Sounds like it was pretty bad. Gramps said it was the first time he saw Ben Berman show any emotion, sitting in his chair, the one by the front window, with the telegram at his feet, ripping at a tear in his suit (Jewish custom, I think) and moaning as he rocked back and forth, back and forth. In his letter Gramps said the Irish would call it "keening." Said it sent a chill up and down his back. Doc Evans had to come over and give Sadie something to calm her. Evans must be in his seventies by now, we thought he was old when he patched up Barney's knee and here he is, years later, treating Barney's mother for something far more serious. Does time ever heal the broken heart of a mother who's not supposed to live longer than her son?

Excerpt from the Diary

The Algonquins, along with the South Alberta tanks, were licking their wounds in a sugarbeet field dubbed the Cabbage Patch after the village in the *L'il Abner* comic strip featured in *The Maple Leaf News*. At first the men from Northern Ontario thought they were in a turnip field. They'd never seen sugarbeets before.

Operation TOTALIZE had been launched the day after Billy, in the cattle pen at Hubert's Folly, had used a 303 round to singe the *Scharführer's* ear.

"I couldn't do it. I just couldn't do it. I wanted to do it. I *really* wanted to shoot the fucker right between the eyes. But I couldn't."

Yates had thrown an arm around Billy's shoulders. "At least you had the satisfaction of seeing the bastard shit himself."

"Ya should have seen him, Willy, lyin' there on the ground curled up in a shit-scared ball. No sneers this time, I'll tell ya. Not a one."

The Algonquins' battle inoculation, their part in TOTALIZE, got underway in the late evening of August 8 with an eager regiment moving up to the start line past a number of French civilians standing by the side of the road in the dusk waving the French flag, *le drapeau tricolore*, and shouting *"Vive la Normandie libre!"*

TOTALIZE had been underway for almost a day, launched with a combined Bomber Command and artillery pounding of Jerry's defence line at Tilly-la-Campagne. The assault phase had been assigned to others whose task it was to break through the line. Once that was done the Algonquins with 4th Canadian Armoured Division would pass through to take their objective, a dot on the map identified as Hill 195, a sloping ridge some eight miles south of Tilly, and the highest point of land between Caen and Falaise to the south.

The Carrier Platoon had been mounted and waiting for hours as had the PBI, ensconced in their own Armoured Personnel Carriers. In operations GOODWOOD and SPRING the Poor Bloody Infantry had gone naked to battle, with the result that German machine guns had chopped them to pieces. For TOTALIZE they were to be clothed in APC steel.

The APCs had once had been Self-Propelled Guns but when the artillery shifted to towed twenty-five-pounders the SPGs were relegated to the scrap heap. Rescued by the engineers for TOTALIZE, SPGs were transformed in record time. The 105-mm guns were removed and steel plate welded over all openings to make a new troop transport called "Priests," presumably because the vehicles were now without guns.

At exactly 2359 hours the long armoured column of 4th Division finally moved out at a pace that turned out to be that of a slow snail. By dawn, the column had only advanced about two miles before it came to a halt, not moving again until night because down the road Jerry was putting up a tough battle against the assault forces.

As darkness fell the Algonquins were joined by the British Columbia Regiment and moved on without a hitch until first light on the morning of August 10, when all hell broke loose.

As the BCR tanks stuck their noses over the brow of a rise just below what they thought was Hill 195 Jerry opened up with his eighty-eights, picking off the Shermans one by one. Pigeons on a wire. To Al it looked like a fireworks display on Dominion Day, the tanks going off like Roman candles, sparks and flaming coloured balls.

Following Gillie's lead the Carrier Platoon gunned through and around the brewed-up Ronsons, Al grimacing at the partially cremated bodies of crews half in and half out of their steel coffins. He yelled at Billy to stop beside one tank where he thought he'd seen some human movement but when he jumped out of the carrier for a closer look it was just a trick of the flames. The stink of burnt flesh, overdone pork, was everywhere. His stomach heaving, Al turned and ran for the carrier, his hand cupped over his mouth.

It soon became clear they were nowhere near their objective. Hill 195 was on the *west* side of the Caen/Falaise Highway and they were on the *other side* at another hill about 2¹/2 miles to the east. Somehow in the confusion of darkness and dust they had taken a wrong turn, bringing them a mile or so west of the hamlet of Quesnay where Kurt Meyer and the tanks of 12th SS Panzer Division were holed up in the dense forest encircling the settlement.

The 12th SS was no longer the formidable force it had been when first encountered by the North Novas on June 7 northwest of L'Abbaye Ardenne, but it still had some 15,000 troops, more than forty tanks, and close to the same number of self-propelled and anti-tank guns. And these were backed up by a *Luftwaffe* flak brigade with sixty eighty-eights, which by noon had wiped out all but two of the nineteen Shermans accompanying the Algonquins.

Once the Canadian tanks had been destroyed, the Hitler *Jugend* turned their mortars on the PBI who had taken refuge with the remaining Priests and carriers in a hollow square made by a hedgerow about six feet high, a bigger version of the cattle pen where Billy had faced off with the SS sergeant.

By 0500 the Algonquins had used up almost all of their field dressings and every last drop of morphine. The dead and seriously wounded in the square outnumbered those who could still fire a weapon and these were fast running out of ammunition. As the day wore on the sickly smell of burnt pork seeped into slit trenches and men crazed by the stench and the shelling were jumping out, screaming curses at the invisible enemy. Some of the wounded, delirious with pain and thirst, had to be restrained from crawling into the worst of the shelling to seek the relief that only death could bring. Even a Tiffie attack in the late afternoon—four Hawker Typhoons, RCAF single-seat fighter bombers armed with four twenty-mm cannon and eight tank-killing rockets—only served to postpone the inevitable. As night fell, reports came in from the perimeter scouts that the SS were massing for an attack, and soon the weary Algonquins could hear the grinding roar of approaching enemy tanks, the shouts of German infantry, and the chatter of Schmeissers. The order to withdraw was not long in coming.

The dead and near-dead were left to the mercy of God, as were the Priests, which were far too slow for the required rapid retreat. The wounded who had a chance, as many as could be, were quickly but gently loaded on the carriers and, with the two remaining Shermans leading the way by tearing a gap through the rear of the hedgerow, the survivors of Operation TOTALIZE made their way back the way they had come, their path in the dark marked by the still-smouldering remains of the Tommy Cookers brewed up that morning.

Even though they were exhausted, there was no sleep that night in the Cabbage Patch at Cintheaux. Not even the Calvados could turn off the sights and sounds of battle—the screams of the wounded echoing in their heads or the fevered cascade of mental pictures, known and remembered faces, men they were forced to leave behind because there wasn't enough room on the carriers; the flash and thunder of battle that penetrated the cotton batting in their ears, reverberations in the brain that had driven many to the edge of sanity and beyond. The more they drank the more sober they got and the more sober they got the less they talked.

At first light they were joined by an old friend, a soldier they had last seen in Scotland, and they managed to rouse themselves enough to hear Popovich's story.

When news of D-Day reached the Devil's Brigade, the Pole had requested a transfer to join his country's army, the remnants that had managed to escape in October 1939, fleeing with only their uniforms on their backs, warmed in the autumn chill by a burning hatred for the Nazi invaders.

Now in 1944 these soldiers were together again, fighting with the 1st Polish Armoured Division, a unit that, in the planning for Operation TOTALIZE, was supposed to be on the Algonquins' left flank. But because the Algonquins had taken a wrong turn in the night, the Canadians and the Poles ended up fighting in each other's hip pockets and not knowing it.

As Popovich told his tale the little leaguers nodded in recognition. Both units had been given a shit-kicking by the 12th SS, with the Poles having had an additional boot in the arse, friendly fire from heaven. The joke about bombing aircraft was when a German bomber was overhead, Canadians ducked. When a Canadian bomber was overhead, Germans ducked. But when an American bomber was in the sky above, everyone ducked. As the Poles found out. Courtesy of the U.S. Eighth Air Force.

"Goddamn pricks came right above us. B-17s. We were at first cheering at them. Then we see opening up bomb bays. Right on top of us." Popovich looked up as if the Americans had come back for another go.

"We see bombs come down, first like sticks all in a row, then spread out making whistling noise. We stop cheering damn pretty fast. Run like hell."

Popovich said he figured about a hundred of his comrades had not run fast enough. Losses to friendly fire combined with the losses to the not-so-friendly eighty-eights had reduced their attacking force to much the same status as the Algonquins beside them.

He shook his big head in great sorrow, staring moodily at the ground. And then suddenly his eyes lit up and he started to smile. "But still we have our fun, eh?"

"Oh, sure, Stan. Lots of fun." Billy was looking at him and wondering if the big Pole was more crazy now than ever.

"Ja, lots of fun. We take prisoners, eh? We take their paybooks. Look to see if they be in Poland in September or October '39."

"And if they were?"

Popovich drew a finger across his throat.

"You killed them?"

The Pole nodded. "Ja, we kill them. We kill them for all of our people they kill. We do not forget what they do to our country. They pay for what they do."

Yates looked at Billy who shook his head. He wasn't about to tell Popovich about the SS sergeant. He didn't want to have to sit and listen to the Pole tell him what he half-believed himself, that he was a damn fool for not doing what he should have done, for not making the son-of-a-bitch pay for killing the North Novas, who were Canadians after all and should have been avenged.

When, later in the morning, Popovich left to rejoin what was left of his unit, Billy was relieved to see the reminder of his failure take his leave. Then it wasn't long before Operation TRACTABLE came along and Billy had other things to occupy his mind.

The three days between TOTALIZE and TRACTABLE were spent getting clean, eating hot meals, reading and writing letters and queuing up to the Salvation Army trucks for chocolate bars, soft drinks and other goodies.

Getting clean was a service provided by the "Chinese Hussars," a.k.a. the army's Mobile Bath and Laundry Unit. It worked like a production line. You went into one tent where you stripped. Off came your dirty, filthy battledress, your grubby, stinking underwear and your foul-smelling socks. You threw them into a pile for washing and then naked as the day you were born you stepped under a shower dispensing the blessings of hot water. There you lathered out the dirt caked behind your ears and in the crease of your neck and underneath your fingernails, around your ankles and between your toes. It was ecstasy, somewhere between orgasm and religious conversion and it was over all too soon.

From the shower tent you followed a duckboard walk to another tent where you went through piles of clean clothes trying to find something that fit, with the more crafty of the men picking up a few extra pieces to trade for fresh eggs, Calvados and, if they were really lucky, maybe a chicken or two.

Sunday morning showers were also a grand show for the locals heading off to Mass, the naked promenade of young men in their prime strutting from one tent to another providing a little diversion for giggling *madames et mademoiselles* who just happened to be lingering nearby.

TRACTABLE had initially gone by the name of TALLULAH until somebody thought that the first name of a well-known American actress might not be an appropriate designation for a combat operation. The plan this time was for a daylight attack—TOTALIZE had taught some lessons—that would form the northern jaw of a trap cutting off the retreating German Seventh Army at Falaise.

Springing the southern jaw was up to the American Third Army, led by
Lieutenant General George S. Patton Jr. The flamboyant Patton, with his ivory-
handled pistols and English bull terrier named "Willy," was a keen student of
military history, his heroes being Alexander the Great, Julius Caesar and William
Tecumseh Sherman. Like Sherman in Georgia, Patton had gone marching
through the German forces in western Normandy so fast and so ruthlessly that
his advance was being called "the American *blitzkrieg*."

For the Algonquins and 10 Infantry Brigade, TRACTABLE began on the
morning of August 14. The hot weather of the previous weeks had now turned
cool and there was a fine mist in the air as the Carrier Platoon took its place in
line with B Squadron of the South Alberta tanks parked in front of them. Al
could see the 4th Canadian Armoured Division's formation sign, a yellow maple
leaf in a green square, painted over the right track of the nearest Sherman. The
green patch mirrored the one the PBI wore on their left shoulders.

TRACTABLE was to be a massive, lightning thrust at the German defenders,
six brigades in all, thousands of men and hundreds of vehicles, trucks, carriers
and Priests, including 500 tanks. Al's friends in the South Albertas said they had
never seen so many tanks assembled in one place at one time. What the Allies
lacked in quality, they more than made up for in quantity.

It was Jerry who had quality. Especially when it came to tanks. The Germans
had three different tanks or *Panzers* in Normandy. The small twenty-ton Nazi
Panzers that had sliced into Poland and through the Low Countries in the early
days of the war were no match for the bigger and more powerful Russian T-34s
on the Eastern Front; and so in August 1942 German factories began to produce
the fifty-five-ton Tiger with an eighty-eight-mm gun. Three months later the
forty-three-ton Panthers started to come off the assembly line and these were
armed with a seventy-five-mm gun. In February 1944 the Germans produced a
third tank, a bigger Tiger, a sixty-eight-ton monster, twice the size of a Sherman.
Dubbed the Royal or King Tiger, it was armed with a seventeen-foot-long eighty-
eight-mm cannon and its turret alone, protected by steel armour more than seven
inches thick, weighed as much as the earlier *Panzer*, the whole kit and caboodle.

The long and the short of it was that in Normandy the thinner-skinned
Canadian Shermans were outweighed, outgunned and outclassed.

In an effort to even the odds, bits and pieces of tank tracks scavenged from
the many derelict Ronsons in the Sherman graveyards have been welded onto the
chassis and turrets of the B Squadron tanks, giving more protection and the look
of bulky alligators. This has been done in spite of bureaucratic protestations
from the Lord High Pooh-Bahs, the chairborne warriors at HQ, gravely shaking
their addled heads because the added weight would substantially reduce the
running life of the tanks.

There has been one other change from TOTALIZE. Al has finally given in to
the importunings of Billy and, to a lesser degree, the rest of the crew. Crow has
lettered a name on their carrier. Hitler's Hearse.

At 1125 hours the artillery fires red smoke to mark the German front lines for Bomber Command, and five minutes later the sky is filled with American B-24s and Commonwealth Lancasters dropping death, a horizon of falling sticks just as Popovich had described them. Then it is the rumble of explosions, a rumble that grows to a roaring wave of sound washing over the brigade as the ground beneath begins to shudder, the aftershock of a series of major earthquakes. All around him, Al can see troops in the assault vehicles stuffing cotton batting in their ears.

At 1140 hours the order comes, "Move now!" At the instant the command is given, Canadian artillery, massed in the rear echelon, begins to fire smoke shells and soon the enemy's forward positions are covered in a thick, milky haze, cover for the charge. Minutes later the first Shermans have overrun the stunned and broken German front line and shouts of *Kamerad* fill the air, Jerry in the hundreds, staggering out of the smoke, hands in the air.

Shortly after noon a long, shuffling column of blue-grey, with a smattering here and there of *Waffen SS* foliage camouflage, is being shepherded to barbed-wire enclosures near Cintheaux. Bringing up the rear of the column is Hitler's Hearse, loaded with enemy wounded, Billy at the controls, cursing about coddling Jerry.

"Whataya think, Al?" Billy was shouting over the rattle of the carrier and the fading sounds of TRACTABLE. "Think Gerald will take care of us like this if we get captured? Last time I looked, Gerald was shooting his prisoners. Bullet in the back of the head. Now we're givin' him limousine service to the rear for rest, relaxation and refreshments. We are a crazy bunch, Al. Crazier'n hell."

It is mid-afternoon when the Carriers return to the front to find the advance has bogged down in the face of toughening German resistance, together with the confusion of trying to navigate in the smoke and now dust whipped up by exploding bombs and hundreds of tracked vehicles.

In order to get to their first objective, the Laison River, about three miles from their start line, drivers are forced to get their bearings from the sun. It is about the only thing they can see.

It is at the river where the yellow haze has settled somewhat that the fit hits the shan. The intelligence reports on the Laison are wrong. It is not "fordable by tanks at all points." It is not bloody fordable at any point. Steep banks and a muddy bottom force the Shermans to idle in confusion at the river's edge waiting for the engineers to find points where banks can be quickly bulldozed and the river speedily bridged with fascines, huge, rolled bundles of brushwood put together especially for such emergencies.

The wait means that the advance piles up behind the tanks and it is this that oncoming bombers, RCAF Lancasters this time, mistake for an enemy concentration.

It all starts when one of the aircraft, looking like a giant dragonfly, peels away from formation and comes in low to drop his bombs on what he has identified as Jerry gathered at the river. With the luck that the God of Mischief often bestows upon fools and the badly misguided, the lone aircraft scores a direct hit on 10 Brigade's ammunition trucks. In a second what is left of the thick yellow dust is breached by a geyser of red and black smoke that serves as a beacon pointing aircraft from each succeeding wave where to drop their bombs. The Canadians on the ground try to warn off the Canadians in the air by firing red and yellow flares but these simply blend in with the Normandy dust and exploding ammo.

The horror goes on for an hour before a lone aircraft from an earlier flight, perhaps one of the first ones to peel off and bomb, perhaps the only one to realize the tragic error, returns to keep watch on the scene of devastation below, shooing off any latecomers eager to get in on the kill.

When it is all over there are close to 400 victims of this round of friendly fire. The families of the Canadians among the killed and the maimed will be told their sons, their fathers and their brothers died or were wounded fighting bravely against the enemies of their country. It would be bad for home-front morale to tell them the truth.

Once again the Carrier Platoon is called upon for transport, gathering Canadian wounded this time, ferrying them back to the Regimental Aid Post, and once again Billy is raging, this time at the fly boys, stupid, gung-ho bastards who are blind in one eye and can't see out of the other.

There is a system to treating casualties and it begins with the SBs or stretcher bearers. It is these brave men who are the first to minister to the fallen. Some of the SBs are conscientious objectors to war. They will not carry a weapon. But they will put themselves in the line of fire to bring first aid to their comrades.

Too many times their dodging runs through falling bombs and exploding shells, exposed to the sights of snipers, are all for naught. The Tommy Cooked are burned to a crisp. The soldier with a shattered head, dirty-grey brain matter oozing out, is beyond help. The kid with a hole in his chest the size of a Popovich fist, a froth of blood bubbling from his lips as he fights for air, has only minutes to live. There is no hope for the men with no legs or an arm torn off at the shoulder, arteries pumping life away in spurting jets of red.

Sometimes it is not so bad. Sometimes the dead have no visible wounds. At a quick glance they look to be having a peaceful post-prandial nap, just waiting for their mothers or their wives or their children to wake them for dessert.

But no one, no matter how loving, will ever be able to wake them for anything anymore and it is the grim task of the stretcher bearers to gather dog tags and jam rifle barrels down in the ground to mark their place; . . . *and in the sky,/ The larks still bravely singing, fly,/ Scarce heard amid the guns below.*

While there is nothing but reverence to offer the dead, the still alive are examined quickly and efficiently where they lie. First, battledress is cut away to get at wounds. If it is a body wound and there is shrapnel in it, the SBs will leave it for the doctors. They have been taught that a shell fragment can be like an iceberg. If you pull at what is exposed, what is left inside can do serious damage to internal organs.

All wounds are liberally doused with sulphanilamide powder, much like a mess cook with a generous hand for flour. Then field dressings are applied. They come in a package with directions. *Tear to open. Extract the dressing. Remove the paper cover along the brown surface. Take the folded ends of the brown bandage, one in each hand. Keep the bandage taut. Apply same and fix the bandage by tying the ends.* Often, more than one dressing is needed.

If a leg is broken, the other one is used as a splint and always there is morphine, quarter-grain syrettes, small, individual, throw-away hypodermic needles that anyone can administer at any time. The wounded who have been given morphine are marked with an "M" on their foreheads so doctors at the RAP will not over-dose them.

There is a triage system in place at the RAP. The walking wounded are treated on the spot and sometimes, when injuries are not too serious, sent back to the front line with a pat on the back. The gravely hurt are examined, the nature and severity of their wounds determined, and notes recorded on a waterproof medical record tied to the soldier's tunic through one of the buttonholes. That done, the wounded man is loaded on a field ambulance Jeep and transported to a casualty clearing station for further treatment. The Jeep is fitted with an overhead frame with room for two stretchers on top and a third on the lower level next to the driver.

The clearing station is a series of tents well behind the lines just south of Caen, where surgeons select those in need of immediate surgery, those whose wounds are so serious further travel would kill them. The wounded who can travel are immediately flown to hospitals in England.

It is this rapid and organized treatment of casualties, from the SBs in the field to hospitals in England, together with the miracle drug penicillin first introduced to the battlefield in Italy in January 1944, that saves the lives of so many men in World War II, men who would have died in droves had they been wounded in World War I.

At the clearing station, doctors and nurses gaunt with fatigue rush to help unload the wounded from Hitler's Hearse. Medical records are quickly checked and the stretchers carried off, some to one tent, others to another. The Algonquins from the Carrier Platoon are quick to give what help they can, but it is assistance they will live to regret because the sights, the sounds and the smells that greet them will haunt them for days.

They hear the groans of men awaiting surgery hooked to intravenous bags, sometimes plasma, sometimes a saline solution to keep them from going into shock, a major cause of battlefield death. They smell the coppery odour of blood and the pungent scent of Lysol used to scrub the floors of the operating tents to rid them of the stench of gore. They see men whose wounds are mental, the traumatized, the shell-shocked, the battle fatigued, slumped on the ground, with blank faces and unseeing eyes. They kneel to offer and light cigarettes that are taken and smoked without any change in expression. It is as if the men are robots wired to do this and this alone.

In a field just beyond the recovery tent where patients are taken for post-operative care, Al stands beside Billy and Yates, bareheaded next to a mound of freshly dug earth as a padre reads from a prayer book while two men with ropes gently lower a blanket-shrouded body into the ground.

"O God, the Creator of all the Faithful, grant to the soul of thy servant here departed the remission of all his sins, that, through pious supplication, he may obtain that pardon which he has always desired, who livest and reignest for ever and ever. Amen."

It is almost dark when Hitler's Hearse gets back to Operation TRACTABLE. The Laison has been crossed and the regiment is dug in a little more than two miles down the road in the village of Olendon about four miles northeast of Falaise. The night is spent in fitful sleep and in the morning there is a cautious move forward to their next objective, the town of Epancy.

Gill has the platoon lay up in a farmer's stone-walled courtyard just outside the town. He is waiting to find out what the brass has in mind for the Carriers in this phase of the attack. In the near distance there is a crossroads and a church with a clock on the spire, hands fixed at twelve, noon or midnight, he doesn't know. But what he does know is that the spire would be a great place for a sniper and he is just about to voice the thought when a sound like a snapping twig tears the air. Gill keels over, slowly, like a falling tree.

Shouting and dragging their lieutenant's body to safety, the platoon takes refuge, some behind the carriers, some tight behind the wall out of the sniper's sight. Al is motioning to Billy and Reggie, thinking of organizing some covering fire so that one of the carriers can move off behind the sniper when he hears what sounds like chalk screeching on a blackboard. It takes a second to register. Moaning Minnies! There is not just a sniper in the tower, there is also an artillery observer.

The first salvo hits but it is on the other side of the farmhouse and the only damage is to buildings, pink clay roof shingles clanging and spattering on and around the armoured vehicles. The stone walls of the house shake with the concussion, a crunching, hammering, deafening roar, strong enough to kill all by itself. The Algonquins have learned that without cotton batting, the next best thing to protect your ears is to keep your mouth open. Shouting also helps. Shouting protects eardrums and is the reason the farmyard sounds like a Cowboys and Indians Saturday matinee at the Empire, whoops and yells punctuating the exploding Minnies, whoops and yells tinged with fear because the men know there is no time to move before the next rockets hit. You only have six seconds from the time you hear the screech to the time you meet your maker.

"Let's get the hell outta here, boys!" Al is shouting above the din. "Reggie, give us some fire on the tower! Keep that bastard's head down. The rest of you into the carriers the minute Reggie starts shooting and give 'em all the gas you've got. Go, go, go!"

Immediately Reggie is up, his weapon resting on the back end of Gillie's Cruiser and the chugga, chugga, chugga of the Bren picks up where the roar of the Minnies left off. Stone chips fly off the church tower as the Canadians roll up into the carriers already pivoting and moving off. Reggie is the last one in and slumps down beside Gillie, who is coming around, his eyes trying to focus. The sniper's round has only creased the side of his helmet, leaving a jagged tin scar and tearing the helmet liner about half an inch from his ear.

The Cruiser is just on the other side of the farmyard when they again hear chalk on the blackboard and mentally count, one-a-thousand, two-a-thousand . . . At six-a-thousand the yard behind them blows up in a hail of cobblestones. Close but no cigar.

The first thing Al does when the platoon finds haven in an apple orchard is to radio in the map coordinates of the church to their FOO. In less than a minute or two the lads are treated to a display of Canadian artistry using twenty-five-pounder howitzers.

A six-man crew can get these big, made-in-Canada guns firing in a little over sixty seconds and hit targets more than seven miles away. If Canadian soldiers are frightened by Jerry's eighty-eights, Jerry is terrified of Johnny Canuck's twenty-fives. Many German prisoners on their way to the rear, stunned and demoralized by an Uncle Target attack of seventy-two guns, ask to see the fabled Canadian secret weapon. So rapid is the artillery fire that they believe the Canadians have developed howitzers that can shoot like a Chicago Piano.

The first rounds from the rear bracket the church. The second rounds demolish it and the audience cheers as the tower clock totters and then swoons in one huge piece to shatter in a thousand pieces on the gravestones in the cemetery below.

Gillie refuses to be taken to the RAP and accepts a cuppa instead. Hungry now, they are just about to open some Muck and Vomit when the wireless crackles and they are told to stop lollygagging about. There is work to be done, bridges, river crossings and junctions to be secured in order to cut off enemy forces rushing to get through the trap before the jaws spring shut. First up is the town of Damblainville and the bridges crossing the Ante River.

Gillie points to Hitler's Hearse, "Follow me," and the two carriers grind their way down the road to Damblainville's main bridge across from the railway station, where Billy and Yates, along with Ross and Dougie Dobson, dismount to have a look at the weathered stone span that looks like it's been around since the Romans brought their know-how to Gaul.

The examination completed, the bridge inspectors clamber up the bank with thumbs up, jumping in the Hearse and the Cruiser to lumber across into the dirty yellow cobblestone station square and park in front of the dirty yellow cobblestone station untouched by shell or bomb and almost as big as its counterpart in Lowvert.

Leaving Gill frowning over his maps, the rest of them go for a stroll across into the *gare* through a canted door hanging from one hinge. Inside is a high-vaulted chamber bisected by a row of benches, back to back, iron frames and wooden slats, open newspapers scattered hither and yon. At opposite ends of the benches, recessed into the walls, are barred ticket windows, four of them altogether, two at each end. Underneath each window are bits and pieces of paper, torn tickets and crumpled train schedules. The entire room has a dusty, unkempt look. It is an eerie, lifeless scene.

Billy can't stand it. He starts to sing, his gravelly voice echoing from the high ceiling. "Mademoiselle from Armentières, Parley-voo? Mademoiselle from Armentières, Parley-voo? Mademoiselle from Armentières, She hasn't been kissed in forty years, Hinky, dinky, parley-voo."

His attempt to add some life to the *gare* is greeted with embarrassed silence. He looks around at his buddies, shrugs and heads around the benches. Pushing open the heavy wooden door on the far side he leads the tour out to the platform in front of the tracks, four sets, straight running in both directions and shimmering in the late afternoon sun as the trick of the eye progressively narrows the space between the rails until in the far distance they come together as one.

In front of them four boxcars sit on the far rails. They look to be higher and longer than Canadian boxcars. Stencilled on the side of each near the door is some lettering: *8 CHEVAUX / 40 HOMMES.*

Close enough to read, they are also close enough to smell. It is an odour hard to identify but Ross comes the closest to describing it. An old shithouse on a hot day.

"Whattaya think that means, eight horses, forty men?" It is Billy's question. He wrinkles his nose as he backs away from the stink. "Think they put men in there? With horses? Jesus!"

There is no answer to his question. Not then.

That night the Carriers lead A Company down the road to Marais-La Chapelle because of an incident at dusk the day before when an Algonquin patrol, shank's mare, encountered another patrol and began to query them on enemy movements, only to discover that the men to whom they were talking were more comfortable conversing in German.

With the noose tightening around Jerry's neck, battle lines are becoming blurred, no one is sure who is who or where as the retreating Germans try to filter through the advancing Canadians, sometimes in the dark even inserting themselves at the tail end of Algonquin columns hoping to avoid detection until they can peel off and away from the encircling Allies.

It is dawn when the column reaches the outskirts of Marais-La Chapelle, and the carrier drivers are having a tough time keeping their eyes open. The rest of the platoon have been able to get some shut-eye here and there, but men at the controls have been on the job for twenty-four hours. More than once during the night a driver in dreamland has angled a carrier into a ditch, where the ensuing lurch snaps everyone awake.

At the crossroads in the centre of the town there is a stone memorial to the dead of the First War overlooked by a casualty of the Second, another crucified Christ, this one with one arm missing. Here the men in the cruiser dismount in a crowd of excited French civilians hailing their liberators.

But the celebration is short-lived. Two truckloads of Germans roar around a corner about 100 yards away. Billy guns the Hearse past the cruiser and Reggie lets loose with a long burst from his Bren. The lead enemy truck veers off the road and explodes in flames. It is enough. The Germans in the second truck pile out, their arms raised in surrender. The count is five Jerry dead, four wounded and fifteen prisoners.

In short order the undamaged truck is looted by the French, an example followed throughout the rest of the day by the Algonquins as more and more fleeing enemy vehicles blunder into the village in the belief that it has not yet fallen to the Canadians. The tension and fatigue of the last few days are forgotten as the spoils of war pile up in the carriers, offerings of a conquered foe—helmets, daggers, medals, red Swastika flags, SS collar lightning flashes and weapons, especially officers' pistols like the coveted Luger and the even more coveted Schmeisser, a cut above the Sten, whose reputation has suffered in Normandy. It has such a bad habit of jamming at crucial times that it comes to be known as "the plumber's nightmare." Since both Schmeisser and Sten use the same nine-mm ammunition, some of the Algonquins arm themselves with the enemy weapon.

The highlight of the celebrations is Billy's bellowing liberation of a German truck containing the contents of a manor house: silver candlesticks, knives and forks and pewter plates, furniture and drapes, paintings and knickknacks of every sort, all of which are immediately and cheaply bartered for fresh eggs and bread, cheese, chickens and bottles upon bottles of wine long buried in village undercrofts to keep them from the clutches of the pillaging Boche.

By the time a tipsy A Company is ready to move on, the Carriers lead what looks like a wagon train loaded with food and drink for a beleaguered outpost manned by starving defenders.

In the days to come there will be very little fighting for the men of the Carrier Platoon. Mostly they will gorge themselves on the spoils from Marais-La Chapelle and watch the slaughter of Hitler's Seventh Army in the Dives Valley.

Their spectator seats are on Hill 240 overlooking the Dives River and the town of Chambois. There on the morning of August 20, 1944, the Algonquins wake shivering in a cold drizzle. Yawning and stretching they look down into the valley, their sleepy eyes widening with astonishment. On the floor of the green dale, a long blue-grey line is snaking its way from south to north, thousands of marching men interspersed with SPGs, tanks, trucks, vehicles and carts of every sort, many of them drawn by horses.

This is the fleeing remnants of a once-proud army trying to escape the closing jaws of the Allied trap and they are in plain view only 500 yards away. Al hears Yates standing beside him, awe in his voice, whispering one of Beth's favourite poems, Tennyson's *The Charge of the Light Brigade*.

> "Into the valley of Death
> Rode the six hundred . . .
> Cannon to the right of them
> Cannon to the left of them
> Cannon in front of them
> Volley'd and thunder'd . . .
> Into the jaws of Death,
> Into the mouth of Hell . . ."

No one speaks. No one moves. Each and every one mesmerized by the sight, holding his breath, waiting for the first salvoes of Judgment Day, the wrath of shelling that is to come, hellfire and brimstone raining damnation upon unsuspecting sinners below.

Al and Willy share a look, a there-but-for-the-grace-of-God-go-I look. Others, like Billy, are grim-faced and clenching their fists waiting for the bastards to get exactly what they deserve, especially the teenaged bastards of the Hitler *Jugend*. This is for Barney and Goody and Creepy and Moose, the lads left behind at Quesnay Woods and the wounded and dying at the casualty clearing station. *Life for life, eye for eye, tooth for tooth, hand for hand, foot for foot, burning for burning, wound for wound, stripe for stripe.*

Suddenly the silence of Billy's rage is shattered by a rumble of man-made thunder behind him followed by a screeching overhead, a prelude to a discordant symphony made up of every weapon the Canadians have—mortars, heavy machine guns, anti-tank guns, tank guns and artillery. In seconds the blue-grey column in the Dives Valley disintegrates, men and machines like marionettes, jerking in flashes of fire and flopping in puffs of smoke. Ammunition blows up in geysers of red and purple. Orange-yellow flames shoot from burning fuel tanks. Bleeding horses run crazed with terror and die in the tangle of their traces.

It is a scene from a gruesome hell far beyond the most vivid of their Sunday School imaginings and even Billy, when he sees the fallen horses, sickens and turns his face from the valley of Death.

When it is all over, the dale is still except for the occasional pop and rattle of exploding ammunition and the crackling of flames. But if you listened hard enough you could hear other sounds, the faint shrieks of dying horses and the distant groans of wounded men.

The Algonquin SBs don't wait for orders to go down the hill on the run with their field dressings and morphine syrettes. Arnie Christensen scrambles after them with his Lee Enfield and while the Canadian stretcher bearers take care of the enemy wounded, Arnie tends to the horses, relieving the pain of valiant animals so well remembered from the lumber camps of Algonquin Park. With tears streaming down his cheeks, he goes to every wounded horse, bends to stroke its nose and then does what has to be done with a single shot to the head.

The jagged teeth of the Falaise trap had closed. The battle for Normandy was over. The good guys had finally won.

Chapter Twenty

AUGUST 22, 1944. Hill 240. Word is Jerry isn't likely to stop running till he gets to the Seine some 60 miles to the northwest so our job in the next few days will be to nip at his heels, keep him moving, make sure he doesn't change his mind. A big change for us, a long distance chase after weeks of hopscotching around in Normandy. Right now we're taking a breather but the sooner we get off this damn hill and get going the better off we'll all be. Dead horses stink like rotten eggs and dead Germans have a putrid sweet smell that leaves a taste of rotten oranges on your tongue. Also seeps into your skin somehow so that you can sniff it on your hands even if you've been nowhere near the valley floor. And a hell of a rotting mess that is, the sunken road clogged with busted equipment and rancid flesh. A maggot's picnic. The bulldozers are out, I can see them from here, digging long trenches and then plowing humans and horses into the holes. Some day, years from now, tourists in fancy cars will drive on this road and admire the scenery with no idea what's fertilizing the hedgerows on either side of them. War correspondents are out and about. Yates said he talked to Matthew Halton of the CBC. Told him the nickname of the Carrier Platoon was "the Suicide Squad" because we were asked to undertake so many dangerous missions. Quite an imagination has our boy Willy. Latest word on casualties is pretty bad. The Regiment started out a month ago at Courseulles with a full complement of 800 or so. Now we're down to about 550. Reminds me of that song we used to sing as kids. "Ten little nine little eight little Indians, seven little six little five little Indians, four little three little two little Indians, one little Indian boy." Going to need some more Indians pretty soon.

Excerpt from the Diary

Matthew Halton filed two reports on the Battle of Falaise, one on the brave Algonquins of the Suicide Squad and the other on the Avenging Allied Angel "whose terrible swift sword had swept the Valley of all things German." More than 200 enemy tanks, 800 artillery pieces, 100 anti-aircraft guns and 7,000 vehicles had been destroyed or damaged beyond repair. Ten thousand Germans were dead along with 2,000 horses pressed into service when supplies of gasoline ran short.

There was no report on the thinning ranks of the victors. At least none that the censors would approve. Between the beginning of Operation GOODWOOD on July 18 and the slaughter of the enemy at Falaise a little over a month later, close to 3,000 Canadians had been killed and 7,000 wounded, the equivalent of ten regiments.

These battle casualties were twenty percent higher than those in comparable British formations because Montgomery had seen fit to assign most of the tough fighting to Johnny Canuck. Not that Johnny was complaining, mind you. As a matter of fact he was damn proud of the job he'd done, especially when word got round what a Jerry general captured at Falaise had said: "With Canadian soldiers and German officers I could have held Normandy forever."

Down to three rifle companies now instead of four and only sixty-five men to a company, the Algonquins were typical in wondering how they were going to do more with less. The one unit in the regiment that was anywhere close to full strength was the Carrier Platoon, and it didn't take a genius to figure out what that meant. To those from whom less has been taken, more was going to be required.

Where they were going to get the energy was another question. Once the adrenaline rush of Falaise had worn off, platoon members felt like the walking dead, skin and bones and hollowed eyes. Al figured he had lost about ten pounds in the last three weeks, ten more than he could afford to lose. What they all needed was a week or so of L.O.B. but the chase was on and being left out of battle just wasn't an option. Aside from fresh air, their only relief when they got to their bivouac area in Monnai was hot food and mail from home.

With his butt on a blanket of last year's leaves and his back to an enormous gnarled tree on the edge of a wood where the carriers were parked, Al was drinking tea and re-reading a letter from Beth, chuckling again at her story of young Sandy telling her he wanted to go to France and help his dad fight those bad Germans.

He had just taken his last swallow when Gill came by with orders for the next morning—hit the road for Bernay and check out reports that Jerry rearguards were setting up near the small medieval town in an attempt to delay the Allied advance.

It was a twenty-mile trip that took them most of the morning to complete. Winding, hilly roads flanked by dense stands of trees offering perfect cover for enemy anti-tank weapons made for cautious going. When the Carriers finally trundled down into the valley and entered the unscathed town they found out their intelligence reports had been wrong again. There were no Germans in Bernay, just Canadians, their brigade brothers, the Links and Winks this time, most of them half in the bag, increasingly the fate of the first Allied soldiers to liberate a town in France.

The Links told the Algoons they'd never seen anything like it. Townspeople lining the long, narrow streets in the pouring rain waving and cheering, some running beside the carriers with flowers, fruit and flagons of wine for the heroes in khaki, strangers who'd come from all the way from Canada to save them from their next-door neighbours.

"Pretty funny, eh? We look in the mirror and see ourselves, a tired, dirty bunch of Canadian guys, scared out of our wits most of the time, and they look up at us and see the rough, tough, fearless liberators of their country. Warrior Kings."

Al's counterpart in the Lincoln and Welland Carrier Platoon was chuckling and shaking his head as he told of the reception the boys from the Niagara Peninsula had received earlier in the day. The sun was shining now and the two NCOs were standing by their vehicles in the cobblestone town square crammed with civilians, many of them clutching reclaimed radios confiscated by the Germans earlier in the war. Behind the crowd, flying the *tricolore* once again, was the Hôtel de Ville, a massive, ornate stone building of four storeys that took up one entire side of the square, causing the Canadians to wonder about the size of municipal bureaucracies in small French towns. Behind the Hôtel de Ville was the 900-year-old Ancienne Église Abbatiale, which Yates and Gill had gone off to explore.

"Well, I'll leave you to it, then," said the Links and Winks sergeant as he climbed aboard his carrier, rousing the rest his crew, who were sleeping off their celebrating. "Gotta catch up with the rest of the drunks in this outfit."

He waved as he headed off toward the Boulevard Des Monts, which would take him out of town along the railway tracks heading for the distant Seine. Al waved back and went off in search of the tourists.

When he found the two tourists they were on the other side of the Old Abbey Church in the middle of a loud and angry argument with a number of men holding three cowering young women.

The moment Gill saw Al he shouted at him to find Reggie. They needed an interpreter, *tout de suite*. The request, even though it was made in English, seemed to calm things down for the moment, but as soon as Reggie arrived the argument resumed more heated than ever.

The women—about seventeen or eighteen years of age, petite and very pretty, two of them dark-haired, one of them blonde—were accused of consorting with the enemy. For that the proscribed penalty was head shaving.

"Wait a minute. Wait a minute!" Yates was shouting to be heard. "We will test them!"

Reggie translated and the men jabbered among themselves until one of them stepped forward and said something to the interpreter, who nodded and turned to the members of his platoon.

"They want to know what you mean by a test. They are very curious about this test."

Reggie was trying to hide a smile and Yates took the opportunity to respond to Gill's tug on his sleeve by whispering in his ear. The lieutenant listened and struggled to nod solemnly for the benefit of the quizzical French.

"Tell them," he said to Reggie, "that we will take them to our doctors and have them examined to see if they are still virgins."

As Reggie rendered the English into French, Al sidled up to Gillie. "Would our doctors include that well-known Lebanese physician, Dr. William Assad, MD, S.O.B.?"

Gillie nodded gravely to Al as he whispered, "Fuck off, McDougal" out of the side of his mouth and bent to hear Reggie's translation of the French response.

"They agree to this test but one of them must come to hear the results directly from the doctor."

That evening at the home of the blonde girl, whose name was Lucie, and whose grateful mother served them a chicken dinner and enough wine to float a battleship, they laughed until their stomach muscles ached regaling each other with their individual impressions of the day's events: the look on the MO's face as they explained what he was required to do; his findings upon examination that not one of the three young ladies was a virgin; and Reggie's translation assuring the French male observer that the doctor had said all three were pure and undefiled and certificates were even now being prepared attesting to that very fact. The certificates, purloined medical record blanks, were signed with a flourish by the very same distinguished Lebanese physician first mentioned by Sergeant McDougal to Lieutenant Gill.

It was good to laugh because it transported them to happier times, the good old days before the nightmares, nervous tics and peculiar behaviours, symptoms of early-stage battle fatigue that now marked them all.

Subsequent encounters with the rough justice meted out by the liberated to consorts and collaborators were not as funny as the story of the Virgins of Bernay. Other stories were worse. Much worse.

At town after town on the way to the Seine they came across other young women seated in their underwear on platforms in town squares, surrounded by jeering mobs, their heads shaved almost to the bone. Signs around their necks read, *"J'étais une prostituée pour les Boches."*

In some places half-naked men who had entertained or done business with the Germans were forced to run gauntlets through the streets, their fellow citizens spitting on them and kicking them as they stumbled along.

And then there were the bodies, men and women, tied to posts, blindfolded and riddled by bullets, citizens of the Republic who had actively collaborated with the enemy, some even with the Gestapo and the SS. Or so it was said.

Found guilty by hastily convened courts, they were executed by hastily organized firing squads, shot by their fellow citizens in the thousands. Between D-Day and the end of the war at least 2,500, and more probably some 9,000, French citizens were disposed of in this way. A good number of them justly.

In the town of le Neubourg the Algonquins came across the body of a fourteen-year-old girl still tied to an execution post. She had told some friendly

Jerries that her father and two older brothers had stored ammunition for the Maquis, the French resistance forces. The grateful Germans promptly rounded up the three men and shot them. When the advance guard of the Lincoln and Welland Regiment had come through the town a couple of days ago, the girl had run off and hid in the woods. But the good burghers had organized a search party, the child was found, brought back to town, tried for her crime at noon and shot an hour later, her mother pleading for her daughter's life until the very end.

All this Reggie reported to them after they had seen the body and asked the questions. They didn't linger in le Neubourg.

Outside Vraiville the Carriers pulled up in front of a lynch mob hammering at the doors of a house, stone with a swayback roof. From what the Canadians could make out from the angry rabble it was the residence of another collaborator about to get his just desserts.

By now they'd had it up to here with mob justice, which, according to Yates, had been a particularly bad habit of the French ever since the days of Robespierre. So Gill had all eight carriers surround the mob and the house. He got their attention by firing a burst from his Sten in the air. Mission accomplished, Reggie shouted instructions to disperse outside the cordon of the carriers.

But the sullen crowd had the scent of blood and refused to budge. Gill, with an officer's impatience for recalcitrants, immediately shouted to the Bren gunners in each vehicle. Before you could say "half-past kiss my ass," the ground around the edges of the mob exploded in tufts of grass and clumps of earth. The Warrior Kings had spoken.

In the ensuing edgy silence Reggie yelled, *"Alors marche! Maintenant! Vite!"* And this time everyone did.

Leaving the Brens trained on the mob, Gill led a contingent up to the door, Billy knocking with the butt of his Lee Enfield and Reggie explaining in a loud voice who had come calling.

After a minute or so the door was unbarred by a small man, graying hair slicked back, wire rim glasses, a white shirt, narrow striped pants and slippered feet. Yates thought he looked like a prissy college professor.

The man smiled, bowed and showed them into a front room that served as a study, dining and living room all in one, a sizable open space dominated by a stone fireplace, a portrait of Hitler on the mantle flanked by Swastika flags.

Billy took it all in and grunted. "So this is one guy we turn over to the mob, right Gillie? No doctor's examination for him, eh?"

The guy in question said something in French to Reggie who turned to his lieutenant. "He wants us to give him a hand moving this trunk."

Reggie pointed to a piece of furniture behind the long low sofa in the centre of the room facing the fireplace. To Al it looked like the cedarwood chest his mother had at the foot of the bed in her bedroom but higher and longer.

"Wait a minute!" Gillie's voice was sharp. He was thinking of booby traps. "Wait just a minute! Ask him about his friend Herr Hitler and the Nazi flags over there."

"And don't forget this!" Yates was holding up a copy of *Mein Kampf* that he'd lifted from its place of prominence on top of the bookshelf to the right of the fireplace.

The man seemed to understand some of what they were saying and smiled as he spoke to Reggie, who translated. "He says if we move the trunk all will be explained."

Reggie looked at the man and then at Gill. "I think it is okay, Gillie."

Once the trunk was wriggled aside—it was far too heavy to lift—the prissy professor immediately knelt and began to roll up the thick braided rug underneath, the puzzled Algonquins watching intently. Then a quick word to Reggie, who went to a bureau on the far wall, opened the top drawer, felt around inside and returned with a wooden mallet, which he handed to the still-kneeling Frenchman who took it and tapped out "shave and a haircut" on the wide boards of the floor in front of his knees.

In a moment the floorboards began to move, a hand from below pushing up a concealed trap door. The hand was followed by a head topped by unruly blond locks.

The Canadians stared open-mouthed, looking like they'd just seen one of Harry Houdini's famous tricks, the escape artist emerging from his chains and a locked trunk in a tank full of water.

Goldilocks, half out of his lair, blinked at his astonished audience before offering a snappy salute. Then he reached out to grasp the extended hand of the Frenchman, who with surprising strength pulled the stowaway out of his hiding place. This was repeated three times until the Algonquins in the room had been joined by four men, one in a beret, dirty white shirt covered in a leather vest, brown culottes and riding boots, and the others in flight boots and blue uniforms with "Canada" etched on their shoulder patches.

"What took you guys so long?"

Goldilocks was the tallest of the three airmen and he was hugging an astonished Gill and cursing them all with an ear to ear grin for being slow, goddamn, splay-footed, Canuck bastards. His comrades grinned at their pilot's good-humoured scorn as they cadged cigarettes from the indulgent PBI.

The tall airman introduced himself as Flying Officer Harold Bremer from Vancouver. With him were his mid-upper gunner, Bunny Etmanski from Winnipeg, and his bombardier, Johnny Dickenson from Sarnia. They were the only surviving members of an RCAF Wellington shot down on D-Day when a Junkers eighty-eight had caught them dropping leaflets warning the French to stay off the highways.

"Certainly glad ta hear that, Harold, old boy," drawled Billy.

"Hear what?"

"That you guys were just droppin' leaflets. Last RCAF fly boys we saw were droppin' bombs. On us."

Before Bremer had a chance to respond, Reggie stepped forward to introduce the fourth man who had come up through the trap door after the Canadians. Except he was a she, her sex revealed when she took off her beret and shook loose tawny hair. For the second time in less than five minutes Algonquin jaws dropped, even further this time when they realized the airmen were as surprised as they were.

The one man in the room who wasn't surprised was their host, who explained through Reggie that the woman was the leader of the Maquis in Vraiville and that she had come to him for shelter late last night as the Gestapo made one last sweep through the town looking for her.

"So this," Yates swept his arm around the room taking in the flags crumpled on the floor, the portrait of Hitler, "and this," holding up *Mein Kampf,* "is all just bullshit. The professor here," he nodded to the Frenchman, "is also with the Resistance, *n'est ce pas?*"

"Perhaps, Private, you will permit me to explain." The woman stepped forward and for the first time Yates registered her looks, thinking she reminded him of Ingrid Bergman in *Casablanca.*

"You will forgive my English. We must blame any deficiencies on my convent education. Monsieur Gresselin," she smiled at the Frenchman, "has for years pretended to be a friend of the *Boche,* and we would say very successfully, as we know from the crowd outside who want to, how do you say, string him up?"

Her audience nodded and bowed their heads to Monsieur Gresselin. The woman continued.

"My name is Raymonde Armorin. Raymond to our gallant Canadian aviators here." She smiled at the three airmen.

"I am the leader of *les Maquisards* in this region. I have succeeded my husband who was betrayed to the Gestapo since a year. They tortured him for many days but he told them nothing and they shot him. I have no life to live now except for revenge. Revenge for my husband. And revenge for my country. I tell you this for the reason I do not want you to make any mistakes because," and here she shrugged expressively, "you see that I am a woman who is not tough enough to do the hard things. Believe me when I say I am very tough. I can kill. I have killed. And I will kill any of you who get in my way."

There was absolute silence in the house, the only sound from outside, the crowd growing restless and noisy. In the stillness, Billy was thinking about why revenge seemed to be such a simple thing for the Poles and the French and such a difficult thing for a Canadian, Yates thought he was falling in love, and Al was tempted to click his heels, salute and say "Yessir!" Gill cleared his throat.

"Madame, my name is Gill. I am the officer in charge of these men. I assure you that you are not the only person in this room who seeks revenge. Many of us have lost dear comrades to the *Boche* as you call them."

Yates smiled to himself as he listened to Gillie unconsciously reproduce the rhythm of the woman's speech.

"So," Gill continued, "we would like to know how we can help you and how you can help us, but before we have that discussion I suggest you go outside and speak to your countrymen before my men have to shoot them."

Madame Armorin smiled at a man she took to be a kindred spirit and reached out to shake Gill's hand before she went to the door, opened it, and stepped outside.

As soon as the door shut behind her Billy stuck the knife in. "Ya know I could never figure out how you guys could bomb yer own soldiers. But now I know. You guys are stupid and this proves it. Ya just spent the night with a good lookin' woman and didn't even know it."

Bremer grinned. "It was dark down there, Flat Foot." He bummed another cigarette from Al, lit it and took a long satisfying drag. "So what's the news? We still winning the war or what?"

In answer, Yates reached into his tunic and pulled out the latest issue of *The Maple Leaf News*. The headline read, **Paris Liberated After Four Years Under Nazis.**

Yates handed the paper to Bremer, with Etmanski and Dickenson reading over their pilot's shoulder. "'August 23, 1944. Paris is free.' In these historic words Gen. de Gaulle's provisional government announced the liberation of the French capital after it had been occupied by the Germans for more than four years— since June 14, 1940."

The article went on to tell how it all happened, how the city had been "freed of the invader's yoke by the citizens themselves after four days' fighting in which 50,000 armed patriots of the French Forces of the Interior and several hundred thousand unarmed civilians took part."

And then Bremer was reading out loud. "Eighty miles away from Paris towards the sea the process of squeezing the Germans out of the Lower Seine pocket went on apace yesterday. Having surged forward all along the line, advancing at some points as much as twenty miles a day, elements of the 4th Canadian Armoured Division, the 'green patch' boys, were well beyond the line of the Touques River southward to the angle of the front where it swings northeast to the Seine. A Canadian Army spokesman said: 'Everybody is going great guns and the situation is changing every fifteen minutes.'"

At that point Bremer stopped reading and looked up. "That's you guys going great guns, isn't it?"

Billy was about to puff himself up in reply when the door opened and Raymonde re-entered the house. She spoke to Gill and the two of them went to the heavy wooden table set against the end wall to the left of the fireplace. There the Maquis leader unfolded a map.

Al picked up *The Maple Leaf News* from the top of the trunk where Bremer had dropped it and started to read again about the liberation of Paris after four years of German occupation. Four years . . .

A long time ago. Four years ago the little league of nations was sitting in the Empire Theatre and watching it all on the screen. Dunkirk in May and Paris in June, Jerry goose-stepping down the Champs Elysées, Hitler posing for pictures in front of the Eiffel Tower.

That was the summer Tony Foligno signed up with the Stormont, Dundas and Glengarry Highlanders to wear a kilt and play hockey for the Canadian Army. That was the summer the rest of them went pickerel fishing and talked about Tubby Martin, Barney pushing up his glasses with a finger and breaking into that big smile of his when reminded of Martin's nickname. That was the summer they decided Hitler was just another bully like Lard Arse and they would take care of the Nazi leader just like they had taken care of Tubby. It was a summer eons ago, before time began.

"Fuck you!" It was one of his sudden shouted curses, one of his verbal tics, his battlefield Tourette's syndrome, which his comrades in the room ignored. It was just Al being Al, but the airmen looked up, as did Gresselin and Madame Armorin, and Al waved a hand in the air, an "I'm all right, Jack" gesture.

"Hey, Sergeant. You off in another world?"

It was a minute or so later and Gill was beckoning him over to the table and the map and Raymonde. It obviously wasn't the first time he had been called and he mumbled an apology.

Gill was pointing to a spot on the map just on the other side of the Seine south of Rouen and about ten miles from Vraiville.

"Madame Armorin has information that our Jerry friends are preparing a major rearguard action here and suggests we get onto them right away before they get a chance to really dig in. If I radio this information to HQ I will be told to wait for a company or two and by the time that happens Jerry will be ready and a good number of our boys will get killed trying to dislodge them. But if we get in there right now before they're set and ready, engage them with a little help from the Maquis and then call for reinforcements if we need to, then that will get things going faster on our end and also throw a monkey wrench into Jerry's preparations. Whataya think?"

Gillie was no longer talking like a machine gun in short bursts. A woman's influence? Al bent over the map and asked the Maquis leader some questions about the lay of the land, enemy numbers and enemy weapons. He was resolved that if he heard the word "tanks" he would tell Gillie it just wasn't worth it. But he didn't so he didn't.

It was late in the day by the time the fly boys had been toasted on their way to the rear and Monsieur Gresselin's hand had been shaken for the umpteenth time. It was even later when Raymonde Armorin, riding in Gillie's Cruiser, signalled them to cut their speed as they approached an intact railway bridge over the Seine near Criquebeuf.

As the carriers geared down to a stop, Armorin looked hard to her left through the haze, part dust and part ground fog, swirling around the trees lining that side of the road. Then she put fingers to her mouth and whistled. Immediately ghostly figures emerged from the tree line, *les maquisards* in various modes of dress, about a dozen men along with two women, carrying an assortment of weapons, Stens and Lee Enfields, captured German Mausers and Schmeissers.

An urgent consult with Armorin, and then Armorin with Gill, and the Maquis were quickly up on the carriers rumbling their way at top speed across the bridge and into an old lumber yard before dismounting for an Orders Group. No sooner had Gill opened his mouth to speak when he was preempted by a series of sudden, rumbling explosions. It didn't take a lifetime to figure it out. The Germans were blowing up the bridge.

Al was standing beside a pile of railway ties and scrambled up to watch in the fading light, trestles toppling from one ballast bed to another right across the width of the broad river. Five minutes earlier he and the rest of the Carrier Platoon had been smack dab in the middle of that bridge, the same bridge whose spans were now tilting like playground slides into the river below.

Sergeant McDougal shuddered and climbed from his perch, head over his shoulder, looking at his lieutenant all the way down. He could see that Gill was furious as it dawned on him the risk he had taken with the platoon because Armorin had fudged the truth.

"Listen, lady! What the fuck do you think you're doing?"

Gill's face was twisted in rage and he was shouting above the fading roar of the last explosion. The Maquis, alarmed at the Canadian's anger, started to raise their weapons until Armorin shook her head at them.

"If I told you the truth you would not have come, Lieutenant. And if we had been wrong about the time we were told the *Boche* would explode the bridge then it would not have been Canadians only killed. Is that not so?"

Gill turned his back on her and stood with his hands on his hips taking in his surroundings, the long tin shed that once housed saws and machinery, the orderly piles of railway ties, together with the scattered mounds of different-sized boards and timbers helter-skelter in the yard, his mind working as he reviewed his options.

At last he took a deep breath and turned back to the woman, holding up his hands, palms out. "Okay, okay. No use crying over spilled milk."

Armorin looked at him inquisitively.

"What's done is done."

She nodded now in understanding.

"But," and here he pointed at her like the schoolmaster he had once been "if you screw around with us ever again, woman or not, I will personally shoot you right between your goddamn eyes. Do I make myself clear, Madame?"

The Madame smiled and nodded that the Canadian officer had indeed made himself clear and the two of them then led their joint forces into the tin shed where the O Group finally commenced.

According to the Maquis, a platoon of German paratroopers was digging in as a blocking unit about 300 yards down the highway at a complex of farm buildings sitting at the crest of a rise. Just behind the barn, silo and house, on the downside of the rise, a number of secondary roads joined the main road running north from the Seine to the Somme and into Belgium. From the crest of the rise the paras commanded a view of the off-road approaches from the farm fields to the west and all of the highway approaches on any of the converging roads from the southwest.

It was proposed that the Maquis, under cover of darkness, infiltrate the German perimeter and take up positions in the old cemetery separating the farm buildings from the western pasture. At first light the Carriers would approach by the secondary roads to draw the enemy's attention with a few Bren bursts.

"And his return fire." Al jumped in. "Tell me again what Jerry's got."

"Small arms only. Mausers, Schmeissers, grenades."

"You sure, Madame? No *panzerfausts,* no anti-tank weapons?"

Madame shrugged. "I am told they have none."

Al looked at Gill, who raised his eyebrows at Madame, who threw up her hands. "Very well. I will ask my people to make certain, *encore,* that this is so. Jacques!"

She called to one of her group, a young man carrying a Schmeisser, wearing a fedora on his head and an SS camouflage jacket draped over his shoulders. Guerrilla chic.

She spoke to Jacques in rapid French and he left the shed immediately while Gill took up the briefing.

"The carriers on the roads," he pointed to the map, "here, here and here will engage with their Brens at long range, gentlemen. Remember you're not trying to kill Jerry. Just get his attention. And while you're doing that the Maquis will attack from the cemetery."

He held up his hand anticipating the question. "Understand, by morning there will be more than the twelve you see here. Madame Armorin says there will be another fifty in the cemetery waiting to join our little force. And," he paused for a moment, "about a half dozen of us. Questions?"

There were none and the only thing left to do was grab a bite and forty winks. Tomorrow was another day and it would start early.

It was no effort at all to drop off into dreamland. They were all bone weary and could have slept standing up if need be. The effort came in waking up when it was still dark and bones still weary.

After tea and hardtack slathered with strawberry jam from Billy's last parcel from home, the Algonquins assigned to the Maquis followed Raymonde Armorin out into a pitch-black and very wet night.

They moved single file through a steady drizzle, each one holding onto something of the person in front. Al, bringing up the rear, had looped an old pair of suspenders through Dobson's web belt and was whispering, "Gitty up, horsy. Nice horsy. Gitty up."

There was light in the clouds in the eastern sky and the rain was easing up by the time the column got to the first gravestones and took cover among them. Once Al looked around through the ground mist for any sign of the promised Maquis reinforcements and saw none he tapped horsy on the shoulder and told him to get to Armorin and find out what the hell was going on. When the Carriers opened up at first light the attack from the cemetery would begin and by the look of the sky, first light was only minutes away. There was no time to lose.

Dobson gave a thumbs up, looked to get his bearings, and then with his rifle clutched to his chest set off in a quick crouching run to a nearby tombstone, where he flopped to check things out before dashing for the shelter of the next grave marker. Al watched him go and a proud smile creased his face. Dobson was a careful soldier, a good soldier.

Dobson's sergeant and hometown friend was about to turn away to reconnoitre the other side of the cemetery when he heard the earth move and Dougie scream.

Chapter Twenty-One

SEPTEMBER 3, 1944. Vauchelles-les-Quesnoy. A line from one of my mother's favourite hymns comes to mind. We used to sing it around the piano. "Solace in the midst of woe." Here, just south of Abbeville, on the east bank of the Somme, our solace is hot food, hot showers, clean clothes, warm beds and all of the Regiment together again for the first time since Hubert's Folly. What more could a man ask after three weeks on the job, 24 dirty hours a day, seven grinding days a week? In the last 10 days not even time to make a diary entry and now that I have the time it's hard to know where to start. Gillie says we will be getting replacements in the next day or so but how do you replace lads you've spent the last four years with or boys like Barney you grew up with or Dougie Dobson whose mother was your grade three teacher? What was it the padre at Borden said about the body having a lot of different parts but still being one body? How do you replace your arm or your leg or an eye or your own right hand? Crow's been around to say hello. Asked him how many notches he had in his rifle. He shrugged and said about a dozen or so. Mostly from tracking and shooting German snipers. Told him we could have used him that day in the cemetery when Dougie was killed. It was…

Excerpt from the Diary

The scribbler was propped up on his knees and the hand holding the pencil had dropped to his lap. He was sitting against a post in the hayloft of a barn Support Company had requisitioned for HQ, sleeping quarters in the loft. There was plenty of room in the barn because all the farmer's cows were in the fields, feet stiff to the sky. Bloated casualties of war.

Al had gone up to the loft for some peace and quiet after the noon meal and sat there now staring up at the sturdy, creosoted beams, the afternoon sunlight shafting through the spaces between the roof boards. He gathered a handful of straw and threw it up, watching the light catch the bits and pieces of chaff drifting like sparkling snowflakes on a lazy-mild winter day. He took a deep breath and blew it out slowly through pursed lips.

Sometimes it helped to write about things and sometimes it didn't. He had a feeling this was one of the times when it wasn't going to help because he didn't have the will to get beyond the words "when Dougie was killed." In Current River he'd told Gillie he didn't want to be a sergeant because he feared giving a man an order that would get him killed. Now what he'd feared had come to pass and he couldn't stop thinking about it, couldn't stop watching it over and over again on the *Movietone News* of his mind's eye.

Jerry had given some credence to the old wives' tale about it being bad luck to walk on a grave by sowing the cemetery with *Schutzenmines*, one of the German anti-personnel weapons Andy Ancaster had gleefully shown them in the Brighton pub. It was a schumine that had lifted the grave under Dougie's prone body, blowing a hole in his shoulder just above the pocket where he carried his copy of the New Testament. But it wasn't the schumine that killed him. It was a sniper following the same advice given to Crow by his instructor at Aldershot.

When Dobson triggered the mine, two of the Maquis rushed to help him. Instantly there were quick shots from the direction of the farm buildings. Al heard the pop of the bullets breaking the sound barrier before his ears registered the crack of the shots.

The two Frenchmen folded like rag dolls and were still. From Dobson there came a piercing and agonized yell, "Al!" And then another pop and another crack, and a red rose bloomed in the centre of his forehead.

Before he could really take any of this in, Al heard the Brens open up on the other side of the farm and could tell that they weren't just trying to get Jerry's attention. The Carriers were attacking.

Flat on his belly on the edge of the cemetery, Al twisted, first to one side and then the other, yelling orders to fall back. Another way had to be found to the farm buildings.

It was Raymonde crawling over beside him who pointed the way, a lane skirting the edge of the cemetery, up and around behind the barn, a sunken path out of sight of the sniper in the silo and likely free of mines because of the fresh vehicle tracks bracketing the grassy median in the centre.

Crawling to the lane, the Algonquins and the Maquis moved cautiously single file along the vehicle tracks, low to the ground like an undulating caterpillar, eyes searching for telltale signs of freshly dug earth and, when they saw anything that might be buried death, carefully probing with their bayonets while all the time the sounds of battle vibrated in front of them, the chug, chug sound of the Brens, the whine and screech of bullets chipping stone and the patter of enemy small arms fire hitting the carriers, hail on a cold tin roof.

They were almost to the courtyard formed by the barn, farmhouse, silo and other outbuildings when the firing stopped and shouts of "*Kamerad! Kamerad!*" could be heard. Was it the paras surrendering?

Al and Raymonde, Stens at the ready, poked their heads around the corner of the barn. The enemy, hands on their heads and surrounded by the Bren gunners from the carriers, were the remnants of a single section, not a platoon, and they were not elite German paratroopers but Mongol conscripts taken from the German incursion into Russia, a ragtag band of expendables left to hinder the Canadian advance, buying time for Hitler's finest to set up on the Somme.

A white cloth tied to a pole emerged from the ground door of the silo. The flag of surrender was followed by a sniper's rifle, scope clearly visible, thrown to clatter on the cobblestones of the courtyard. Then a soldier appeared, blue-grey framed in the doorway, hands in the air. He took one step forward before Billy shot him.

His body pitched forward, head bouncing on the pavement stones. Two of the Maquis, cursing and screaming, rushed over to empty their weapons, the corpse greeting the fusillade with a macabre jerking that kept time to the beat of thudding bullets. The other prisoners, expecting the sniper's fate, fell to their knees, hands clasped in supplication, begging for their lives, and for a heart-wrenching minute Al felt a bloodbath would be unstoppable.

Then he heard Gill shout, "Cease fire! Cease fire!" It wasn't much, but it was enough to break the spell, enough to drag men, their nerve ends raw, back from the edge of a cliff.

Al walked over to his lieutenant and told him about Dobson. Gill walked over to the sniper's body and kicked it hard. Then he turned and beckoned Al through the gate on the road side of the courtyard, pointing down the hill to a smoking, overturned carrier.

"Panzerfaust," he said. "Three of our guys gone." He spit out the names. Chaisson, Bowman, Smith.

Al swallowed and looked away with the same expression on his face as he now had in the hayloft, the same sad, vacant stare, as Yates, climbing the ladder, poked his head over the edge, showing a grin. "Oh, Auntie Em! There's no place like home!"

Al looked blankly at his friend and then was startled by a loud, excited voice taking off on Foster Hewitt. "Oh, and that was a *fantastic* save by McDougal in the Leaf's net! Now Archibald behind the net picks up the puck, passes it up to Assad, over to Carriere streaking down the right wing, Carriere across ice to Berman, over the blue line to Foligno! Foligno is around the defence! He shoots! He scores!"

McDougal, from the Leaf net, was down the ladder in a flash to throw his arms around a grinning Tony Foligno who dropped his kit bag, stepped back and offered a parade ground salute.

"Corporal Tony Foligno, Sergeant. Reporting as a replacement to the Carrier Platoon from the 4th Division holding unit, sir!"

Sergeant McDougal winked at the corporal, stepped back himself, straightened his back and farted, the crump of a muffled grenade blast. Yates, his head hanging over the edge of the loft, whistled in appreciation and Tony burst into laughter.

"Better check your underwear on that one, Al. And speaking of shit," Tony was looking at his goaltender with a critical eye, "you look like shit."

"And you, *paesano*, look like a real fashion plate all set to go dancing and wow the ladies in your spiffy uniform and polished boots. Yates, come down here and meet the best dressed Wop in France and be careful you don't cut yourself on the sharp creases of the man's battledress."

The three of them found a stone bench along the opposite wall, got out their smokes and sat down for a chat, Yates listening as Tony and Al filled in the blanks for each other since Tony had gone one way and the rest of the little league of nations another. There was silence when Al finished telling how Barney had bought the farm, Tony reaching to shake Willy's hand when he heard how the American had eased Barney's passing with a reassuring lie about Goody Noseworthy.

Later that evening Tony held court in the barn on various and sundry matters ranging from what he'd been up to since the little league had last convened, to the subject of manpower shortages in the Canadian Army, information he had gleaned from personal observation and overheard conversations while hobnobbing with the high and mighty, including, he said, the Honourable J. Layton Ralston, the Minister of Defence, on a recent fact-finding tour of Normandy.

He told how his knee had taken a long time to heal sufficiently for combat duty. For a while he thought he would be invalided out of service and sent home to Lowvert. But bit by bit the knee got better and with a little help from his CO he was assigned to HQ duties. Eventually early in 1943 he wangled his way to 1st Canadian Div as a driver cum interpreter for the division's commander, Major-General Guy Simonds. He was with Simonds in July for the invasion of Sicily and the later fighting in the Italian peninsula. In September when Simonds was hospitalized with a bad case of jaundice and succeeded by Brigadier Chris Vokes, Tony wangled his way to England.

"Couldn't stand Vokes. Acted like he was Montgomery's twin brother complete with horsetail swagger stick. Even had a fake English accent. Arsehole."

With Simonds back in the picture in 1944, taking over 2nd Canadian Corps in preparation for the invasion of Normandy, Tony hooked up with him again but a motorbike accident just outside of Caen—he'd borrowed a Don R's Norton for a spin—wrenched his other knee, which meant a month in hospital back in England with his leg in traction. Two wonky knees was a definite ticket home, a blighty for Canada, but Tony used his army hockey connections to call in some favours and presto, the necessary paperwork was completed to get him to 4th Div's holding unit to await assignment.

"Don't suppose it's an accident ya got assigned to us, eh? I mean there must be what, fifteen other outfits in this division?"

Tony winked at his interrogator. "It's not *what* ya know, Billy."

"Yeah, yeah. Same old Tony. But listen, this ain't no picnic, son. Maybe ya shoulda gone home."

"No siree, Billy boy. Gotta do my bit."

They could tell from the expression on his face that he meant it.

"So you said something about the reasons we're fighting at half strength?"

The question came from Willy Yates and the answer made them shake their heads in disgust. As Tony told it, the manpower problem was, first and foremost, a snafu by Canadian military planners. They'd goofed. From the beginning. Too many men had been recruited for the RCAF and the RCN and not enough for the army. So right off the bat there weren't enough PBI to do the job.

Then the number of infantry casualties for the Normandy campaign had been grossly underestimated, which meant that, after three months of fighting, there were about 2,000 fewer Flat Feet than predicted.

And that wasn't all. The number of wounded able to return to their units had been grossly *over*estimated. The original prediction was fifty percent. In fact, returnees amounted to a little over ten percent.

Finally, the military planners in Ottawa hadn't the foggiest notion as to how really bad the fighting was going to be, Moaning Minnies and eighty-eights, shrapnel and schumines and a "well-trained, well-equipped and battle-hardened" enemy.

"You know what the army's manual has to say about hours of work?"

"Tell us."

"Says twelve days of combat are to be followed by four days of rest."

Groans and laughter.

The end result of hard fighting, no rest and the enervating effect of friendly fire was hundreds of casualties due to battle exhaustion. Something else the planners had neglected to factor into the equation.

It was Yates who broke into the quiet after Tony finished. "So, Corporal Foligno, O Great and Wise One. You have just told us there are no reinforcements out there and yet we've been told we're getting some tomorrow. Please square the circle for these your humble servants gathered here."

Tony grinned. "Well, Brother Yates, you of course know that the Canadian Army," and here he blew a mock fanfare on an imaginary trumpet, "has the highest proportion of rear-end warriors of any fuckin' army in the whole damn fuckin' world."

The Great and Wise One went on to explain that the ratio of the rear end to the front end in Johnny Canuck's army was about three to one. For every soldier like them on the sharp end, there were three on the other end. And that was before a shot had been fired. As soon as the fighting began, seventy-five percent of the casualties—naturally—were from the sharp end so that now, three months after D-Day, the ratio was more likely to be about six to one.

"So what that means is that the brass, confronted with the obvious, have decided that our reinforcements will be coming from the rear-end warriors."

"Yessir, Private Yates, and guess what that means?"

Before anyone chanced an answer there was a blaring of an automobile horn outside, followed by shouts and whistles. On the other side of the barn door, waiting for their inspection, was a captured version of Hitler's answer to Henry

Ford's Model T, the bubble-shaped Volkswagen, or "people's car," with its air-cooled twenty-four-horsepower rear engine and front-end trunk. This Volkswagen, a captured staff car, had a canvas top and a spare tire mounted above the trunk just below the windshield. The car was so light that a group of laughing soldiers was lifting it up by its four wheel wells and moving it from place to place in the barnyard, showing off as successive groups of their comrades came by for a look.

In the midst of all the fun Yates picked up the thread of the conversation. "Here's what I think it means."

"What what means?" Al asked the question but Tony nodded, instantly tuned in to Willy's waveband.

"It means that starting tomorrow we are going to be getting a bunch of guys who don't know shit from shish kebab when it comes to fighting."

The next morning, watching the rear-end warriors clambering down from their transport and lining up in formations that would have embarrassed the little league on their second day at Camp Borden, Al could see that Yates had been spot-on. Plucked from their jobs as cooks, carpenters, truck drivers, shoemakers, mechanics, clerks and pencil pushers in general, the reinforcements were dumped into holding units and then randomly assigned to depleted regiments as front-line troops.

Gill made an appearance and stood watching with his sergeant for a minute or two. "Forty-eight hours, Al. To make fighting men out of this lot. Find out which ones are ours. ASAP. Get them ready."

The three men assigned to the Carrier Platoon knew nothing of Northern Ontario. Louis Cormier hailed from Grande-Digue, New Brunswick, Woody Williams from Kelowna, British Columbia, and Whitey MacLeod from Shawville, Quebec. While it was easy to understand their lack of enlightenment when it came to God's country, the backwoods and the mine, it wasn't so easy to fathom their wide-eyed innocence with regard to the profession of arms.

Cormier, who spoke very little, if any, of the king's native tongue and shouldn't have been sent to an English-speaking regiment, not in a million years, evidently had never seen a grenade before because he didn't know you had to pull the safety pin if you wanted the damn thing to explode.

Williams darn near blew Billy's foot off with a Sten because he didn't know how to turn the knob and engage the weapon's safety. When asked where he got his weapons training he sheepishly said he'd never had any; he was a cook.

MacLeod was a bit of a know-it-all and pretended he was a savvy and grizzled veteran, but was exposed as a numbskull when he asked Ross about the makeshift dish he used to bring water to Captain Max of the RCFF.

"Hey, where'd ya get the American helmet? At Falaise?"

"Yeah at Falaise. 'Cept it's a German helmet."

When their forty-eight hours of training were over, Al took all three of them aside and, with Reggie translating for Cormier, told them to keep their eyes and ears open and heads down.

"You lads are gonna have to learn on the job. If you're not sure about something, ask. Ask and ye shall receive. Cormier, you stick close to Reggie. You *comprenez?*"

Even before Reggie finished translating, Cormier was smiling and nodding his head. He wanted to please. Al smiled back but called Reggie aside and told him to talk to Cormier like a Dutch uncle to make sure he understood *everything*. Al didn't want the rookie pretending he knew what he was doing when he didn't.

As Al turned to go, he saw Williams hanging back. "Sarge, can I talk to you for a minute?"

"Sure."

"Listen, I appreciate what you've tried to do for us in the last two days and I want ya ta know I'll do my best. And I want ya ta know I appreciate the welcome you boys have given us. Including us, and all that. I know it can't be easy. After all, the only reason the three of us greenhorns are here is because you boys lost some of your buddies. And we're never gonna replace them."

Al stepped back and looked at Williams, thinking for the first time how hard it must be for an outsider to fit in, a man who hadn't been to the same places as the rest of them, didn't know the same people and hadn't been a part of the same stories. The funny ones or the sad ones.

"Look. It's Woody, isn't it?

"Yessir."

"Jesus, Woody, don't yessir me. I'm just a sergeant. And don't yessir Gill, either. He'll think yer talkin' about somebody else. A general or something."

"Yessir." Then Williams caught himself and grinned. "Okay, Sarge."

"Okay, Woody."

Sergeant McDougal stepped forward and threw an arm around Williams's shoulders. "Let's you and I go for a stroll while I tell ya about a padre's sermon I heard once when we were doin' our basic training at Camp Borden."

At dawn the next morning the Carriers hit the road with a good number of groggy lads tuckered out after spending much of the previous evening in the fleshpots of nearby Abbeville. Passing through their first map reference, the town of Saint Riquier, Al takes note of the statuary fronting its abbey, faces eaten away as if leprosy were an affliction of stone as well as flesh, the ravaged medieval bishop with no legs, the Blessed Virgin Mary with no arms.

Then the road to Hesdin, straight as an arrow, past the detritus of a fierce battle in the flatlands on either side, tilted telephone poles, wires hanging down, garbage in the ditches—empty ration and ammo boxes, jerry cans and tin cans, bits and pieces of blowing paper—burned-out tanks and trucks bulldozed off the road into the fields and, here and there, temporary burial grounds, some mounds with crosses, others still with helmets hanging on upturned rifles bayoneted into the earth, this war's gloss on the glorious dead of the First, slaughtered by the tens of thousands at the various battles of the Somme.

A railroad crossing demonstrates Jerry's ingenuity, the tracks rendered useless by a device coupled to the rear end of a locomotive and hooked down and in like an eagle's beak, a perfect instrument for ripping up ties and rails.

Past the ruined crossing, the convoy eating up the miles on a road thickly forested on each side, Gillie's Cruiser comes upon a dangling road sign announcing the town of Fauquembergues. At Fuckimberg (Billy's translation) the Carriers are about fifteen miles from their destination of St. Omer, which the convoy approaches along the crest of a ridge, the red tile roofs of the town now visible in the valley below as the green of trees gives way to bald rolling hills of brown slashed here and there by the white of chalk underneath, a marker to remind them that they weren't far from the Channel coast, in fact less than fifty miles southeast of Vera Lynn's White Cliffs of Dover. The greenhorns take note. The old-timers pay no attention.

Their route now parallels the torn tracks into St. Omer, past a World War I British cemetery, a statue of a navel officer in a cocked hat, and then into the heart of the town, the usual narrow streets of cobblestone and the usual street-crowding buildings, but ornate this time, intricately carved stone fronts and virtually all with balconies.

Their orders are to rendezvous at the railway station with a British agent who had been parachuted into France two months before the invasion to coordinate resistance activities along the coast. The agent is from Special Operations Executive, the name given to those brave men and women dedicated to clandestine warfare, sabotage and subversion in German occupied Europe. Founded in 1940 by Prime Minister Churchill to "set Europe ablaze," the SOE address in London, known only to a select few, is on Baker Street just a few doors down from the fictional address of another unconventional champion of justice, the legendary Sherlock Holmes.

The SOE is the brains behind the sabotage of the German war machine in France, teaching railroad workers how to disrupt signals or disable a *plaque tournant*, and holding clandestine seminars on how one tiny cube of sugar dropped in a gas tank can freeze an engine when the sugar caramelizes on the pistons. When sugar is scarce a potato wedged in an exhaust pipe will, at the very least, blow a hole in the muffler. If you're lucky it can also direct deadly carbon monoxide into the driver's compartment.

The SOE is already a legend among the PBI, its work, in Eisenhower's words, "the equivalent of fifteen divisions," and the Canadians are looking forward to meeting an agent in the flesh.

But hopes are dashed when there is no SOE operative to greet them at the station, a squat cylinder of stone looking like an oversized hat box; but there is a reception committee comprised of the mayor and several members of the local

Maquis, now *persona non grata* in the eyes of the Algonquins, their own experience confirmed by stories from other regiments, the Argyll and Sutherland Highlanders reporting the loss of a man when the trigger-happy French mistook him for a German and shot him.

Gill delegates Reggie to deal with the St. Omer Maquis, who are quite clearly miffed that an officer has no time for them. In a minute Reggie reports back with information of a German concentration on the other side of the canal to the east of the town. All bridges over the canal have been destroyed but the French are offering to show where and how a crossing can be made using a Dutch barge. However, once Gill finds out where the barge is located, his reply is thanks-but-no-thanks-the-platoon-will-look-after-it-see-you-arseholes-later.

It is late in the afternoon when they find the barge and get it floated down to where Jerry has blown up a bridge but left the concrete approach ramps pretty much intact. Once the barge is turned sideways to the current and anchored, planking linking it to the ramps on either side is nailed, wired, roped and ultimately prayed into place, enabling the Suicide Squad to rumble across and fan out in search of Jerry before the sun goes down, Louis Cormier sitting close to Reggie in Hitler's Hearse along with Williams under Al's watchful eye.

As events will prove, it will not turn out to be a peaceful evening. Long before the moon rises Tony Foligno will get his first real taste of battle and one of the three rookies, after only one fighting day on the job, will end up with his name inscribed on the regiment's casualty list for the first week of September 1944. The other two will follow in short order.

The first to make the list is Whitey MacLeod from Shawville. He has smooth-talked his way into taking a turn at the wheel of his assigned carrier and makes the rookie mistake of taking the shoulder of the road to avoid a burned-out Royal Tiger.

It is one of Jerry's favourite and deadly tricks to pack the shoulders around road wrecks with Tellermines. This is a flat, cylindrical, pressure-covered, anti-tank device packing an explosive charge powerful enough to blow a carrier and everyone in it arse over teakettle. Some Tellermines are set to go off when the first track or tire rolls over them while others only detonate after a pre-set number of vehicles have depressed the pressure cover.

All carriers, including those of the Suicide Squad, have a Suicide Seat. It is the driver's seat, right above the bogie wheel, which, nine times out of ten, is the first pressure contact with a Tellermine. So all drivers, for their own preservation, have learned either by near-death experiences or word of mouth to swing away early and take a wide loop around a road wreck. It's one of those things you don't think about because it's just one of those things you know—if you've been around for a bit.

MacLeod, curious as to what one of the monsters looks like up close and dead, is almost on top of the Tiger when he swings his vehicle hard to the left to go round. The explosion flicks the carrier up off the shoulder of the road and over the shallow ditch, where it comes to rest on its side.

Al gets to the crumpled vehicle before anyone else, with Woody Williams right behind him. MacLeod is still in his seat as if glued to it. He is white-faced and unconscious, both legs blown off just above the knee, torn arteries spouting blood.

Al turns to Williams and yells for his web belt, anything that can be used for a tourniquet, but Williams is frozen. Yates and Billy arrive on the run to help stop the worst of the bleeding and MacLeod is quickly loaded onto another carrier along with four of his comrades, bruised and concussed and maybe a broken arm or two, but otherwise healthy in comparison. The carrier turns and roars off, back to the closest RAP, all of the watching veterans knowing it is a race that MacLeod will not win. He has left too much of his blood behind, pooling and thickening now in the corner of the tilted carrier.

Gillie is all for pushing on with the six carriers left. He gets no argument. Everyone knows there is a job to be done. Find Jerry.

This doesn't take long. Up over a hill past stooks of hay in the fields, the Carriers gear down at a crossroads, tilled lands at all four points of the compass smelling of sheep manure. The shelling starts immediately.

It isn't entirely unexpected. Jerry is nothing if not predictable and does what he always does when retreating from strong defensive positions like hills or crossroads. He zeroes in on the position just vacated and the minute there is any sign of advancing Allied forces in and around these spots, he lets loose with everything he has. This time it is eighty-eights, *wham wham wham*, three black airbursts about fifty feet above the point where the four roads join, sheets of orange-yellow flame shooting down.

The Carriers waste no time in wheeling back over the hill out of sight, where Gill hand-directs a dismount and take cover signal. In a minute he and Corporal Foligno are burrowed next to Hitler's Hearse talking to Al, Gill asking for his best guess about the eighty-eights. Are they static emplacements or tank mounted?

Al shook his head. "Jesus, Gillie, the name is Al McDougal, not Swami McDougal. How the hell should I know."

Corporal Foligno is listening hard and remembering a story he'd heard of King Tigers in the early days of the invasion just east of Caen when twelve of the monsters annihilated a British armoured brigade, knocking out twenty-five Shermans, fourteen half-tracks and a dozen carriers in less than ten minutes.

"If they're King Tigers then this is no place for us." Tony was sweating and speaking rapidly. "Shit, I don't like this. Let's get the hell outta here."

Al looked over at his boyhood chum and was startled to see a man whose head seemed to be shrinking into his neck and whose eyes reminded him of the night at Camp Shilo when he and Billy had frozen a deer in the headlights of their Jeep.

Yates had just wiggled in beside them. "Look, it's getting dark. If there are tanks up there, pretty soon they'll be hunkering down because they won't be able to see a damn thing. So why don't we hide the carriers, lay low for a bit, then send a foot patrol out to take a peek."

Gill nodded and the carriers were driven off among the stooks, where the lads quickly covered them with hay and then settled down to wait for the stars to show themselves.

Once he'd seen to the camouflage of the Hearse, Al went looking for Tony, but couldn't find him anywhere in the lengthening shadows. He asked around but no one had seen the corporal, not since the confab about the eighty-eights. Frowning now, Al stood and racked his brain, trying to figure out where Tony could possibly be. Finally, muttering a frustrated oath, he returned to the Hearse, tucked himself into the shallow slit trench he'd dug underneath the rear end, and lay down using his helmet as a pillow.

He must have dozed off because the next thing he knew it was pitch black and someone was tugging at his boot.

"Al! Al, wake up, goddammit. Gillie wants to talk."

For an instant he didn't recognize Billy's voice but when he did he shook himself and wriggled out from under.

"Seen Tony?" Billy asked.

"No, you?"

"Nope, and Gillie's lookin' for him."

"Jesus, Billy." And Al voiced the thought that had been worming its way into consciousness even before he'd drifted off to sleep. "What if he's gone AWL?"

"Tony? Absent without leave? You gotta be kidding. What the hell for?"

"No, no! Wait a sec."

And Al told Billy of the fear he'd seen in Tony's face at the Hearse and not being able to find him later. "I'll bet ya, Billy, this is the first time Tony's been really close to what Jerry has to offer. Driving around with the hoity-toity brass all the time, it's not bloody likely that he's seen a man get his legs blown off or ever been shaking in his boots under an exploding eighty-eight. Not in a month of Sundays, eh?"

"So he's scared." Billy shrugged. "Christ Al, we're all scared. You, me, Yates, Arnie, Ross, Reggie. Tout la gang. Even Gillie. We're scared every minute. We get butterflies in our guts every day. We jump at any little noise. Hell, the guys jump when you fart."

Al snorted but Billy was right. Fear was their close companion. Every day it was mirrored in their eyes, etched on their faces. It was in the way they walked, most of the time hunched over, heads swivelling like kids in the dark wondering if the bogeyman is lying in wait behind that bush or around that corner.

If Gill had been looking for Tony he seemed to have forgotten all about it by the time Al got over to the cruiser and knelt to listen to his lieutenant outline just what he wanted from the patrol.

"Take Foligno with you. And Cormier and the cook from B.C. Give them a chance to see what stumbling around in the dark in No Man's Land is all about."

Al had two hours to kill before the patrol was to set out and took the time to thoroughly brief Williams and Cormier. When he was certain he'd dotted all the I's and crossed all the T's he could think of, he heaved a sigh.

"Okay, you two guys go rest up while Reggie and I explain to this fine gentleman what we're gonna do tonight."

The fine gentleman was Billy, who had turned up just as the briefing came to an end. The moment the two rookies were out of hearing, Al turned to Billy. "Any sign of Tony?"

"Nope. I mean where could he go? Nothing but fields around here, fields and haystacks."

"Well, nothing we can do about it now. We," Al flicked Gill's flashlight on his watch, "are off to see the Wizard in about one hour and the greenhorns are comin' with us, so listen up."

They left the hay-covered carriers under a full moon. The advantage was they could see where they were going. The disadvantage was so could Jerry. But then that's what life was all about. Choices.

Their route was northeast through the stubble of the fields to a stand of tall trees on the brow of a rise, a distance of some 1,500 yards. If there were any German tanks hanging around that's where Gillie figured they would be laagered for the night. Somewhere over the rise.

It was past midnight when they got to the trees, towering, gloomy sentries standing tall in the moonlight. If Crow had been with them Al would have sent him in through the sentries but he wasn't so he fingered Arnie for the job.

For the most part, the early going was easy for the Swede; the underbrush had been cleared away and the trees widely spaced, certainly enough for a tank or two to manoeuvre through, so all Arnie had to do was dodge from tree to tree, watching for wires that might trip a booby trap. But the deeper into the woods he went the less moonlight there was to guide him and he was almost at the point of having to plant one foot in front of the other when a sound drifted through from the other side of a dense thicket looming in front of him. His head went up like a startled rabbit, straining to identify what he'd just heard.

After a second or two he got it, the haunting, sensual voice of a woman singing a brooding, sentimental song the homesick on both sides vocalized when they were in their cups. But this time "Lilli Marlene" was in German.

Arnie scuttled around the thicket to the tree line closest to the music, dropped on his belly and, with rifle cradled in his arms, elbowed his way to a small clearing where he found himself looking down into a shallow gully at the familiar shape of a Royal or King Tiger with its long telltale eighty-eight-mm cannon. He was close enough and the moon was bright enough to see the white-outlined black cross on the turret just above and to the right of the tank's number—"17," with the distinctive slanted cross through the seven.

Both the turret and driver's hatches were open and the music was coming from inside, Arnie guessing that the Tiger's wireless was tuned into German Armed Forces radio. The tank crew were sprawled all over the tank's surface, some listening to the music and others dozing. As Arnie's eyes swept around the Tiger he could see silhouettes on the ground. He took them to be a sleeping infantry patrol attached to the tank and counted nine men in all, crew and patrol, with maybe one or two others inside the tank.

There didn't seemed to be any guards posted or any sense that there was a war going on. It looked as if Jerry was on peacetime maneouvres whiling a warm night away listening to music under the stars.

There was something seductive about all of it and the Swede felt himself falling under the spell, a peaceful moonlight communion with the enemy and his music, "Lilli Marlene" followed by a piano, notes high and clear rippling up the side of the gully, something by Beethoven, Arnie thought, although he wasn't altogether sure. He came from a musical family and although his knowledge of music beyond the songs of the camboose was good, it wasn't that good.

Then, as he listened, he thought of the beer-fuelled discussion they'd had one night in England, Thetford, if memory served, Willy Yates declaiming, cataloguing the great names of German culture, the writers, the philosophers, the composers, blind Beethoven among them, and then asking how such a people could fall for a madman like Hitler.

The spell was broken. Arnie shivered and then quietly crabbed his way backwards from his observation point and, once out of earshot, retraced his steps in double time.

After a surprisingly brief discussion, Al letting everyone have his say, it was agreed that they would attempt to eliminate the menace facing the platoon by taking out the tank at dawn using the advantage of surprise and the rising sun behind them. It would have to be quick and dirty before the tank crew could react.

"Too bad we didn't have a PIAT." While Arnie had been gone they'd been talking about tanks and anti-tank weapons and Woody Williams had been listening.

"Son," drawled Yates, "with those fuckin' Tigers you might as well go after them with a peashooter."

Then playfully back into his good-old-boy persona for the first time in months, Willy turned to Al and asked with his best Old South accent, "Sarge, suppose we all play a little game of Shilo softball here."

Al looked at him with a bemused expression as he continued. "Let's say you all keep Jerry busy by comin' at him and shootin' from the sun where it'll be hard for him ta see ya and ol' Willy Yates here gits ta layin' just above 'em where ol' Arnie was. Don't ya suppose I could drop a couple of strikes right down the hatch? So ta speak, Sarge?"

Al chuckled. "Well, I reckon ya could, Willy. I reckon you bein' a prize softball pitcher and all, you most likely could just pop one o' them there grenades down a hatch or two." Al accented the first syllable so it came out "gree-nades."

Right after the sun came up, blinding bright, Yates got his third gree-nade right down the tank commander's hatch and disabled the Tiger. The first two lobs had bounced off the turret and gone off harmlessly as far as the tank was concerned but the combination of the two exploding bounces and accurate fire from the rest of the Algonquin patrol put most of the surprised Germans down quickly while inducing the survivors to drop their weapons and surrender without delay.

At a signal from their sergeant, the Algonquins rose up, spread out and advanced down from the mouth of the gully toward their prisoners as Yates clambered down from his perch above, his eyes on the Tiger.

Suddenly he saw movement in one of the lower hatches, the one above the tank's machine gun, and shouted a warning. Instantly Al extended his arm and gave the hit the ground signal. As he dropped he looked to his left and saw Cormier grinning and waving back at him and thought, *Jesus Christ, he doesn't understand*. Al got to his knees to yell and point frantically to the ground. Reggie was also shouting in French. But it was too late. A sound like tearing paper ripped from the Tiger and Louis Cormier, an Acadian from New Brunswick, gave up his life for his country and a king who didn't speak his language.

Chapter Twenty-Two

SEPTEMBER 8, 1944. Somewhere near Bruges. We are now in Belgium and they're telling us there's hard fighting ahead, that the honeymoon of liberating grateful towns is all over. Some honeymoon! Word is Jerry still occupies the heart of Bruges and we don't want to blast him out for fear of doing a Caen to one of the most beautiful cities in Europe. In the Middle Ages it was not only the capital of commerce in Northern Europe, it was also the capital of culture, architecture and the arts and even today is "home to the work of some of the most famous painters of the fifteenth century, men like Memling and van Eyck." Think that's how you spell the names and thank you, Mr. Yates. Gillie says Jerry is definitely finished running now and is going to stand and fight in order to deny us the use of the inland port of Antwerp which Montgomery is horny to have because his supply lines for the final push into Germany will be a hell of a lot shorter and our job of bringing this shitty war to an end will be a hell of a lot easier. As usual, it will be up to the Canadians to persuade Herr Hitler's gang to move along. In the meantime, while we're waiting to boot his arse back to the Siegfried Line, Yates and I have had a chance to explore the suburbs of the city where you wouldn't know there is a war on. Last night, clean battle dress and freshly scrubbed, we went to a restaurant and had what was definitely a black market meal—oysters (first time for me), steak and artichokes with a half dozen different kinds of cheese (names I never heard of) for dessert. While we were eating, a beautiful young woman—a very thin version of the actress, Katharine Hepburn—played the violin, her open case at her feet, diners dropping in money as they left. Yates was so taken with her and the sad music she played that he invited her over to our table when she took her break. To make a long story short, she told us her name was Ruth, she was 19 years old, she was from Brussels and the only surviving member of her family. She last saw her mother and father and older sister in 1941 when they were taken away to a concentration camp. Ruth was a Jew. When we left, Yates and I gave her all the money we had.

Excerpt from the Diary

For the first time in two months, Reggie had his guitar out, singing a Jimmie Davis song: "Come sit by my side, little darlin'/ Come lay your cool hand on my brow/ Promise me that you will never/ Be nobody's darlin' but mine."

Al, together with Billy and Yates, wandered over to lean against the Hearse with Reggie and sing the chorus. "Nobody's darlin' but mine, love / Be honest, be faithful be kind/ Promise me that you will never / Be nobody's darlin' but mine."

When the song was over they sat in silence until Reggie spoke. "That was his song, ya know? Louis Cormier's."

Al thought to himself it was also Reggie's, thinking of Charity back home in Lowvert.

Reggie chuckled. "He could sing it in English, every damn word."

"But he couldn't speak English."

"Yeah, but he could sing that song in English."

"Poor bastard."

"Yeah, poor bastard."

They'd brought back two bodies that morning, Cormier's, on a makeshift stretcher covered with a German blanket taken from the Royal Tiger, and Woody Williams's, upright and held there by Arnie on one side and Billy on the other. There wasn't a mark on the boy from B.C. but his arms dangled uselessly at his sides and his legs dragged behind him like broken hockey sticks. In fact his whole body seemed to be disjointed with no brain in command and no muscles to obey. He was alive but his mind was gone. All circuits blown.

"That's what happens when ya try to make a soldier out of a cook in two days." Billy spat venom. "Fuckers responsible for this should be strung up by the balls."

On the way back with Cormier and Williams they'd run into Tony. He fell in beside them just as they came out of the woods and took over one end of the stretcher from Yates. He said nothing to them and they said nothing to him.

The Germans were frightened out of Bruges by the Algonquins' CO, Lieutenant Colonel Bob Bradburn, who sent messengers to his Jerry counterpart via captured Jerry MOs bearing threats of dire consequences, including the fabled rapid-firing Canadian artillery should the defenders be reluctant to move PDQ.

By noon of September 12 reports were coming in that the enemy was packing up, taking with him several thousand wounded still recovering from the battle of Normandy. As the invaders left, the empty streets were soon filled with cheering Belgians waving the red, black and yellow flags of their country, celebrating the salvation of their city.

By this time, most of their Canadian saviours had long since moved on, leaving only the higher ranks behind to bask in the glory of preserving a monument to European culture while lesser mortals were on their way to what 4th Armoured Division believed would be the main German defensive positions protecting the long estuary leading into Antwerp.

On the way members of the Carrier Platoon have noted a change in scenery. Gone are the hills, hedgerows and woods of northern France. Here in western Belgium the land is flat and barren, reminding them of the Manitoba prairie. Only farms and villages break the line of the horizon and the trees are straight-tall and evenly spaced poplars marking the routes of the many canals, the principal one being the Leopold, which runs in a semi-circle from Zeebrugge on the west coast to the Savojaard Plaat on the east coast. The crescent formed by this waterway encloses the area around the coastal town of Breskens and so the Canadians choose to call the half-circle, "the Breskens Pocket." The Pocket protects Jerry's rear and the Leopold protects the Pocket and it is at the Leopold that the 245th Infantry Division of the German Army lies in wait for the regiment from Northern Ontario.

At the small town of Sijsele about three miles south of the Leopold the Algonquins meet up with members of the Belgian underground, nicknamed the "White Brigade" because they have taken to wearing white butchers' coats. But the Canadians, fresh from the Maquis in France, are wary of a quick embrace and make no commitments.

The Carrier Platoon is sent out by the light of the silvery moon to reconnoitre possible bridgings of the Leopold, places where the engineers can go to work laying down an "overgrown Meccano set," a.k.a. a Bailey bridge, for the South Alberta tanks, which will then cross and fan out in both directions to drive Jerry from the area.

The platoon recommends the site of an enemy-demolished span in the little town of Moerkerke, a tight grid of narrow streets and red brick buildings abutting the canal just northeast of Sijsele. Once across, Intelligence reports the going will be easy. Jerry is thoroughly disorganized, he has scarcely any equipment, he is taking desperate refuge behind the canal, little resistance will be encountered, probably only scattered small arms and sniper fire, and that would come from the area to the right of the crossing because Jerry has flooded the area to the left. This is one of his favoured defensive tactics in a land of canals and polders—low-lying, sodden fields reclaimed from the sea.

An O Group is held in the afternoon of Wednesday, September 13, at 1700 hours in Moerkerke's community hall, where the assault plan is quickly laid out.

The briefing maps show there are actually two canals at the chosen crossing point, the Leopold itself and le Canal de Dérivation de la Lys. The latter, they are told, is a holding canal, like a siding in a railway yard where barges are gathered and held until there are enough of them for a full "train." The Dérivation Canal will be the first waterway the Algonquins will have to navigate.

Companies A for Able, B for Baker, C for Charlie and D for Dog, once again ninety-men strong, thanks to another cull of cooks and clerks, are to embark at 2130 hours. Transport will be rowboats of the canvas-sided, wooden floor variety, capable of holding eighteen men. The boats will be trucked to Moerkerke and off-loaded at the red brick church of undetermined denomination pointed out on the map. From there they will be portaged to the banks of the Dérivation Canal where volunteers from the Links and Winks will be waiting to ferry their Ontario brethren to an easy night of flushing Jerry down the toilet.

On the far bank of the Leopold the plan of action is simple. Able Company will land just to the right of the blown bridge and take all the buildings on the left of the north road in front of the flooded polders. Seventy-five yards to the right, B Company will say goodbye to the ferrymen, clear the buildings on the right and push forward a platoon to secure the intersection between the north road and the east road some 400 yards beyond the Leopold. Next in line, C Coy will hold the canal area to the right of B and assist in securing the east road. D will do the same for C.

But, as Robbie Burns phrased it, *the best laid schemes o' mice an' men, / Gang aft a-gley* and the next day when it was all over, a stunning forty-two percent of the assault force, 153 Algonquins, were either dead, wounded or missing in action.

It took a day or so to piece together the whole story and Al took pains to do it because, as he muttered to Yates, he was "goddamn mad." Mostly he was goddamn mad that so many good men had been chewed up and spit out because of God's continued indifference to the conflict between the forces of good and evil. But he was also goddamn mad because, once again, the Intelligence guys had screwed up.

"Halton's not gonna report this on the CBC and it's not gonna make the papers back home, but it's gonna be in the diary, Willy. It's gonna be there so that some day when somebody wants the truth there'll be a place they can find it."

So he talked to the men, mostly fellow NCOs he'd come to know, sergeants who'd managed to get back to Moerkerke in one piece.

Kelly from D Coy said his CO had told his men the assault was going to be a piece of cake, it was going to be a walk along Sunnyside Beach. "Can ya believe it, McDougal. A walk on the beach, fer Chrissakes!"

D Company made it across the Dérivation Canal without any trouble, the Links and Winks paddling furiously like veteran *coureurs de bois*, supporting artillery pounding away at the enemy, the New Brunswick Rangers firing their machine guns above the boats—everyone doing their bit to make sure the Algonquins were delivered to their objective in good time and good shape.

But that was as good as it got. When the supporting fire ceased and the lead boat touched shore the first man out to secure his vessel with tether rope and spike was the wireless operator, his number eighteen radio strapped to his back. Straightening up after jamming the spike into the ground, both he and his radio were cut in half by an enemy machine gun, severing all communication links with HQ. Right then and there D Coy was doomed.

Scrabbling up the canal bank past the sprawled body of their comrade, lifeless legs dangling in the water, the assault force came to the top and stared. Snafu!

Ninety feet in front of them was another canal. Somehow, word had not been passed down to them that there was more than one.

Back down they slid, past their dead comrade a second time, uprooting spikes and grabbing tether ropes, hauling and pushing boats up and over the strip while their Bren gunners sprayed covering fire. The rush across the island to the next canal was a surge of shouting men, jostling and cursing each other and the stupid bastards who forgot to tell them what they needed to know.

Once again it was down a bank. Once again across the water. Once again the Links and Winks paddling, harder this time, deeper thrusts into the water, grunting with the effort.

At last on the enemy's side of the Leopold, they poked their heads up to get their bearings, their objective being a line of trees on their right, tall shadows in the dark. The instant the arty barrage lifted they sprinted for the line, diving for cover as three German machine guns, strategically placed, suddenly opened up, red tracers searching out the Canadians flat among the tree trunks. The signature chatter of the guns marked them as MG34s capable of firing 900 rounds a minute. So much for predictions of little resistance and scattered small-arms fire.

Frantic attempts were made to dig in, but as fast as they picked and shovelled down, water seeped up into their holes. In it above their knees, the men of D Coy returned fire. Somewhere in the field in front of them between the bursts of automatic weapons, they could hear a wounded Jerry, over and over again, the voice of a boy in pain calling for his mother. *Mutter, hilf mir, Mutter, hilf mir.*

Around 2300 hours the counterattacks began, the Germans coming at them in the dark from the east road, every hour on the half hour, or so it seemed. So much for intelligence reports of a disorganized enemy taking desperate refuge behind the canal.

In the silence after each attack was beaten off, the pitiful cries of the wounded German pierced the night and the nerves of the frayed Algonquins, who took to shouting back, "Shut the fuck up!" and "Hurry up and die, you bastard."

Just after midnight the bastard obliged and the counterattacks stopped as suddenly as they had begun.

The rest of the night was spent in an eerie silence until the first light of the new day illuminated thick, rolling ground mists, the height of a man, folding in upon them. You couldn't see a thing.

About 0800 hours what they couldn't see, they heard: the *wham, wham* of eighty-eights, the shells exploding in the trees above them. Now the cries of the wounded were in English, their voices distorted by the fog, the stretcher-bearers trying to find them.

Kelly, the sergeant, saw one of his Bren gunners crawling out of the mist shouting for ammo. Just as Kelly reached to hand him a couple of magazines, the man's head burst like a ripe melon thrown up against a concrete wall. A lucky shot. The MG34s were firing at sounds, the wounded calling for the stretcher-bearers, men yelling for ammunition.

While he was telling Al the story, Kelly was absent-mindedly picking off bits and pieces of the Bren gunner's brains stuck to his battleblouse.

At 0900 hours the fog began to lift, and fire from the eighty-eights increased, plumes of dirt and cherry-red flame erupting all around them. Kelly's officer bellied in beside him to tell him to "get the platoon the hell out of here." He was still speaking when he was shot in the forehead.

Kelly told Al he would never forget the lieutenant's face staring at him. Three eyes. For the rest of the battle the lieutenant's corpse on the lip of the slit trench served to shield the D Coy sergeant from enemy fire. *This is my body given up for you.*

At 1000 hours Jerry attacked again, wave after wave, and the Canadians began to run out of ammunition. Given the intelligence report, there had been no thought of bringing any extra.

And now with the wireless gone, there was no way to call for more. The order was not long in coming, "One round, one German."

At 1100 hours the enemy was discovered sneaking in along the canal behind D Coy, forcing the lads to fight on two fronts to avoid encirclement. By now they were scrounging weapons and ammo from the enemy dead.

At 1200 hours what was left of the company was enveloped by smoke put down by their own artillery. The brass had decided to call it a day and laid on cover for the withdrawal. But D Coy had no way of knowing that a retreat had been ordered and thought the smoke might be to mask the advance of reinforcements crossing to help them. So they fought on.

By 0230 hours with no reinforcements and no more ammunition, theirs or Jerry's, it was obvious their situation was hopeless and, section by section, they began to surrender, jettisoning their weapons and standing, hands in the air, in response to German commands given in guttural English.

The only man in his platoon to make it back, Kelly survived by pretending to be dead, just another body in the field, and when Jerry marched his captives off, he retreated in a crawl through the dissipating smoke, stripped off his boots and swam back across the two canals.

The situation with C Company, next up the line, was little different. The riflemen in C got the message of two canals but, in traversing the island between the Dérivation and the Leopold, were surprised by the sudden appearance of daylight, dangling enemy parachute flares lighting up the darkness around them. As one of the C Coy NCOs put it, "You could've read a newspaper. It was that bright." And another, more ominously, "It was almost as if Jerry was expectin' us, ya know."

By 0200 they had reached their objective and dug in, slit trenches stretching along the west side of an irrigation ditch. Settling down to wait for the South Alberta Tanks to rumble over the expected Bailey bridge, they could hear muffled voices from the other side of the ditch and then a call, "Hello comrades, come to me here."

No one was fooled and the next two hours were spent exchanging insults with Jerry on the other side of the ditch, C Coy's expressed with Brens and number thirty-six grenades, Jerry's with his MG34s and potato mashers.

Right on time at 0400 hours, their spirits rose when they heard the rattle of a tracked vehicle coming towards them from their left. The bridge was obviously finished. The Shermans were coming.

But in fact there were no tanks because there was no bridge. Not then. Not later. Not ever. The enemy had the bridge site zeroed in and each time the engineers made the slightest movement toward it, shells rained down. It was hopeless.

What C Company took to be a Sherman turned out to be an enemy bulldozer leading a column of infantry who charged through the fog with fixed bayonets only to be cut down in waves, the Canadians ceasing fire when German stretcher bearers with Red Cross armbands came out to mark their dead and pick up the many wounded.

Then the waiting began, none of the Algonquins daring to move because the slightest twitch got Jerry's attention. Trying to keep muscles from cramping, the Charlie Horses wondered if the ditch running behind them back to the Leopold was deep enough to give them cover for a withdrawal, which the handwriting on the wall said was their only hope.

At a little after the noon hour, as they were beginning to count the last of their ammunition, the company was hit by friendly fire. Al wrote word for word what he was told. "The combination of both enemy and friendly artillery fire made moving out of the question. It would have meant certain death for us to leave the protection of our slit trenches."

The speaker was a plain-talking sergeant from Oak Lake, Manitoba, who'd signed on in the war's early days with the Princess Patricia's Canadian Light Infantry. Wounded in Italy, he'd taken a Tony Foligno route to the Algonquins and was now sitting in front of Al wringing his beefy hands, his pock-marked face creased in grief, one of only a handful of men from C Coy who made it back, forced to leave comrades behind.

B Company's story took only seconds to tell. The lads suffered so many casualties in the crossing alone that they had to abandon their objective altogether, tuck in with Able and share another shock of discovery—the area to the left of the proposed crossing was not flooded. What Intel said was water was waving fields of grain, leaving an exposed left flank that Jerry was quick to exploit, coming through the rye at first light with Schmeissers and Mausers held high across their chests. Soon there were firefights in and around the cluster of buildings hugging the road. One of A Coy's riflemen came upon a young boy in short pants standing in a water-filled ditch holding the limp body of a woman, keeping her head out of the wet. The boy was crying. The woman was dead. She was his mother. Shot by the Germans.

Able Company took a number of prisoners, who were put to work carrying out Canadian wounded, a task they cheerfully took on. For them the war was over.

Other enemy prisoners were not so cooperative. A group of six, bearing three stretchers of Algonquin wounded and guarded by a corporal and a private from the remnants of Baker Coy, were halfway across the island strip between the two waterways, headed back to the RAP in Moerkerke, when the Germans dropped their burdens and turned on their guards, knives flashing in the darkness. It was all over in a matter of seconds. Four soldiers lay dead or dying, three of the enemy and the B Company private, whose last name was Roy, a downy-cheeked boy from Brandon, Manitoba, a knife thrust up through the ribs and into his eighteen-year-old heart.

There was no time to learn Roy's first name because he was one of the new recruits dumped off thirty minutes before the assault began, barely enough time to record his dog tag number and get him to his assigned boat.

Two of the Germans managed an escape and the one remaining pleaded with the corporal, begging for his life in broken English. It was a plea that fell on deaf ears.

By now Al had heard enough to start thinking that the operation never had a chance, his gut feeling that the Germans had been ready and waiting for them, a feeling reinforced by Jerry knowing where to set up his defence lines on his side of the Leopold and where to shoot on the other—his mortars and artillery zeroed in on the bridge site, the crossing points and Regimental HQ in Moerkerke, including the RAP across the street, where Father Tom Mooney had become a statistic, the fourth clergyman killed in action since D-Day and the first Roman Catholic padre to be killed in the battle for northwest Europe.

So when news of treachery began to circulate, it made a lot of sense. Gill's story was that the Moerkerke community hall where the O Group had been held on Wednesday afternoon had been bugged. A simple transmitting device hidden in the piano by a Belgian collaborator was all that was needed to KO the attack.

It took Al forty-eight hours to get the story all down on paper and forty-eight hours was how long it took for the regiment to shrug off the Leopold, take a deep breath and ready itself for action once again, not much time to grieve; but then grief was a luxury no soldier on the front lines could afford.

On the offensive once again, what was left of the various rifle companies went off with various squadrons of Swatty Wotherspoon's South Alberta Tanks to do armoured sweeps of the area surrounding the Breskens Pocket with the Carrier Platoon's newly acquired flame throwers getting a bit of a workout frying up Jerry squirrelled away in barns, lurking in drainage ditches and holed up in fortified trenches dug into the sides of dikes.

On Sunday morning, September 17, Al looked up from his tea to the sound of aircraft glistening silver in the sun, a thousand fighters escorting C-47s and towed gliders in the hundreds, all of them jam-packed with paratroopers and their equipment en route to Holland to seize key bridges at Eindhoven, Nijmegen and Arnhem. This was *Operation Market Garden* and it was Montgomery's plan to bring Hitler to his knees.

The key to success was the huge highway bridge over the Lower Rhine at Arnhem. Seizing the 2,000-foot span was the job of the British 1st Airborne Division, while the American 82nd Airborne tackled Nijmegen and their countrymen in the 101st dropped at Eindhoven. At Arnhem the Brits were to suffer the same fate as the Algonquins at the Leopold and for many of the same reasons, including Jerry knowing what to expect. The Germans had discovered a copy of the assault plans for the entire operation in a wrecked American glider near Nijmegen.

Despite nine days of valiant fighting against overwhelming odds, wresting the crossing from German hands proved to be what Montgomery's subordinate, Lieutenant General Frederick Browning, had predicted when he first saw the plans for *Market Garden*. Arnhem, he said, was going to be "a bridge too far."

The headline in the September 28 continental edition of London's *Daily Mail* succinctly told the tale. **230 Hours Of Hell.** The 1st Airborne lost 7,500 men proving, for what it was worth, that Browning was right and Monty wrong.

This same edition of the *Daily Mail*, on the same front page, second column from the left at the bottom, reported the death of the founder of the Angelus Temple of the Foursquare Gospel built in Los Angeles in 1923 at a cost of $1.25 million. Born in Canada, the most publicized Christian evangelist in the world, Aimee Semple McPherson, was fifty-three years old when she died in Oakland of what the paper said was "heart disease."

But none of this was known on that Sunday morning in Belgium, not to the Algonquins craning their necks between bites of jam-covered hardtack and slurps of sugared tea, nor to the cheerful families on their way to early morning Mass.

The show of force in the sky gave everyone a lift and it was one the Algonquins badly needed after the Leopold. Maybe the rumours supposedly coming from the British War Office were true, that "organized resistance under the leadership of the German Armed Forces is likely to cease by the first week in December 1944."

Al was talking about the possibilities with Yates and Billy when Gill called them over. He was bending over a map unfolded on the fender of the Cruiser.

"Captain wants us here." He pointed a finger at a village on the banks of another canal about three miles northwest of Moerkerke. The name of the village was Damme.

"Damn?"

"Da-mmay, Billy."

"Da-mmay, dummy."

"Da June and da July, too."

As far as HQ was concerned there was nothing special about the village except their ignorance of it. The Algonquin sweeps with the South Albertas had passed it by and the brass thought it would be prudent to check it out just in case.

"We'll be taking two Belgians. White Brigade—" Gill was brought up short by disapproving grunts.

"Look," he made an effort to speak more slowly, "I know what you're thinking, but these are men we picked out. I've talked to them, father and son, level-headed, both of them. And from Damme. We'll be better off with them than without them."

As he helped in the gassing up, hefting jerry cans of petrol to Yates who passed them on to Billy, Al felt a great weariness wrap around him, a coiling python squeezing his chest until he had trouble breathing. He turned and leaned back against the Hearse trying to calm the hammering of his heart, a frightened animal in a cage thumping against the wire desperate to escape. He didn't have a good feeling about this excursion.

He was still trying to breathe normally when the three carriers wheeled down the road between the flooded polders on either side, Gill leading with his driver, a replacement by the name of Blakeney, and the two men from the Belgian Resistance in the Cruiser, their white shirts and armbands of red, black and yellow a colourful contrast to Canadian khaki. Arnie, Reggie and Ross were in the second carrier, while Al rode with Billy and Yates in the Hearse bringing up the rear.

As they rumbled out of a long curve, the road straightened into a boulevard lined with tall trees that looked just like the poplars along the Leopold. At the end of the boulevard was a sandstone-coloured bridge over a wide irrigation ditch and across the bridge on the left a church, with the village of Damme beyond.

Built of the same sandstone brick as the bridge, the church looked like a smaller version of L'Abbaye Ardenne with a square bell tower rising about 100 feet, louvred openings at the top, a perfect site for an OP.

Al took all of this in as the carriers approached the bridge and stopped with engines idling. It was early in the afternoon, sunny and very quiet. You could hear the rustle of leaves and the buzzing of bees.

He hopped out of the Hearse and jogged up to the Cruiser where Gill, his head down, was listening to Edouard, the father of Robert.

"It is too quiet, *monsieur*." Edouard was shaking his head. He looked worried and Al took comfort from that. A worried man would be a careful man.

Gill glanced at his sergeant and then back to the Belgian. "Very well. But you understand that we cannot report back that 'Damme is too quiet.'"

He spoke very slowly and distinctly as one does when one is not certain how fluent the other is in your language. "We must," and here he was talking with his hands as well, "we must have more than that, we must look around a bit?"

"*Oui*, but we must do so very carefully, *monsieur*." The word "very" came out as "veray." Al was all for being "veray" careful.

The three of them talked a bit more about the situation, Robert listening gravely beside his father. In the end their decision was to bring just one carrier across the bridge, leaving the other two on the Moerkerke side with Blakeney guarding them, getaway cars if needed.

So Billy took Gill and the Cruiser over the bridge with Reggie on the Bren, all eyes front. The rest of the patrol was crunched down walking on either side of the carrier, weapons at the ready, safeties off, Edouard leading Ross and Al on the left side and his son, Robert, leading Arnie and Yates on the right.

The bridge rose to a hump in the centre, just enough of a rise to have hidden something that would have made them even more careful had they seen it clearly from the Moerkerke side. Now on the Damme side what had appeared to be a simple grass-covered hillock at the foot of the bridge was recognized as something more, grass and earth covering a sandstone brick shelter. It looked like it could be a free-standing root cellar and before the war that's probably what it was, but now it was a German pill box and as soon as the Algonquins came down the decline the MG34s opened up. It was an ambush.

All three men on the left side of the Cruiser were hit immediately, Edouard and Davy Ross, a ripping stitch across their chests, flinging them both aside like rag dolls. Al, half-turned toward the slewing carrier, felt two red-hot pokers lance into the flesh behind his collarbone. He stumbled with the searing pain and the coppery smell of blood as another round clipped the side of his helmet setting off a clanging in his ears and a film of scarlet misting in his eyes. When something hard slammed into his back he felt himself falling into a pit of darkness. His last conscious thought before he hit the ground was that Ross was dead and there would be no one to look after Captain Max of the RCFF.

Chapter Twenty-Three

September 17, 1944

Allan McDougal, face gray with pain, came to a groaning wakefulness in a gloomy dungeon. Or so it seemed. The only light came from four apertures above his head covering all four compass points like arrow slits in a castle keep. He was half-sitting, half-lying on a dirt floor, the smell of a dank gardener's shed, a mixture of potting soil, decaying grass cuttings, oil and gasoline. Willy Yates was cradling his head and Billy Assad was holding a canteen to his lips and speaking to him, his voice urgent.

"Al, Al, it's okay, it's okay. Max will be fine. Ross made a deal a long time ago with some guy in the Signals Platoon. If somethin' happened the guy would take the cat. Here, try and drink some water."

Al took a sip and then shook his head to clear it. Big mistake. Pain shot through his shoulder and into his neck. Gasping, he reached very slowly to where it hurt, his touch telling him there was a field dressing covering the throbbing. His fingers came away feeling sticky. Blood.

Yates was quick to reassure him. "It's just seepage. You're gonna be fine. We'll talk to them. Get you to a doctor."

"Them?" Al asked the question with his eyes.

Yates sighed. "For you the war is over, Al. For you. And me. And Billy." He sat down beside him to tell him the story.

Besides the MG34 in the root cellar, there were riflemen in the bell tower. The machine gun killed Edouard and Ross right away. Yates figured it was Jerry in the tower who'd shot Al. And Reggie.

Again Al asked with his eyes. In response, Yates shook his head and then looked away. Charity Noseworthy, dark-haired, pretty and young, with her boy, Martin, waiting for Reggie in Lowvert, waiting with strangers in a strange land far from her family in Newfoundland, soon to get a telegram from the Minister of National Defence, Reggie's insurance, his guitar and whatever else remained of his twenty-five years on God's green earth stuffed in his kit bag. *Pack up your troubles in your old kit bag and smile, smile, smile. / While you've a lucifer to light your fag, / Smile boys, that's the style. / What's the use of worrying? / It never was worthwhile, / So pack up your troubles in your old kit bag, and smile, smile, smile.* It was a moment or two before Yates found his voice and started talking again.

The men in the Cruiser were fish in a barrel for the riflemen in the tower. Gillie was hit in the leg, just above the knee, shattering bone, Billy grabbing him and pushing him over the side. Then reaching down to wrench the Bren from Reggie's lifeless hands, he vaulted over himself and got some return fire organized, spraying the tower while Yates and Robert chucked grenades at the root cellar.

At the same time, Arnie hauled a protesting Gillie down to the water and half-dragged and half-swam his officer back to where Blakeney was waiting on the other side to give him a hand. Billy's hard-breathing, shouted instructions to Arnie had left no room for discussion.

"Leave the fuckin' Hearse for us. It's our good luck charm. We'll use it to get outta here. Ya can bet on it. But you and Blakeney bundle Gillie in the other one and make tracks. We'll cover ya. Ya hear me?"

Arnie had nodded and shaken Billy's hand, a message in his firm grip and understanding eyes. You're full of shit, Billy. You got as much chance of getting outta here as a snowball in hell. But you've been a good pal and a good soldier. Skol!

As soon as they heard Blakeney gun the carrier away, the rearguard ceased firing. No use wasting ammunition. For the most part Jerry took his cue from them, only the riflemen in the tower, every few seconds or so, clanging a round or two off the Cruiser to keep the three of them heads down.

Yates and the Belgian ignored the admonition, crawling to check on comrades, worming their way around and under the canted Cruiser, one track up on a stone mile marker by the side of the road.

Robert returned white-faced, and Yates with Al, dragging his unconscious body by the legs. Sheltered from Jerry's prying eye, he examined his friend, noting the nasty welt above his left ear and the dark stain on the battleblouse at the collarbone. He set to work ripping open the blouse and tearing away the undershirt to examine the wounds, two purple red puckers about an inch apart oozing blood.

Breaking open a packet of sulpha, he sprinkled it on and around the bullet holes before applying a field dressing, tying it tightly under Al's arm. Billy held up a syrette of morphine, but Yates shook his head. "Not now. Let's wait and see if he needs it when he comes around." A bullet clanged off the Cruiser and Yates ducked. "If we're going to get out of here in one piece we're going to need Al up and running with all his marbles."

His last words were punctuated by a series of rapid shots from the tower then the machine gun opened up again and Billy, hands over his ears, looked at Yates who nodded back in understanding. The only reason for this fusillade was that Jerry was up to something, shooting to pin them down while others moved in.

It didn't take long to prove their instincts right. Schmeisser rounds from the underbrush above the drainage ditch to their right and shouts from the down-slope of the bridge behind them made it clear the jig was up. The shouts were in broken English, a rough translation being *Für euch ist der Krieg zu Ende.*

There was another exchange of glances between the two Algonquins and they surreptitiously unclipped the last of their grenades, hiding them under the carrier, indicating to the Belgian that he should do the same. Jerry shot men who surrendered with grenades clipped to their web belts. Jerry was very safety conscious.

As if to demonstrate the point, all three of them were roughly but thoroughly searched before being marched off toward the church by a dozen grim German soldiers, Billy using a fireman's lift to carry Al, head lolling to one side. Behind them the young Belgian was prodded and cursed in guttural German. When he stumbled, one of his captors, a small man—red, angry face above the field-grey of his uniform—used the butt of his rifle to hit him repeatedly on the upper back.

The bell tower of the church was enclosed by a wall of brick about fifteen feet high and the same sandstone colour. A gate made of weathered planks, vertical and bound by black iron bands, was set in the wall. As soon as the Algonquins had been prodded through this gate, Yates felt his stomach lurch at what was inside—an enclosed garden, flowers and linden trees. *All hope abandon, ye who enter here.*

When the door creaked shut behind them, Billy carefully lowered Al to the ground under the shade of one of the trees. When he stood and glanced around, he looked at Yates, who shrugged. If this was it, then that was that.

"Where's the kid?"

Yates had no time to answer before the garden door banged open, two hulking specimens of the Master Race barging through led by the red-faced, angry Napoleon screaming at them and pointing in the direction of a low door in the bell tower. By the stripes on his arm, two upside down Vs, Yates figured him for an *Unteroffizier*, a corporal who thought he was a *Generalfeldmarschall*.

Billy leaned down to pick up Al but this brought on more screaming from the field marshal, who pushed Billy aside, leaving his two underlings to reach down, grab Al by the arms, and start dragging him to the tower.

Billy was on them in a second, throwing a hip check into one and using both hands to shove the other staggering away. A rifle shot exploded at his feet, the corporal screaming again, advancing with his weapon pointed now at Billy's head, his finger tightening on the trigger.

At that moment the garden door was shoved open and an *Oberleutnant* stomped through, shouting at the corporal, who stood stiffly at attention just in time to get a royal chewing out and the back of the lieutenant's hand across his face.

Then the *Oberleutnant* gestured to the Algonquins, who picked up their comrade and carried him through the tower door where he came to consciousness shouting through his pain about Max the cat.

When Yates finished bringing Al up to date, the three of them brooded in silence, the only sound the frantic buzzing of flies, fellow captives in the tower.

Each man was ashamed at being captured, each afraid of what was going to happen to them, each worried about their families when the telegram arrived. Al figured his father would be the first to know.

"MINISTER OF NATIONAL DEFENCE DEEPLY REGRETS TO INFORM YOU THAT B55379 ALLAN McDOUGAL HAS BEEN OFFICIALLY REPORTED MISSING IN ACTION SEVENTEENTH SEPTEMBER 1944 STOP WHEN FURTHER INFORMATION BECOMES AVAILABLE IT WILL BE FORWARDED AS SOON AS RECEIVED STOP"

The door banging open and the reappearance of Napoleon was almost a relief. While his two henchmen stood to one side with rifles pointed, the corporal ordered the prisoners to stand and then made the rounds with a gleam in his eye, introducing himself by punching Al in his wounded shoulder, spitting in Willy's face, and standing nose-to-nose with Billy before kneeing him in the groin.

It was only after these greetings that the corporal got down to the business at hand, the looting of personal possessions—cigarettes, Belgian money, rings, watches, and their boots, Grebs made in Kitchener, an Ontario city settled in the nineteenth century by German Mennonites who called it Berlin.

When the corporal and his goons left, a wincing Allan McDougal slumped to the ground. He looked at his stocking feet and then at his wrist, a band of white where his watch had been, and thought to himself that when it came to watches, if it wasn't for bad luck he wouldn't have any luck at all. He vowed that in the next war he wouldn't bother with a timepiece. He'd use the sun. Like Crow.

His musings were interrupted by a commotion outside, marching boots and sharp commands. Quickly, Billy on his knees, Yates above him, were peering through the gaps in the door planking. They couldn't see everything but saw enough to stop looking.

The young Belgian, tied to a linden tree, was naked except for a sleeve ripped from his white shirt and tied around his chest, the red, black and yellow armband, the colours of Belgium, serving as a target over his heart.

Yates and Billy had scuttled over to sit beside Al and do what they did when they were kids and didn't want to listen to what the world was insisting they should hear. They hunched over and put their hands over their ears.

"They're gonna shoot the kid."

Al nodded. He'd figured that one out for himself when he'd noticed young Robert wasn't with them. It was German policy to shoot any Resistance fighters they got their hands on. No ifs, ands or buts.

Outside in the garden the harsh command was given. *Feuer!* The crash of a rifle volley echoed its way inside the tower room, loud enough to be heard even by insulated ears. All three of them flinched and swallowed.

Later that evening, when they were rousted out of their dungeon and led away past the execution tree smeared with blood, they were told by other POWs that Robert had joined his father in death, both their naked bodies dumped into the irrigation ditch. The other prisoners were Lake Superiors captured earlier and now swelling the ranks of the dejected to a column of fifteen being herded away from Damme deeper into the Breskens Pocket.

Billy and Yates walked alongside Al who moved slowly, his head cocked to one side, angled toward the wounds in his shoulder, the only way he could bear the pain.

Marching as best they could in their socks through the village and then along the canal leading deeper into German-held territory, both Billy and Yates pestered the *Oberleutnant*, every chance they got, begging him to get Al to a doctor. Each time the officer brushed them off, pretending he didn't understand, until the sun went down and the column was ordered into a barn for the night. There he called the three of them aside.

"Would you like a smoke, gentlemen?"

He took off his helmet and laid it next to a pail sitting on a barrel beside a water pump. He was an older man, fair hair combed back from a high forehead, bushy eyebrows, a straight, longish nose overseeing a square jaw. His eyes twinkled as he offered cigarettes from a black metal case. Lucky Strikes.

"Your American allies are most generous with their cigarettes when they are captured. As I'm sure you were with yours."

The Algonquins lit up courtesy of three German matches. "An old custom, is it not? I believe from the first time our countries fought. In the War of 1914. One match for one cigarette so as not to give a sniper enough time to, I believe the expression is 'draw a bead.'"

"Your English is very good, Herr *Oberleutnant*." Yates gave the word its German pronunciation so it came out "Ober-loit-nant."

"Thank you, Private. I learned to speak English, and a bit of French, in Montreal, where I studied engineering at McGill University. Before the war, of course."

He whistled a few bars of the McGill Redman's fight song. "But that, gentlemen, is a story for another day."

He turned to Al. "Sergeant, I beg your indulgence. If you can stand the pain for a few more days we will be far enough into Holland and I will see then that you get the best medical care the German Army has to offer to a brave Canadian soldier."

He took a long last drag from his cigarette, dropped it and ground it under his heel. Then with what Yates would later swear was a wink, clicked his heels, thrust out his arm and said, "Heil Hitler."

It wasn't until a week later that the promise to Al was kept, seven days constantly on the move, shank's mare to Breskens, barge across the fogbound Westerschelde to Flushing, then by foot and by truck to Breda, a city east of Arnhem, the POWs tucked in the middle of an enemy column heading deep into German-held Holland, a column forced to hit the ditch two and three times a day to dodge strafing and rocket-firing Tiffies. It wasn't only the Germans who prayed for inclement weather. *O God, Heavenly Father, who by thy Son Jesus*

Christ hast promised to all them that seek thy kingdom and the righteousness thereof, all things necessary to their bodily sustenance: Send us, we beseech thee, in this our necessity, such moderate rain and showers, that we may be delivered from the vengeance of the RAF, the RCAF, Polish Spitfires and American P-51 Mustangs. All this (which, when you think about it, Old Boy, isn't very much) we ask in Jesus' name. Amen.

The prisoners were a tired, starving lot by the time their hosts showed them to their quarters on the outskirts of Breda, a military drill hall not unlike the Timmins Armoury, where the little league of nations had first signed up in August 1940, a bedsheet-sized poster on the back wall featuring the head of a snorting bull moose biting Hitler's ass, the five of them standing under it, right hands raised, swearing a solemn oath "to serve in the Canadian Active Service Force so long as an emergency of war, invasion, riot or insurrection, real or apprehended, exists, and for the period of demobilization after said emergency ceases to exist, and in any event for a period of not less than one year, provided His Majesty should so require my services."

His Majesty's part of the bargain consisted of clothing—khaki-coloured wool pants and tunics along with underwear and high-top boots; two fireproof, hexagonal discs on a necklace—dog tags with name, regimental number, blood type and religion; and a paybook informing them they would be remunerated at the rate of $1.30 per day.

Now, in the Breda hall, Al was wondering if the Canadian government would be paying him for being a POW, as he bent to his first real meal since being captured—if you could call a piece of black bread and a thimble-sized piece of potato floating in a mess tin of watery barley soup a real meal.

In the old days Billy would have dumped it all on the floor, but after seven long, tough days of living on the kindness of strangers, drinking water rationed to a swallow or two a day and chewing slowly—to make them last—the few hardtack biscuits they had among them, the bread and soup tasted like the best meal he'd had in years.

If not for the generosity of sympathetic Dutch women who had blessed them on their way with smiles and waves and handouts of food when they had little enough to feed themselves, Billy wondered if the POWs would have made it. He remembered the women with a fond smile, pushing past the German guards to hand out pears, apples and buns.

After their bread and soup, the three Algonquins sat on the concrete floor of the drill hall and unwrapped their battered feet bound with whatever they'd managed to scrounge from the Dutch. Al's wound was paining him, beating in time with his heart, and Yates had to help him with his foot wrappings, leather gauntlets like those worn by motorcyclists, fingers and thumbs cut to make room for his toes, the forearm coverings up over his heels and tied with a bit of string around each of his ankles.

He sighed his thanks to Willy and reached inside his blouse to touch his wound, the bare skin next to the last of the field dressings that Yates had wrapped round his shoulder three days ago. His exploring fingers felt a warmth that should not have been there, a heat that signalled an infection. He grimaced and resolved to raise hell as soon as the after-dinner entertainment was over. Tonight it was to be provided by the Gestapo, on hand for interrogations because of *Market Garden*.

One by one the POWs were taken to a small room just inside the street entrance to the drill hall and one by one they were returned and segregated from their fellows who had yet to be interrogated.

Except for three pieces of furniture, the room, about ten feet by ten, was bare and lit by a single, very bright bulb hanging from the ceiling. In front of a long wooden desk was a chair. It was empty. Behind the desk was another chair. This one was occupied by a man whom Al recognized right away. It was all those movies he'd seen since 1939, films featuring nasty men in dark, ill-fitting suits, ferret-faced with wire-rimmed glasses. Except this man spoke without a trace of the heavily accented English that Hollywood assigned to evil men of German extraction.

"Please sit down, Sergeant McDougal."

The Gestapo had their army paybooks, so it was no surprise to be addressed by name and rank. When he sat, even with his head to one side, Al noticed that the lighting in the room also followed Hollywood's script, his chair so placed that the glare was in his face, leaving his questioner's in the shadows.

"Permit me to check some details with you, Sergeant." Ferret face was writing on a legal-sized pad. "Your regimental number is B55379?"

Al nodded, trying to remember through the throbbing in his shoulder and the ache in his feet just what it was that the Geneva Convention required him to tell his captors.

The German looked at him. "That is a 'yes' then, Sergeant."

"Yes."

"Very good." The German wrote something on the pad. "And you are with the 2nd Canadian Infantry Division, are you not?"

"No, sir. The 4th Canadian Armoured." Then Al remembered. Name, rank and number only. Bastard.

The Gestapo agent smiled. "Quite so."

Then he began to ask questions about the Belgian underground, questions that Al was suddenly having difficulty hearing because the German's seventy-eight-rpm voice was being played at thirty-three rpm. He caught sight of his inquisitor looking at him, his quizzical smile fading as the light above him dimmed and the four walls of the room began to squeeze in and out like an accordion.

A day and a half later, when he finally swam up from under, Allan McDougal was in a German military hospital, a nurse bending over him. She wore a starched white cap with a red cross on it, her uniform narrow stripes of blue on white, covered with a white apron tied at the waist. She was bathing his forehead with a cool, damp cloth and smiling.

The hospital had been set up in a school to treat casualties from the *Market Garden* fighting around Eindhoven. The classroom where Al lay on a canvas cot was full of American paratroopers from the 101st Airborne Division, a cocky bunch who'd taken their objective "without firing a shot. Just waved the Stars and Stripes and the Germans turned tail and ran."

The speaker was a grinning American, an airborne master sergeant by the name of Visser whose right leg below the knee was hamburger thanks to shrapnel from an eighty-eight. Impervious to pain, he lay in the cot next to Al's, chain-smoking and talking, a steady stream of conversation from lights on until lights out.

"Got yourself a bad shoulder wound there, partner. Nurse told me when they brought you in. Just caught the infection in time. Had to slice you open. Drain it. Nice gal, that nurse. She's Dutch. Name's Annie. Speaks English pretty good. Docs here are all German. Not bad guys but short on supplies. Except for acriflavine. Only problem is they're amputation happy. Annie says don't ever tell 'em you got a headache. Want a smoke?"

The first days of consciousness went by in a blur, Annie nursing him, Visser talking to him and himself sleeping. He slept in the morning after breakfast, coffee made from roasted acorns and a piece of black bread. He slept in the afternoon following lunch, more make-believe coffee, another slice of the same bread and a piece of sausage. And he slept after supper, bread again and soup, mostly potato. He was exhausted from months of fighting—no rest and little sleep—fatigued by sorrow and enervated by pain in his shoulder and his feet, bruised and cut. The more he healed the more he slept, and the more he slept the less he yelled in his dreams—curses, names, warnings. After awhile he told Annie he felt like Rip van Winkle and she asked if Mr. Van Winkle were Dutch.

He wondered about Billy and Yates, where they were. Still in Holland somewhere? Off to a POW camp in Germany? He knew that if not for him, they might not be prisoners today. If not for him they would have tried to escape when they were still in the Pocket. In the first few days. The best time to try it. When the Tiffies were at them. Just roll away from the ditch when the rockets and strafing forced heads down, when Jerry had no mind for prisoners, too busy trying not to shit his pants. Would have been easy. Hide in the underbrush. Wait till dark.

He wondered too why he was still alive and Ross and Reggie were dead, all three of them on the same side of Gillie's Cruiser when the shooting started. Who or what had slammed into his back, shoving him to the ground out of the line of fire? He fell asleep pondering all possible answers, natural and supernatural.

One morning when he awoke, the cot beside him was empty. Visser was gone. When Annie came to shave him as she did every morning, she said it was gangrene and the German doctors had no choice if Visser was to live.

When he felt well enough to read, Annie brought him books from her doctor father's library, including a thin volume of verse from the soldier poets of World War I. Al read the introductory notes, how Rupert Brooke died of dysentery and blood poisoning on a troopship bound for Gallipoli; Edward Thomas killed in action on Easter Monday, 1917; Isaac Rosenberg, a year later on April Fool's Day; and Wilfred Owen, a week before Armistice Day, November 11, 1918. The only survivors of the carnage were Ivor Gurney and Siegfreid Sassoon; and Gurney spent the rest of his life in a mental hospital.

When he was well enough Annie got him up and walking in the wooden shoes her brother had made "especially for the Canadian at the hospital." She took his arm, carefully leading him between cots past a German medical orderly administering a bedpan to a sightless soldier from New Jersey and then around a group of paratroopers, all with legs broken from the jump, arguing about the War between the States. Through the classroom door she walked him up and down the corridor past children's crayon drawings, windmills and tulips, still tacked on walls painted an industrial green. After years of army boots, it took him some time to get the hang of walking in clogs, but soon Annie kissed him on the cheek pronouncing him a veteran.

When she asked him if he'd read any of the poems, he shook his head but promised to do so that afternoon and once he started he couldn't stop because the poems spoke of things he now knew well.

He read Owen:

> *Having seen all things red,*
> *Their eyes are rid*
> *Of the hurt of the colour of blood forever.*
> *And terror's first constriction over,*
> *Their hearts remain small-drawn.*

It was exactly what Yates had said to him on the road after their capture, his definition of a dead comrade being "a close buddy you pretended you'd never really met."

Allan read Sassoon and thought back to what he'd been told about the snafu at the Leopold.

> *"Good-morning; good morning!" the General said*
> *When we met him last week on our way to the line.*
> *Now the soldiers he smiled at are most of 'em dead,*
> *And we're cursing his staff for incompetent swine.*
> *"He's a cheery old card," grunted Harry to Jack*
> *As they slogged up to Arras with rifle and pack.*
>
> *   **
>
> *But he did for them both with his plan of attack.*

He thought he was falling in love with Annie, not just because patients always fell in love with their nurses, but because she was so kind to him. Sure, she was kind to all of the men in the classroom-ward, laughing and joking with the Americans, but with him there was always something more, the books, the shoes, the smiles and her touch lingering on his face when she shaved him so that he pretended he needed her help long after he had more than enough energy to do it himself. He wanted to be her patient forever.

But early on the morning of Friday, October 6, the beginning of the Thanksgiving Day Weekend in Canada, two years after the sinking of the *Caribou*, Allan's time with Annie came to an end. Along with a dozen of his fellow American patients well enough to travel, he was marched off for transport to a prisoner-of-war camp in Germany.

Annie was on hand in the ward to say farewell and he wanted to hug her fiercely, but thought that even the sympathetic German medical staff would frown on her for that. Instead he handed the book of wartime poems back to her, pointing to the inside cover where he'd used a pen borrowed from the orderly to inscribe his address in Lowvert and the first few lines from the poem he'd penned in his wife's autograph book before he'd gone off for basic training at Camp Borden. "A friend is a gift that you give to yourself, that's one of the old time songs. So I put you down with the best of them, for you're where the best belongs."

At the train station their *Wehrmacht* guards lined them on the concrete platform facing the tracks and there, with much heel-clicking and many "Heil Hitlers," they were turned over to other escorts for the rest of their European guided tour.

Al's heart sank when he recognized who was replacing the *Wehrmacht*, the lightning flashes on collars and the death's heads on caps. Then he did a double take when he saw the officer commanding the new guards, a spitting image of Hauptmann Kaputt.

But this German officer was an *Obersturmführer*, an SS lieutenant, and although he spoke the same precise English as Kaputt, his voice was different, oily, even more condescending and higher-pitched, so much so that a couple of the Americans could be heard making kissing noises.

The lieutenant had been boasting to his captive audience about the failure of *Market Garden*, striding up and down in front of them, rubbing it in about the "bridge too far," snapping a swagger stick against his breeches to emphasize his point-by-point description of the battle prowess of *Der Führer's* finest against the pitiful lackeys of Churchill and the Jew-loving Roosevelt.

When he heard the lip-smacking behind him he was in mid-stride and mid-sentence. Letting the rest of what he was saying go, he brought his raised foot down slowly, turned and smiled. Then, ever so deliberately, he walked back down the line to where he thought the sound had originated. Reaching out with his stick he held it out underneath the chin of one of the Americans.

"You wish to say something," he looked at the American's arm, "Private?"

"No, sir."

"Good! Because you must not speak when a German officer is speaking." And with that he reached back with the swagger stick and lashed the airborne private across the face.

Their *strafe* or punishment for making fun of a German officer was to stand on the platform for the rest of the morning and into the afternoon, when thunderclouds moved in from the west and they were drenched with a cold, hard rain. They pissed their pants standing at attention. Warmer rain.

Train-spotting helped to pass the time, rolling stock coming and going, hospital trains with German wounded going home, troop trains heading the other way with reinforcements bound to shore up the defences along the water approaches to Antwerp. The Battle of the Scheldt was at its height.

It was late afternoon, the sun breaking through clouds to reveal a shimmering rainbow, the Biblical sign of God's pledge to the descendants of Noah that there would be no more divine acts of wrath and that henceforth forever and ever Amen, the God of Israel would be a loving God to all his people, when a freight train creaked and rattled across their line of vision on the far track, boxcars with lettering, *8 CHEVAUX / 40 HOMMES.*

Al could see clawing hands stretching through the ventilation louvres on the upper corners of the boxcars as they juddered to a stop and SS troopers converged, sliding back doors and shouting to those inside, backing up their threats with leashed and growling German shepherds, called Alsatians by the Brits because they couldn't bear to have such loyal and handsome animals associated with the enemy.

Even though Al and the Americans were a fair distance away, a terrible smell was wafted to them from the open boxcar doors, a foul and putrid odour worse than Falaise borne on the cries of the damned from the depths of Hell.

One or two of the Americans gagged as empty wheelbarrows were brought up by civilians in ragged clothes, men with yellow stars sewn on the breasts of their jackets.

Bodies were carried to the edge of the boxcar doors and then hauled out by the yellow-starred men. Mostly the bodies were small. Al guessed children and babies. He could see flashes of yellow on their clothing, bundles of rags marked with the sign of David piled high in the wheelbarrows, arms and legs every which way like sewing needles stuck in a pincushion.

In a minute the wheelbarrows pushed by Jews were full of other Jews, and boxcar doors were slammed shut and cries were muffled and the stink gone and all that was left was another soundtrack to be filed away in the horror archives of the mind, another image with all the makings for future, roll-your-own nightmares.

When darkness came their *strafe* was deemed sufficient and they were ordered inside the station to wait. It turned out to be an all-night wait, a hard rest catnapping on the stone floor. But better than the alternative.

In the morning, one of their number was given a very dull knife to use as a handsaw to carefully cut equal portions from a small sausage and loaf of black bread, breakfast eaten slowly and washed down with tepid water from an outside tap. Afterwards they were lined up on the platform once again.

The first train that morning was another eastbound freight, three locomotives pulling another long line of the same boxcars each with the same capacity, eight horses or forty men. Or, if circumstances warranted, 100 Jews.

This time the train was on the nearest track and as it ground to a stop a few paces directly in front of them and SS guards with their dogs moved in from either end of the station, Al steeled himself for a reprise of yesterday's grim scenes.

But then it hit him. Hit all of them at once. There wasn't a whisper from the train, no clawing hands stretching through the ventilation openings. This was an empty train. These cattle cars had come for them.

Quickly the doors were pulled open to confirm what they had already guessed and just as quickly they were herded inside, pushed by rifles jammed in their backs, dogs snarling at their heels and harsh shouts of 'Raus! 'Raus!

As soon as the last man was through, the sliding door behind him was rolled shut and secured, the sound of a locking bolt slammed through a steel staple, signifying incarceration. In the semi-darkness of the interior they stood stock still until their eyes adjusted, enabling them to pick out, in the floor in the middle of the boxcar, a large wooden tub.

"What the hell's that for?" one of the Americans asked, and another closer to the tub answered, "By the smell of it, I'd guess it's our latrine, boys." And it was.

The only light in the boxcar came from the ventilation louvres, one on each side at either end. These were openings about three feet long and one foot wide with two narrow bars running the length of the opening. When inspected by the tallest of the Americans reaching up, the bars were found to be made of steel and wrapped with barbed wire. His curse of discovery was interrupted by a lurch, throwing everyone off balance as the train began to move. At the same time, the cattle car door was jerked partway open and then slammed shut again. In the interval a box had been thrown at their feet. Wrapped in brown paper and tied with string, once lengthwise and twice crosswise, the box was stamped with the insignia of the Cross of St. John. It was the first Red Cross parcel any of them had ever seen.

Red Cross parcels for POWs came from different countries and the contents varied slightly, but generally included tins of stew, meat rolls, Spam, vegetables, and butter, as well as tea, coffee, sugar, biscuits, prunes, raisins, chocolate bars, cheese and soap. You could tell the country of origin by the contents of the parcel; for example, the parcel on the floor of the boxcar had Spam and no vegetables, which meant it was Canadian and not British.

It was clear to the thirteen prisoners in the cattle car that the contents of the Red Cross parcel would have to be doled out bit by bit with attention to justice and equality for all. Being a Canadian, Sergeant McDougal was assigned the task.

It would be five days before the sergeant and his twelve companions, locked in their rolling cell, would again see sun and moon and stars of night, five days of frequent stops and starts, each stop taking on another Red Cross parcel and another group of POWs as if the Germans were boasting of the vast number of the defeated and demoralized in their hands.

But it was the vast number of prisoners in their cattle car that most concerned Al and the Americans. Forty-eight hours after they had been shoved on board in Breda, their numbers had increased to seventy-five, shoulder to shoulder, crammed in a space for forty. Some of the seventy-five were sick, all were hungry but too nauseous to eat, the smell of tightly packed, unwashed men and the reek of a wooden tub full of piss and shit driving all thoughts of food from their minds.

With the last influx of twenty or so there was no longer any room to sit down, and it wasn't long before Al could sense a rising panic in the crammed car. There was no time to lose. Someone had to take charge.

He still couldn't crane his neck, so he edged his upper body, first to one side, then the other, looking for the biggest and tallest soldier closest to him. Once he'd made his choice, he spoke rapidly and earnestly and the soldier nodded, as did others who could not help overhearing the one-way conversation.

The biggest, tallest man closest to him turned out to be a kilted lance corporal from the Argyll and Sutherland Highlanders of Canada and when he raised his voice, Al knew he had chosen wisely and well.

"Now, lads, hear me out." The big man said it twice, the second time in a roar that brought instant silence to the car.

"Lads! We need to bring some order to this feckin' mess."

There was a certain accent here. "Feck" for "fuck" a definite indication that while the Argylls might be from the highlands of Hamilton, Ontario, the L/C himself was not that far removed from other highlands elsewhere.

"We need to deal with our situation here." The word "situation" was rendered as "sitcheeation."

"None of us is takin' kindly to Gerald packin' us in like sardines here in this godforsaken space."

Al nodded ruefully to himself, thinking of all the train rides he'd been on as a boy, as a young man, as a soldier—the T&NO, the CNR and the CPR— complaining of this and that when trains were late, conductors brusque and washrooms dirty. He vowed to himself that if he ever survived all this, he would never again speak ill of a Canadian railway.

The L/C was speaking again in a voice used to authority. "Now we can deal with it like a bunch o' frightened girls or we can deal with it like soldiers o' the king. What will it be, lads?"

There was a general consensus they would deal with it like soldiers of the king, even the Americans whose ancestors had fought like hell against George III. And so all orders they received from the Highlander were followed to the letter.

The first was to crowd everyone together at one end of the car, leaving a space at the far end. The three rows nearest that space sat down. For two hours. The L/C timed them as best he could without a watch. Then the next three rows of standees replaced the sitters. And so on.

And this was how they travelled for four more nights and three more days, sometimes strafed by their own aircraft, sometimes shunted to sidings for endless hours, a long, hard, desperate journey sustained by the hope of a better life to come.

Chapter Twenty-Four

October 22, 1944

The first thought in Allan McDougal's head when he saw the camp through the pine trees was one of relief. Anything was better than the cattle cars.

The second thought was that prison camps must be the same the world over, Camp Q in Northern Ontario, Canada, and *Stalag* 12A just north of Frankfurt, Germany, were almost cookie-cutter copies of each other, at least at first glance, the same rectangle of land enclosed with the same barbed wire, the same dirt road around the outer edge, the same wooden guard towers on the four corners with machine guns and searchlights, the same low-lying barrack huts, except that here German brick replaced Canadian lumber.

Once off the prison train, stinking, stiff-limbed and lousy, the new arrivals had been lined up in front of the boxcars and counted, not once, not twice but three times, to make sure no one had escaped along the way, a possibility that had not occurred to Al or anyone else among the unwashed seventy-five, all their energies focused on surviving.

But what had not even been considered by some was actively pursued by others. In one or two of the cars, prisoners had fashioned primitive tools from the tins in Red Cross parcels and hour after hour, with the patience of Job, dug away at floorboards to loosen them enough for a hand to get a grip, for fingers to pull and pry, tugging one board off and then another, opening a space big enough for a man to drop through whenever the train slowed enough that it could be done with a reasonable chance of success, a prospect measured by not losing a leg or an arm to a cattle car wheel.

No one was sure how many had made it, numbers varying depending on who was whispering the story. But the best guess was that of the many hundreds who eventually ended up in the cattle cars in the last few days only a dozen or so had gotten away before Jerry, in one of his periodic dog checks underneath the boxcars, had discovered loose floorboards.

The entrance to the camp was through a flimsy gate of crisscrossed, weathered boards interlaced with barbed wire that looked like it could be blown open by a stiff breeze. Through this gate the prisoners were ushered into the outer compound or *Vorlager*, past a guardhouse with two sullen armed guards accompanied by one of the omnipresent, snarling shepherds.

Inside the *Vorlager*, a fenced-in area tacked on to the camp proper, the column was counted once again, checked and re-checked against a number of lists, in what was becoming a familiar display of Teutonic efficiency. That accomplished, the column was quick-marched off to the right toward a group of Nissen-like huts, where they were separated into groups of fifteen. The promise of the huts was that their filthy, stinking uniforms would be burned and replaced by other uniforms, fresh and clean, once they had stripped for a shower and delousing.

For the first time since he had been captured this was an order Al was happy to obey. He was still with his American comrades from the hospital in Breda and when he started to shrug off his grimy, fetid tunic the Yank beside him reached out a restraining arm telling him to stop. The Americans had heard about "showers" in Nazi camps and were not about to be "cleansed." Instead they staged a sit-down strike. Right then and there.

It took a demonstration by one the guards going into the shower room and turning on the water in full view of his onlookers before anybody moved. But when they did, it was with a boyish enthusiasm. Even though the water was shivering cold it washed away filth and grime and gave them a new lease on life. Godliness was next to cleanliness.

From the showers they went naked into a another room where they were dusted with DDT powder to rid them of the carriers of typhus, *Pediculus humanus*, otherwise known as lice, tiny black, blood-sucking creatures looking like cinders, hitchhikers who had first announced their itching presence a day or two after the prisoners had been herded on the cattle cars.

Freshly scrubbed and powdered, they were then photographed, fingerprinted and dog-tagged, this time with a *Kriegsgefangener* or POW identity disc. Al's regimental number was replaced with his kriegie number. B55379 became 9036.

Lastly they were given a stern warning. No escaping. Jerry, once burnt, was twice shy.

A little over six months before, on the night of March 25, 1944, seventy-six Allied officers had escaped from a POW Camp for airmen, *Stalagluft* 3, just outside of Sagan, a small railroad town in Germany about eighty miles southeast of Berlin, close to the border of Poland. Like Monteith, Sagan was in the middle of nowhere.

The escape was over a year in the making and involved hundreds of men working at scores of different jobs, everything from forging documents to the lighting and ventilation of tunnels.

The digging got underway in April of 1943 when three tunnels were started, Tom, Dick and Harry. Tunnelling was supervised by Wally Floody, a Canadian fighter pilot from Toronto, who before the war had been a miner in Algonquin country, the goldfields of Kirkland Lake and Timmins.

In September, when Jerry discovered Tom, Dick was abandoned and Floody concentrated all efforts on Harry. Running thirty feet below ground, Harry was lit by a tap into the camp's electrical system. Sand dug from the tunnel face was carried in wooden trolleys pulled by ropes along wooden rails back to the tunnel entrance underneath a stove in one of the huts. There it was bagged and turned over to men whose job it was to get rid of it by hanging the sand bags inside their pants and then going for a walk around the prison compound. As the men walked they loosened a drawstring at the bottom of the bags and the sand trickled out bit-by-bit, losing itself in the compound earth.

The problem of circulating fresh air in Harry was solved by bellows fashioned from kit bags pumping air through ducts made from powdered milk tins taped together.

The Escape Committee had thought of everything, even rest stops. There were two along the 336-foot-long tunnel: The first widened space between the entry shaft and planned exit shaft outside the wire was called Piccadilly, the second Leicester Square. It was a long, long way to Tipperary.

The plan was for 120 prisoners to get out, but a premature discovery of the exit limited the number to seventy-six and these instantly became the object of a massive manhunt.

Only three of the seventy-six made it and fifty of those recaptured, six Canadians among them, were lined up and shot by the Gestapo on direct orders from an infuriated Führer. As a hedge against Allied reprisals, the executions were said to have occurred while "resisting arrest" or "attempting to escape."

In 1963, Hollywood made a movie about Tom, Dick and Harry. Called *The Great Escape*, it starred Richard Attenborough, Steve McQueen, James Garner, Donald Pleasence, David McCallum, James Coburn and Charles Bronson. In the film, the Americans and the Brits were portrayed as having played prominent roles in planning and pulling off the breakout. There was no mention of a Canadian by the name of Wally Floody.

But in the real world of *Stalag* 12A in October 1944 Jerry was still smarting from Sagan in the spring. And so the warnings after the fingerprinting were to the point. If you escape and are captured wearing civilian clothes you will be shot.

Jerry knew very well that no escapee was going to advertise his status by wearing a uniform, so the edict was heard as it was no doubt intended to be heard. "If you escape you will be shot."

It was after the warning and late in the afternoon before the *Stalag* clerks finished processing the latest batch of prisoners, who were then separated by nationality and rank before being shown to their quarters in the inner compound.

Dressed now like a refugee from an international military rummage sale, the baggy pants of an American paratrooper and the battledress blouse of a British infantryman, but still in his wooden shoes from Holland, Allan McDougal was led down a cinder path between rows of huts, in the gaps between, a playing field, a game of softball in progress.

At Hut 38, the escort used his Mauser to point to the ground telling his prisoner to stay put. Then he turned and marched away as a Canadian soldier stepped through the hut door.

"I like your shoes, Sergeant."

Al looked closely at the speaker and then broke into a wide grin. It was the NCO from C Company, one of the men who'd told him the story of the debacle at the Leopold Canal. The sergeant stuck out a big right hand.

"McCafferty, Fergus. Charlie Company."

"Yeah, McCafferty. I remember. What the hell are you doing here?"

Al grinned and shook McCafferty's hand warmly. Seeing a familiar face made him feel like it was Old Home Week in Lowvert.

McCafferty chuckled. "Well, about a week after the snafu at the Leopold a bunch of us got together and said 'Piss on it, let's take the rest of the war off. Head off to Germany and see how the other half lives.' And so we found us a bunch of Jerries who were happy to accommodate us and here we are! Come on in. You're messing with us."

Al followed Fergus inside the hut, down a poorly lit corridor past a series of numbered doors. At number 12 he stopped and straight-armed the door, pushing it open and ushering his guest into a large room made small by the clutter of bunk beds, four doubles and one triple, each of them hung with drying clothes, mostly socks and underwear. Scattered here and there were wooden benches and homemade chairs grouped around a large table covered with an oilcloth like the linoleum on his mother's kitchen floor. A black, pot-bellied wood stove stood in the corner, a kettle simmering on top.

Fergus pointed to the top bunk of the triple. "That one's yours. New guys get the top ones. It's warm. Heat rises. But so do smells. Wood chips in the mattress. Not too bad when you get used to it. Anyway you won't be here long."

Al sat at the table and absent-mindedly fingered a pack of dog-eared playing cards.

He was only half-paying attention to his host, who was still talking as he took the kettle from the stove and poured water into a cup. McCafferty used a homemade metal spoon to stir in a cube of instant tea taken from a battered tin on the table, a tin that had once contained Klim powdered milk. Then he set the offering in front of the new kid on the block, threw a leg over the bench, and sat across from him.

"So what happened to you guys, anyway? Arnhem Sunday, wasn't it?"

Al took an appreciative sip of tea and nodded as McCafferty continued. "We could hear the firing. Some of us wanted to swing down there and see if you lads needed a hand, especially when Christensen got back with your lieutenant, but we were told to stay put. Christensen was fit to be tied. But *befehl ist befehl.*"

"What?"

"Oh, sorry. That's Jerry talk. Hear it a lot around here. 'Orders are orders.'"

"Lieutenant Gill. He all right?"

"Far as I know. Took him into the RAP right away. Last I heard he was gonna be airlifted to Blighty."

Für euch ist der Krieg zu Ende. Thinking of Gillie, Al spoke the words mostly to himself.

"What?"

Al took another drink of tea and stood up. "Hey, McCafferty, you're not the only one who spreckenzee *Deutsch*. It means 'For you the war is over.'"

He went over to the window opposite the door, a washbasin and a bar of soap on the counter below, and looked out at a long wooden wall behind a barbed-wire fence.

"That's the American compound you're looking at there, McDougal. Behind that wall. The goons don't want us to be talkin' with the Yanks through the wire so they threw up the barrier."

Just then Al remembered with a start what McCafferty had said a few minutes earlier. "What did you mean when you said I wouldn't be here long?"

"They didn't tell ya?"

When Al shook his head, McCafferty explained. "This is just a transit camp. Prisoners are in and out of here on a daily basis. When Jerry gets enough of us together he ships us out to a permanent camp. Me and the rest of the guests in Room 12 been around for a couple of weeks now and we figure we'll be on our way any day. And you'll be comin' with us."

Any day turned out to be two days later. Early in the morning their hut was invaded, not by their regular guards, but by the Hitler *Jugend*, juvenile thugs high on fanaticism and testosterone, banging on doors with rifle butts and screaming.

McCafferty had scrounged a pair of army boots for Al, who was down on one knee lacing them up when one of the Nazi boy scouts bowled him over with a boot to his wounded shoulder and then stood over him roaring at him to get a move on. *Schnell! Schnell!*

The pain that seared through his neck and down his arm was nothing to the rage that suddenly took hold of him, a volcanic anger erupting from deep inside him where he didn't know he'd stuffed it.

Had not one of his roommates helped him to his feet and wrapped him in protective arms as he hustled him out to the parade ground, Allan McDougal would have been a dead man. He would have launched himself at the kid to gouge out his eyes, stomp in his ribs and kick him repeatedly in the balls, to beat him to a bone-breaking, bloody death and he would have been shot before he even started.

Out on the parade ground, he stood between McCafferty and Williamson, the man who had saved his life. He was trembling and taking in great gulps of air, trying to calm himself, conscious now of the ache in his shoulder, an ache he dared not touch, since they had been ordered not to move, not even blink.

And there they remained for two hours, like trees in a winter forest, without expression, frozen in a wooden silence, 300 men, mostly British paras from Arnhem along with a number of scruffy contingents representing the Commonwealth—New Zealanders, Australians, a handful of turbaned Sikhs from India, and the Canadians from Hut 38, Room 12.

Al used the time to stare at nothing, concentrating on blocking the pain in his shoulder while he sniffed at his new-found rage.

At another time in another place he would have been frightened by the intensity of it, but here he welcomed it because he sensed a power that he could use to keep him going.

In England, in his delayed reaction to the *Caribou*, Kathleen had taken him to the comfort of her bed, and later, when Barney and Goody were killed, the lads had rallied around each other. Like poles at the top of a teepee they had leaned on each other and held each other up.

But now there was no Kathleen, no little league, no Yates. Sure, he knew he could count on the lads with him now. Williamson had proven that. But he sensed he was going to need more and maybe rage was going to be it.

The first test came at the railway siding and he gave himself a solid passing grade. While others sagged like deflating balloons when they saw what they hoped they would never see again—the waiting cattle cars, sliding doors open, wooden wash tubs inside—Allan McDougal kept his back straight, his face firm, his spirit armoured with a "Fuck-you-Jerry" resolve.

This time the train was shorter in length. Marching under guard down the length of it with his fellow POWs, Al saw only the one locomotive and tender coupled to a half-dozen freight cars with their doors shut, all of them marked with red crosses painted in white circles. These were followed by flatcars loaded with aircraft wings and fuselages, tanks and trucks. The five cattle cars were next and then two passenger cars at the very end of the train where a caboose would have been in Canada. The cattle cars were marked "POW" in large white letters on either side of the doors and the passenger cars bore the same red crosses as the freight cars. Al could see that these last two cars were crammed full of enemy soldiers, many of them hanging out the windows exchanging cigarettes with some of the Hitler *Jugend* at track level.

As the prisoners watched, the flatcars were covered with heavy tarps also marked with red crosses painted in white circles. It didn't take a genius to figure out what was going on. Jerry was trying to ward off the increasingly bold Tiffy attacks on everything and anything that moved in Germany. If Allied pilots could be convinced that this was a hospital and prisoner-of-war train, medical supplies in the boxcars and ambulances on the flatcars, then safe passage for Jerry's men and matériel was almost guaranteed.

In groups of sixty, rows of twelve, five abreast in front of each cattle car, the POWs were counted for a third time that morning and then, at a shouted order, prodded up and inside with rifles jabbing at their backs. When the last row was aboard, loaves of black bread, enough for two slices per man, were thrown in behind them. Food for the day or food for the trip? Nobody knew. And nobody knew how long the trip was going to be.

Al flinched at the next sounds, the screech of the rolling door, the final thud as it slammed shut and the clink of locking bolt shoved into place. But he got hold of himself instantly, a self-administered and stern admonishment—no further signs of weakness would be tolerated.

With sixty occupants there was a bit more room this time but still it was necessary to organize standees and sitters, and Al found himself among the first twenty to sit, his linked arms holding his knees in tight to his chest to minimize the space he occupied. McCafferty was next to him.

"You never did tell me how you were captured, Fergus."

Fergus obviously didn't want to talk about it because he answered with a question about something else entirely.

"Ya know what really happened at the Leopold, dontcha? Why Jerry gave us a shit-kicking?"

"You mean the community hall being bugged."

"Uh, uh." McCafferty shook his head. "That's a bullshit story. The real story, as I heard it and on good authority, is that some horny officers got themselves laid by a couple of real good-looking Belgian girls who just happened to be German sympathizers from the air base at Maldegem. It was all pillow talk, the stupid bastards bragging to the girls about what we were gonna do to Jerry the next day when we crossed the canal."

McCafferty kept talking, but Al tuned him out. He didn't care if Monty himself had been the source of these ejaculatory revelations. As far as he was concerned, scrunched up on the floor of the cattle car, the screw-up at Leopold might as well have been the fall of Troy. It was all ancient history.

It was the next day and his fourth shift of sitting before the train even moved, and then barely getting up steam before it was attacked by two marauding Tiffies. The fly boys were either ignoring the train markings or were, as Billy had put it, "blind in one eye and unable to see out of the other." Given his experience in such matters, Al opted for the CNIB explanation. The Canadian National Institute for the Blind.

The Tiffies didn't do much damage, just enough to hold things up for several hours while the track in front of them was repaired, a delay that frustrated the experienced escape-minded among them, keeping them from working on a raised floorboard their overseers had forgotten to nail down. The sullen, delinquent Hitler Youth were patrolling outside, up and down the stationary line with their mean shepherds, and no one wanted to give man or beast an excuse to be nasty.

Once underway again, the train travelled without interruption through the evening and into the night. By this time two of the floorboards were completely free and all of the bread consumed. They were a hungry lot, but more than that, parched and very thirsty. They'd had nothing to drink since leaving the camp and that was thirty-six hours ago.

When dawn came it was the Tiffies who came to their aid. This second attack was a sustained one, the aircraft repeatedly dive-bombing the train, disabling the locomotive and prompting the soldiers in the passenger cars to rush forward and open the cattle cars, ordering the prisoners to take cover in the ditches along the track where the brave Hitler *Jugend* were already cowering.

There was water in the ditches, dirty water, garbage floating in it, a greenish scum covering it, a smell of decay rising from it, and when the Tiffies departed, some of the thirsty prisoners drank, cupping the ditch water to their lips as if it were spring water, fresh and clear and pure.

It was good to be outside, to stretch constricted limbs, to look up and see the sky. But not for long. They were on the outskirts of the bombed city of Erfurt and soon were surrounded by an angry crowd of citizens, mostly women and most of them looking to be in their fifties. At first the women simply stared. Like visitors to a zoo in front of a cage holding exotic, wild-looking animals, their expressions were a mixture of fear and anger because these animals were of the same species as those who had rained death upon them.

It was the women with children who began to call them names. *Englander Schweinehund* and, for those who knew a bit of English, "Englander babykillers." Al thought to himself wryly that if Billy had been around he would have objected to being called an Englishman. He missed Billy.

The name-calling emboldened the women and they stepped closer, the Hitler *Jugend* laughing and egging them on until they began spitting in the faces of the babykillers. Al thought he would rather be clubbed by a rifle butt than be degraded by another human being spitting on him.

He saw he wasn't the only one to think this way. A prisoner to his left, one of the Australians, lunged in anger at a grandmother with a child in her arms who'd just spewed a gob of phlegm in his eyes. To the cheers of the mob, the Aussie was clubbed to the ground by rifle butts.

It was the soldiers from the passenger cars, the regular *Wehrmacht*, who saw that the situation had escalated to dangerous levels and hurried to hustle the prisoners back inside where they spent the rest of the day and the following night locked in the unmoving cattle car waiting for Jerry to find a locomotive that worked.

For many of the prisoners who'd drunk from the ditch it was a sickening wait. First they were racked by severe stomach cramps. Then it was diarrhea and in no time the washtub was close to overflowing. Al didn't know which was worse, the sight and smell of the tub or the poor bastards who didn't make it to the tub before their bowels let loose.

He had been one of the few who had steeled himself against drinking the water and now he wormed his way to a corner, as far away from the tub as he could get, distancing himself from voyeuristically witnessing the humiliation that was the everyday lot of a POW, freaks in a midway performing the most personal and private bodily functions in front of others. "Step right up, folks, and see the man take down his pants and defecate in a washtub. See the tears in his eyes. From the pain of his cramps, for sure. But also, ladies and gentlemen, because he is so ASHAMED! Yessir, ladies and gentlemen. ASHAMED! And you can see this shame, right here on our stage for one thin dime, that's one-tenth of a dollar. So step right up, folks! Step right up."

When the worst of it was over, word went round that the men working on the floorboards were grateful for the spitting women. If not for them, the boarding would have been more orderly and most probably preceded by an inspection of the cattle cars, a search for anything out of the ordinary, a close look at the floorboards. Every cloud has a silver lining.

There were also rumours of their destination, a conversation among the guards overheard by one of the Brits who knew more German than he let on. They were en route to *Stalag* 8C just across the road from the now-famous *Stalagluft* 3 at Sagan, a junction point on the main rail line running southeast from Berlin. They would be in Sagan in another day or so.

The rumour was both right and wrong. Right about their destination. Wrong about how long it would take them to get there. It wasn't until five days later, a Sunday, that their train pulled into Sagan.

Shaky and unsteady on their feet, sick, starving and dehydrated, they were counted off in raggedy lines on the platform in front of the Sagan freight sheds, dirty-red brick and corrugated tin, much like the dock sheds in Halifax where the Algonquins had waited to board the *Empress of Scotland*. The count came to 283. Twelve had died on the trip.

Some of these had been weak and sick to begin with while others, unable to cope with the barbarity of their days and the depravity of their nights, had simply curled up and willed themselves to die. An endless sleep was far more preferable than a living hell.

Five had been shot trying to escape, all from Al's cattle car, McCafferty among them. The attempt had been made in the evening of the day after leaving Erfurt when they had been shunted to a siding to allow a troop train to pass on the main line. As soon as the cars slowly screeched into the siding and before the Hitler *Jugend* had time to get out with their dogs, the floorboards had come up and five men dropped through to the tracks to hide and wait for night among the rushes in the ditch.

Al held his breath, hoping not to hear what he expected to hear, shouts and shots signalling failure. He thought the escape was a stupid idea, concluding that it was just another way of giving up. Instead of curling up and waiting for death, the escapees were going to go after it. They knew they were too weak and too unprepared to make a successful break. So did Al. So did everyone.

But there were no shouts and no shots. At least not right away. There was only the noise of a railroad siding, the screeching click and clack of passing trains and, in the intervening silences, the hissing of steam along with the crunch of boots on the cinders and crushed stone of the track bed, patrolling Hitler *Jugend* keeping an eye on their charges. These being the only sounds, every listening man in the boxcar exhaled.

Truth be known, they were thankful for the diversion the escape provided. Wondering about the fate of their comrades on the lam and fantasizing about their making it—wine, women and song in Paris—occupied space in minds that would otherwise have been corroded by acidic thoughts eating away at what little spirit remained. If the lads outside accomplished nothing else, if they didn't get beyond the track bed ditch before the dogs got them, they had at least, for one brief shining moment, managed to transport their comrades left behind to a far more happy place, far, far and away from the reality of their godforsaken lives—the overwhelming stench of overflowing piss and shit, the frenzied scratching at the constant itch of blood-sucking lice, the endless, hopeless craving for food and the desperate longing for water, forcing some of them to drink their own urine.

In that sense the escapees did not die in vain when night fell, the shouts came and the searchlights caught all five of them running for their lives, the dogs at their heels. It was a race quickly lost to the Mausers and Schmeissers of the salivating, pimply-faced kids who, fresh from the kill, would have turned to make life miserable for those remaining in the cattle car if they'd boarded and found the loose floorboards. But they stayed away. The smell was too much even for them.

Stalag 8C was *Stalag* 12A all over again, the same *Vorlager* or outer compound and the same drill of repeated countings, dumping of clothes, showers and delousing. This time you got the same clothes back smelling of disinfectant and this time the warnings about escapes were both oral and written—posters on the walls of the hut, blaming England for a new, bold typeface, Nazi policy toward **"All Prisoners of War!"**

Because England was no longer "fighting in an honest manner" and no longer "practising the rules of sportsmanship" but now resorting to "gangster commandos, terror bandits and sabotage troops," then it was no longer possible for Germany to follow the Geneva Convention with regard to escaped prisoners of war.

Therefore there were now "death zones," broadly interpreted, in which escaping prisoners would be "in constant danger of being mistaken for gangster commandos, terror bandits and sabotage troops." And if they were so mistaken they would be "shot on sight all suspected persons."

The last lines of the stern message, again in bold typeface, tried to leave a lasting impression. **"In plain English: Stay in the camp where safe you will be! Breaking out of it is now a damned dangerous act."**

Squinting at the poster, Al didn't have the energy to guffaw at the laughable plain English or shake his head at the breathtaking hypocrisy. He wished he did. He wished Yates were here to parody the whole business, to do his-finger-under-the-nose-for-Hitler's-moustache routine, a hank of hair falling over his forehead as he goose-stepped around spitting out his best imitation of the ranting Führer fulminating about the sportsmanship of cattle cars and the kindhearted conduct of the helpful young men in the Hitler *Jugend* and the generous and humanitarian treatment of the Jews and the fair and honest bombing of East

London's innocents and the thoughtful, benevolent torpedoing of women and children on the *Caribou*.

Billy would have been on the floor laughing. Thinking about it, Al could barely manage a smile.

It would take him ten days to recover, longer to forget the taste of his own urine, in large part because the consistency and smell of the camp's *soupe du jour* served as a daily reminder.

Mangel soup was the main meal of the day, ladled out at noon from the bottom half of a wooden barrel. The soup was made from beets grown by the Germans to feed their cattle. Some of the lads thought it tasted a bit like a sweet consommé but Al thought they were out of their minds. These were the same guys who were of the opinion that the one cup of acorn coffee that served as breakfast wasn't half bad, while the majority of their comrades used it to shave, a habit that eventually left them looking like they'd just come back from a couple of weeks of sun worship in the Mediterranean.

A slice of bread came with the soup, not the ubiquitous black bread they were used to, but a more doughy-looking substance said to be mostly made from potato meal with a little bit of sawdust thrown in for flavour. Al thought it was the other way around. When it was available, a dollop of marmalade from a Red Cross parcel helped the bread go down.

Not only was Jerry not now following the Geneva Convention with regard to escapees, he was also not abiding by the rules when it came to feeding POWs, who were supposed to be issued the same daily rations as German garrison troops. In fact no one could survive for long on what the 10,000 or so inmates of *Stalag* 8C were given to eat. If it hadn't been for the Red Cross parcels they would have slowly starved to death.

Living quarters were long, narrow huts clustered in the centre of the 300-square-foot compound, the soil sandy like Camp Borden's. The huts themselves were clustered around a good-sized pool of water, not for swimming but in case of fire. Constructed of pressed-concrete blocks about the size of large bricks, each hut slept approximately 100 men in long rows of three-tiered bunk beds along the walls, the same wood-chip-stuffed mattresses as at *Stalag* 12 A.

Each mattress rested on half-inch wooden slats. Where once there had been four of these slats per bed there were now only two and sometimes none. Bed slats were in great demand for cribbing tunnels and the needs of the Escape Committee meant that many a mattress sagged dangerously on a frame of rope.

The bunks were so close together that you had to shuffle sideways to get between them. What space was left on the walls was adorned with masturbation aids—pinups of Hollywood's finest, mostly Rita Hayworth, Betty Grable, Lana Turner, Dorothy Lamour and Veronica Lake.

The prisoners in the hut comprised a little league of nations much larger in number than that of the Lowvert Maple Leafs and with different countries represented. Here it was Brits, South Africans, Australians, Kiwis from New

Zealand, Indians from India—Sikhs and Hindus, muleteers from the Italian campaign captured during the battle for Ortona—along with about a dozen Canadians Al was just getting to know by his third night when he was allowed to gather round with the rest of his hutmates to hear the BBC news correspondent report on the progress of the war.

Because Jerry was known to put stool pigeons in among the cats, all new arrivals got the third degree from the POW Security Committee. You were kindly invited to sit on one side of a table while three members of the committee sat on the other side. You were offered a smoke and then right after you'd lit up you got the rapid-fire questions about your regiment, its officers and where it had trained; about your country, its leaders, its politics, its geography and the games your people played—hockey, baseball, football. What was a double play? What was an offside in hockey? In football? Who was Foster Hewitt? Who was Turk Broda? And Wayne & Shuster was the name of a prestigious Toronto law firm, true or false?

Al answered this last question with a rendition of "When the swallows come back from Kapuskasing" and then a question of his own. "Where's Kapuskasing?" He passed the test.

There being no Eaton's catalogues in eastern Germany, or in neighbouring Poland for that matter, there were only a few clandestine radios in the camp. They had arrived early in the war, in bits and pieces, different components hidden in different Red Cross parcels. Disassembled during the day, the various parts secreted in different huts, the radios were put together each evening in time for the news from jolly old England at 1800 hours, Greenwich time.

One man from each hut was called to listen to the news at a central location that changed daily. When the news was finished, this man returned home and stood in the centre of his hut to await the "All Clear" from two lookouts, one at each end of the hut, watching for goons.

Al could see that their correspondent was a little guy, the spitting image of Mickey Rooney in his Andy Hardy days, the quintessential All-American boy. When Mickey got the signal from the lookouts he cleared his throat and began to recite from memory in a Cockney accent.

"Here is the official BBC Evening News for Wednesday, October 18. Bomber Command continues to bring the war home to Germany. Air Chief Marshall Arthur Harris reports . . ."

Young Mickey went on to describe raids on Dortmund and Duisburg—twice in sixteen hours—and the continuing success of the campaign in Greece, British forces having just liberated Athens. Meanwhile, in Europe, Canadian forces were making steady progress in the battle to drive German forces from the Scheldt.

The evening news report was followed by tea at the table in the centre of the hut and a confab as to how much of what they'd just heard was true and how much of it wasn't. Given that there was general agreement among the discussants that the first casualty of war was truth and a consensus that propaganda was not something invented by the Germans, there was some scepticism expressed about the news from the Scheldt, especially by a burly corporal from the Royal Hamilton Light Infantry who was reporting on conversations he'd had at the transit camp with regimental comrades captured during the early days of fighting for the town of Woensdrecht.

"Listen, you guys. At Woensdrecht the Rileys came up against some pretty tough Jerries. Paratroopers. Von der Heydte's boys. Lads said they got the bejesus kicked outta them. And let's not forget the poor, sad buggers of the Black Watch."

The corporal was reminding them of what was already being called "Black Friday," the Friday of October 13, when the Montreal Regiment was ordered into combat with an attack plan that made no sense, to fight a battle among the polders they could not win against an enemy who could not lose.

At the end of the day the Black Watch casualties numbered 183 and the survivors stumbled back to base, where a scheduled showing of the movie *We Die At Dawn* was hurriedly cancelled.

"So Harry, you don't believe this stuff about 'steady progress,' then."

"Could be, Smitty, but I have my doubts." The corporal grinned and nodded. "Ever since that big victory at Dieppe."

"Oh yeah that, quote, daring and triumphant raid unquote, when half the regiment was wiped out?"

"Yeah, that's the one, Smitty. That's the one. Except it wasn't half the regiment wiped out. It was *two-thirds*. And it was 'a daring and triumphant raid that taught us valuable lessons about invasion tactics, lessons that saved thousands of lives on D-Day.'"

"Right, Harry. I forgot that one. The biggest fuckin' lie of all."

"Smitty, Smitty. Watch your tongue. Not a lie." Harry did an exaggerated tsk-tsk-tsk. "An explanation. True it was dreamed up after the fact when the shit hit the fan and it was cover-your-ass time. But ours is not to reason why—"

"—ours is but to do and die." Al completed the line for Harry and told him about getting down on paper what really happened at the Leopold Canal because he was afraid the true story would never be told. Harry winked at him.

"Ask yourself this, my young man," Harry was older than all of them, Al figuring him for about forty, "ask yourself this. Who writes history?"

Smitty groaned, shook his head and gave Al a look. "Now you're in for it, lad. You are about to get the 'What Is History?' lecture from Professor Harry Hounam of the Hamilton School of Economics. Professor Hounam has a BA, a 'Bullshit Always' degree that he conferred upon himself one night a couple of months ago when we were both very, very drunk on Calvados."

Harry cleared his throat and proceeded as if Smitty hadn't spoken. "History is usually written by some namby-pamby ivory tower guy who sits at a desk and never gets his hands dirty or his feet wet because all he does is pore over second-hand information. Then he writes it down and somebody calls it history and we read it and think that's what really happened. But it isn't, is it? It isn't history. It's his story. Get it? It's the twist that the guy gives it, or what he leaves out, or what he thinks is important and what he doesn't. You know the history of French Canada written by a Frenchman is gonna be a hell of a lot different then the history of French Canada written by an Englishman and neither so-called 'history' will be what really happened. Ya know that old saying, eh, McDougal. 'There's three sides to every story: Your side, my side, and the truth'?"

By the end of the discussion generated by the monologue it was clear that Harry Hounam and Smitty Anderson had adopted Al McDougal, who liked them both, Harry because he reminded him of the best of Billy Assad and William Butler Yates—he was cynical and smart—and Smitty because of the twinkle in his eyes and the chuckle in his voice when he played Edgar Bergen to Harry's Charlie McCarthy.

The next morning the two Rileys took the Algonquin sergeant for a "circuit bash" or walk around the wire, Harry insisting that Al needed to build up his strength because sooner or later Jerry was going to be squeezed like a pimple by the Allies coming from the west and the Russians coming from the east, and when Jerry popped it was going to be every man for himself. And if a man had to make a run for it, then a man wanted to be in shape, eh?

The route around the circuit was clockwise on the beaten path following the perimeter fence and there were twenty or so others taking the air with them, the air getting colder by the day. Al was still dressed in his American para pants and his British army tunic and he was shivering. When Harry noticed he promised to scrounge up a greatcoat for Al before the day was out.

There were two fences enclosing the compound, each about ten feet high and separated by an eight-foot gap filled with tangled rolls of rusted concertina wire, so thick in places you could barely see through it.

On the far side of the outside wire was a clearing, stumps here and there uprooted in the sandy soil. It was an area too exposed for the exit shaft of a tunnel and an excellent field of fire for the goons in the towers. Jerry had learned a thing or two from the Great Escape.

About thirty feet from the inner fence was a single strand of wire strung on short posts a foot or two off the ground.

"Warning wire," said Smitty. "Step over this and you're shot."

He nodded up at the goon towers. Just then, as if to illustrate the point, a soccer ball bounced over the warning wire. The prisoner running after the ball stopped short before calling up for permission to go after it. Not until the guards in the towers on either side indicated that he could do so did the POW move and both goons watched him like a hawk while he gingerly stepped over the strand, picked up his prize and turned back to the game.

Farther along the wire, Al noticed other groups of POWs in other sections and asked how many different compounds there were in the camp. Harry said he thought there were around six or seven, with the Russian being the biggest.

There were three or four different American compounds—he grinned and said that when the going got tough and the tough got going, the Yanks surrendered— and two officers' compounds, one American and one Commonwealth. He also said he thought there were some other Algonquins in their compound and promised he would ask around that afternoon to find out where they were exactly.

Tuckered out after one circuit, Al excused himself and found his own way back to their hut, where he climbed up on his bunk and lay down, wondering if the other Algonquins in *Stalag* 8C might know what happened to Yates and Billy. He dozed off hoping.

Chapter Twenty-Five

November 10, 1944

Alan George McDougal found himself standing in front of a series of tables set end to end and covered in starched white linen, one long groaning board of food beginning with oysters on the half shell, just like the ones he'd eaten with Yates at the black market restaurant outside of Bruges. He smiled, remembering Willy telling him how oysters helped you keep it up all night.

Next to the oysters were shrimp and Solomon Gundy, smoked salmon and a dozen different salads together with several plates of various mouth-watering cheeses, hardtack biscuits on the side, a combination that struck him as being a curious conjunction of the sublime and the ridiculous, as was the next table, opened compo ration cans and the contents of Red Cross parcels decorously arranged—Neilsen's Jersey Milk chocolate bars, Frey Bentos corned beef, Clover Leaf salmon, Klim powdered milk, Atlas prunes, sardines, and the ever-mouth-watering Snake and Kidney pie together with the always tasty and flavourful Muck and Vomit.

He shook his head and wrinkled his nose as he passed on to pans filled with bacon and sausage and real—not powdered—scrambled eggs. He took generous helpings of the breakfast food, piling it beside the shellfish, pickled herring and salmon, a heaping plate even before he got to the ham, scalloped potatoes and mustard pickles; the roast turkey and cranberry sauce with mashed potatoes and gravy, turnip, peas and carrots, the meat carved by his father and the vegetables served by his mother, who was surprised to see him when she looked up with plate extended to his empty left hand.

Next to Myra, Pietro Foligno was smiling at him as he offered a spatula bearing a thick square of lasagna oozing mozzarella cheese. Nodding his thanks, Al set down the overflowing plates, one from each hand, and reached for a bread knife to saw off a slab of homemade bread still warm from the oven, reminding him of the bread the farmer's wife had served them just outside Monteith on that cold winter day of hunting Jerry escaped from Camp Q.

After slathering the bread with butter, he looked up to see a grinning Barney Berman handing him a plate of potato latkes and Joe Assad offering *kibbeh* and black olives along with a waterglass full of dandelion wine. He shrugged his shoulders and flashed a goofy grin. He had no room on either of his plates. Not even for a teaspoonful. He just stood there, his eyes wide and ranging down the rest of the table, scanning all the desserts, the chocolate cakes, the apple and lemon meringue pies, the trifle, the ice cream—homemade strawberry and vanilla—the fruit, along with coffee and tea in steaming silver flagons. And then at the very end, a waving Tony Foligno, his arm around Kathleen O'Halloran, who was holding up a bottle of *grappa* in one hand and a fistful of fat, Churchillian cigars in the other.

When he woke, it took him a moment to get his bearings and figure out what it was that had trolled him up from the depth of his sleep. By now he was used to the air-raid sirens, the faraway muffled crump of falling bombs and the grind and screech of shunting freight cars in the nearby railway yards at Sagan. Train noises were increasing with each passing week. Jerry was getting ready for something.

Al lay quietly in his bunk wrapped in the greatcoat Harry had managed to find for him, paying two packs of cigarettes to a Sikh who'd got it from a Russian for one pack. Cigarettes were the camp currency and the Russians the camp merchants, because they were out and about on work parties every day, meeting the locals whose taste for Canadian and American smokes—not to mention Jersey Milk chocolate and real coffee—exceeded their fear of trading with the enemy.

The lives of these Russian traders were nasty, brutish and short. The Germans worked them to death. Literally. Not that there was anything to live for. If by some fantastic improbability they survived captivity and were returned to their homeland, they would be executed by their own government. As far as Uncle Joe was concerned, getting captured was a capital offence.

Each day, cheerfully fatalistic in their blue and white vertical-striped jackets and pants, the Russians marched by Al's compound on their way to work and trade. And each night some of them didn't return. But there were lots of them and when one merchant collapsed, another stepped forward to take his place. For that their fellow POWs were eternally grateful.

Al's greatcoat had a strong horse smell to it and was a boarding house for lice, but it kept out the cold and that was all that mattered. He snuggled into it. There was very little heat in the hut during the day and none at all in the freezing nights, the daily supply of firewood and briquettes made from compressed coal dust being insufficient for twenty-four hours of sustained warmth.

He was still trying to figure out what sound had wakened him when the camp searchlights came back on, the beams roaming up and down the wire and playing over the huts, light seeping through the blackout shutters and sliding over his fellow *kriegsgefangenen*, or "kriegies" as they called themselves. Idly scratching at the lice in his crotch, he raised his head and took in a lung-full of stale bunkhouse air, slowly exhaling and watching a searchlight beam catch the fog of his breath.

And then he got it. What had wakened him was a new sound, the rumble of faraway thunder. But not thunder. Artillery. And not from the west but from the east. The Russians were coming.

The next day was bright and cold, a high blue sky crossed with the vapour trails of more Allied bombers over the German heartland. After the ritual of morning *Appell* or roll call in the parade square and a great deal of pointing at the sky for the benefit of their captors—the bolder kriegies gesturing to the east and shouting, "Russki Komm,"—one of the British padres stepped forward to remind them of what day it was; and so, on this eleventh day of the eleventh month of 1944, Allied prisoners bowed their heads in a moment of silence for their fallen comrades. *They shall not grow old, as we that are left grow old: Age shall not weary them, nor the years condemn. At the going down of the sun and in the morning / We will remember them.*

After prayers, Al wanted to go back to bed, where he found it was easier to cope with the pangs of hunger, but forced himself to join Harry and Smitty for some stamina-building circuit bashing even though he knew the exercise would give him more of an appetite.

"Ya know, boys," said Smitty after blowing into his hands to keep them warm, "I'm beginning to forget what the old Abort looks like."

The Abort was the lavatory block, two huts down from theirs, a forty-hole version of the outdoor privies many of them knew from home. The pit underneath the forty holes was pumped out every few weeks by "the honey wagon," a large cylindrical tank mounted on a flatbed and pulled by a team of sway-backed horses. POWs quickly learned to make themselves scarce when the wagon came round. The farther away you were from the smell the better off you were. Also, and even more importantly, the less likely it was you would be conscripted into manning the pump that sucked "honey" from the latrine pit into the wagon tank, a gagging, retching job if there ever was one.

"When's the last time you had a crap, Smitty?"

When you lived on a starvation diet, bowel movements were few and far between and thus major events deserving of recognition.

Smitty affected a Western drawl in response to Harry's question. "Why, ah can't rightly say, pardner, but I marked it on the wall beside my bunk and I reckon it was last Monday."

"And today being Saturday that makes it five days since your last dump. That's pretty good, Smitty, but I hear there's a South African in hut six is up to eight days."

"Do tell," said Smitty. "Do tell." He turned to Al. "And you, Sergeant McDougal of the Yukon, when's the last time you had a bowel movement, lad?"

Al clutched the collar of his greatcoat at his throat. "Whenever it was, Smitty, I damn near had heart failure. The biggest rat I've ever seen hanging around to bite my balls."

The Abort was infested with rats and before you sat down to do your business you were well advised to administer a hard kick to the front of the hole to scare off any of the loathsome creatures hanging about. On the day in question, the Algonquin sergeant had forgotten to do so and his revelation brought a song to Smitty's lips, a *Stalag* version of "The Quartermaster's Stores."

"There were rats, rats as big as alley cats, / In the hole, in the hole. / There were rats, rats as big as alley cats in the shitty *Stalag* hole."

They walked on in silence for a bit before Al got talking about his dream and that got them going on a POW's favourite topic. Food fantasies.

Most food fantasies in the camp took the form of grandiose post-war plans having to do with the opening of a restaurant, a bakery, or some form of food supply business. The would-be restaurateurs had worked out elaborate menus, while the bakers could spend hours telling you about the different kinds of breads, rolls and pastries they would offer, fresh daily. Those planning a food supply business were vague on details as to how such a business would operate but very specific in terms of the various and often exotic foods they would market to retailers.

Harry said he was going to settle in Britain and open a restaurant in London specializing in peas and faggots. Al asked what a faggot was.

"You mean you've never eaten a faggot?"

"Not yet, but I've got my eye on you, Smitty."

Smitty blew Al a kiss as Harry explained that faggots were chopped pig livers mixed with seasoning and onions, then rolled into balls and deep fried. Al shook his head.

"You're going to make a living selling peas and pig livers?"

"Absolutely, dear boy, absolutely."

Smitty grinned and circled his index finger by the side of his head.

That evening the stove was the centre of eager attention. Not only was there food to eat, there was fuel for cooking with enough left over to do some serious heating. It was a red-letter day.

But first things first. All the windows were opened to clear the air, the stale musky odour of a company of unwashed bodies and the acrid haze of cigarette smoke.

Once the air inside was freezing fresh, the windows were shut and the stove fired up, this one being a black, cast-iron rectangle standing on end and resting on a tiled floor. There were two fireboxes, one larger one at the bottom for heat and another smaller one at the top for cooking. A metal stovepipe ran from the back of the stove into the wall and then up through to the chimney. It was just such a stove that had camouflaged the trap door leading into the shaft of a tunnel named "Harry."

The fuel had been dumped in a huge pile outside the hut by the goons that afternoon, bits and pieces of leather from the tops of shoes, leftovers from the death camps. If you looked closely you could see eyelets and the remains of buckles. Evidently Jerry believed in the old adage, *Waste not, want not*.

If the POWs had European Jewry to thank for hot food and warmth on this Remembrance Day, they had Russian slave labourers to thank for their food. Cigarettes for potatoes. Thirty spuds in all and all of them unfit for human consumption.

Al shook his head remembering Dougie Dobson's father and his potato harvests, dusty burlap bags full of only the best, any bruised or soft ones separated out and saved for pig swill.

When their thirty pig-swill potatoes were boiled and carefully sliced, there was enough for one mushy piece per man. Spread with a little margarine one of the lads had been hoarding, each man's ration was nibbled slowly to preserve the sensation as long as possible. Licking his fingers, Allan McDougal imagined his ancestors pushing back from the table, one step ahead of the famine.

The conversation that night was about the body found floating in the fire pool that morning, the third in the last ten days. No one was saying very much except the obvious. These were no accidents. None of the three had gone for a skate on thin ice.

It was pointed out that each time a body was found, Jerry came and quietly took it away, no fuss, no bother. There was no special *Appell*, no complaint from the Allied POW command, no nothing. The consensus was that the floaters could not sing "When the swallows come back from Kapuskasing." But the question was how come there were so many of them so often.

It seemed that the potatoes had been a harbinger of good dietary things to come because the next day's soup had meat in it. Maggots.

Al thought back to the last Christmas the Lowvert little league of nations had been together and Billy's dad talking about curing meat in the sun at Slaughterhouse Lake, stringing up the sides of beef in a screened-in hut the way the Indians had taught him, and how careful you had to be to ensure it didn't get maggoty; but even if it did, some camp cooks swore on a stack of Bibles that there was no finer tasting dish than meat boiled with maggots.

As he skimmed God's little creatures, well boiled and white, from the soup in his mess tin and sipped what was left, Al thought the cooks were right. It wasn't half bad.

That afternoon, at mail call, he got his first parcel from home. Using his initial issue of German postcard forms, he had written to his wife and his parents on his second day at *Stalag* 8C to let them know he was safe and sound, short breezy notes so as not to worry the recipients or the German censors.

To Beth he had written on a card labelled *Kriegsgefangenenlager*, "Hope you and the wee (ha!) lad are well. Am fine myself. Getting fat and lazy here. Do a lot of sleeping and reading. Hope to hold you in my arms soon. Give Sandy Jr. a hug for me. Lots of love, Al."

On another *Kriegsgefangenenlager* he'd pencilled a similar note to his parents. "I am fine and contented and looking forward to the day we can sit together on the front steps and watch the sun go down on Ames Lake. Have lots of new friends here but don't let my old friends in Lowvert forget me. Keep smiling and your chins up and DON'T WORRY about me. All my love, Allan."

The parcel was in response to his cards and the contents the work of many hands. Thick wool socks. Three pair. Brown, gray and navy. Beth's knitting. Two were set aside for personal use by Hounam, Anderson & McDougal Co., Ltd., and the other for in-house bartering.

Underneath the socks were his father's contributions. Cigarettes and chocolate bars. Neilsen's Jersey Milk. Five of them.

Because their guards would damn near offer to shoot *Der Führer* for a chocolate bar, Al wanted to reserve all five to trade, but Smitty persuaded him to set two aside for their hutmates. He told Al he was thinking of Christmas.

Wrapped in tissue paper was a navy blue knit toque and a wool vest also in navy blue, along with gloves, two pair, hand-knit, one pair in thick brown wool and the other in wool of many different colours—navy blue, brown, green and yellow.

Al smiled as he held the technicolour gloves up for his comrade's inspection. Smitty whistled.

"Very original."

"Very my mother. I grew up with gloves like this. Whatever wool was left over was used for gloves." Waste not, want not was a cross-cultural thing.

Al handed Smitty one pair of gloves and Smitty told him to keep the other pair and the vest. The toque went to Harry, which left the rest of the company without headgear, but Smitty said not to worry, that would be taken care of.

In the evening the BBC News brought tidings of great joy. The battle for the Scheldt was over. Thanks to the First Canadian Army the water route to Antwerp was open and now that the Allies' supply problem had been licked, Eisenhower was predicting the Nazis were on the ropes. The British padre led them in three cheers for the "Caneyedians." Hip, hip, hurrah! Hip, hip, hurrah! Hip, hip, hurrah!

Roosevelt had won his fourth term as president of the United States, Russia had renounced its neutrality pact with Japan and, somewhere off the coast of Norway, the RAF had sunk the German battleship *Tirpitz*. Harry led them in three cheers for Roosevelt, Stalin and the good old RAF. Hip, hip, hurrah! Hip, hip, hurrah! Hip, hip, hurrah!

As November slid toward December, a routine settled in, a routine that chipped away at morale, a little bit here, a little bit there.

Every day they were fed rumours of food, Red Cross parcels arriving momentarily. But they never did.

Every day the camp tannoys or loudspeakers broadcast enemy propaganda, excited proclamations of new weapons—V3 rockets that could reach America and aircraft that flew faster than the speed of sound—planting seeds of doubt among some of the prisoners some of the time, even those like Smitty, who claimed the Nazi News was total bullshit.

Then there were the repeated and earnest enemy entreaties that made a lot of sense to some kriegies—entreaties urging America and the Commonwealth to join Germany in the fight against their common enemy: Bolshevism.

Arguments ensued. And fist fights. When you lived cheek to jowl with ninety-nine other guys from whom there was no escape—a prison within a prison—it didn't take long before molehills became mountains. Politics aside, one man might hold his cigarette between his thumb and forefinger and eventually that would infuriate another man. Or one man might have a habit of clearing his throat every time he spoke. Another might be in love with the sound of his own voice and never use ten words when 110 would do. Yet another might laugh too loudly. Or shout in his sleep. Or pass gas, a truly rotten-smelling fart that in the good old days would have been the occasion for much mirth.

Each and every day there was the personal battle to stay warm and to keep as clean as possible. There were no showers or baths in the compound, only a long, galvanized trough with one cold-water tap for 500 men.

Each and every day was a battle against lice and loneliness and a fear that wore a dozen different faces. There was fear of what the future would bring. Would they end up in the hands of the Russkies who shot their own? Or the Nazis who, when the end for Germany finally came, might do unto the kriegies as they had done unto so many others—Jews, Gypsies, Jehovah's Witnesses, homosexuals and the mentally retarded?

There was also the fear of getting sick, in their weakened state, succumbing to anything that came along. In the week after Remembrance Day there was an outbreak of diphtheria in one of the huts and all of them had to be inoculated. Marched to the camp hospital in the *Vorlager* they were ordered to take off their pants and move down the assembly line of German medical orderlies, the first swabbing a bare thigh with alcohol, the second jabbing in the hypodermic needle, the third hooking up a vial of serum to the needle, the fourth injecting the serum and the fifth removing the needle.

The fear of physical illness was often outweighed by the fear of going *Stalag*-happy. Different men reacted to the stress of POW life in different ways. It wasn't unusual to see men talking to themselves, sometimes furtively, sometimes in lengthy animated conversations, or a big tough guy in his bunk sobbing like a baby. And there was the occasional suicide, men who had reached the end of their tether, rushing the wire, inviting the goons to shoot them. The goons always obliged.

Al figured they were all *Stalag*-happy. More or less. Had to be. It was just that some were more happy than others.

He was beginning to understand what had driven Hauptmann Kaputt at Camp Q, indeed any man who was ever locked behind bars or wire. The planning that went into an escape, the digging of tunnels, the manufacture of primitive weapons and tools, the forging of documents, the gathering of food, the making of civilian dress, the production of maps—all the cloak-and-dagger preparations that went into an operation—was almost more important than escape itself because it gave everyone something to do, everyone something to believe in, everyone something to live for.

But in the early days of December 1944 there was none of this to sustain the lads at *Stalag* 8C. First of all, it was winter and no time to be traipsing about on the other side of the wire leaving footprints in a cold and foreign land.

That was the main reason the powers that be were not authorizing any excursions to the countryside, that together with diet and the winding down of the war. Because of starvation rations the chances that men would have the energy to make good on an escape were virtually nil. Furthermore, given that the war would soon be over, it was probably a good idea to stay put. Better the devil you knew and all that.

The sense that no one was going anywhere was obviously shared by the ferrets, the Third Reich equivalent of the scouts at Camp Q. At *Stalag* 8C the ferrets wore black, belted coveralls, carried flashlights and what looked like long screwdrivers. The first time Al saw one of these goons he thought he was looking at a camp electrician. It was Smitty who put him right.

"You saw a ferret. That's the name we give to the goons who ferret around trying to catch us doing things were not supposed to be doing. *Verboten* things."

"Escaping would be one of those *verboten* things?"

"Hey, you're pretty smart for a Northerner!" Smitty spoke with mock surprise.

"That's why the flashlight. For crawling around under the huts looking for suspicious piles of dirt. And what you thought was a screwdriver is a probe. Ya know, like sticking a toothpick into a chocolate cake to make sure it's done. Except the ferrets are making sure that underneath the dirt there's no wooden slab covering any tunnel shaft."

Al nodded and told Smitty about the scouts at Camp Q. But unlike the Monteith scouts, the *Stalag* ferrets always seemed to be bored to tears. He mentioned this to Smitty one day when the two of them were entering their hut after some circuit bashing and looked up to see the spitting image of Ichabod Crane, a ferret so stupid they called him "Mortimer Snerd," idly walking up and down the rows of bunks using his probe to direct a desultory poke under the palliasses of the top bunks as he passed by.

"Yeah, they're bored all right. They know there's nothing going on. Nothing serious anyway." Then Smitty whispered something to Al, who looked up at Mortimer and grinned.

While Al manoeuvred the ferret to the back of the hut, where he took his time in transferring two Sweet Caporals from his pocket to Mortimer's, Smitty busied himself at the hut entrance, so that when Mr. Snerd opened the door to leave, a strategically placed tin of sardine oil was dumped all over his head.

Smitty was nowhere to be seen at the time and Al was hiding behind a bunk shaking with laughter. For the first time in months.

Morale was given a bit of a boost in the second week of December when the *Stalag* 8C Christmas Lice Race was announced. On the chosen day, the camp stove was lifted off its tile base to free up space for a racetrack and lice were plucked from underarm and pubic hair where the conditions for optimum growth were most favourable. For lice racing, bigger was better. Easier to see.

One Canadian whose nickname was "Turp" proudly displayed a louse that was at least an eighth of an inch long. Turp said the louse's name was "Leaping Louse Louise." Because of her size, Louise quickly became the favourite.

Asked why "Louise," Turp replied that it was only the female of the species that sucked your blood, and given how big Louise was, her sex was obvious. When Harry suggested he was getting lice mixed up with mosquitoes, Turp winked and said it was true of all insects, animals, mammals, birds, fish, snakes and ladders as well as *Homo sapiens*. It was *always* the females who were the bloodsuckers. Turp would brook no argument.

But in the end, Turp was the only one to rally to the cause of female names. Other racing lice were resolutely masculine: "Armpit Art," or "Pubic Phil," "Larry Louse," or just plain "Hairy."

Two lice were raced at a time. As soon as bets were down—so many cigarettes on Louise, so many on Hairy, or whoever—the lice were positioned on the tile's start line.

When the official starter yelled "Go!" a lit cigarette was placed in close proximity to a louse derrière. The first louse to be thereby persuaded to cross the finish line was declared the winner.

Euphoria from the lice races and thoughts of Christmas kept their spirits up for a good number of days, as did reports that a still was operating somewhere in the camp and there would be enough Kickapoo Joy Juice around to make the festive season a joy for everyone in Dogpatch. And this time, more credence was being given to the rumours of Red Cross parcels. Santa's bag was said to be full of them.

All in all it was promising to be a grand old time of eating, drinking and making merry. According to Smitty the only thing missing was a Mary to make. So when Hitler's Great Blow hit the Americans in the Ardennes it really took the wind out of their sails.

The first news of the German offensive was broadcast with great fanfare from the camp tannoy during morning *Appell* on December 17. The goons who had sullenly put up with jibes about the Russians coming and churlishly endured fingers pointing to the vapour trails of Allied bombers now got their own back and they did it with kicks and rifle butts and grinning taunts, "Churchill *Kaputt*" and "Roosevelt *Schweinehund* Jew."

Even Mortimer Snerd got his licks in. As the prisoners broke from *Appell*, the tall, lanky ferret made a point of coming up to Smitty and jabbing his probe up under the Riley's chin.

"I know you are believing I am much stupid, *Kanadisch*." His Adam's apple was bobbing as he spoke. "But I am not more stupid than you think."

And with a knowing smirk and firm nod of his head, Mortimer took his leave. He did not hear Smitty's *sotto voce*, "Oh yes you are, arsehole."

The German offensive was designed to split the Allied armies and recapture the port of Antwerp. In the first few days it succeeded brilliantly. Even the nightly BBC News acknowledged it to be so.

Seventeen German divisions supported by artillery and Royal Tiger tanks attacked along an eighty-five-mile-long front, pushing the outnumbered and inexperienced American defenders back and back until the line on the battle maps ballooned some sixty-five miles westwards, giving the action a configuration and its name. The Battle of the Bulge.

The battle featured a few Jerries familiar to the inmates of *Stalag* 8C. Harry Hounam's old friend from the Battle of the Scheldt, Colonel Friedrich Von der Heydte, led paratroop drops behind the American lines, spreading fear and rumours of other drops deep into Belgium and even into France.

And the murderers of 156 Canadian prisoners of war—the 12th SS Hitler Youth Division minus the butcher of L'Abbaye Ardenne, Kurt Meyer, who had been captured by Belgian partisans in early September—were out in force and up to their old tricks.

But it was other SS units under the command of *Obersturmbannführer* Joachim Peiper who were the most savage.

The patrician Peiper, blond and blue-eyed, came from an old German family, a long line of proud and distinguished military officers. He was described by those who knew him as educated and sophisticated. He was known to speak fluent English and had a good sense of humour. When the Battle of the Bulge was over, troops under his command had murdered 353 helpless American prisoners of war and 111 innocent Belgian civilians.

Near the town of Malmédy, eighty-six American POWs from Battery B of the 285th Field Artillery Observation Battalion were led to a snow-covered field by Peiper's soldiers, lined up, and mowed down with Schmeissers and MG 34s. When the firing stopped, officers roamed among the bodies checking to make certain no one was left to tell any tales. One of the favoured ways of doing this was to laughingly kick the fallen in the balls. If there was any reaction, the stricken GI was put out of his misery with a shot to the head.

Two days after Malmédy, Peiper's brave and fearless troopers shot and killed eight more POWs and ninety-three Belgian civilians near the village of Stavelot—men, women and children—the children because the supermen of the Third Reich became annoyed with the tears of little boys and little girls.

Once word of Malmédy and Stavelot got around, the last days of the Battle of the Bulge, and the rest of the war for that matter, saw a precipitous decline in the number of SS prisoners taken by the Americans.

At *Stalag* 8C, work on Christmas preparations proceeded with one eye on the wall beside the stove and the other on the table in front of it. On the wall was a hand-drawn map of western Germany, France, Belgium and Luxembourg. Here, each evening after the BBC News, the fortunes of war in the Bulge were charted using crayon markings—red dots for the attacking Germans, blue for the defending Yanks. In the early days the map looked like it had measles.

On the table were the ingredients for the much-anticipated POW Christmas cake, bits and pieces of stale *Stalag* black bread, crumbled and mixed with powdered milk. All this was watered and left to soak until it was soggy enough to form something resembling dough.

A lack of baking powder stumped the chefs for a bit until someone hit upon the idea of using Jerry-issued tooth powder. It worked like the real thing. Mainly because it *was* the real thing. Almost.

The cake was put in the oven when the German siege of Bastogne was in its sixth day. About the same size as Lowvert, Bastogne was a market town in Belgium where seven paved roads fanned out in all directions, many of them key routes to Antwerp. For this reason, the Germans had to have it and the Americans had to hold it.

The cake was baked in four mess tins, two serving as cake pans and the other two as pan tops. When it came out of the oven, Al understood why Smitty had wanted to keep two bars of Jersey Milk out of the barter pool. The cake was iced with chocolate bar shavings on the day the tannoy announced that the number of cowardly American soldiers who had surrendered to the brave Grenadiers of the Third Reich was 7,000. With more to come.

Once the cake was sprinkled with "nuts"—the kernels from prune pits—it was ready for display with the understanding it was hands off until Christmas Eve, when the BBC reported that the defenders of Bastogne had received an ultimatum from the commander of the German armoured units surrounding the town. "There is only one possibility to save your encircled troops from total annihilation and that is the honourable surrender of the town."

The ultimatum was delivered to the commander of the U.S. forces holding Bastogne, Brigadier General Anthony C. McAuliffe. His reply was "Nuts!"

On Christmas Eve, after Christmas worship and a carol sing, which Allan McDougal refused to attend, fearing memories and sentiment, the cake was cut and distributed. One paper-thin slice per man. Ambrosia. Food for the gods.

At Bastogne, famished Americans were also feasting thanks to a break in the weather permitting C47 cargo planes to drop ammunition, medical supplies and food—red, blue and yellow parachutes like Christmas tree ornaments floating from the winter sky.

Christmas Day was a Northern Ontario December day, bright and crisp and even, just like the home brew, a concoction made from raisins and sugar saved mostly from the Red Cross parcels of summer, long before they had become so few and far between. Foresight is always a wonderful thing.

At the beginning of December, the raisin and sugar mixture had been dumped into a soup barrel filled with water, where it boiled and bubbled for weeks. Harry Hounam said it reminded him of the witches' brew in *Macbeth* and said he wouldn't be surprised if it had similar ingredients. "Eye of newt and toe of frog, / Wool of bat and tongue of dog."

In the days just before Christmas, the sludge of the ferment was strained through a towel and then distilled a second time until it looked a bit like Calvados. There was some concern among the higher-ups of POW command that too much of a good thing could be trouble. Drunken prisoners challenging belligerent goons flush with the arrogance of success in the Ardennes was not something they wished to see. But as there was barely enough of the brew for one swallow per man, and since, as Harry said, one swallow does not a drunk make, there were no problems.

The swallow came in a ceremony before Christmas dinner. Santa had not disappointed. At morning *Appell*, Red Cross parcels were distributed, one parcel to be shared by three men. Al and Harry and Smitty brought their gift back to the hut, where they joined their comrades in raising a cup of kindness, a wee dram of Joy Juice, to family, friends and comrades, the church militant and the church triumphant, the living and the dead.

As Al raised his mug, he thought again about Billy and Yates. Mostly he tried not to think about his pals, but there were times when he couldn't help it. The Algonquins Harry had mentioned, lads who might know somebody who might know somebody who knew the Carrier Platoon, had turned out to be recent reinforcements who had barely got to know the guys in their own sections before they were captured.

He shook his head and joined his comrades in sipping the brew. Immediately the hut erupted in a fit of choking and coughing. Liquid fire.

On Boxing Day, when the kriegies had finished sifting through the BBC and German news reports, they figured out the bodies in the fire pool.

On the first day of the Battle, nine German commando teams led by SS *Obersturmbannführer* Otto Skorzeny began infiltrating American positions wearing captured American uniforms, driving American Jeeps and speaking American English.

They were so successful in spreading disinformation, confusion and fear behind the lines that Eisenhower was surrounded by guards and confined to quarters at Versailles, the Yanks convinced an assassination team was on its way.

At the same time, all over the field of battle, jittery American MPs checked and double-checked for fear that the soldier who said he was a farm boy from Iowa was really a Kraut from Hamburg. Who was Babe Ruth? Who was Mickey Mouse's girlfriend? Who was Betty Grable's latest husband?

And so the mystery of the bodies in the fire pool was solved. They were German commandos masquerading as recent Allied POWs to brush up on their English and North American ways in preparation for the blitzkrieg through the Ardennes.

On the day after Boxing Day units of the 4th Armoured Division of the American Third Army broke through the German lines to link up with the "Battered Bastards of the Bastion of Bastogne."

On New Year's Eve the BBC News reported that Lieutenant General George S. Patton was leading an attack against enemy forces in the north of the Bulge; and late on the afternoon of New Year's Day itself the camp tannoys blared forth an account of a massive *Luftwaffe* attack over Belgium, Holland and northern France. Scores of Allied airfields were "totally annihilated and more than 500 aircraft destroyed."

But that was the last the kriegies heard of the triumphal German offensive in the Ardennes. The air raids were Hitler's last gasp and after January 1, 1945, the Nazi News suddenly began featuring reports from other fronts.

Not that Hounam, McDougal & Smith, Co., Ltd., noticed. The partners now had other things to worry about.

Chapter Twenty-Six

January 8, 1945

At the beginning of the new year the old world was coming to an end and everyone in *Stalag* 8C knew it. Both kriegies and goons.

Apocalyptic signs and heavenly portents were everywhere. When the winter sky was blue and high it was interlaced with more and more vapour trails, more and more B24s and B17s, more and more Halifax and Lancaster bombers dropping death on more and more German cities, rendering buildings into rubble and people into ashes. *Earth to earth, ashes to ashes, dust to dust; in sure and certain hope of the Resurrection to eternal life, through our Lord Jesus Christ.* Or, put another way, *Für euch ist der Krieg zu Ende.*

And the Russkis were indeed coming. Not only was the thunder of artillery from the east getting louder with every passing night, but now in the dark kriegies were able to see the muzzle flashes of the guns on the eastern horizon. And with every passing day the reports brought back by the Russian slave labourers were more and more graphic. Rumours of atrocities on both sides were cheerfully conveyed, demoralized German troops, stampeding in retreat from Poland, shooting prisoners of war and inmates of concentration camps, including women and children, while the invading Russians, drunk on vodka and victory, were raping and then bayoneting all the women they could lay hands on. In this they were but following the dictate of Lenin: "Push out a bayonet. If it strikes fat, push deeper."

The terrible storm signalled by the rumbling artillery and the advent of vengeful hordes from the steppes was driving people westward, German refugees this time, passing by the camp, some walking with their families, some with their cattle, some riding bicycles, some pushing baby carriages or pulling sleds and children's wagons crammed with whatever they could carry through the ice and snow. From time to time the more affluent appeared with horse-drawn wagons and carts filled with household possessions—chairs and tables, beds and mattresses, crates and boxes, trunks and suitcases, squawking chickens perched beside shivering children huddled together with fearful mothers clutching bundled-up babies.

It was a Monday morning and Al was circuit bashing with Smitty and Harry when they stopped to watch in silence, the wire separating them, one group of war victims from another. As he stood there, a spectator at a ghastly parade, Al's memory took him back five years to the Empire in Lowvert watching the

Movietone News, the same scene of frightened people fleeing from a heartless enemy.

But there were different players this time. Then it was the people of Poland running from the descendants of the savage Goths. Now it was the offspring of the savage Goths running from the spawn of Ivan the Terrible.

Sergeant McDougal thought of Private Popovich, wondering if he were still alive, imagining the Pole standing here with him and watching the suffering of the very same people who had torched his homeland a few years before. Al could almost hear Popovich cursing the German refugees, shaking a fist at them, jeering at them, "How you like it, you fuckin' cocksnuckers!"

And suddenly he was himself yelling, shaking both his fists, swearing and jeering in a jumble of German and English.

"'Raus, 'Raus, you *verdammter schweinehunde. Für euch ist der Krieg* just starting. I hope you enjoy every fucking minute of it, me, and Barney and Reggie and Goody, Davy Ross, Dougie Dobson and all the other poor bastards who'll never see Canada again. Fuck you! Fuck every last fuckin' one of you!"

And then he was weeping and Smitty had his arms around him and Harry was dragging both of them away from the goon in the nearest tower whose machine gun had started to swivel toward them.

Back in their hut after calm had been restored they quietly continued their preparations for the inevitable. As Harry had explained it, there were at least 20,000 Allied prisoners in the camps around Sagan and it wasn't bloody likely that Jerry was going to let the Russians liberate and possibly arm that many men. Ergo the POWs were going to be marched away to the west and sooner rather than later.

When he was asked about the buzz going round regarding Jerry's plans for them, that they would all be shot like the fifty lads from *Stalagluft* 3, Harry's matter-of-fact response was chilling but reassuring.

"Are you crazy? It would take them a month of Sundays to kill all of us and believe you me, even if they wanted to, they wouldn't. They know the jig's up. They're not gonna do something obvious like shooting us this close to the end of the war because the same thing would happen to them. Nope, they're gonna march us out of here. And boys, that will be bad enough! Mark my words."

All of their planning for the march out of *Stalag* 8C had been governed by one principal question. What was necessary to survive?

The first and foremost answers were easy. An army on the march in winter, even an army of kriegies, required good boots, a change of socks and warm clothes.

Hounam, McDougal and Smith Co., Ltd., had done its best with the resources available—the parcels from home and skillful bartering—but their success was mixed. Al, for example, had the boots McCafferty had scrounged for him at *Stalag* 12A. They were still in good shape because he had taken care to take good care of them, even more so now when the need was going to be greatest and improvident hutmates were on the lookout for boots left lying about. Al wore his to bed.

Boots he had, but only one pair of real socks, the brown ones Beth had knitted. His other pair were *Stalag* socks, which weren't really socks at all but pieces of grey cloth the texture of a diaper that you wrapped around your feet. They were better than nothing, but not much.

All three of them had greatcoats and all three of them had gloves, thanks to the knitters of Lowvert. Smitty had the brown pair and Al the technicolour, while Harry had traded the navy blue toque for a pair of sheepwool-lined flying gloves to go with his sheepwool-lined flying helmet. When he was all decked out in his travelling duds he looked a bit like an eccentric World War I flying ace all set to do battle with the Red Baron.

For the other members of the Company, headgear was a problem, Smitty and Al reduced to fashioning kerchiefs out of stitched-together foot wrappers, making them look like the female impersonators at the South Alberta Christmas party in Maresfield in 1943.

If good boots and warm clothing were the first essentials of an army on the march in winter, then food was a close second. The more enterprising among them had been hoarding food for some time now, damned hard to do given how little they had. But self-denial and shrewd bartering had left a few of them with a fair collection of tinned goods from Red Cross parcels—salmon, sardines, corned beef and cheese, along with hard biscuits, dried apples and prunes. However, most of them would have to make do with a lot less.

By mid-January the lads who'd made the Christmas Cake were well into the production of their very own version of the foodcakes every red-blooded Canadian schoolboy knew was a North American Indian tradition: pemmican.

Made from dried meat, pounded and mixed with fat and berries and anything else at hand, pemmican was for natives and *coureurs des bois* alike, a staple of Canada's early days. Crow had once made some for the little league and Al remembered the wild meat taste, a little like moose meat he thought, but Crow told him it was beaver.

Stalag pemmican was a product of Red Cross parcels from Canada, a meatless version of the original, there being no bear, beaver or moose in the POW camp. It consisted of black bread crumbs mixed with Klim powdered milk and shaved Jersey Milk chocolate, Atlas raisins, and prunes (pitted). Melted margarine was poured over all these ingredients to form a paste that when pressed into little bars and cooled, looked like a plug of chewing tobacco. According to those who taste-tested the first lot, there were also other similarities.

But whatever the flavour, *Stalag* pemmican was supposed to be nourishing and one could pack a lot of it without sacrificing much room, another concern of an army on the march. If you should take only what you could comfortably carry, then what exactly did you take and what did you leave behind?

Some solved the problem by refusing to make the hard decisions, fashioning large knapsacks and stuffing them with all their kriegie possessions together with as much food as they could get their hands on. Others hammered together sleds made from bunkboards, some of them complete with runners bottomed in tin. These too were packed to overflowing.

But the Company decided to travel light, guessing that knapsacks and sleds would only serve to sap strength from men who had none to spare. They would take pemmican, tea, and as many cigarettes as they could stuff into one carrying sack for all three of them, the sack a leg of Russian long johns tied tightly at the ankle.

The cigarettes were a necessity, if not for personal use, then certainly for bartering. There was a big market for Canadian smokes in Germany and the Company figured they could trade fags for food when they ran out of pemmican.

The sack also contained some of their personal stuff—letters, photos, Harry's Bible, Smitty's rabbit's foot, their mess tins, spoons, razors and shaving soap.

Harry insisted they shave every day they were on the road. "Good for the soul," he said. What he really meant was that it was a form of self-discipline, something that would go a long way to ensure their survival.

The pampered kriegies in *Stalagluft 3* were the first out, on Groundhog Day, professional courtesy, thanks to fat Hermann Göring, the *Luftwaffe* chief of many medals, who had a soft spot in his heart for fly boys no matter their nationality. The scuttlebutt was that the airmen were sent west by rail and there was much muttering among the PBI about preferential treatment. None of the mutterers seemed to remember their own experience of rail passenger service in Germany, the quality leaving much to be desired.

It was a good thing the PBI had prepared themselves to leave on a moment's notice because that was all they were given. Six days after the departure of the air force, the army kriegies were awakened at 0400 hours by goons they had never seen before, soldiers in grey-green anoraks, the lightning bolt insignia on their helmets, Hitler's nasty boys with rifles at the ready, bursting into the huts banging rifle butts on bunkbeds and shouting "'*Raus! 'Raus! Schnell machen!*"

Since the middle of January it had been so cold in the hut that they all slept fully winterized, coats and scarves and mitts and toques and boots on, so when the shouts came in the early hours of February 8, no one had to get dressed to go out.

But some were slower than others at coming awake, tumbling out of their bunks, getting their bearings and grabbing their packs. These men paid a price. They were punched and kicked, some even beaten about the shoulders with truncheons.

Once outside, the prisoners took their places on the parade ground in the face of a biting wind driving a pellet snow across the searchlight beams lighting up the fog of their breath. The weather had the look and feel of a coming blizzard and it was very cold, Al guessing it to be about fifteen degrees below zero.

It had been his turn that night to sleep with the sack of their belongings and now he lowered it from his shoulder to the ground between his legs, blowing into his cupped hands and then digging into his coat pocket for his footwrapper kerchief. Flipping the wrapper over his head, he tied the ends firmly under his chin. Then he hooked up the collar of his greatcoat and tucked his kerchief ends inside before putting on his gloves to join his comrades in the stamping of feet and swinging of arms, the universal exercises of men trying to keep warm.

This was the only movement the kriegies were allowed to make for the next eight endless hours and it wasn't long before Al's wounded shoulder was aching from the rhythmic arm swinging. The grumbling in the restless ranks grew louder when some of the lads tried to light up and their cigarettes were knocked from their mouths by cursing SS troopers. *Rauchen verboten!*

The cold and the menace of their wary guards gradually imposed a silence that was spooky and, to Al, puzzling until he identified what noise was missing: the nightly serenade of shunting freight cars, the screech of steel wheels on steel rails and the rapid chug-chug-chug of locomotives getting up to speed. The Sagan rail yards were quiet as a tomb.

It wasn't until just before noon and they were damn near frozen stiff that their wait came to an end with the arrival of their regular guards and a surprising announcement, "*Achtung, achtung! Rotes Kreuz, Rotes Kreuz!*"

The gratitude of the prisoners lost some of its oomph when it was learned that one Red Cross parcel had be shared among three kriegies. When Harry handed him theirs, Al knew there wasn't enough room in the Company sack for anything more, so he told Smitty to open the parcel and divvy up selected tins among their various pants and coat pockets.

They were in the middle of doing this when the order came to move out. *Fertig machen!*

It took them—500 kriegies, five abreast—half an hour to straggle clear of the *Vorlager* gates, thirty minutes of putting one foot in front of the other before their toes started to tingle with circulating blood.

At five abreast, the Company found itself expanded to include two Brits, a glider pilot captured at Arnhem and the padre who had led their prayers on November 11. Once through the gates and about halfway up the rise leading west, all five of them turned, as if on cue, to look back on the dreadful place that had been their life—the goon boxes, the wire, and row upon row of dreary unpainted huts, some of which were now on fire, burning hard and fast in the wind, an act of defiance, an "Up yours, Gerald!" from departing guests.

Not every voice was raised to join the ragged cheer when word of the flames spread. Those who saw the march as an adventure or a taste of freedom after months and sometimes years of captivity were happy to give the raspberry to *Stalag* 8C. But others had a perverse fondness for what had been their family home and viewed the march with a certain foreboding. Despite all the shittiness of the camp—the cold and hunger and dirt, the breakdowns, sickness and death—it was a known place, a familiar place, where strong and durable friendships had been forged in the fires of hardship. And now, out in the cold, literally and figuratively, these prisoners were at best apprehensive; at worst, scared to death.

When the Company topped the rise, breathing hard from the long, slow climb, and just before the first trees of the pine forest, they saw that the ditches on either side of the road were strewn with flotsam and jetsam—furniture, baby carriages, cooking grates, a crate of dishes, an open suitcase spilling dresses and women's underwear—discards left in the roiling wake of German refugees now joined with kriegie knapsacks and sleds, cast-off blankets, clothing and food, mostly Red Cross tinned butter, margarine and powdered milk, all of it thrown away.

This was the detritus of failed hopes, the expectorate leftover from biting off more than one could chew. It was obvious that the place of all these leavings was a mount of revelation, the point where reality tapped you on the shoulder, refugees and kriegies alike, the height of land where the eyes of all were opened and they could see clearly what was really necessary for salvation and what wasn't. What possible use was a can of powdered milk on a forced march in the middle of winter?

Al saw one of the kriegies from his hut, a man he remembered clothing himself in a vest and two bulky sweaters underneath his greatcoat, now struggling to divest himself of the vest and one of the sweaters. It wasn't that the man was too warm; he was too weighed down. He was just one of the many from *Stalag* 8C who also left their mark on the hill.

But not everyone was a convert to reality. Smitty shook his head and pointed at the lads stooping to gather food and clothing, sleds and packs, stuff that others had just abandoned. It was a case of those who through force of circumstance or poor planning had left the camp with too little, seeing their chance to cash in on those who had finally seen the folly of leaving with too much.

After the hill, the column was through the tree line, and all kriegies were grateful for the sheltering pines, nature's windbreaks against the blowing snow. Soon they fell into the familiar rhythm of the route march, their eyes fixed on the five pairs of boots in front of them, watching the snow flicking off soles, keeping a lookout for the icy patches formed by the weight of all the other marchers who had gone before, and the break in the ranks when a man's feet slipped out from under him.

They quickly learned that a fallen man was fair game for a kick or a rifle butt so any man on his ass was instantly hoisted to his feet and dragged along by his comrades, down and up in one fluid motion.

Yet all too soon their weakness showed. Men on starvation rations with not even a smidgen of breakfast in their bellies had little stamina for a route march and by mid-afternoon, the pleas for a rest were echoing up and down the column.

Their guards paid no attention, prodding them on, threatening to shoot anyone who failed to keep pace. *'Raus! 'Raus!* Russki Komm!

When darkness came, a cold winter blackness reminding Al of Lowvert in January, playing road hockey under the street lights, waiting to be called in for a hot supper, the column was out of the woods and circling a small town, smoke from chimneys rising straight up in the now windless night. About halfway round the town, the five men in the Company felt the pace slowing and the ranks in front of them bunching up. At long last, they were stopping.

Their first night on the road was spent on the grounds of a soccer pitch fenced with a high brick wall topped with broken glass. This and the cold, together with a fatigue that sucked marrow from bones, was enough to discourage those who just hours ago had been bravely speaking of escaping that very night.

The Company set themselves down in a corner of the pitch, up against the brick, huddled around a small fire set deep in the intersection of the two walls as far away from the goons as they could get. The fire was fuelled with twigs and bits of wood that Harry, in his wisdom, had thrust upon them in their *tour de forêt*.

As the flames got going, socks came off wet feet and were held by the fire to dry. The glider pilot produced a miniature combination stove and kettle he'd fashioned from three powdered milk tins soldered together. The two bottom tins, punctured here and there to provide a draft, constituted the stove and soon the cleanest snow they could find had melted to a boil in the top tin kettle. They sipped their tea as hot as they could bear it and shared a tin of sardines and half a biscuit each. Their first and only meal of the day.

After supper they slept, huddled together for warmth like puppies in a basket. Just before he drifted off, the padre, curled up behind Al, tapped him on the shoulder and asked if he could find room in the sack for his bottle of communion wine. Al said sure and good night in the same breath.

In the morning they were wakened by the shouting of their SS guards, "*Fertig machen! Fertig machen!*"

But getting ready to march after a cold night on hard ground, even for the PBI who were somewhat used to it, wasn't easy. Legs had to be persuaded to move but not before feet were cajoled back to life. Some had made the mistake the night before of taking their wet boots off to let them dry out. By morning the boots were leather popsicles. On Harry's instructions the Company had changed their socks before the evening meal and put their boots back on. This was the reason they were able to leave the stadium in their boots while others were forced to march in sock feet.

As far as Al could tell from the angle of the sun on this second day, a clear day after yesterday's storm, the column was headed in a southwesterly direction, some said toward Dresden. At mid-morning the suddenly merciful guards gave them a ten-minute rest, which Harry insisted they use to shave. With a nod to the padre Smitty told Harry to fuck himself, they were going to eat first, a bite of pemmican, a piece of Red Cross cheese and some cold tea saved from supper the night before.

In the afternoon they passed frozen bodies in the ditches, the blue and white striped clothing of Russians from the work camps, the *arbeits lager*. Kriegies who got a close look insisted the Russkis had all been shot.

That night they were herded into a farmyard and hived off, most into the large barn, but some into other outbuildings, the Company in the empty pigsty, a long, low hut separated into pens with a floor of mud and dirty straw, Red Cross parcel food rationed out for supper. There was no tea in the pigpen because there was no water in the pigpen. The pump was broken.

The next day the column marched past a barbed wire enclosure, a vast space eerily empty except for a number of horse-drawn wagons and military vehicles—one or two Volkswagen Jeeps, a few trucks and about a half dozen *Schützenpanzerwagens*. These semi-tracked carriers, a larger version of the Canadian Bren carriers, were used to ferry *panzer* grenadiers into battle alongside their tanks.

It was obvious there had once been buildings behind the wire; the kriegies could easily make out foundations and what remained of structures that had been bulldozed away, a fallen chimney, scattered piles of bricks, bits and pieces of long boards, shattered a yellow-white where they had been torn and twisted from walls, evidence that the place had been flattened not all that long ago.

When the Company passed by they couldn't see any grenadiers about and Smitty speculated that the stench from the enclosure had driven the Jerries to abandon their vehicles in search of breathable air. No one could figure out just what the god-awful smell was but the explanation that came the closest to pinning it down was that the place had been a rendering plant, a factory where aging horses were boiled into glue. No one asked why a glue factory would need to be surrounded by barbed wire.

After several nights of sleeping in barns and more often in the open in the middle of farmers' fields, their accomodations improved near the town of Lübben, where they were billeted in a Lutheran church. It was here that Al saw a ghost with his arm around a limping Jesus Christ.

That night in the church, the 500 dirty and disheveled worshippers, Christ Eaters and Song Singers alike, had offered diffident praise to God for a half-decent place to lay their bodies, which were everywhere—on and under pews, in the organ loft, in the choir, on the steps leading up to the pulpit and behind the communion rail in the sanctuary. One man was even sleeping on the altar itself, giving the communion table the appearance of a sarcophagus, the carved stone body of an ancient divine resting on top to mark the place of his earthly remains underneath.

The Company had been one of the last to get in and were slumped around a big stone font in an alcove near the front door, where they picked through what was left of the pemmican, stifling the urge to eat every last crumb that remained. But *carpe diem* wasn't such a hot idea in these circumstances.

Professor Hounam, shorn of his greatcoat but with his flying helmet still on his head, swept an arm toward the altar and proceeded to deliver a lecture on what a vicious anti-Semite Martin Luther was and how this explained Hitler and the Jews. His class of four were too tired to pay him any attention.

Al looked around at the interior of the church, feeling it warming up with the body heat of his fellow marchers. He wondered how long they could keep going. The column that had started off from *Stalag* 8C in step, "left-right-left" was now like an accordion, sometimes bunching up, sometimes opening up until a mile separated the front ranks from the stragglers in the rear. He figured it was only a matter of time before men began dropping out and there was no doubt in his mind what the SS would do with those who did.

He was repacking the Company sack when he looked up at the sound of the entrance door creaking open and admitting the ghost with Jesus.

The ghost was Willy Yates, who was a lot thinner than he was when Al had last seen him but still recognizable. It was Billy who took Al's breath away and stung his eyes with tears.

Billy's once sturdy fire hydrant frame was skeletal, his battleblouse and filthy pants hanging from him as if his body were a clothes tree. His head was drooping, his face bearded and drawn, the image of Christ in agony on the cross. "*Eli, Eli, la'ma sabach-th'ni?*" *which being translated is to say, "My God, my God, why hast thou forsaken me?"*

But when Willy noticed Al and bent to speak to Billy, his head came up and when he saw his chum from Lowvert, his cracked lips broke into a trembling smile that broke Allan McDougal's heart. *And behold, the veil of the temple was rent in twain from the top to the bottom.*

First Al hugged Billy, not hard, because Billy was as light as a feather and Al had the feeling if he squeezed too tightly his friend would break in two. When he turned to embrace Yates, his wet face next to Willy's wet face, he clung to the American, much as he had after the sinking of the *Caribou.* Neither of them spoke. Both of them stepped back from each other at the same time, both of them attentive to Billy, getting him bedded down on a pew, Al taking off his greatcoat and draping it over his friend's shivering body.

It was only then that he spoke to Yates, telling him there was a water tap in the sacristy. While Willy went off for water, Al went in search of the glider pilot's stove to make some tea. As it was brewing he had another idea and made his way over to the padre to get his permission.

When he returned he reached into the Company sack for the communion wine and poured a bit into a tin cup, handing it to Yates, who lifted Billy's head and gave him a sip. *The Blood of our Lord Jesus Christ, which was shed for thee, preserve thy body and soul unto everlasting life: Drink this in remembrance that Christ's Blood was shed for thee and be thankful.*

When Billy drifted off in a fitful sleep, Yates told Al their story.

The two of them had ended up in *Stalag* 4B on the east bank of the Elbe River just northwest of Dresden, where they had volunteered to work in the woods, Billy's idea, more chances to escape.

As it turned out they did escape, not through working but by playing, a hockey game on a creek running through the forest lot where they were cutting trees. The game was arranged for the noon break of a workday, kriegies against their good-natured keepers, older men like the veterans in Canada's Home Guard, fatherly types who took them to work, watched over them with an indulgent eye and brought them home again after work, their craving for Canadian smokes and Canadian chocolate satisfied for another day.

There not being enough skates to go around, Billy suggested that while others played, he and Yates would gather wood for a fire to keep the players warm in between shifts. This was hailed as a splendid idea by the guards and soon there was a good-sized bonfire roaring on the banks of the creek, a fire that required more and more wood from farther and farther away.

Jerry didn't notice that Billy and Yates did not return from their last foray into the forest. Their absence was covered by other kriegies who kept the fire blazing and managed to fake the cursory head count after the game. It wasn't until end-of-the-workday *Appell* that the two Algonquins were missed and even then it took three counts to get it. By that time they were long gone.

It was dark when they came out of the woods into cultivated land, the frozen stubble of last fall's corn crop in the fields. With the aid of a bright moon, the North Star and farm fences, they found the river. It was Yates who guessed that German farms along the Elbe would be no different from Canadian farms along the St. Lawrence, the homestead would be a strip of land running up from the water. Therefore, if they followed the fences west, they would eventually come to the Elbe.

It was one thing to find the river, another to cross it. Any bridge would be well guarded, and the prospect of running the ice floes like Eliza and her baby in *Uncle Tom's Cabin* was not all that appealing. So they would look for a boat or a raft, something they couldn't do in broad daylight, and since it was getting on toward the rising of the sun they had to find somewhere to hole up to wait for it to go down again.

The best they could do was to burrow under the roots of some alders along the riverbank. The only food they had was what they could carry without raising suspicions—a few tins of this and that, bully beef, sardines, raisins, some biscuits and two Jersey Milk bars.

At dusk they came out of their burrow like a pair of muskrats and began searching the shore, slow going as they stumbled over roots and slipped on jagged slabs of ice. They thought of themselves as lucky fellows when they came upon a broken-down boathouse and found two skiffs tied up inside. One was stove through but the other looked like it had possibilities. It wasn't until they were in the middle of the river, rowing hard, that they discovered the wish was father of the thought.

Yates didn't know if the boat started to leak all of a sudden or had been leaking steadily since they'd launched it but by the time they were at the point of no return on the wide and fast-flowing Elbe, it was clear they would have to swim for it.

Yates said that this was the beginning of the end for Billy. They both survived the ice-cold water, minus their boots, their food and all their winter clothing, dumped so they wouldn't sink like a stone, but once on shore, exhausted and freezing, Yates could see that the dam had burst. Billy's fierce heart that had defied death and horror, fear and degradation, and had sneered at months of wire, lice and dirt, cold and malnutrition, had finally been gnawed away.

The only thing they could do was give themselves up to the first Jerry who came along and that turned out to be an old man on a bicycle riding the shore path, some sort of village bobby armed with a rusty pistol that Yates was sure had not been fired since the days of the Austro-Prussian War.

But instead of turning them in, the bobby took them to his home, a thatched-roof, greystone cottage on the edge of a wood high enough above the water to keep spring floods from reaching the door. There Billy was stripped of his wet clothing, wrapped in several warm blankets and ensconced in a stuffed chair beside the fire, where he was fed hot soup by the policeman's brother, who spoke very good English because he had been a POW in England during World War I.

His name was Walter and, while Billy dozed, he told Willy, himself swathed in a comforter borrowed from a bedroom, how well he had been treated by the English and how he had wanted to stay after the war was over. He said their situation—and here he pointed to himself and his brother as well as to the two Algonquins—was very dangerous. The cottage was not far from a major bridge held by the Hitler *Jugend*, who regularly patrolled the area and if the "little bastards" found the two *Kanadisch* at the cottage all four of them would be executed. He drew his finger across his throat to underline the point.

But when Yates told him he understood and he and Billy would be on their way as soon as their clothes dried, Walter shook his head vehemently.

"*Nein! Nein!* You vill not go!"

He had seen in Billy what Yates had seen. He stood and beckoned the American to the woodbox in the kitchen. Underneath there was a trap door into a root cellar and Walter told him that's where he and Billy would go at the first sign of the *schweinehunde*.

The two of them stayed in the cottage for three days and in the end it wasn't the fear of the *schweinehunde* that forced them to leave. It was Billy's dysentery.

Dysentery was the soldier's sickness. Its symptoms were bloody, with painful and frequent diarrhea followed by dehydration and exhaustion. It was caused by a fighting man's environment, dirt and shit and piss, polluted water, mess tins never properly washed, filthy hands, germs galore.

Dysentery usually cleared up over time when a soldier was strong and healthy to begin with. But it could kill if a soldier was weak and malnourished to begin with.

Billy came down with it the day after the Elbe and it was his necessarily frequent trips to the outhouse that compromised security, this and the times he didn't make it, convincing Yates that they were abusing the brothers' courageous hospitality. It was time to go, time for Walter's brother to turn them in.

Billy was bundled into a pushcart with a bottle of schnapps, a sausage and a loaf of real black bread. The cart and Yates were pointed down the road toward *Stalag* 4G at Oschatz. But not before the American's hand was vigorously shaken by both brothers and Walter had kissed Billy on the forehead after fussing over him like a mother tucking her baby boy into the warm blankets of his carriage.

"There's good in all of us, Al. Those two Jerries risked their lives for us. Didn't have to. I'll never forget them."

Yates had finished his story and was making sure a wheezing Billy was covered on the pew beside them. In the confusion of *Stalags* being emptied, refugees cramming the roads, and the armies of the Third Reich in full retreat, it had taken them five days to find a Jerry to whom they could surrender. By then Billy had a rattle in his chest that Yates was sure was pneumonia.

That night in the church built by followers of the vicious anti-Semite, Martin Luther, their sleep was interrupted by Bomber Command over Dresden, a city the world knew for its delicate porcelain, a metropolis of some 600,000 people swollen to a million by refugees from the East, many of whom had never heard an air-raid warning.

Bombing Dresden was Churchill's idea. Or so it's been said. He wanted to send a message to Stalin, a note of appreciation for Russia's fine effort on the Eastern Front. Allied ground forces might be a bit mired in the mud of the Western Front but there was nothing in the way of Allied air power. Bombing the cities of East Germany would be proof positive to Uncle Joe that the Americans and the English were keeping up their end of the bargain. An added bonus was that the air strikes would also bugger up the transport of German ground forces moving to counter the Russkis in the east.

On the night of February 13 the British dispatched two waves of Lancasters to Dresden, 772 planes dropping 2,656 tons of bombs, seventy-five percent of which were incendiaries. The next day it was the turn of the Americans, 311 B17s or Flying Fortresses delivering 771 tons.

The British incendiaries created a firestorm, a tornado of flame that roared through the old city incinerating everything in its path, Hiroshima before Hiroshima, charred skeletons, buildings and people. The Brits had done to Dresden what Jerry had done to Coventry.

The morning after Dresden was torched, Billy was dead. It was the first day of Lent in the year of our Lord nineteen hundred and forty-five. It was Ash Wednesday.

Remember, man, that thou art dust and unto dust thou shalt return.

Chapter Twenty-Seven

February 14, 1945

Nein!

This was the quick, harsh answer to the padre's request to bury Billy in the churchyard. The Company would build a fire over the site and thaw the frozen ground so they could dig. But the Russkis were still coming and permission was denied.

However, their need to perform some parting ritual was greater than their fear of the shouting guards. Al couldn't remember whose idea it was, he just stood in a stupor and watched as Yates and the rest of the Company, ancient priests of an atavistic and solemn liturgy, stripped Billy of his lice-infested blouse and his shit-stained pants, washed his frail, dirty body with snow and then wrapped it in white linen altar cloths from the sacristy. Tied around his shroud at the neck were his dog tags and a note in German requesting the pastor of the church to bury this brave Canadian soldier. *Bitte.*

The padre led them in a recitation of the Twenty-Third Psalm even as they were driven out the door by the impatient goons, shouts of *Schnell! Schnell!* riding above their quiet murmuring and the padre's strong voice, "Surely thy loving kindness and mercy shall follow me all the days of my life and I will dwell in the house of the Lord forever."

Their penance for the forty days of Lent was more marching, some 250 miles of it, a twisted and twisting pilgrimage of prayer and fasting into the heart of western Germany.

The fasting was involuntary. Both the Red Cross food and the pemmican were long gone and the only sustenance they had was what they could get by hook or by crook.

On the other hand, their prayers were voluntary and mostly imprecatory, calling down the wrath of God upon the goons who guarded the flanks of a flight that, with each successive day, was turning more and more into a Death March as kriegies succumbed to starvation and exhaustion, sickness and the casual cruelty of their SS escorts, who sometimes shot the weak for sport, their favourite targets being men with dysentery rushing to get their pants down by the side of the road.

In ministering to flagging strength and sagging spirits, the British padre used up all his communion wine without ever once celebrating the sacrament according to the rites prescribed by the Church of England.

The route from the church had been toward Leipzig and away from Dresden, probably by design, because rumours of thousands of incinerated German civilians were making the rounds. The further Allied prisoners were removed from the revenge of the *volk* the better off they would be, even though their lower-class status as PBI stood them in good stead. If they'd been fly boys guarded by the SS, the revenge of the *volk* would have been the least of their worries. As it was, the days following the firebombing had been tense and the kriegies had gone out of their way not to antagonize their guards.

Cigarettes sustained them for the first week after Billy's death, currency for the only food the populace had to offer, the ubiquitous German *kartoffel*. For a week the Company ate nothing but these *pommes de terre*, these apples of the earth, mostly raw or boiled, but sometimes roasted and once fried. Nothing was left over, not even a peel. Once more Al thought of the stories of starving Irish ancestors scrabbling for the same survival food a hundred years ago. History was like baked beans. It had a way of repeating on you.

As soon as their smokes ran out they were forced to move farther down the food chain. With the weather warming up, greens had begun to sprout by the side of the road and these were often gathered for supper. Grass and weeds. Salad but no salad dressing.

Once, on the outskirts of Halberstadt, they got lucky when the glider pilot spotted a lump of brown in a garbage dump by the side of the secondary dirt road that snaked its way toward the advancing Americans. The column stayed away from the main highways where any and all traffic would be seen as targets of opportunity for Allied fighter pilots.

The brown lump turned out to be half a loaf of very stale black bread, soggy on the outside but hard as a rock in the centre. Once the muck and mould had been carefully picked off, the Company had a treat for supper. Salad *and* bread. And not just any bread, but bread *a la poubelle*.

When they slept in barns the menu varied, often including corn on the cob, picking out the grime-encrusted cobs from the pig swill, washing them off as best they could and eating them raw. A poor man's corn boil.

Late one afternoon in early March the Company was getting ready to bed down in a hayloft when Smitty spied a nesting hen. Before you could say "cluck cluck" he had tackled the bird and wrung its neck.

In no time at all the chicken was skinned and gutted. Head and feet, wingtips, entrails and feathers were buried under the hay while the carcass, wrapped in Smitty's footwrapper kerchief, was stuffed in the bottom of the underwear leg to await a more propitious cooking time.

The next morning the kriegies were lined up for early *Appell* and the order to march was just about to be given when an SS officer halted proceedings. Jumping up on a farm wagon, he reached down and hauled another man up beside him. Then the officer harangued the POWs in German, the translation passed on down the line.

"This fellow," pointing to the farmer beside him, "has lost a chicken!"

No one in the Company could figure out how one single, solitary bird could be missed so soon.

"The prisoner who stole this chicken must admit his guilt for the sake of his fellow comrades!"

Smitty shared a look with *his* fellow comrades that said quite clearly that this was the biggest crock of shit he'd ever heard.

The officer waited for a response and when none was forthcoming, he shook his head. "Very well, you will all be searched and the guilty party will be appropriately punished!"

The Company had taken to sharing the burden of the sack each hour and on this the first hour of the day it was the padre's responsibility. The sack was between his legs as the guards came down the rows frisking kriegies and peering into their homemade knapsacks.

The Company never did understand how the goon missed the chicken. The padre, imbued with a generosity of spirit the others scoffed at, was certain the guard had seen it and had pretended he hadn't. Smitty said it was luck. Courtesy of his rabbit's foot. The others thought either the goon was just plain dumb or a very pious man who couldn't bring himself to believe a padre would violate the Eighth Commandment.

When at long last the chicken search was called off and the column finally marched away, the relief among the members of the Company was audible. Six men, now that Yates had joined the firm, let out their breath as one. There was no doubt in any of their minds what "appropriately punished" meant.

They carried the hen for nine days before the opportunity came to cook it and by then the bird was well on its way to putrefaction, which was the reason their fellow kriegies wouldn't let them near the pots over the cooking fires. So the men of the Company scraped off the rotting parts of the bird, divvied it up, and ate it raw. As Harry put it, it was "foul fowl," but Yates was the only one to upchuck.

On St. Patrick's Day, the Death March halted for the last time at *Stalag* 9B near Fallingbostal just south of Bremen in the northwest corner of Germany. Neither the glider pilot nor the padre made it, their bodies left behind to mark some corner of a German field as being "forever England."

The padre had wasted away in a couple of weeks after the last drop of his communion wine was doled out. It was as if he had a fast-acting cancer. Harry said he died of too much caring.

They buried him at night under a pile of rocks in a field, reading from his *Book of Common Prayer* the words he had used for so many others since the day the 500 had marched away from 8C.

The glider pilot went in twenty-four hours. Over six feet tall and big-boned, he liked to brag about his prodigious appetite in the good old days back home in Yorkshire. When his wife served him tea he would always tell her, "Nettie, just pour my portion in a pail."

It was hard for a man like that to last very long on portions that wouldn't even fill a teacup. One Monday morning his knees and ankles began to swell, making walking very painful. By the end of the day he was in agony, he could barely move, his eyelids had turned a purplish red and his speech was slurred.

They laid him down beside the well in the cobblestoned courtyard of a bombed-out country home, their bivouac for the night. In the waning light they could see lice crawling from his body like hordes of desperate rats deserting a sinking ship, black dots wriggling up his neck and face, clinging to his eyebrows. As fast as Al brushed them away, more took their place. The next morning when the Company wakened, all the pilot's lice were gone.

Only 400 emaciated men managed to stagger through the gates of 9B and most of these were sick with coughs, colds, fevers and dysentery. The Company, sitting on the ground in the *Vorlager* waiting to enter the delousing/shower hut, was no exception. Both Rileys had racking coughs, Yates had a bad cold and Al was skin and bones. He figured he'd lost fifty pounds since he'd first set foot in France and was damn close to looking just like Billy in the church, no fat and no reserves to fight any illness, no reinforcements ready to be called to the front lines if things got tough.

After delousing, their next stop was a storage shed where the contents of several hundred Red Cross parcels, British, Canadian, American, Australian and some Indian, had been dumped in a pile. As the representative of each group entered the shed he was given an allotment of tins from the assortment. The result was that Harry brought back victuals from a British parcel—bully beef, mixed vegetables, plum pudding, Nestlé condensed milk, tea, sugar, hardtack biscuits and two packages of British Players cigarettes.

Harry distributed all of the food he was given, as did most of the group representatives. Most, but not all. That evening, their first in *Stalag* 9B, they found out what happened to a British sergeant who'd kept some for himself, two American chocolate bars and some Indian cane sugar.

When the sweets were discovered stuffed in his pants, his fellow Brits picked him up by the scruff of his neck and the seat of his pants, dragged him to the open privy pit—eight feet long, six feet wide and four feet deep—and threw him in. Face first.

Trust and honesty were the most basic values in the kriegie credo. Violators were prosecuted. Always. No matter what.

That night, after lights out, the Company caucused and came up with a quick and unanimous decision. Canada would act.

In a minute they were out of the hut, Al and Yates reaching down into the pit and pulling the Brit out of the slime. Standing in it up to his thighs he was too far gone to get up and out all by himself.

They stripped off his clothes soaked in nauseating, grey-coloured muck and washed him with water relayed in mess tins from the tap outside their hut, his hair, his eyebrows and his face, especially around his nose and mouth. It was above and beyond the call of the Golden Rule; and Smitty said afterwards, as they were washing shit from themselves, that he was going to put them all up for VCs.

The Commonwealth's highest award, the Victoria Cross, was given only for conspicuous acts of bravery. With Willy's help Smitty made up witty citations for each of them, citations typical of the real thing, complete with the traditional rhetorical flourishes and gilded phrasing designed to excite the homefront. An action could not just be brave; it had to be "an outstanding example of military courage." A grenade could not simply be thrown. It had to be "fearlessly hurled." And so on.

They chuckled at Smitty's words, his repeated and varied references to dung, "gallant men fighting fearlessly against the fierce forces of feces" being one of the better lines, but their laughter was mostly to cover their embarrassment at feeling sorry for a common thief covered in excrement. They felt a little better when the senior British officer in the camp sought them out to say thank you. The man had to be punished, mind you, but not degraded. That wasn't the job of Empire men, eh what? That was bloody Jerry's job, now wasn't it?

Eight days later, bloody Jerry's job came to an end and so did a good number of bloody Jerries.

It was the beginning of Holy Week when they first heard thunder from the West. Al was in his bunk, his forehead beaded in sweat, his knees drawn up, fighting a wave of cramps, knowing that he would soon once again have to drag himself up and out to the privy. Yates was with him and had been since the night they'd rescued the British sergeant and Al's dysentery had come on with a vengeance, forcing him to spend most of his days with scores of other men at the open pit, a barked log running lengthways serving as a toilet seat. You sat on this shit-encrusted log with your ass hanging over the hole and did your business.

Yates had been told that charcoal was the best bung in the world and so the Company was fast burning bits and pieces of wood to make it, with Yates then crushing it and spoon-feeding it to Al.

For the rest of his life, Allan McDougal would be unable to sort out what was real about the events of Holy Week in 1945 and what was a story woven from the strands of his feverish dreams; what he was later told; and what he, in his more lucid moments, had actually witnessed from his ringside seat. In the end, he would come to the conclusion that his memory of those hectic days was a blend of fact and fiction, truth and wish-fulfillment and in that sense, very much like the many stories of the war told back home when it was all over, stories of villains and heroes that more often than not featured "an outstanding example of military courage."

The night skies in the last Holy Week of the War were lit up by artillery flashes, the day skies filled with Allied fighter planes—Tiffies, Hurricanes, Mustangs and P-47s—shooting up roads and railway tracks and anything that ran, walked, crawled or otherwise roamed the face of German earth. To make sure the fighters didn't take to strafing the camp, permission was sought and enthusiastically granted to make a sign consisting of three very large letters carefully cut from a roll of tarpaper and anchored with stones in the parade square just a few feet from the privy. The sign read "POW."

The SS, their forced march of the starving prisoners to *Stalag* 9B finished, had melted away with the last of the snow, leaving behind a bunch of older goons, the same smiling, phlegmatic *Volkssturm* or Home Guard types who had been Yates's and Billy's keepers at 4B. After a couple of days, a few of these had dumped their weapons and gone home. Of those who remained, some stayed well outside the wire, as far away from their charges as they could get without abandoning their posts, while others worked hard to be seen as comrades in adversity, sharing what little food and few cigarettes they had. *Kein Essen, keine Zigaretten, alles kaputt.* "Nothing to eat, no cigarettes, all is ruined."

For these guards the hope was that they would win some grudging respect when the time came that they would have to change places with the men on the other side of the wire and be forced to say *Ich bin ein Gefangener jetzt.* "I am a prisoner now."

Back in Canada on the morning of April 1, Easter Sunday, and Sanford Berkett McDougal's fifth birthday, the Reverend Mr. Payne of the Church of England in Lowvert, Ontario, offered prayers for all prisoners of war and murmured words of comfort to the McDougal family as they left the church following the celebration of the Resurrection of Jesus Christ.

Meanwhile the birthday boy's father was dozing in his bunk in a *Kriegsgefangenen* near Fallingbostal lacking the energy to lift his head and fearful of opening his eyes because, when he did, the walls of the hut seemed to be moving, in and out, like a bellows being ever so slowly and rhythmically squeezed.

So he wasn't sure if he was in a feverish dreamland or the real world when Willy Yates came bursting into the hut at the break of dawn shouting, "They're here! They're here!"

The camp had wakened to find itself surrounded by Sherman tanks, their seventeen-pounder guns sticking through the wire. The white stars painted on the tanks confused some of the kriegies, who were yelling that the Russkis had finally come, but they were quickly told don't be a fucking idiot, it's the Americans.

And it *was* the Americans. God bless America and George Patton's boys who stuck their heads out of turrets and hatches wanting to know why the prisoners were just standing there, not moving a muscle. One of the kriegies started to explain about the warning wire and then burst into hysterical laughter because the warning wire was now ancient history.

But even so, the mind could not persuade the feet to move and when the laughter died the kriegies were still rooted to the spot until the silence was broken by the squawking of the tank radios and the gunning of motors as the Shermans roared straight through and over the wire, dragging and tearing it to pieces. It was only when the tanks were inside and swiveled around with their guns pointing out that the prisoners moved; and when they did, many of them burst into tears.

Was George S. Patton Jr. there? Many swore he was, with his ivory-handled pistols, standing ramrod straight in a circuit-bashing Jeep, taking the ragged salute of the wildly cheering men, prisoners no longer.

Was it true that the Yanks brought battlefield justice to 9B? There were a good number of men who said they'd seen this with their own eyes. A half-dozen of the SS goons from the Death March had been captured and were dragged into the camp on the run, all of them tied in a line and the line anchored to a Jeep moving at a pretty good clip. When some of the kriegies recognized four of the Nazis as guards who had shot prisoners on the March they yelled and pointed. As quick as a flash the four were lined up with their backs to the privy pit and then, one after the other, shoved in with a rifle butt. Then the rifles were turned around and triggers pulled. Harry said he felt sorry for the shit.

Al had no trouble believing this story because it fit with things he heard later, tales of Americans liberating death camps and once they'd recovered from puking their guts out at the sights and the smells, summarily executing every Nazi goon they could find.

Sergeant McDougal was particularly fond of the story of the officer with the American Third Army who arrived at a death camp to find the SS camp commandant waiting at the gate. Clicking his heels and saluting, the *Sturmbannführer* formally presented a list of all his staff and every inmate in his care, together with the numbers tattooed on their forearms. The list, in triplicate, was gravely accepted by the American officer as he peered over the SS major's shoulder at hundreds of stick-limbed bodies in blue-striped rags stacked beside a bulldozed burial trench.

With the handover of the camp completed, the Nazi was politely thanked and graciously invited to ride in a Jeep with two GIs who drove him into the woods outside his death camp and shot the *schweinehund*. In the nuts first of all. Or so the story went. The GIs had friends who'd been in the Battle of the Bulge.

Then there were the accounts of the cake served by the Yanks as a luncheon dessert. By noon American Army trucks bearing dixies of hot beef stew and enough coffee to float an ocean liner started to arrive at 9B and the kriegies lined up with their mess tins for their first real meal in a coon's age. Of course they were all sick as dogs, their stomachs being unable to cope with more than few spoonfuls of anything, but the really interesting story to come out of that lunch was the tale of the cake.

In fact there was no baking for dessert that day, no cake, no cookies, no pie, just tinned fruit. Peaches mostly. But with the stew there was a lot of white bread, something the kriegies hadn't seen for so long that they mistook its white fluffiness for angel food cake.

Every time Al came to his senses, Yates was beside him, spoonfuls of charcoal succeeded by spoonfuls of broth, a kriegie bunk replaced by a stretcher carrying him to a Jeep that took them to the airfield at Fallingbostal and a gutted Lancaster from Bomber Command that flew them, twenty-seven prisoners at a time, to a hospital in England.

His last view of Hitler's Third Reich was on the way to the airfield, German soldiers left behind by their retreating comrades, grenadiers of the Third Empire bound hand and foot and strung up to lampposts beside the road. Around their twisted necks were hand-lettered signs reading *"Der Überläufer"*—"The deserter."

The hanged soldiers were just baby-faced kids, recent conscripts, old enough to read the handwriting on the wall and smart enough to go AWL when they did. But not smart enough to avoid the men in black leather coats, the *Geheime Staatspolizei*, the Gestapo.

Child eyes bulged wide open in death, blackened tongues sticking out, the tips of their scuffed boots dangling just inches from the ground. So near and yet so far.

Yates had finagled his way on the plane with the stretcher cases and kept up a running in-flight commentary on the view from on high, men and *matériel* flowing into Germany for the last push, the ship traffic on the North Sea, the coast of England—*Oh, to be in England / Now that April's here*—the descent through wispy white clouds to an RAF base somewhere in Northumberland.

"Big place, Al. Looks like a small town."

Yates was shouting over the roar of the bomber's engines as he peered out of the top turret, describing streets, the triangle of runways, the hangars, the barrack H-huts, and Quonset huts that he took to be workshops, dozens of them, the whole complex surrounded by a high screen of hedges.

The next time Al opened his eyes he was lying on a stretcher in a British uniform, his second change in three days. One of the first things the Americans did for the POWs, right after they burned their kriegie rags, was get them deloused, cleaned up and into fresh GI duds. But crabs were like old soldiers, they never died. So the Brits were repeating the cycle, hoping the little bastards would at least fade away.

When he looked around, Al saw that he was one of many, row upon row of stretchers resting on individual pipe frames above a concrete floor, the smell of Lysol, doctors and nurses bustling about.

The next time he opened his eyes was three days later. He was in a bed this time with a needle in his arm and a tube snaking up to an intravenous bottle. Liquid refreshments.

"Welcome back, soldier." Yates was bathing his forehead with a cool cloth. "For a while there, we thought we were going to lose you."

Al motioned for some water and after he had sipped, croaked out a question. Yates nodded. "This is a hospital. Fourth Canadian General Hospital in Farnborough. South of London. Flew down here day before yesterday."

Another hoarse question. Another nod. "Last time I saw them was in the Naffi up in Northumberland. Eating and smoking like there was no tomorrow."

Al had asked about Smitty and Harry, and Yates had told him that he'd last laid eyes on them in one of the canteens run by the Navy, Army and Air Force Institute.

The talk of eating prompted a request and before you could say "Jack Robinson" Yates was back with refreshments. While Al, propped up with two pillows at his back, sipped sugared tea through a straw and nibbled at a chunk of cheddar, Yates told him that he was being treated for the lingering effects of dysentery, malnutrition and peripheral neuritis.

He had moved to the foot of Al's bed, picked up his patient's chart and was pretending to read from it while he recited bits and pieces of what he'd heard day after day from doctors making their rounds.

"Peripheral neuritis is a condition caused by malnutrition. The chief symptoms are swollen joints, knee jerks, muscle spasms, physical exhaustion and general numbness," and here he grinned, "especially between the ears. Treatment to consist of plenty of bed rest and frequent visits from Dr. Dart."

It proved to be an accurate description of Allan McDougal's care for the next ten days, especially the visits from the MO nicknamed Dart, so christened because of his manner of injecting penicillin. He would pull down your pajama bottoms, grab a hunk of your ass in one hand, hold the hypodermic between thumb and forefinger of his free hand, take careful aim and throw the hypo just like a dart into the bull's eye of your bunched-up cheek. Then he would depress the plunger, pull out the needle and pat your ass, all the while whistling "On Ilkla Moor baht 'at."

By the end of the ten days, the Algonquin sergeant was feeling much better thanks to Dr. Dart and all the nurses and orderlies and cheerful volunteers, mostly overly made-up middle-aged women bearing tea and cigarettes, newspapers and offers to bathe you, shave you and cut your hair, not to mention other more basic needs: "Oh, love, do ye need a battleship?" Bedpan. Or "Ah, love, would ya be needin' a duck?" Urinal.

The first time Al heard the latter question he thought he'd been asked something else and blushed when he declined.

By the third week in April he had been moved to the 1st Canadian Nuthouse, where the nurses all wore blue uniforms with white aprons and spent most of their time warding off advances from randy patients who were clearly on the road to recovery. Listening to Foster Hewitt on the radio, Allan McDougal cheered the Toronto Maple Leafs to their Stanley Cup victory over the Detroit Red Wings. God was in his heaven and all was right with the world.

The 1st Canadian Neurological Hospital, a.k.a. the "Nuthouse," was in Basingstoke about fifteen miles west of Farnborough. When the war was at its worst, the CNH was a treatment centre for severe cases of battle exhaustion, but now it also served as a hospital for convalescents where patients like Allan

McDougal were fed six small meals a day to bring them, bit by bit, back to the land of the living with some meat on their bones.

When he was carried off the Lancaster in Northumberland, Al weighed ninety pounds. By the end of April, when he discharged himself from Basingstoke, he tipped the scales at 109 and was gaining at the rate of a pound each day. He took to calling himself "Two-Ton Tony."

The doctors at Basingstoke wanted Two-Ton to stay while they dug around in his neck and shoulder looking for lead, but he and Yates had planned a trip and there was no holding them back. They'd been cooped up too long.

On the train to Glasgow the Canadian exchanged bets with the American as to when the war would end. Now that Roosevelt was dead, Yates was wondering if the new man, Truman, would keep the heat on or let nature take its course. The world had not yet been told that Hitler had committed suicide that very day in the *Führerbunker* deep beneath the rubble of Berlin. A bullet through the top of his mouth.

While Willy dozed, Al reached into his pack and pulled out the newspaper clippings his father had sent over, stories from the *Timmins Daily Press* about his soldier son—the report of him missing in action, the news of his capture.

A former resident of Louvert, Sergeant Allan McDougal is now reported to be a prisoner of war in Germany. The Louvert man was with the crack Algonquin Regiment of Northern Ontario through most of the heavy fighting on the continent and it was in close action with the enemy that Sgt. McDougal fell into enemy hands

There was news of his time in the *Stalags*:

Bearing the date "December 17, 1944" a letter has been received by the family of Sergeant Allan McDougal, now a prisoner of war in Germany. The letter contained no information beyond the fact that he was well. Since the letter was written it has been learned that the prison camp, Stalag 8C, *is one of many evacuated from the path of the Russian forces to an unknown location in Western Germany.*

Al sighed and folded the articles. Every time he glanced at them he felt he was reading about a stranger, another man using his name, rank and serial number.

The clippings he could not bear to read again were the obituaries his father had saved. Barney's. Reggie's. Billy's. Instead he just held them in his hand and stared out the train window at passing sheep on the hillsides, taking some comfort that there were no clippings bearing the names Frank Archibald or Tony Foligno in the section of the paper devoted to **DISTRICT CASUALTIES.**

In Glasgow they stayed at a gargantuan Victorian rooming house near the university. The front door handle was knee high and the roof sprouted sixteen pot chimneys. They rode the underground to George Square and visited with the pigeons perched on Gladstone, Robert Peel, Robbie Burns and Thomas Watt. "You know what? Yeah, he invented the steam engine."

From Glasgow they hitched a ride to Inverary, where they'd trained in January 1944, and after a stay of a few beers moved on up to visit the three forts built by the Brits in the Middle Ages to contain the warring clans—William, George— and Augustus on the shores of Loch Ness, where they spent a peaceful and restful night at the Benedictine Abbey pretending to believe Brother Paul, who swore several solemn oaths that Nessie really was.

Back in Glasgow they found a U.S. Air Force Dakota bound for Londonderry and hopped on board. Both of them wanted to see Ireland before they went home.

History records that Saint Columba established a monastery in Derry in the sixth century AD to minister to the needs of the people. Some 1,400 years later, during the Second World War, some 150 public houses had been established in the city to assuage the thirst of soldiers, sailors and airmen. Willy Yates and Allan McDougal were determined to have a go at sampling all of them, starting from Waterloo Square and going up the street of the same name where you could move from one pub to another without going outside. They were all connected by inside doors.

They got as far as Paedar O'Donnell's, where they sat on high stools at high tables under a sign advising "Guinness is Good for You." A bunch of the locals in the far corner were pointing at them and muttering about "Black and Tans," the name given to English veterans of the First War recruited in the 1920s for ten shillings a day to cross the Irish Sea and sort out the Dogans. Their uniforms were army khaki and police black and they murdered mayors and priests, shot children and cows, and picked at scabbed-over hatred until it began to bleed all over the green of Ireland.

Two of the mutterers swaggered over and stood with arms folded at the table of the Algonquins. Both of the Irishmen were young, one tall and skinny and subservient to the other, shorter and more muscular. Yates guessed he was a longshoreman.

"So Brendan? What do ye make of these grand gentlemen?" The short one spoke out of the side of his mouth to the tall one who just grinned. His role was to be the straight man.

"Oh aye, not Black and Tans, Brendan. Too smart lookin'. No Brendan, I'll be thinkin' they'll be more like Auxiliary Cadets. You'll be rememberin' Brendan from yer Irish history, Seamus à Caca and all that, that the Cadets were killers like the Black and Tans but a fair better quality."

Neither Yates nor Al said a thing. As if some unseen battlefield signal had been exchanged between them, they both downed their beers, wiped their mouths with the back of their hands, nodded politely to their visitors and excused themselves. They'd had enough of fighting.

It was a fine night so they decided not to return to their lodgings at the Salvation Army Hostel on Bishop Street but to take a walk down to the river, weaving their way through concrete tank obstacles still in the thoroughfares. At the Foyle they followed the railway tracks on the lower level of the double-decker Craigavon Bridge across the river and then up to the naval base at Lisahally docks. There they persuaded a pretty nursing sister to give them a bed for the night in a Quonset hut that served as the base hospital. Just before he fell asleep Al glanced at a calendar tacked to the wall above his bunk. It was May 6.

The next morning at breakfast—Shredded Wheat, bacon, tomatoes and toast (with marmalade)—there was great excitement. Two enemy U-boats had surrendered to the Royal Navy and were docking this very minute. As the shouts in the mess hall died away the Algonquins gulped the last of their tea and rushed outside to watch the subs tie up, black flags of capitulation tied to their periscopes. Yates read off the U-boat numbers stencilled on their conning towers, *U-1009* and *U-1305*. Anchored just behind them was the ship that had brought them in, the Canadian frigate *Thetford Mines*.

That afternoon Al wrote to his father. "This morning we saw two Jerry subs and their crews being taken off and put on a train for Belfast where they are to be interrogated. Seemed queer to see them prisoners again for a change. The bastards were a pretty scruffy bunch but still damn cocky, turning their backs on the press photographers trying to take their pictures. Willy and I would have liked to have had the job of guarding them. Many a good kick in the arse we had from Jerry and it would have been nice to return the compliment."

The conversation between Al and Willy had been about more than a few kicks in the arse but Al didn't want to alarm his mother, who would probably be reading this letter over his father's shoulder.

The next day they were back across the river when the official announcement was made. Germany had surrendered. The war was over.

The two of them followed the crowds downtown to The Diamond where Londonderry's memorial to the dead of the First World War was located and there, in the afternoon, they listened to Churchill over the tannoy, his familiar voice breaking when he came to his peroration, "Advance Britannia! Long live the cause of freedom! God save the king!"

Then the two soldiers linked arms with the people next to them and sang "Roll out the Barrel" and "Bless Them All"; "Pack Up Your Troubles"; "On Ilkla Moor baht 'at"; and "Tipperary" over and over again with a slight word change in the chorus. On VE day it was "a long, long way to good, old Derry."

At six in the evening they listened to the king's speech and when the sun went down jumped ten feet in the air when fireworks began exploding in the sky above them—Roman candles, rockets and star shells the city fathers had been hoarding for just such a day. An early Guy Fawkes celebration.

Once he'd recovered, Yates started to sing a few lines from "The Star Spangled Banner," the ones about rockets' red glare and bombs bursting in air.

Later the two friends stood, their arms around each other's shoulders, watching as a huge bonfire was lit in the centre of the square. When the straw-stuffed dummies of the three Axis dictators were heaved into the fire, the crowd shouted as one, a great visceral roar of triumph.

But then as sparks in the night sky danced away from Chancellor Adolf Hitler of Germany, Prime Minister Benito Mussolini of Italy and Prime Minister Hideki Tojo of Japan, a hush came over everyone, each reveller suddenly alone with his own memories, his own joy and sorrow, his own hopes and dreams. In that moment of silence in Derry, Allan McDougal thought of duty, promising himself he would visit Lindfield before heading home. His mind lingered on that last word savouring the memories it evoked, wondering how his family in Canada would choose to celebrate the end of the war in Europe.

As for William Butler Yates, he was thinking of some scattered lines from Shakespeare's *King Henry the Fifth*.

> *This day is call'd the feast of Crispian:*
> *He that shall live this day, and see old age,*
> *Will yearly on the vigil feast his neighbours,*
> *Then will he strip his sleeve and show his scars,*
> *And Crispin Crispian shall ne'er go by,*
> *From this day to the ending of the world,*
> *But we in it shall be remember'd;*
> *We few, we happy few, we band of brothers.*

He looked at his brother Allan McDougal and smiled as a voice whispered in his head, *Für euch ist der Krieg zu Ende.*

THE END

The author on the shores of Loch Ness

About the Author

G.F. McCauley was born and reared in Cochrane, Ontario, where he began his working career digging ditches for what was then the Ontario Department of Highways. Since those early days he has held many jobs and been fired from a few, including that of member of Parliament for Moncton, New Brunswick. He lives in Ottawa with Máire O'Callaghan, Maxmillian O'Callaghan, Sierra Muldoon and Muffet McGregor O'Toole. The latter three are cats.

To order more copies of

send $29.95 plus $6.50
to cover GST, shipping and handling to:

GENERAL STORE PUBLISHING HOUSE
Box 28, 1694B Burnstown Road
Burnstown, Ontario, Canada K0J 1G0
Telephone: 1-800-465-6072
Fax: (613) 432-7184
www.gsph.com

VISA and MASTERCARD accepted